MW00635740

POINT OF SIGHS
by Melissa Scott

"In this slow-burning fifth fantasy procedural set in the city of Astreiant (after 2014's Fairs' Point), Adjunct Nicholas Rathe and his lover, Guard Captain Philip Eslingen, are once again drawn into unsavory matters of murder, corruption, and intrigue. ... Scott's world is atmospheric, moody, and richly detailed; the emphasis on trade disruptions, tea, and institutional graft provides an intriguing angle for the relatively leisurely plot."
—*Publishers Weekly*

FAIRS' POINT
by Melissa Scott

"Centered on a crime that could occur only in Astreiant, *Fairs' Point* takes many unpredictable, impressive twists and turns on its way to the conclusion. And, if the reader deduces a guilty party slightly ahead of the protagonists, that doesn't make the mystery any less fresh or imaginative. In its mystery–in all its parts–*Fairs' Point* is, like its predecessors, a pleasure."
—Cynthia Ward for *Locus*

POINT OF DREAMS
by Melissa Scott & Lisa A. Barnett

"A warmly inviting story where astrology and magic work, and ghosts sometimes name their murderer."
—*Romantic Times*

"Readers of police procedurals will recognize the form of *Point of Dreams*, if not the details, which are necessarily changed by the fantasy setting.... Scott and Barnett blend the genres deftly, transposing their mystery plot seamlessly into their magical world.... *Point of Dreams* is a thoroughly rewarding reading experience."
—*SF Site*

POINT
OF SIGHS

POINT OF SIGHS

MELISSA SCOTT

❄ LETHE PRESS ❄

Published in 2018 by Lethe Press, Inc.
6 University Drive • Suite 206 / PMB #223 • Amherst, MA 01002 USA
www.lethepressbooks.com • lethepress@aol.com
ISBN: 978-1-59021-645-3 / 1-59021-645-8

Set in Jenson and Ornatique.
Cover and interior design: Alex Jeffers.
Cover artwork: Ben Baldwin.

Cataloging-in-Publication Data on file with the Library of Congress.

CHAPTER ONE

IT HAD BEEN raining for the better part of a week, a thin cold drizzle alternating with colder, heavier downpours that were rapidly stripping the last of the leaves from the trees. Autumn had set in early and hard, and Nicolas Rathe was glad for once to be home by his own stove, stockinged feet stretched to the fender. Rain rattled like pebbles against the shutters, the draft bending the candles' flames, and the basket terrier Sunflower lifted his muzzle from his crossed front paws. Philip Eslingen lifted his head, too, but quickly returned his attention to the flatiron heating beside the kettle. Behind him, his new-made captain's coat hung on its stand, carefully arranged so that the crosspiece completely filled the padded shoulders and the full skirts hung without creasing. Silver lace and silver buttons caught the flickering light, bright against the fine midnight-blue wool. Rathe still had his doubts about the ultimate utility of the newly formed City Guard, but he had to admit that Eslingen wore the uniform exceedingly well.

As he watched, Eslingen laid a shirt on the table, holding the fabric taut with one hand while he ran the iron over it with the other. The air smelled suddenly of hot linen and the herbs it had been washed with, and Rathe tipped his head to one side.

"I thought you paid your laundress for that."

"We don't draw actual pay until the middle of Galeneaon," Eslingen answered. "And what Coindarel calls maintenance doesn't maintain very much at all. And anyway, this is only my second-best."

Rathe refrained from pointing out that the point of second- and third-best shirts was that no one expected them to be uncrumpled. "I didn't know we had an iron."

"We don't." Eslingen flipped the fabric, rearranged it neatly. "I borrowed it from the weaver downstairs."

"I was having trouble imagining you riding through the League with a lump of iron in your saddlebags."

Eslingen laughed. "You'd be surprised. When I was senior sergeant, I had a sempster's box and smoothing stones and a gauffering iron for the company's use. Of course, I also had a seamstress and three laundresses on the rolls, so I wasn't expected to use them myself except in emergencies. But Coindarel likes his men looking neat."

Evidently. Rathe swallowed a word that might have rung too sharp—Coindarel's new Guard encroached on the prerogatives of Astreiant's Points, charged with enforcing the same city laws, and Rathe had been a pointsman too long to take that comfortably—and Eslingen went on, apparently oblivious, "Do you want me to do yours, too?"

"Think it would do much good?" Rathe asked, with a wry grin.

"Probably not." Eslingen set the iron back on the side of the stove, began folding the shirt ready for the clothes-press. That was another piece of furniture Rathe had not owned before; his entire wardrobe lived in a single chest, winter on one side and summer on the other. "I've never known a man who could make a shirt wrinkle just by looking at it. It's as if your clothes take one look at you and surrender."

There was, regrettably, enough truth to that to make Rathe shrug. "It's not like it matters what a pointsman looks like."

"Not even an Adjunct Point? You're second-in-command of Point of Dreams, don't you need at least one good suit—and what about the Chief Points?"

Rathe looked up at that, but Eslingen's expression was purely curious. "All right, if you're chief at Temple Point or City Point, you spend enough time dealing with the regents—or the queen's court, at Point of Hearts—that I suppose someone might care. But the rest of us, especially us Southriver points—we're like the rat-catcher. People want the job done, but they don't want to spend much time with us while we do it."

"Many a woman's been grateful for a good rat-catcher," Eslingen said, lightly enough, but there was a faint line between his eyebrows. As Rathe watched, he found a limp roll of paper and carefully flattened it on the table, then reached for the iron again.

"Philip, what on earth—"

There was a soft hiss and a smell of scorched paper, and then Eslingen had set the iron on the back of the stove to cool. "I bought some broadsheets on the way home. Maybe you can explain this one to me."

Rathe took the sheet carefully, the paper warm and brittle to the touch. It was recently printed, the ink dark, lines still sharp in spite of the rain, and he looked automatically for the printer's license at the bottom of the page. For a wonder, the seal was there, and even legitimate—half Astreiant's broadsheet printers skipped buying their license even for relatively innocuous projects—and it looked as though someone had spent the money to commission the woodcut illustration, rather than re-using an old block that was only tangentially related to the subject. But that subject.... The print showed a flat-faced fish with an ugly, underslung jaw and a mouthful of needle-sharp teeth plus two more that jutted up like tusks, rearing up out of the water to balance on its belly and wide-spread, hand-like fins. Beneath it, oversized letters read: *A New Sighting of an Old Curse, or, New Dangers in the Waters, Portending a Rise of All Tides and Other Prognostications Merrily Expounded.*

Rathe skimmed the text, his frown deepening. Some of the river-folk, mainly sailors and bargemen idled by the early autumn, claimed to have seen greater dogfish swimming in the Sier, though the greater dogfish had been extinct for centuries, if indeed it had ever existed at all. The broadsheet writer was happy to claim that its reappearance meant a winter of disaster for the city, and in particular for its sailors—and I'm glad, Rathe thought, that I'm not in Point of Sighs to deal with this one. Point of Sighs and Point of Graves and Customs Point were responsible for the docks on the southern bank of the river, not Point of Dreams.

"What in Tyrseis's name is a greater dogfish?" Eslingen asked. "Besides exceedingly ugly."

"They say it's a handmaid of the river spirit, the spirit of the Sier," Rathe said. "The Riverdeme, they called her. She used to take a certain number of drowned men every year to share her bed, but nobody's believed in that for, oh, at least three hundred years. When they built the bridges, she was bound, and her power faded and she with it. There is such a thing as a dogfish—lesser dogfish, if you want to be precise—but it doesn't look anything like that."

"That's comforting," Eslingen said. "Or—what do they look like?"

"They're about as long as my forearm, with a face like one of those pug-dogs they breed in the Western Reaches. Undershot jaw, and little nasty teeth. When I was a boy, they'd take most of our bait fish in a single bite."

"Charming."

"And they're not in the slightest bit edible," Rathe said, mildly surprised to find an old grievance so sharp. "They're full of tiny nasty bones and taste like mud."

Eslingen drew his chair closer to the stove, and settled in the pool of lamplight. "This thing has the jaw, according to the drawing. So do you think that's what someone saw?"

Rathe shrugged. "It's possible. Or it's possible someone was drunk and telling tales, and an enterprising woman wrote it up for prophecy. Or made it up out of whole cloth. It's been a grim autumn."

Eslingen nodded, still studying the broadsheet, and Rathe sighed. The autumn westerlies had set in almost ten days early, ending the Silklands trade; battered caravels had been straggling in all month, sails in tatters from fighting the gales, and rumor said a good dozen had put in to the smaller ports along the coast to the south, and were sending their goods by land rather than try to make the mouth of the Sier. The tea trade was hurt worst of all, each of the great houses vying to bring the last best thinnings, the Old Year tea that they could sell for midwinter prices. There was already talk that the tea blenders were bidding against each other in every factor's hall, and there was even a rumor that Three Ships was cutting their ordinaries with tea from southern Chenedolle. It would be a hard winter indeed if they were reduced to that.

"Do you think it could be an omen?" Eslingen asked. "Though I notice they don't say anything the astrologers haven't already said."

"If someone's seen a greater dogfish, it might mean something, if only that the Sier's running high." Rathe reached for the broadsheet, and Eslingen handed it across. "Oh, I like that. 'Prognostications Merrily Expounded.'"

"Disasters sound better in rhyming couplets?" Eslingen began, and was cut off by a knock at the door.

Sunflower bounded to his feet, barking wildly, and Eslingen scooped him up one-handed. "Who's there?"

"Adjunct Point?"

Rathe recognized Sohier's voice, breathless from a quick walk, and unlatched the door. "Sohier?"

She was wearing a sailor's oiled hood and shoulder cape over her pointsman's jerkin, but beneath it her skirts clung damply to her soaked stockings, and a bead of water dripped from the end of her lovelock where it straggled from under her hood. Out of the corner of his eye, Rathe saw Eslingen grimace, and take a tighter hold on the dog.

"Sorry to disturb you, sir," she said, "but the chief says, you're needed."

Rathe gave a resigned nod, reaching for the jerkin he'd discarded when he'd come off duty a little after six. The winter-sun would be rising soon, but in this weather, its light would never pierce the clouds. Sohier was carrying a shuttered lantern, he saw with approval, and shrugged back into the damp leather. "What's the trouble?"

"The adjunct from Point of Sighs is claiming a point on Mattaes Staenka, and the chief wants some of us there to supervise."

"The tea family," Rathe said, and Sohier nodded.

"He's the son—there's two older sisters, their mother died last year and Meisenta and Redel hold the business in shares, or so I hear."

Money, and a lot of it, Rathe thought. Many of the tea merchants preferred to live in the nicer parts of neighboring Point of Dreams, rather than among the warehouses and shops and factors' barns that made up most of Sighs. "What's the claim?"

Sohier winced. "Murder."

"Astree's tits, Sohier." Rathe stopped. "You're serious."

"I'm afraid so. That's why Trijn wants you there."

To be a buffer to one of the district's richest families: that was more in Trijn's line than his. "Why doesn't she go herself?"

"She was friends with the mother," Sohier said. "Sighs is being… touchy."

"Who did they send?" Rathe slung his truncheon at his belt.

"Their Senior Adjunct. Dammar."

Rathe swore again. Edild Dammar had a bad reputation even outside his own station, was reportedly a man who demanded fees at every turn, and still somehow never managed to stay bought.

"Do you want company?" Eslingen asked.

Rathe hesitated, then shook his head. "No, this is Points business— Points politics."

"I'll keep the bed warm, then," Eslingen said, and Rathe smiled in spite of himself.

"Not with the iron, please."

"I promise not to scorch the sheets," Eslingen said sweetly, and Rathe heard Sohier choke.

He found his own rain cloak and drew it close, the fabric still chill and smelling of the street. "All right, let's go. You can tell me the details on the way."

The rain had slacked off again, to Rathe's relief, though he kept his hood up, hunching his shoulders under the damp fabric. Sohier opened the lantern's shutter all the way, casting a fan of light across the wet cobbles, and gave him a sidelong glance.

"It's an odd business. The Staenkas are a quiet family, generally."

"So tell me about it."

"There's not much to tell, just yet. Dammar says he was called to a tavern in Point of Sighs, known to be frequented by tea traders, where he found the body of a tea ship captain currently under contract to the Staenkas. The man—bes'Anthe, his name is, was, Ketel bes'Anthe—was seen quarreling with Mattaes Staenka, though I'm not sure he said what about. Mattaes stalked out of the tavern in full view of everybody drinking there, and they found the body in the garden about an hour later."

"That's not much to call a point on," Rathe said. If it was his case, he'd certainly want to talk to the boy, but it didn't sound as though there was enough to justify an arrest.

"I suppose they think he went back after?" Sohier sounded doubtful herself. "There's usually a gate by the privies, he could have come in there."

"No point in speculating." Rathe pulled his hood further forward as they turned into the wind.

Like all the points stations, Point of Dreams had once been a garrison and an armory, and in the rainy night its walls loomed large, blocking the end of the street. Magelights flared on either side of the gate, and a cloaked figure emerged from the narrow watch-box at their approach.

"Sohier—Adjunct Point. The chief's waiting."

I expect so, Rathe thought, but waved an acknowledgement and ducked through the gate. The courtyard was empty except for puddles, though enough light fell from the station's unshuttered windows to make it easier to avoid them. The main door was open, and even from outside he could see the fire built high in the enormous fireplace. There were more people than usual in the main room—more pointsmen, he amended, two women and a man sitting on a bench pulled close to one of the stoves, and another man leaning on the mantel of the fireplace, scuffing his feet on the stone hearth. They were all strangers, thought he thought he had at least seen one of the women before.

"Point of Sighs," Sohier said, under her breath, and he nodded.

An equal number of their own people had found reason to be in the main room, though only Maeykin had the sense to at least pretend to be mending the leather wrapping on the handle of his truncheon. The rest were clustered by the largest of the stoves, eying the group from Point of Sighs like dogs watching trespassers. Per Maillard, the duty point, looked very glad to see them.

"Adjunct Point! The chief says you should go straight up."

"Right." Rathe handed his wet cloak to Sohier, and started up the stairs. The door to Trijn's workroom was open, spilling magelight into the hall, and he could hear an unhappy rumble of conversation as he approached.

"—a respectable merchant-resident." From the exasperation in her voice, Trijn had made the argument more than once already, and Rathe rapped on the doorframe.

"You sent for me, Chief?"

Trijn glared at him from her place at the worktable. She looked as though she'd been called out from a party, in a fine wool skirt and bodice trimmed with an almost frivolous line of maiden's-knots. Her hair was pinned up under a lace cap, but the fashionably loose curls that framed her face were frizzed with damp. "Come in and close the door."

Rathe did as he was told, and pulled a stool away from the wall.

"This is Edild Dammar, out of Point of Sighs—Senior Adjunct there." Trijn reached for her pipe, discovered it was cold, and scowled deeply. "He claims he has reason to call a point on a resident of our district."

"I have reason and evidence, Chief Trijn," Dammar said. He was, Rathe guessed, only a few years younger than Trijn herself, a broad-shouldered, bull-necked man who was managing to ignore the discomfort of soaked stockings and cuffs.

"So Sohier said," Rathe said. "On a tea merchant's brother?"

Trijn gave him a sour glance. "On Mattaes Staenka. His sisters, Meisenta and Redel, they've held the business since midwinter."

"He was seen quarreling with the tea captain," Dammar said.

"And by your own account was seen to leave," Trijn said.

"But no one else had any argument with bes'Anthe," Dammar said, "and there's no denying the man was found dead in the garden not an hour later."

"Dead how?" Rathe asked.

"Knife between the ribs," Dammar said. "Neat enough, but not—experienced. Not professional, certainly."

"I take it no one saw him come back," Rathe said, and was unsurprised when the others both shook their heads.

"No sign of him," Dammar said, "but the place was busy as a beehive. The price of tea has risen like a rocket, and everyone's trying to make a decent price."

7

"And that's what they quarreled over?" Trijn's eyes narrowed as she held a sliver of wood to the nearest candle and used it to relight her pipe.

Dammar shrugged. "We don't know. No one claims to have heard. It's one of the questions I'd like to ask him."

"You were wanting to call a point," Trijn said.

"And still am," Dammar answered. "But I'll admit there might be evidence against it."

Trijn sighed. "Go with him, Rathe. And don't take every woman in the station. No need to make a spectacle of it."

And that was also typical of Trijn, Rathe thought. She came of a good merchant family herself, and preferred to cater to their sensibilities where she could. From the look of him, Dammar was considering a protest, but wisely swallowed it. "I'll bring Sohier," he said aloud, adding, to Dammar, "She's my usual second."

"My second's Bertelan tonight." Dammar grimaced. "And I'd like to know how we're expected to call the point with only four of us."

"If there's the need, the boy will come quietly," Trijn said. "I'll guarantee it—as will Rathe."

And how in Astree's name am I supposed to do that? Rathe swallowed the words, knowing that Trijn had probably already warned the Staenka household—and knowing, too, that a merchant's son was more likely to come quietly than most of the folk southriver.

"We need a fifth," Dammar said.

"If you do, it'll be one of mine," Trijn answered. "I won't have Sighs running roughshod over my neighborhood."

Dammar made a noise that was just shy of a snarl, but managed a nod. "I'll leave the rest of my people here, then."

"As you please." Trijn waved dismissal. "A quick word, Rathe."

"Yes, Chief." Rathe rose, waited until Dammar had left the room, and then, at Trijn's gesture, closed the workroom door. "He'll think you're ordering me to cross him."

Trijn snorted. "And so I am. Well, no, not if there's enough evidence against the boy. But Meisenta Staenka is an honest woman, and I want her troubled as little as possible."

"What do you know about the brother?" Rathe couldn't keep an edge out of his voice, and Trijn frowned again.

"Nothing against him. He's but young, they only took him into the business after Chera died. She was by way of being a friend of my sister's, though I don't know if Meisenta's kept up the connection."

"She'd be a fool not to." Trijn's sister was the grande bourgeoise herself, chief of Asteiant's regents, the council of merchants-resident that governed the city's day-to-day business.

"Meisenta goes her own way," Trijn said. "Well, go on, get this over with."

"Right, Chief," Rathe answered, and headed for the stairs.

It didn't take long to collect the others and head out into the rain again. To his surprise, the Staenka family lived not in the street of nice houses that bordered Point of Hopes, but in a mixed neighborhood closer to Point of Sighs. Still, the house was a good one, three stories tall and only two rooms wide, but brick with solid stone in the corners. Iron gates closed off the alleys that led presumably to a garden at the back. There was a stone ship between two lighthouses carved above the door: entirely appropriate for a tea merchant, Rathe thought. Lights showed in what was likely a parlor window, and Dammar swore under his breath.

"If the brat's run—"

Before he could finish, a cloaked figure detached itself from the shadows beneath the wall, opening its own lantern to reveal a pointsman's truncheon at his side. Rathe lifted his own lantern, focussing on the other's face, and recognized Leenderts, the senior man on the night watch.

"Rathe. I hoped the chief would send you. The boy's still there—"

"No thanks to you," Dammar said. "Or your chief."

"This is Edild Dammar of Sighs," Rathe said. "The body's on their books."

"Adjunct Point," Leenderts said, warily.

Dammar ignored him, and pushed past all of them to climb the four steps to the door. He slammed the knocker hard against its plate, one, twice, and the door swung open, plucking the knocker from his hand before he could strike again. A tall man in a coat so plain and precisely cut as to mark him as a superior servant looked out at them.

"Dammar, Point of Sighs. I want a word with Mattaes Staenka."

The steward hesitated, and Rathe took a step forward. "Nicolas Rathe, adjunct at Point of Dreams. Chief Trijn sent me as well. If we could speak to the household? There's a man dead in Point of Sighs."

"Dead?" For a moment, the steward looked shaken, and then his mask of calm returned. "If you'll come in, pointsmen—Adjunct Points—I'll inform Madame Staenka."

"Thank you," Rathe said, riding over whatever Dammar might have said, and they shouldered awkwardly into the stone-floored hall. The steward closed and barred the door behind them, then disappeared through a door halfway down the hall. In the light of the single magelight lantern, Rathe could see that the console table and stand were old but good, expensive pieces well maintained, and even the benches were neatly made and impeccably polished. But then, the Staenka family had a reputation for excellent goods at corresponding prices.

The steward reappeared a moment later, the pause barely long enough to preserve the fiction that they were not expected. "This way, Adjunct Point."

The Staenkas were waiting in what had to be the main parlor, a fire burning in the old-fashioned fireplace and half a dozen candelabra lit on the tables. There were magelights as well, small ones backed by mirrors, but the shadows were still deep in the corners. There were five people in the room, Rathe saw, but one drew the gaze, a woman sitting straight-backed in a tall chair to the left of the fireplace. Her skirt and bodice were too dark to read as anything but black in the flickering light, relieved only by a small square collar of exquisite lace. There was another narrow band of lace at her cuffs, and the slipper that peeped out from beneath her hem embroidered with silver thread. She was not beautiful, long-faced and hook-nosed, but the hair that showed beneath her sober cap gleamed golden in the firelight.

"Adjunct Point Dammar, Point of Sighs, and Adjunct Point Rathe, Point of Dreams," the steward announced. "And three others."

"Thank you." The seated woman had to be Meisenta Staenka, the elder sister, Rathe thought. "Drowe says you spoke of a dead man."

"That's right," Dammar began, and the woman lifted a hand.

"And which are you?"

Dammar blinked, visibly taken aback, but rallied quickly. "Dammar of Sighs, mistress, and the body is on my book."

She turned one palm outward. "Tell your tale. Please."

"This evening, a tea captain, one Ketel bes'Anthe, was found dead in the gardens back of the Bear and Bush," Dammar said. "Word is, he was under contract to your house."

"Aucher?" Meisenta did not turn her head, but the man standing beside her chair cleared his throat nervously.

"Yes. That's right, we'd hired him this year."

"My husband, Aucher Gebellin," Meisenta said. "I am sorry to hear that, Adjunct Point. Go on."

"bes'Anthe had been stabbed and left for dead by the privy gate," Dammar said. "When I spoke to the servers, they all said that they'd seen him talking to a young man, and that he and the young man had argued.

In fact, the quarrel was serious enough that the young man stormed out of the tavern almost without paying. The house knife had to chase him down to make him settle his score."

"And you have a name for this young man," Meisenta said.

"Mattaes Staenka," Dammar answered. "He's well known about the place."

"Mattaes?" Meisenta did not look away—in fact, Rathe thought, his attention sharpening, she didn't seem to be looking at anything at all, as though she were at least night-blind.

A figure stirred in the shadows, stepped forward, and emerged as a slight young man in an embroidered dressing gown. That was a nice touch, Rathe thought, implying that he'd been dragged from his bed, but less convincing with the rest of the household still fully dressed. "I was at the Bear and Bush, yes." He was older than Rathe had thought at first glance, not really a boy any more—maybe twenty-five, with fair hair receding from his high forehead. "And I certainly argued with bes'Anthe. But I left him unharmed."

"What time did you come home?" Rathe asked, and saw Meisenta's mouth open. "Rathe, mistress, Point of Dreams."

She inclined her head in thanks, and he was more certain than ever that she didn't see him. "Mattaes?"

He shrugged. "I came straight back, but in this weather—I think the clock struck half-past eight while I was changing clothes."

"We'll want to see those clothes," Dammar said sharply.

"Redel," Meisenta said. "See to it, please."

"With your permission, mistress," Rathe said quickly, "I'll send Sohier with whoever collects them. That way there's no chance of—misunderstandings."

"That's outside of enough," the third woman said. Where the Staenkas were all golden-fair, she was dark, her hair piled up in a coronet of braids.

"It's for Mattaes's sake as much as anyone's, Elecia," Meisenta said. "Yes, Adjunct Point, you may send Sohier."

Rathe nodded to his second, and the younger Staenka sister—Redel—crossed the room to tug at a bell-rope. Sohier joined her, and when the door opened, disappeared with the servant.

"Can anyone vouch for when you arrived?" Dammar asked.

"Drowe?" Mattaes sounded doubtful. "Our steward, that is. And I had hot water brought up to my room."

"I saw him about a quarter to nine," Redel said. "He hadn't been in long, his hair was still wet."

"And bes'Anthe was found dead when?" Rathe looked at Dammar.

"Near ten o'clock. And it's not so far to the Bear and Bush that he couldn't have gone back again."

"Can anyone vouch for you after you came in?" Rathe asked. "Witness that you were in the house?"

Out of the corner of his eye, he saw Dammar stiffen, and then relax with an effort.

Mattaes shrugged again. "I—I don't think so? I was still angry, I didn't want to talk to anyone until I could think straight."

"Someone must have seen you," Redel said.

"Why? I was in my room, trying to dry out. I didn't have anything to say because we hadn't settled anything—"

He stopped abruptly, and Rathe said, "What did you argue about?"

"Business." Mattaes cast a wary glance at his brother-in-law. "You'll have heard that the tea harvest was light this year, and the sea lanes closed early—"

"I sent him to make an offer for the part of bes'Anthe's cargo that was not already bespoke to us," Meisenta said. "And before you ask, I sent him because it's time he took his share in the business, man or not."

Mattaes blushed, the wave of color visible even in the lamplight. Before Rathe could question him, the parlor door opened again, and he looked back to see Sohier with a bundle of clothes in her arm.

"You'll want to see this, sir." She tilted the mass to expose a man's shirt, tugged out the sleeve to reveal dark stains at the cuff and spattered up the arm.

"Blood," Dammar said, with grim satisfaction, and Sohier nodded.

"I don't find any on the coat," she said, "but there might be some by daylight."

"Blood?" Meisenta said, and in the same instant, Mattaes said, "Let me see that."

Instantly, Dammar put himself in front of Sohier, and Rathe lifted a hand. To Meisenta, he said, "My second has found blood on your brother's shirt, the one he discarded in his room."

"Let me see," Mattaes demanded again.

Dammar clenched his fists, and Rathe touched his shoulder. "Let him look. But no touching."

Dammar grimaced, but stepped aside, and Sohier held up each of the pieces. They were well made, expensive fabric cut plain, just what Rathe would have expected in this house. Mattaes shook his head.

"That's not my shirt."

"The maid said it has the house laundry mark," Sohier said.

"Well, it's not the shirt I was wearing." Mattaes looked around as though realizing for the first time that he was in trouble. "It's isn't! I swear, I gave this one away weeks ago."

"I'm calling the point," Dammar said.

"Wait." Meisenta rose from her chair, and instantly Aucher was at her side, ready to guide her if needed. "Show me."

Sohier held out the shirt, and Aucher said softly, "In front of you."

Meisenta took three steps forward, then stopped, hand outstretched. "I cannot see. May I touch it?"

"No harm in it, surely," Rathe said, to Dammar, who flung up his hands.

"If you must. But I'm still calling the point."

Meisenta ignored him, running long fingers over the fabric, then pinching at the stains. They were stiff under her fingers, and her mouth tightened. "I see."

"It's not the same shirt," Mattaes said desperately, but his sister ignored him, her attention on Dammar.

"You're Point of Sighs, of course. I would be willing to pay a fee for your inconvenience if he could be held at Point of Dreams, where we can see to his upkeep."

Dammar hesitated, and Aucher moved to a tall sideboard, unlocking the front panel and lowering it to reveal a bookkeeper's desk. Most of the arched compartments held neatly folded papers; the empty spaces looked like missing teeth, but he ignored them, fumbling with the inkstand. For a moment, Rathe thought he was going to offer a vowel, but instead Aucher unlocked a larger lower compartment and drew out a purse as big as a fist. Dammar's eyebrows lifted, and Sohier and Bertelan were both wide-eyed—and no wonder, Rathe thought. Even if it held only copper coins, there had to be two pillars in that worn bag, a month's salary for a common pointsman, and he would lay money himself that most of the coin would be silver.

He saw Dammar swallow hard. "Well. Under the circumstances...."

"Thank you, Adjunct Point, that's very gracious of you." Meisenta nodded, and Aucher pressed the purse into Dammar's hand. "And you, Adjunct Point Rathe—"

"I don't take fees," Rathe said. "We'll hold him at Point of Dreams, but he's Sighs' case, madame."

"Understood." Meisenta inclined her head in regal acknowledgement. "Mattaes, put some clothes on, and go with them. We'll see you well housed."

"Meis—" He stopped abruptly. "All right. I'll go change."

"And I'll go with you," Leenderts said smoothly.

"What happens now?" Redel asked, as the door closed behind them.

"He'll be held until the next court sessions," Dammar said. "If he confesses, it'll go easier on him. Times are hard—"

"And in the meantime, Sighs will try to prove his story, or find someone who saw him at the tavern after he left," Rathe said. He kept his voice as neutral as possible, but Dammar sighed anyway.

"I doubt we'll find anything. It's a clear point, madame, I'm sorry to say."

Meisenta retreated to her chair, and they stood in silence until Mattaes and Leenderts reappeared, Mattaes now bundled in a hooded cape. As they headed back out into the dark, Rathe managed to brush up against the prisoner, and felt the wool damp against his palm. Not that it meant much, but it seemed as though the cloak had had time to dry out a little. Outside, it was still raining, and they paused in the middle of the street to adjust hoods and lanterns. Dammar tugged his own cloak tighter, hunching his shoulders against the wet.

"Rathe. I'd be willing to share the fee if you'll let me take him on to Point of Sighs for the night. You could have him back in the morning if you really want him, but by then I guarantee you we'll have enough to make the point stick."

Rathe took a deep breath, anger washing over him. "You took Madame Staenka's fee." He let the rest of the accusation hover—it was bad enough to take fees, but to take them and break the agreement was outside the pale—but Dammar merely shrugged.

"If she wants to pay me, that's her business. And before you get too righteous, consider that I'm doing no more than you do yourself. I go my own way, without favor. If they're fool enough to offer—well, a fool turns aside."

"I keep my word," Rathe said, hearing his voice tighten. "And since you've made it my business, I'll keep yours for you."

"It's a waste of time. The boy knifed him, that's obvious. It's just a matter of getting a confession." He spread his hands, the light from his lantern flashing from the puddles and wet cobbles. "All right, we'll do it the hard way. But I'll find the witnesses, make no mistake."

If he lost his temper now, Rathe reminded himself, it would give Dammar an excuse to contest the arrangement. "I'm sure you will."

"And I'll tell you now—and Trijn. This is Sighs' business, not Dreams'. If I catch any of your people on my patch—"

He broke off, and Rathe lifted his own lantern. "Was that a threat, Adjunct Point?"

"A statement of fact, Adjunct Point." Dammar showed teeth like a pocket terrier, pale and sharp in the lantern light. "And Astarac won't take kindly to your interference."

"Chief Astarac can take that up with Chief Trijn," Rathe said. To his relief, he could see the walls of Point of Dreams ahead of them, the magelights flaring from the gatehouse.

Dammar saw it too, and shook his head. "On your head be it. I'll take my people home, then—since I know I can trust you to lock him up."

For that, Rathe thought, I'm tempted to lodge him at the nearest inn, with whatever company he'd like. "That's the agreement."

Dammar flourished a bow. "I'll leave you to it, Adjunct Point."

Sohier swore under her breath, and Rathe glanced sideways. "And how much of that did you hear?"

"Enough to know he doesn't stay bought." Sohier shook her head. "Do you really think he did it?"

"Mattaes?"

Sohier nodded.

"You found the blood." Rathe sighed. "I don't know what to think, not without a lot more information. Which I'm unlikely to get, given it's Sighs' point and Dammar's warned us off. Come on, let's get inside and get dry."

CHAPTER 2

PHILIP ESLINGEN RESTED his elbows on the fence that bordered the new riding ring, grateful for the breeze that sent the clouds scudding across the sky. Only the day-sun was up now, but the mare in the ring had taken offense at the flickering shadows; the training sergeant, Sendoya, leaned back at the end of the long line, turning her into the light. She steadied then, and he clicked his tongue, sending her back into a steady walk.

"She moves well," Matalin Rijonneau said, leaning against the fence himself, and Eslingen nodded.

"Good bones, too. But she'll need another year, maybe two, before we can trust her."

"At that rate, we'll all still be afoot when we get our commissions." Rijonneau was the City Guard's second captain, a deceptively willowy Ajanine, one of the hundred sons of impoverished nobility whose mothers had bought them a horse and a sword and sometimes a breastplate and dispatched them into the world. Rijonneau at least seemed to know his business—but then, the Prince-Marshal Coindarel rarely promoted incompetents, however pretty.

"Better than trying to take her into a crowd," Eslingen answered, and Rijonneau laughed. They were both stripped to shirtsleeves for the work at hand, and Eslingen guessed he was as dust-streaked as his fellow captain. "Who else do we have to see today?"

"Only one more horse, thank Seidos," Rijonneau answered. "But we're to meet with Estradere and the Prince-Marshal to talk over the candidates."

Eslingen sighed. Every noblewoman at the queen's court was vying to get a son or a nephew appointed to the new Guard, which carried the status of a commission with little risk they'd be sent into battle. He was determined to get people who would be willing to work for the Points—it was one of the promises he'd made Rathe when he took the captaincy—but in practice that meant offending more women of rank than seemed wise.

In the ring, Sendoya brought the mare to a stop and moved in to stroke her long neck, murmuring praise. Out of the corner of his eye, Eslingen saw movement by the stables, turned to see the youngest of the candidates, Balfort de Vian, being boosted into the saddle of a heavy-muscled near-black gelding. Sendoya led the mare away, and the boy—he really was a boy, only seventeen, a striking beauty and the son of one of the Queen's Wardrobe-keepers—edged the gelding through the gate.

"Who's this one?" Eslingen asked, and Rijonneau consulted a slip of paper.

"Prince Crow. Ten years old, supposedly trained to the cavalry."

"We've far too many kings and princes in this bunch," Eslingen murmured, thinking of the mount he'd claimed for his own, King of Thieves, and leaned his weight against the fence.

"Give us a couple of circuits to settle him," Rijonneau called, "then you can put him through his paces."

De Vian lifted a hand in acknowledgement, and edged the gelding into a neat trot, moving clockwise around the ring. Eslingen eyed the gelding's sleek muscles, the arch of his neck and the easy gait, and heard Rijonneau sigh.

"Very pretty."

"The horse or the boy?"

"They're both very nice to look at," Rijonneau said, "but I know I can't afford the horse."

That struck a little close to home: Eslingen had earned his first commission in the marshal's bed. "I expect the dealer wants a pretty price."

"So she does, and then some. Still, Coindarel swears he'll pay for what we need—"

"I'll believe that once he's seen the bill," Eslingen said. It wasn't that he thought Coindarel would go back on his word, or stint them if he could help it, but well-trained horses didn't come cheap. Even in the autumn after the campaign season was ended and impoverished troopers were willing to sell animals they couldn't afford to feed, most would rather go hungry themselves than give up a well-trained mount.

Rijonneau grinned. "Well, there's that. I wonder what nasty habit this one's going to have?"

"Cribbing," Eslingen said.

"No sign of that so far."

"Biter."

"Not near as bad as your beast."

"King of Thieves doesn't bite," Eslingen said, with mock dignity. "He merely takes."

"Buttons, ribbons, hats, sleeves," Rijonneau agreed. "Oh, that's nice."

Eslingen nodded, watching Prince Crow stop neatly from a canter, de Vian nearly motionless on his back. He heard de Vian cluck to the horse, the shift of weight invisible, and Prince Crow moved into a lovely high-stepping trot. De Vian brought him back across the ring with a half pass, then moved into a canter and a series of neat lead changes.

"School movements," Rijonneau said, but Eslingen could hear the desire in his voice.

"The seller warrants he's seen battle."

"Yes, but how did he stand it?" Rijonneau gave a wry smile. "Oh, I'll admit he's a beauty, and I'd love to have him for my mount. But one must be practical."

Eslingen shrugged. "My advice will be to buy him, if you want a practical word. We're not going to find so many horses this well trained that we can afford to pass them by." He lifted a hand to catch de Vian's attention. "Balfort! Bring him over, and tell us what you think."

De Vian wheeled neatly and cantered back across the ring, sliding to a stop beside the fence. "Oh, Captain, he's lovely! Mouth like silk, supple in the shoulders. The Marshal has to buy him."

"I'll tell him you said so," Rijonneau said, and bright color flooded de Vian's ivory skin. He looked even younger on the big gelding, slight and hatless, chestnut hair fraying from its queue, the blush still staining his high cheekbones, and Eslingen suppressed a sigh. He couldn't imagine de Vian calling a point on a foreigner, let alone wading into a fight. Still, pretty boys had been belying their looks since time began, and a little honest enthusiasm did no one any harm.

In the distance, the clock at Manufactory Point struck noon, and Eslingen pushed himself away from the fence. "We should give him a try ourselves if he's that good, but not today. Finish exercising him, Balfort, and when you're done make a note of anything we should know about. In the meantime—you and I have an appointment with the Marshal, Matalin."

They collected coats and hats, and stopped in the stable yard to draw water from the well and sluice off the worst of the dust, shivering in the chill. Eslingen shrugged into vest and coat and loosed his hair from its ribbon, while Rijonneau finished washing his face, wiping his hands on the skirts of his coat.

"And I could wish we had a pump, not a well," he said, "and I'm none so fond of barracks living."

Eslingen grunted agreement. The companies he'd served with had always been billeted on civilians in the towns where they were stationed, which had its disadvantages, but also offered certain freedoms. "At least we only have to be here when we're on duty."

"That's right, you've a leman to think of," Rijonneau said, with a quick grin.

Eslingen spread his hands. "One has obligations."

"And ours is to the Marshal," Rijonneau said, regretfully, and collected his hat.

Barracks and stables had been part of a caravansary built some years before by a Silklands merchant-venturer to house her Chenedolliste family and business. The stables were ordinary enough, but the residence was Silklands style, long and low, with a roofed arcade running along the side that faced the courtyard. That allowed most of the newly-partitioned rooms to have their own door and windows, and the old shop and common spaces had been converted into a dining hall, armory, and workrooms. Coindarel had taken over one of the workrooms, and Eslingen was pleased to see that someone had sent for the noon meal from the Ship, the best of the neighborhood taverns. There were three big pies as well as a pitcher of wine, and as he took his place at the table, his own sergeant, Faraut, nudged him and passed him a knife. Eslingen cut himself a generous slice, glancing around the table to see who was still missing. Coindarel himself was there, of course, genial at the head of the table, and Sendoya and Rijonneau's sergeant Vaulevenarges, which left only Coindarel's own Master Sergeant, Patric Estradere. Even as he thought that, however, the door opened, and Estradere appeared, murmuring an apology as he took his place at the table's foot.

"About the horses," Coindarel said. "That's quite a list you've given me."

Over the course of the meal, Estradere took notes with one hand and ate with the other. Coindarel complained about costs, but, as Eslingen had expected, agreed to most.

"I won't pay more than a petty-crown for that gray mare." Coindarel poured another cup of wine. "She's too young. She's barely trained."

Eslingen heard Faraut sigh—she had had her eye on the little mare—but he couldn't argue with Coindarel's reasoning. Both King of Thieves and Prince Crow had made the main list and that was all he would ask for just now.

"That brings us to the more difficult question," Estradere said. "The company itself."

"There are twenty-five places, and nine of those are filled," Coindarel said. "The rest—well, now you've seen them. Is there anyone you don't want?"

"Bertelieu," Eslingen said promptly. "His sixteen quarterings have gone to his head, and he won't take orders. I don't want a man who won't work with the points."

Rijonneau nodded agreement, and Estradere reached for another list. "Shall I strike him?" he said, to Coindarel, and the Prince-Marshal nodded.

"Aldemayor," Vaulevenarges said, and Rijonneau nodded again.

"Same reason."

"Pallianne," Sendoya said. "I hate to say it, she's more than willing, but—her stars are against her."

"She's the one who keeps getting hurt?" Faraut asked, and Sendoya nodded.

"She's been kicked, stepped on, thrown once—nothing broken, but her wrist swelled up like a melon. She's like to get herself killed."

"Her mother is the Grand Silvan of Tscharn," Estradere said. "It would please her majesty if she remained on the rolls until she chose to leave herself."

"Yes, but she won't," Sendoya said.

"Perhaps one of the captains could have a word with her," Coindarel said. "Otherwise, she stays."

Eslingen sighed. That would probably fall to him, as the senior captain, and that was never a pleasant conversation, telling someone that their dream went against the stars of their birth. And some people did make their way in unlikely professions, against their natal horoscopes, but it was never easy.

"We're still five over," Estradere said. "Anyone else?"

There was a moment of silence, and finally Rijonneau said, "What about de Vian?"

Even his own sergeant gave him a startled look. Eslingen said, "I've seen nothing wrong with the boy."

"I'm not saying there is. There's nothing wrong with him or any of the rest of them." Rijonneau spread his hands. "But nor is he that much better than anyone else, and he's only seventeen…." He shook his head. "If he's even that, I'm not sure he hasn't added a year. If we let him go, he could apply again when he's older."

Eslingen grimaced. If he'd been turned away at fourteen, when he'd run away to join a company, with no more skills than what he'd learned growing up in a stable—but de Vian wasn't a motherless boy from Esling, he reminded himself. "He has enthusiasm. And he's willing to learn."

"Have you been giving lessons, vaan Esling?" Coindarel smiled meaningfully, and Eslingen felt himself blush.

"He came to us knowing more or less what a good fencing master teaches his middling students, and now he's seventh or eighth best in the company. At his age and build, that's doing well."

Faraut looked up from her plate. "I've been giving him extra lessons, sir—and before anyone asks, not that kind—and he's been more willing to work than most of those sixteen-quartering bastards. Begging your pardon, sir."

Rijonneau made a face. "Who do we get rid of, then? I'm not averse to keeping him, but you heard the man, we're still over strength."

Estradere turned over a sheet of paper. "The boy's sister is the Vidame d'Entrebeschaire—the mother was a Mistress of the Queen's Wardrobe, received the title on retirement. She's dead now, and the sister is trying to place him respectably—she did not inherit her mother's place in the Wardrobe. There are two other brothers to provide for."

"All right," Rijonneau said, "not the boy."

Eslingen nodded in agreement. Maybe that was what had caught his attention, besides the boy's looks: de Vian had flung himself into every task as though he was looking for a home.

"Well, sort it out among yourselves," Coindarel said. "I can't and won't fund the company at this size—you'll have to rid yourselves of some of them."

Eslingen and Estradere nodded.

"In the meantime…." Coindarel rose gracefully, the skirts of his long coat swirling. "I'm sure you have plenty left to do."

COINDAREL HADN'T BEEN wrong about that, Eslingen thought, as he made his way west along the Sier's northern bank. At least it was early enough still that he could spend an hour at the baths, and maybe even spend the extra demming for the masseur. He could feel the day's work in back and seat and thighs. It was too early yet for the hot-nut vendors to be out, but the apple-men were present, elderly men from the country with baskets on their arms and knitted caps shaped like their goods. Eslingen slowed his pace as he spotted a man selling the small, sweet fruit called love-knots, and happily paid a demming for three. He tucked two into his pockets, heedless of whether it might spoil the fabric, and bit into the third, eyes closing as he tasted the familiar crisp sweetness. Juice ran down his chin; he wiped it with the back of his hand, then licked his fingers before tossing what was left of the core into the nearest midden. He wondered if Rathe liked them: one of the many things they'd not yet learned about each other.

"Hsst! Captain!"

Eslingen looked up sharply, hand drifting toward the knife he wore beneath his coat. There weren't many people in Astreiant who knew him by that rank, and not all of them were friendly. For a moment, he couldn't tell who called, but then a man moved in the shadow of a doorway. Eslingen blinked, recognizing a sailor's knitted tunic and wide trousers, and then the straw-colored hair triggered memory: Young Steen, captain of the *Soeuraigne of Bedarres*—a man with ties to both Eslingen's old employer Hanselin Caiazzo and to the honest work of the riverfront.

"Steen."

"A word with you, if I might."

"All right." Eslingen wiped his fingers again on his breeches. "I'm headed to the Hopes-Point Bridge—"

"I'd rather talk here. And—maybe more privately."

Eslingen glanced over his shoulder, wondering what had put Young Steen's hackles up. No one seemed to be paying any attention to them, but he lowered his voice anyway. "The tavern?"

Steen nodded. "They'll let me in with you."

It was, Eslingen realized, the sort of place that catered to the wealthier merchants-resident, perhaps even to the elegant clerks of All-Guilds, who served the regents. But Steen was right, the rich blue coat and silver badge of the City Guard would ensure their acceptance, even if he winced a little at the thought of the prices. He pushed through the door into a warm, dimly-lit room, a bar and serving hatch to the right, and a generous fire burning in the hearth at the back of the room. Most of the tables were empty, only a handful of women sitting close to the fire, and another pair tucked into a corner, a branch of candles and what looked like an account book between them. The tavern's knife, homely and deceptively slim, looked up from his stool by the door, flexing corded hands, but then recognized Eslingen's uniform and relaxed again. Eslingen nodded in acknowledgement, and took Steen's elbow to steer him toward a corner table.

"So what's going on?" He broke off as the waiter popped out of the shadows, and ordered a pint of wine and, as the waiter remained, hovering, a plate of bread and cheese. He saw the waiter's lip curl at his frugality, and added, "Apple fritters?"

The waiter bowed. "We have that, sir. Will you have the cheese with that?"

Eslingen nodded, and the man scurried away.

Steed's unease was evident as he looked around. "Not the sort of place plain folk go to drink."

"You didn't want to be seen," Eslingen reminded him, and Steen sighed. He looked more prosperous than he had the last time Eslingen had seen him, tunic and trousers of better quality, clean and unpatched, but there was no mistaking him for anything but a sailor. And maybe more than a sailor: he wore three silver bracelets on each wrist, and a set of gold earrings, one with a pendant pearl, more jewels than an honest man could afford. But then, rumor said that Steen, like his father and grandfather before him, was what Astreiant called a summer-sailor and everyone else named a pirate. Certainly Eslingen's old employer, Hanselin Caiazzo, who had at least a finger in most things illegal around Customs Point, had been happy to employ Steen's father. "You're looking well—and well-off. If this is summer business—"

Steen shook his head. "I'm keeping to the common trade just now. I've made a good bargain with my owner."

The waiter returned with wine and plates, and Eslingen poured for both of them, watching Young Steen's nervous hands as he plucked a fritter into steaming pieces. "It's about the docks," he said, without looking up. "Which I know isn't your business, or Rathe's, but Sighs is too well-fee'd to look into anything, and I haven't the money to top the offer."

Eslingen nodded.

"Understand, there's always extortion on the docks," Steen said. "It's a cost of doing business, we all pay it, and our goods get put ashore quick and neat."

"And if you don't pay?" Eslingen asked, when it seemed Steen wasn't going to continue.

Steen shrugged one shoulder. "Then it takes forever to get unloaded, and things go missing, and sometimes something gets broken, too. Or someone has an accident. But it's different this year." He leaned forward, lowering his voice so that Eslingen had to lean forward himself to keep from missing anything. "This year, they want twice what they charged last year, and they want it in coin, not goods. That was how most of us paid, we're coin-poor until we unload and things get sold, so we'd bring a few extra barrels of wine or bolts of fine silk or whatever we'd been trading in, and the dock bosses would take that for their payment. But this year, unless you've got tea to trade, they want silver coin only, thank you, and twice as much. And they don't stay bought like they used to, either."

Eslingen nodded again. "Not a good situation, I see that. But you said it yourself, this isn't Guard business. We deal with foreigners and nobles, and these sound like homegrown trouble."

"They are."

"And I'll happily share the news with Rathe, but I know what he'll say. This happens in Point of Sighs, it's Sighs' business. Unless—I don't suppose you or your owner lodge outside of Sighs?"

"Jesine's family lives northriver—Dame Hardelet, my owner, that is. City Point is her station, but they don't deal with trade. They've made that clear. Where I lodge, you might stretch a point and call it Point of Hopes, but—" Steen shook his head. "I don't want to go to the points directly. Jesine's increasing, and a pregnant woman's too easy a target. And, yes, they've made that threat explicitly."

Eslingen tipped his head, hearing something in the other's tone. "Yours?"

"Yes." Steen grinned like the sun breaking through clouds, as though the mere thought was enough to drive off the worry of the dockside gangs. "The stars say it's a girl, to be born at midwinter."

"Felicitations." Eslingen couldn't help matching the smile.

"Now you see why we can't risk a complaint," Steen said, his smile fading. "The *Soeuraine* is her biggest ship, true enough, but she's got part-interests in half a dozen more, and she's up and down the docks day-long right now. It would be too easy to hurt her. That's why I didn't want to be seen with you."

"If no one complains," Eslingen said, "there's not much the points can do. You know that."

"Someone might. If you think Rathe—or you—would be willing to listen, I can put that word out. Discreetly, mind you, and you'd have to promise discretion—but I thought someone ought to know."

Eslingen sighed. "I'll tell Nico. But I can't promise it will do any good. The points are...territorial."

Steen drained his cup, and pushed himself away from the table. "You'll forgive me if I leave separately."

"Probably wise," Eslingen said, to his retreating back, and rested his shoulders against the wall.

He took the time to finish his wine and the rest of the now-cold fritters and the bread and cheese, then tipped the waiter more than he deserved, and stood in the tavern doorway for a long moment, adjusting hat and gloves, while he took a careful look along the length of the street. From what he'd seen while he was in Caiazzo's service, he believed every word of Steen's complaint, and had no desire to add to the young captain's troubles. There were similar gangs in Customs Point, though most of them knew better than to trouble Caiazzo's people, but he'd seen what they'd done to women who didn't have that protection. There were no obvious knives in sight, however, just the usual evening traffic making its way along the Mercandry where it paralleled the Sier, a few masts rising above the tiled roofs, ships' hulls glimpsed at the end of the alleys between the factors' halls. Most of them were still brightly lit, mage-lights and lamplight showing at the ground-floor windows, and where the double doors gaped open to let in a breath of air, he could see the halls crowded with women in fine wools and the occasional velvet: the merchants-resident worked by the clock, not by the light of day. The thought was steadying, after Steen's fear: there would certainly be knives in plenty, but they'd be at their employers' sides, not stalking the streets.

He paused again at the foot of the Hopes-point Bridge, pretending to look at a broadsheet posted outside one of the bakeshops. Where other such shops had gardens out back, a pier jutted out over the river, tarred wood and tattered awnings over a scattering of empty benches. Lanterns bobbed in the freshening breeze, magelights glowing behind the painted paper. The tide was half out, though he couldn't have said whether it was on the fall or rise: a wet beach of mud and stone and less wholesome debris lay beneath the pier, and he wrinkled his nose as the wind carried the smell. On the far side of the river, stretching east from the foot of the bridge, lay Point of Sighs, the docks so crowded with ships that the masts looked like a leafless, near-limbless forest. House-pennants flew from their tops, and from the warehouses and factors' towers, but in the gathering dusk, it was impossible to make out color or design. The *Soeuraine of Bedarres* would be somewhere among them, though, and the extortion gang, too, moving along dock and street and foreshore like gargoyles along the housetops. It was very much Point of Sighs' business, but he'd learned long ago that not every station kept their books as clean as Point of Dreams. Or, more to the point, as Rathe himself: he was the exception to the rule that the points worked harder if you paid an extra fee.

He glanced around, seeing nothing that made him think he'd been followed, that his conversation with Young Steen had been noticed, and joined the stream of people making their way across the river. Maybe Rathe could think of something clever. At the end of the bridge, he turned west, deliberately turning his back on Point of Sighs, and threaded his way through the twilight streets. The winter-sun wouldn't be up for another couple of hours; it would be full dark, thieves' dark, before then, and he was unsurprised to see a pair of pointsmen walking patrol along a section of Lacemakers' Street.

Another patrol was leaving as he reached the gates of Point of Dreams, and he recognized the young woman who held the gate for him as the woman who'd come to collect Rathe the night before. "Still on night duty, Sohier?"

She gave him a quick grin in answer. "Only till the end of the month. If you're looking for Rathe, I think he's down the cells."

"Thanks." Eslingen crossed the courtyard, nodding a greeting to the runner hauling water from the building's well, and pushed through the door into the main room. He didn't recognize the man at the duty point's desk, but the man seemed to recognize him, and came to his feet at his entrance.

"Lieutenant—I'm sorry, Captain vaan Esling! Would you mind waiting a moment? I know the chief would like a word with you."

"The chief?" Eslingen repeated, but the man—Ivelin, he remembered, too late—was already clattering up the stairs toward the workrooms. Eslingen moved closer to the fire, casting a look around to see if he knew anyone else, but the handful of pointsmen still present were bent over their work, mending gear or scribbling assiduously in a set of tablets, refusing to meet his eye. One woman stood apart, still in her leather jerkin over a shortened skirt that showed a hand's breadth of striped stockings above the tops of her shoes. Not part of Dreams' contingent, Eslingen thought, from the way the others left space around her, but he didn't think he'd seen her before.

"Captain vaan Esling!" Ivelin came back down the stairs, ready to resume his post. "The chief says, would you go up, please?"

That was unlikely to be Trijn's actual wording, but Eslingen appreciated the attempt at tact.

"Actually, I was here to see Adjunct Point Rathe."

"He's there, too," Ivelin said. "If you please, Captain?"

There was no point in arguing. Eslingen made his way up the stairs, to see the workroom door standing open at the end of the hall. It swung wider as he approached, and Rathe looked out, scowling.

"Oh, good. Come on in."

There was no chance to ask questions. Eslingen could see Trijn at her table, paper spread out in front of her, and a stocky man sat opposite her, his frown even deeper than Rathe's. "Chief Point," he said, with a half bow that was meant to include the two men as well.

"Captain." Trijn spoke the word with a sort of relish, as though she was aware of and enjoyed the joke: Eslingen was no more expected to bear a commission than he was entitled to the aristocratic version of his name. "You've arrived conveniently."

"Have I?" Eslingen asked, but she ignored him, gesturing to the stranger at her table.

"Captain vaan Esling, allow me to present Adjunct Point Dammar, of Point of Sighs. Adjunct Point, this is Captain vaan Esling of the City Guard."

"And what in Astree's name does the City Guard have to do with this?" Dammar caught himself. "Your pardon, Captain. A pleasure to meet you."

"And you," Eslingen murmured. He let his eyes drift sideways to where Rathe leaned against the door, arms folded, but Rathe no sign of what this was or how he wanted it played.

"Were you aware that there was murder done in Point of Sighs last night?" Trijn asked.

Eslingen hesitated, but could read nothing in Rathe's expression. "I had heard that much, yes."

"Adjunct Point Dammar called the point on Mattaes Staenka last night, and he, as a resident of Point of Dreams, lodged in our cells overnight," Trijn said. "Today his sister has sent to request bail, and has offered a sufficient surety that I'm inclined to grant it."

"Which I protest," Dammar said. "And I have my chief's authority to do so."

Trijn dipped her head. "So you do. And she's welcome to take it up with the surintendant. But unless you have more evidence than you had last night—"

"There was blood all over the boy's shirt!" Dammar's color darkened toward apoplexy. "And I'll lay money he's not offered any explanation."

"He insists it's not his shirt," Rathe said. "And we took another look at the laundry mark by daylight: it's not his, and not a match to any of the shirts in the house."

"The Staenkas are well-respected merchants-resident," Trijn said, "and have offered more than adequate assurances, including a note of hand for sixty pillars as a pledge for his appearance to answer the point. I see no reason to treat them any differently from any other household of their rank."

"That's your prerogative, of course," Dammar said, tight-lipped, "but I promise you, Astarac will take this to the surintendant."

"And so she may, with my blessing." Trijn showed teeth in an approximation of a smile. "But for now and until the sur himself rules otherwise—Mattaes is free to leave."

"If that's the way of it, Sighs should keep the note," Dammar said.

"It's inscribed to Point of Dreams," Trijn answered. "They're residents here. You've no real rights to them save what I give you—"

"And what good is a bond that goes to fee a family friend?" Dammar demanded.

Rathe moved then, the barest shift of weight, jerkin whispering against the wood panels. Trijn shook her head, her eyes narrowing, but fixed her attention on Dammar.

"Be that as it may," she said, "and I'd suggest you not make that accusation again, Adjunct Point, you agreed to let him be held here, so you've no right to it, either. I suggest that the City Guard hold it for us, until the surintendant decides otherwise. Or until it can be returned to its maker."

This time Eslingen looked openly at Rathe, and caught the quick twist of his lips that meant reluctant agreement. "If that would resolve this problem for the moment," he said carefully, "I would of course be willing to oblige."

"Excellent." Trijn shoved a roll of paper across her desk. It was taped and triply sealed, a neat secretary's hand crossing the seam where the folds overlapped, certifying that the document had been signed and sealed before and with the full knowledge of Meisenta Staenka. That was unusual—surely Meisenta herself should have endorsed the note—but he took it anyway and slipped it into the cuff of his coat.

"You'd better hand that over to your colonel straightaway," Dammar snapped.

Eslingen lifted his eyebrows. "At this hour? As soon as I may."

Dammar stiffened. "Hardly reassuring. If you're going to let the brat go, Chief Trijn, I'll take him home."

"I'll just come along," Rathe said, and Trijn lifted a hand.

"I think we can ask Captain vaan Esling to see to that as well. If you'd be so good, Captain."

Eslingen hesitated. This was exactly what no one wanted from the City Guard, interference in what was entirely the Points' business. And yet he couldn't very well refuse Trijn's request, particularly when he saw exactly how it made things easier for everyone. "I'm certainly willing to do it as a favor to Sighs and Dreams," he said, "though I think we can all agree that it's not properly our place to intervene."

Trijn nodded. "Well spoken. And thank you."

"We'll keep you company, Bertelan and I—" Dammar began.

Trijn lifted a hand. "No, no, Adjunct Point, we've handed this off to the City Guard. Let the good captain handle it."

Out of the corner of his eye, Eslingen saw Rathe relax again.

"You'll not send your man, then, either?" Dammar rubbed his chin.

"Nor will I," Trijn said.

"I've got business here still," Rathe said. His eyes slid sideways, and Eslingen tipped his head forward: message received. He'd come back here once he'd delivered the Staenka boy.

"You'll not send him out onto the streets at full dark carrying a note of hand like that," Dammar said.

"And who but us would know who had it?" Eslingen asked. He pulled the packet from his sleeve. "But as it happens, I think you're right. I'll ask Chief Trijn to keep it for me until I can lodge it in the Guard's strongbox."

Dammar opened his mouth again to protest, then seemed to realize that he'd backed himself into a corner.

Trijn gave a thin smile. "I'll send word to Chief Astarac once he's safely lodged at home. The agreement is that he won't leave the house without my permission. And Astarac's, of course."

There was nothing more to say, Eslingen thought. Dammar recognized it, too, and managed a strangled agreement before he turned on his heel and stalked away. Eslingen could hear his boots loud on the boards of the hall, and repressed the desire to be sure that he was gone. "Chief Point—"

"I'll keep the note for you," Trijn said, "but in the meantime you'd best get the boy home."

The cells at Point of Dreams lay below the street, in a stone vault that had probably once been a part of the cellars. It was well lit, mage-light and lamplight both, but the cells were small and the stone walls held the autumn damp. They were scantily furnished, just a wooden cot and mattress, and Eslingen suppressed an old anger. Rathe had spent too many nights here after the midwinter masque almost a year ago, the point called even though Rathe—with Eslingen's help—had managed to stop a plot that would have resulted in the queen's death and chaos to the realm. In fact, it was because he'd stopped it, killed the noble behind the conspiracy, that he'd been locked up. If it had been an ordinary woman....

He was becoming as much of a Leveler as Rathe, he thought, and dredged up a smile for the duty point. "A bond's been set for Mattaes Staenka. I'm to escort him home."

Mattaes proved to be older than Eslingen had expected, or at least old enough that a night and day in the cells had left a fine stubble on his cheeks. His clothes were crumpled, and he'd been using his cloak for a blanket, but he seemed otherwise untouched by the experience. He followed Eslingen quietly enough, but at the top of the stairs he hesitated.

"You're no pointsman."

"Philip vaan Esling, captain in the City Guard." Eslingen sketched a bow. "Your—sister, was it?—your kin have posted a bond, at any rate, and I've been asked to take you back to them."

"On terms," Trijn said, coming down the stairs to join them. "You're to remain at home, in the house, unless either I or Chief Astarac of Point of Sighs grants permission for you to leave. Are you clear on that?"

"Yes, Chief Point."

He sounded docile enough, Eslingen thought. It was no wonder everyone seemed to think of him as a boy.

"Phelis will light your way," Trijn went on, gesturing to a runner who waited with a lantern. "She knows the direction."

Eslingen gave her another bow, grateful he wouldn't have to ask the way. "Thank you, Chief Point. We'll be on our way."

It was full dark now, the streets nearly empty: most women were snug at home or settled into a tavern or a cookshop to wait out the hours of thieves' dark before the winter-sun rose. The area around the station was generally safe enough, and the wealthy residential neighborhoods hired their own knives and watchmen for the weeks when the winter-sun rose later and later, but even so Eslingen was glad of the knife at his hip. He would have preferred a proper sword, but the city's laws limited the length of blade that could be carried in the streets. His own might be a finger's-width beyond that limit, and he certainly didn't want to argue the question with any of Rathe's fellows.

Phelis opened the lantern's shutter all the way, casting a fan of light across the beaten path. Eslingen did his best to divide his attention between his footing and the alleys that gaped between buildings, and was unsurprised when Mattaes lurched suddenly against him. Eslingen steadied him, and felt the young man shiver under his touch.

"Are you all right?"

He felt Mattaes shrug. "I suppose. Not hurt, at any rate."

He might have been referring to his stumble, but there was something in the taut stance that suggested a more general meaning. Eslingen felt his eyebrows rise. "And were you expecting to be, after your sister paid the fee to lodge you at Dreams instead of Sighs?"

Mattaes darted a glance at him. "I wasn't sure the fee would hold. Or that I'd get bail."

"And yet here you are."

"Yes." It was hard to tell in the dim light, but Eslingen thought the other's smile was wry. "I've never had—none of us have ever had much dealing with the points."

Eslingen could think of no good answer to that statement: everything that came to mind either seemed to blame the points, or gave Mattaes too much credit. He said instead, "You're from the tea-house family? I've seen your shop on the Mercandry."

There was a movement in the shadows that might have been a nod. "That's us. It's my sisters' business, really."

And that was only to be expected, in a family with two competent daughters. "And it's your own tea captain you're supposed to have murdered?"

"I didn't kill him." Mattaes sounded tired of defending himself. "And bes'Anthe's not really our captain, not exclusively, which only makes things worse."

Eslingen made a noncommittal noise, hoping to keep him talking, but Mattaes said nothing more, following in Phelis's wake as she turned onto a residential street where trees stretched over the garden walls. Rathe would know exactly what to ask, how to keep him going, Eslingen thought, but he himself had no idea what he was doing. He cleared his throat, searching for the right words. "Was that why you argued—since he wasn't your regular captain?"

"That was part of it. You'll have heard that the season closed sooner than usual?"

"Yes."

"Our usual captain is somewhere down the coast, or at least we hope he is, Meisenta hasn't actually had word yet. He stayed to try to get a few extra chests of the Old Year, which he does every year—we're known for Old Year blends, there's no one in the city who makes better than us." Pride seeped into the boy's voice at last.

"So I've heard." Eslingen had never actually tasted any of the Old Year teas, which sold for a silver pillar an ounce, two weeks' wages for most women.

"Meisenta never puts all her eggs in one basket, she had our Silklands factors ship home two-thirds of the yearly purchase with other captains, and bes'Anthe was one of them. It was a good deal for him, he's not worked much in the tea trade before this, but Aucher said he came well recommended. And then he had the nerve to demand extra fees from me. Said he had unexpected expenses!"

Eslingen's attention sharpened at that. If the gang Young Steen had mentioned was affecting the tea captains.…"What sort of expenses?"

He felt Mattaes hesitate, saw one shoulder move again in a shrug. "I wouldn't know—he didn't say."

"Surely he had some accounting to give you."

"If he had, he didn't share it with me." Mattaes lifted his head. "Good, we're almost home."

He lengthened his stride, not quite running, but Eslingen had to stretch to keep up. Phelis darted up the steps ahead of them to slam the knocker against its plate, and a moment later, a severely dressed man peered out at them.

"Yes—?"

"I'm home, Drowe," Mattaes said, and for just an instant the servant's face relaxed into unmistakable relief.

The servant nodded at Eslingen. "Very good, sir, thank you for bringing him—"

"I'm Captain vaan Esling of the City Guard and my warrant is to give him into his sister's hands." That was stretching a point, he knew, but he wanted to see the rest of the family.

"Very well." Drowe retreated into the hall. "If you'll wait here, I'll inform Madame Staenka."

"She'll be in the parlor," Mattaes said, and once again he sounded as if he might collapse. "It won't be long."

"This way, if you please, Captain?" Drowe beckoned from a door half-way down the hall, and Eslingen tapped Mattaes on the shoulder.

"Let's go."

This was not the formal parlor, Eslingen saw at first glance. This was the family's room, a fire lit on the hearth and another more effectively in the tall iron stove tucked into one corner. The floor was thick was carpets, the scent of lavender rising from them with every step, and a collection of small tables was piled with books and sewing baskets and balls of yarn. A tall, sharp-nosed woman sat beside the stove, and a dark-haired man sat beside a branch of candles, a book closed on his finger to keep his place, while another fair woman had risen from her seat by the hearth, threads still clinging to her skirt. He made a general bow, and the standing woman said, "Captain vaan Esling, you said?"

Eslingen bowed again. "At your service."

"And why is it the City Guard's business to bring my brother home?" That was the seated woman, her eyes wandering even as she turned her head to him: blind or so short-sighted as not even to see shapes beyond the reach of her arm.

"I'm acting at the request of Chief Point Trijn. As this is properly Point of Sighs' business—their body, their point—she felt having the Guard escort him would remove any question of undue favor from his home station."

"Sweet Heira," the standing woman said. "Still more trouble than you're worth."

"Leave me alone, Redel," Mattaes said tonelessly.

The seated woman—she had to be Meisenta, the elder sister—ignored them both. "Is Point of Sighs determined to pursue this?"

"They have a dead man on their books, madame," Eslingen answered.

She made an impatient sound. "You know what I meant, Captain. Do they still place the blame on my brother?"

"At the moment, yes. I don't know what evidence they have, or whether anything new has been found since last night."

"Hah." Meisenta's hands tightened on the arms of her chair, then relaxed as though by an effort of will. "Surely we will be able to convince them of their error."

"If an error has been made, I'm sure they'll find it," Eslingen said. "In the meantime, Chief Point Trijn asked me to review the details of the bail agreement before I give Mattaes into your hands."

"I understand them," Meisenta said.

"Mattaes is not to leave this house without Trijn's express permission," Eslingen began, and Meisenta frowned.

"I said, I understood."

"And I hope you'll forgive me, madame, but it's my duty to restate the terms." He waited, and she waved a hand.

"Go on, then."

"Your brother is not to leave this house or its ground without permission from Point of Dreams," Eslingen said, "though Chief Astarac at Point of Sighs can also release him. Your note of hand is to be held by the City Guard and will be returned to you once he makes his appearance before the judiciary or the point is dismissed."

"Very well," Meisenta said. "You may tell Chief Trijn that I intend to keep my brother close at home, and he will be at her disposal should she have further questions. And I'm sure this unfortunate business will be cleared up shortly. Thank you for your time and efforts, Captain."

Eslingen made her his most courtly bow. "Delighted to be of service, madame."

Redel pushed herself away from the fireplace. "I'll walk you out, Captain."

That was hardly necessary. Eslingen swallowed the words, and let her lead him to the door. In the hall, she paused, glancing over her shoulder at the half-open door, and lowered her voice.

"My sister can be a bit abrupt. But her thanks are sincere."

"I never doubted it."

"What should we do to help Mattaes's case? I know it looks bad—that bloody shirt. But I can't believe he'd harm anyone."

"The points will be asking questions," Eslingen said. "Tell them what you know. Point of Dreams wants to believe you, even if Sighs doesn't."

"Or at least Meisenta's fee'd them well over the years." Redel laid a hand on his sleeve. "It was good of you to stand between them for us. Would you be willing to act as our representative, speak for us—for Mattaes— to both sides?"

Eslingen winced. This was exactly what Rathe had feared would happen once the Guard was established, women trying to use it against the points to further their own ends. And while Rathe would certainly agree that there were questions about this point, he'd also be right to say that it was a bad precedent. And yet this was a chance to get the Staenkas to cooperate with the investigation. "The Guard has no right to interfere in the points' work," he said. "Our responsibilities are different. But I'll do what I can."

"That's all anyone can ask," Redel said. "And I assure you, we will be grateful."

"I don't take fees."

But the door had already opened into the night.

CHAPTER 3

B Y THE TIME Eslingen returned to Point of Dreams, the clock had struck eight and the dinner Rathe had ordered from Wicked's had grown cold in its basket. It was also raining again, the winter-sun and the waxing moon both hidden by clouds, and he was feeling more than a bit put-upon by the time he'd shrugged his still-damp cloak over his shoulders. Eslingen was looking a bit frayed himself, though, and Rathe buried his annoyance in making sure the oilcloth that lined the basket was snugged tightly in place. At the door, Eslingen balked, staring out into a driving rain that splashed from the puddles and turned the muddy cobbles dangerous underfoot.

"I thought it was slacking."

"Not noticeably." Rathe watched a sheet of rain drive across the court-yard, caught in the magelights. "And not looking likely to any time soon. We can sleep in the cells, or dry off when we get home."

"I've seen your cells once today," Eslingen said, and settled his hat more firmly on his head.

They made their way through nearly empty streets, the rain beating down on them. At least the wind was at their backs, Rathe thought, hunching his shoulders to tip his hood forward. He was grateful for his boots as well, a good secondhand pair that Eslingen had insisted on buying for him: shoes and stockings would be soaked through already by now, but he was only just beginning to feel the damp on his toes. "So you got Mattaes back to his sister in good order?"

Eslingen slipped and splashed into a deeper puddle, righted himself with a curse. "Yes. And I've another bit of news for you. You remember Young Steen?"

"The summer-sailor?" Rathe squinted into the rain, glad that piracy was not his business. That was a matter for the pontoises, the boatmen who had jurisdiction over the river and its docks.

"I gather he's honest now. Mostly," Eslingen said. "His owner's taken him for her man, or at least to father her child, so he's staying on the right side of the law."

"That's a change for that family."

Eslingen laughed. "He might find it a tad safer."

Young Steen's father and grandfather had been pirates as well, and both had ended up murdered. "So what did he want?"

Eslingen glanced behind them, and sputtered as a gust of rain struck him in the face. "Damn this weather. He said he was having trouble with a gang on the docks—that all the captains were."

"There's always graft on the docks," Rathe said. "And that's Point of Sighs' business, not mine. Or the pontoises."

"I hadn't thought of them," Eslingen said. "But, anyway, Young Steen says it's worse than usual this year. The gangs are demanding bigger fees, and they want to be paid in cash, not kind."

"And it's still not my business," Rathe said. "Who's his owner—one of the Hardelets, wasn't it? She's got money enough to fee Sighs well enough to get the problem stopped."

"Apparently she doesn't think so. She's increasing, Steen says, and the gang's threatened her directly."

"Nasty." Rathe shook his head. "But we're already at odds with Sighs over this murder. If we try to interfere with this, Astarac will have every reason to go straight to the sur."

"I told him there wasn't much you could do," Eslingen said, "but he said he wanted someone he trusted to know about it. Do you think the pontoises might be able to help?"

Rathe winced as another blast of wind-driven rain lashed across his shoulders. "They claim the parts of the docks that extend into the river. Though, like the women at Sighs, they're not always the most honest."

"I hear they stay bought," Eslingen offered.

"Which I'll admit is more than I can say for Sighs." They were at their own gate at last, and Rathe fumbled with the latch. "I can talk to the cap'pontoise, if you'd like."

"I can't see how it would hurt," Eslingen began, and swore again. Rathe glanced back to see that one of the trees outside the weaver's door, weighted down with apples and rain, had swept the hat from Eslingen's head. He clapped it back onto his dripping hair, and released another stream of water to drip from nose and chin. Rathe suppressed his laughter, and hurried across the courtyard to the stairs that led to their rooms. Eslingen pressed into the lobby beside him, soaked and squelching, and Rathe closed the door again behind them.

"Come on, we can get you dry upstairs."

They felt their way up the familiar stairs, not bothering to light a lamp, and Rathe worked the lock of his own rooms. It was equally dark inside even with the shutters open; he heard Sunflower struggle out from his favorite corner between the clothes press and the chest, and then he'd struck a spark and gotten the first candle lit. He heard a wet slap and a yelp behind him, glanced back to see Eslingen methodically discarding his soaked clothes while Sunflower bounced back and forth around the growing puddles. The Leaguer's lips were tightly compressed, as though he were holding back some particularly pungent comment, and Rathe looked away, concentrating on lighting the rest of the candles.

When he looked back, Eslingen had stripped naked—even his small-clothes appeared to be soaked—and he was squeezing water out of the ends of his long hair. Rathe grimaced in what he hoped would be taken for sympathy, and moved the kettle to the front of the stove before starting to build up the fire. "When you say your stars are bad for water...."

"Yes." Eslingen's voice was tight, but he made an effort to smile. "Apparently it applies to rain, too, at least this time of year." Sunflower approached the piled clothes with a growl, and Eslingen snatched them up, disappearing into the narrow bedroom.

Rathe coaxed the fire to life, found the tea chest and teapot and had everything waiting by the time Eslingen returned. He had wrapped himself in his brocade dressing gown and combed out his hair so that it lay like black satin across his shoulders. Sunflower frolicked at his feet, and Rathe reached automatically for one of the bits of dried biscuit they kept for bribery. "Settle."

Sunflower snatched the biscuit from his hand and retreated under the clothes-press. Eslingen quirked a smile. "Got anything for me?"

"Do you need to be bribed to sit by the stove?"

"Not I. Not today." Eslingen seated himself at their battered table, stretching bare feet toward the raised bricks where the stove rested. "Sweet Tyrseis, what a night!"

"The water's almost hot enough," Rathe said. "Then we'll have tea."

"I'd rather have something a bit stronger."

There was a note in his voice that made Rathe look more closely. Eslingen had drawn the gown tight around himself, arms pressed hard against his sides as though to keep from shivering. "That could be arranged."

He found the bottle of *menthe*, the neck crusted with sugar, worked the stopper free and poured a small glass. Eslingen took it with a nod of thanks, and tossed it back in a single swallow. Rathe lifted an eyebrow, but filled it again.

"Are you all right?"

"Cold and wet and tired of being wet." Eslingen's smile was wry. "All my planets are in their detriment, and the moon's in the Dolphin for at least another week."

"Can we hope it'll be better then?" The kettle was bubbling; Rathe found a cloth and filled the teapot.

"It's square to retrograde Tyrseis, too," Eslingen said.

The retrograde movement intensified the negative effects that came with a challenging square: you didn't have to be a follower of broadsheet astrology to know that much. Rathe grimaced again. "Drink."

Eslingen lifted the little glass in salute, though this time he took only a small swallow. "It's such petty things. I bought an oiled-silk parasol, and the first gust of wind split the fabric. I can't walk under any building's eaves without the run-off landing on me. If there's a puddle, I'll stumble into it, and if I can't get around, it'll be knee-deep. I tell you, Nico, I'm sick of it."

Like Istre b'Estorr at Ghost-tide. Rathe swallowed the words, knowing they wouldn't make anything better—Eslingen was still touchy about the necromancer, for all that b'Estorr and Rathe had never been more than friends—and poured the tea instead. "Here. This'll warm you."

"Thanks." Eslingen accepted the cup, sipped cautiously at the steaming liquid. "Ah, that's good."

He was starting to relax, Rathe saw, and settled himself across the table, the teapot and the candles between them. "As it happens, it's the Staenkas' ordinary. They give value for the money. And, speaking of whom—did you get Mattaes settled? Sighs didn't try anything on the way?"

"No, nothing," Eslingen answered. "I took him back home, gave him into his sisters' care—repeated Trijn's rules for them—and that was pretty much it. Do you think he did it?"

Rathe shrugged. "I don't know. There's that shirt to consider."

"Which he says isn't his." Eslingen said. "He doesn't seem like the sort."

"No more does he." Rathe topped up their teacups, and saw Eslingen frown.

"I nearly forgot. We talked a little on our way back to the house. Mattaes said he'd quarreled with the captain over the captain's claim for extra expenses, and I wondered if he'd run foul of the same gang that's threatening Young Steen.."

"That's worth following up on," Rathe agreed.

Eslingen sighed. "There's one more thing. Redel Staenka asked me to act for the family in this."

Rathe stiffened. This was exactly what he had dreaded from the moment the Guard had been created, one more interested party able to interfere in the points' investigation. The points were granted the right to enforce the queen's law, not anyone else, and if they were imperfect—and the gods knew they were often less than entirely honorable, or even fully honest—at least their rights and role were clear. The Guard was supposed to deal only with the nobility, and with foreigners, not with citizens of the city. "What did you say?" He was pleased that his voice was steady.

"I told her the Guard had no right to do such a thing."

But. The word hung in the air between them, clear as daybreak, and the trouble was, this was exactly the sort of exception where someone from the Guard might make a difference. He himself couldn't go into Point of Sighs, not without considerably more backing than even Trijn was able to give him, never mind willing, and without being able to act, there was no telling whether Mattaes was wrongly accused. Trijn would make use of Eslingen without a second thought, and damn the precedent—and that was exactly how the pontoises had given way to the points, case by case, year by year. And yet—it might still be the best chance of proving the boy's guilt or innocence.

"I don't like it."

"I didn't think you would." Eslingen leaned forward, resting his elbows on the table. "Look, Nico, I'll follow your lead on this."

"I knew this would happen. Damn it, Philip."

"If you say no, I won't do it."

"That's not the point."

Eslingen moved closer to Rathe. "Then what is?"

"We need your help—I need it, Trijn needs it, and the Staenkas need it, because Dammar's determined to see that boy hang."

"He's not that much of a boy," Eslingen said. "Let's talk to Trijn in the morning, and if she says yes, I'll have a word with Coindarel. Surely there's a way to make this work."

Rathe sighed. "You're right, damn it. We can figure something out."

Eslingen nodded. "In the meantime—it's late, Nico, and I'm cold, and I swear I'm wet under my skin."

"I expect we can do something about that," Rathe said, and was rewarded with one of Eslingen's slow and knowing smiles. "Let's to bed."

As RATHE HAD expected, Trijn was more than willing to make use of the Staenkas' unexpected request, which did no more to improve his temper than the scudding clouds and the cold draft that whistled through the gaps in the rattling windows.

"I'll need to have Coindarel's permission," Eslingen said, carefully not looking at Rathe, "but then—I'm at your disposal, Chief." He paused. "Did you want me to take the bond to him as well?"

"Yes," Trijn answered, and drew the packet out from under a pile of papers "And I'd like a bit more detail in young Mattaes's story. So the sooner you get the Prince-Marshal's permission, the happier I'll be."

Eslingen bowed. "If you'll excuse me?"

Trijn waved her hand, and Eslingen withdrew, with only a fleeting glance at Rathe. Rathe caught the rolling eye, however, and tightened his lips to keep from grinning.

"Sit." Trijn pointed to the nearest stool. "I know your mood, but even you have to see this is a gods-sent gift."

"That the Staenkas want Philip's help?" Rathe seated himself. "I see that it makes things easier, yes, but—well, you know my arguments."

Trijn nodded. "Most swords are double-edged, Nico. But I trust Eslingen more than most. I could take you off the job if you'd like, and give you my word I'll lay no blame. Astree knows we've work enough in hand."

Rathe hesitated. It was what he ought to do, he supposed, but he hated to give up any point, least of all one where birth and status complicated matters so thoroughly. And when it came down to it, he and Eslingen worked well together. More than that, he trusted the Leaguer more than he trusted most people, points or not; any help Philip gave him would be whole-hearted and honest, and his own would be the same. And that brought him back to the same tangle, giving away the Points' hard-won authority, and yet.... He shook his head slowly. "No. I'd like to keep this on my book. There's something very odd about it."

"I hoped you'd say that," Trijn said. "You're the best I've got, and Eslingen's your leman, and I'd hate to waste any of that. And, speaking of that—did he get any more news when he delivered the boy?"

Rathe sighed. "Not exactly, but—yes, there's another matter to consider. Except it's properly Sighs' business."

"Joy." Trijn reached for her pipe.

"You remember Young Steen?"

"Old Steen's son, the summer-sailor?" Trijn nodded.

"That's him. He's gone somewhat respectable, it seems, and yesterday he pulled Philip aside with a tale about a new extortion gang working the docks, one that wants to be paid in coin and isn't taking no for an answer."

Rathe went through the rest of Eslingen's story. Trijn listened without comment, smoke veiling her face, but when he had finished, she shook her head. "Eslingen's right, that's Sighs' business entirely, and it sounds like Young Steen knows it perfectly well. And that is inviting the Guard to interfere in how we run our stations."

"And I agree," Rathe said, "though I'd like us to consider passing some word to the surintendant—"

"Can't. Not while we're fighting them over the Staenkas."

Rathe let that go. "But there's another piece of it that may apply. Philip thinks Mattaes and the tea captain may have quarreled about this."

"Does he now?" Trijn lowered her pipe.

"It's not certain—Philip wasn't certain, the boy didn't want to talk about it, and there wasn't time or place to ask more questions," Rathe said. "But I think it's worth pursuing."

"I'll go that far. You're still on good terms with the cap'pontoise, aren't you? Cambrai?" She touched flame to the pipe's bowl, coaxing the embers into brighter color.

"Euan Cambrai," Rathe said. "And yes."

"I'd think a word with him wouldn't come amiss."

"Agreed."

"As for Mattaes…." Trijn squinted at him through the cloud of smoke. "This murder is not our business but this morning I had a formal request from Astarac that one of our people check personally on the boy each day, to assure ourselves that he is keeping to the terms of the bond. I'd like you to handle that today, and to explain the procedure to Meisenta."

And if he happened to find time to ask a few questions about dockside extortion, no one would need to know. Rathe didn't need to have the rest of it spelled out. "I can do that, Chief. The usual routine?"

"Yes, and write a note for me to co-sign once you've done it." Trijn waved her hand again, though Rathe wasn't sure whether it was dismissal or to clear some of the smoke. "And talk to Cambrai."

Sohier was still on the night watch, and the rest of the junior points seemed burdened with a busy day's work, so he checked the duty point's book and collected his truncheon before heading out. The rain had finally stopped, but the wind was up, whipping bits of straw and scrap and dead leaves down the length of the street, while women clutched awkwardly at hats and hoods. Overhead, the scudding clouds showed a few scraps of blue, but there was a weight to the air that hinted at more rain to come. Rathe made a face, and turned toward the Staenkas' house. Better to get that over with first, and then he'd be in a position to take a low-flyer home from the Chain if the weather turned. If he had to go that far to find Cambrai.

By daylight, the street where the Staenkas lived looked more prosperous, each walk and short flight of steps scrubbed until the stone gleamed, the narrow dooryards swept clean of leaves and debris. With the main sun up, the watchman's box was closed and locked, but he could tell that his presence was noted. Within the hour, everyone on the street would know that the points had visited the Staenkas again.

There was nothing he could do about that, and he refused to feel guilty: either the boy would be proved innocent, or not, and only the facts would determine that. He climbed the stairs to the main door and knocked. The butler answered quickly enough that Rathe suspected someone had warned him, and invited him into the hall without hesitation.

"Though if I may say so, Adjunct Point—it is Adjunct Point Rathe, is it not?"

Rathe nodded.

"Dame Redel is at the counting house, as she usually is during the season."

"My business was with Madame Staenka, I believe," Rathe said. "And also to Mattaes. I'd like to speak to her, but I will need to see him. In person."

"Madame is in the stillroom." Drowe threw open the door to a small room that seemed to serve as a library rather than a parlor. "If you'll wait here, sir, I'll see if she can meet with you. In the meantime, I can send Master Mattaes to you if that would serve."

The room was long and narrow, and the stove was unlit; the upper shutters of the one long window were folded back, but the cloudy light barely seemed to lift the shadows. The main piece of furniture was a single long table strewn with books: he doubted he was going to be offered tea and cakes, or any of the other amenities of a polite visit. Most of the books on the table dealt with botany—as did most of the books on the shelves, or so it seemed at first glance. Appropriate for a tea family, he thought, but it seemed odd that they weren't kept closer to the stillroom. Except that if Meisenta was the tea-mistress, as she seemed to be, receipt books would be of no use without someone to read them to her, unless she'd devised some other way of keeping her notes. Some blind women did, or so he'd heard.

The door opened behind him, and he turned to see Mattaes hesitating in the doorway. "Drowe said you needed to see me, Adjunct Point?"

"Point of Sighs has requested that we check on you daily. To be sure you've kept your bond."

"But we already gave our word," Mattaes began, and stopped, scowling. He was clearly dressed for a day at home, a plain shirt and breeches patched at the knee beneath a loose coat. "Not to mention the bond itself."

"Understood," Rathe said. "But—as you know—Point of Sighs has rights in this. They're going to demand that you fulfill every requirement to the letter."

"There's not much else I can do," Mattaes said. "Well. Here I am."

"Duly noted. Someone will come from Dreams each day—not always at the same time—and when they do, they'll need to see you in person."

"Oh, very well. Meisenta won't be pleased."

"Chief Trijn asked me to explain the situation," Rathe said. "And we've another matter on our books that touches the docks, and I wondered if I might ask you a question or two about that."

Mattaes shrugged. "You can ask, certainly, and I'll do my best. But I'm no expert."

"They're very general things," Rathe said. "About how things usually work on the docks. For one—I gather there are sizable fees to be paid when a cargo is brought ashore?"

"Yes." Mattaes's voice remained indifferent.

"Who pays them, generally, the captain or the cargo's owner?"

"It depends. If the captain's on retainer to her owner, then the owner generally pays. If the captain's carrying goods for several merchants, then she pays and generally the merchants reimburse her. Or if she's bought her own cargo at a venture, then she pays or sometimes the factor pays."

"I've heard a rumor that the dockers are asking for higher fees this year." Rathe glanced sideways as he spoke, and was unsurprised to see Mattaes's gaze flicker.

"I've—there's been talk, but I don't really know about that."

"But didn't you say your sister asked you to handle such matters for the family now?"

"But our ship hasn't come home yet. So far, it's been the captains' business, not mine."

"Was that what you argued with bes'Anthe about?"

Mattaes flinched. "I—that's not exactly—"

Rathe lifted his eyebrows, and Mattaes stopped, flushing.

"Well, yes, that was part of it. He said we owed him for the extra he'd had to pay, and I told him he was a fool, and he threatened to take our cargo—our cargo, that he'd bought with our money—to the factors and get a better price. I told him if he did, we'd have him up before the regents, and by the time we were done, no one would ever hire him again. But I didn't kill the man."

Rathe let the denial lie, not knowing whether he believed it or not. "What do your sisters say?"

Mattaes rolled his eyes, looking younger than his years. "They chide me for not paying him. And they're probably right."

"Was he asking more than usual?"

"I may be new to the business, but I did handle the factors last year, and I know what's proper," Mattaes said, indignantly. "bes'Anthe was trying to squeeze the family for almost twice as much as last year.."

"Had he paid out money already, or was he trying to get you to pay what he owed?"

Mattaes blinked. "I—I don't actually know. I thought he wanted to be paid back, but now that you ask, I don't think that's what he said…. He might have said he couldn't pay? I don't remember."

"If he owed the dockers money, it gives someone else a reason to want him dead."

"I hadn't thought of that." Mattaes frowned, but shook his head again. "I'm sorry, Adjunct Point, I can't remember exactly what he said."

Surely a guilty man—or even someone more worldly—would pounce on the excuse, Rathe thought, but he wasn't sure what it meant that Mattaes didn't. He said, "I've also heard a rumor that the people who want higher fees aren't taking no for an answer. And they want to be paid in cash."

"Now that may be true. bes'Anthe was determined to be paid in coin."

Rathe considered him for a moment, trying to frame his next question, but the door opened behind him.

"Excuse me, Adjunct Point," Drowe said, "but if you've satisfied yourself as to Master Mattaes's whereabouts, Madame will see you."

The servant's tone suggested an order rather than a request. In any case he'd run out of useful questions. He reassured himself with the notion that the dead captain was Sighs' business, not his—though he'd certainly drop a word in Cambrai's ear. "Thank you," he said, and followed Drowe from the room.

The man led him down the long hall, beneath the formal stair that led to the upper floors, then past the door that led to the kitchens. Light spilled from the doorway, and Rathe could hear cheerful voices, but Drowe ignored them, pausing instead to knock at a closed door. In most wealthy houses, that door would give on the courtyard, or perhaps a covered walk that led to the privies, but instead this one swung back to reveal an enclosed hallway, its walls neatly painted to resemble paneling. A small woman peered out at them, a long canvas apron covering skirt and bodice, and a twist of scarf confining her hair.

"Thank you, Drowe. Madame says she'll see him now."

"Very good, dame." Drowe sketched a bow and turned away, and the woman favored Rathe with a brisk smile.

"I'm Hyris Telawen, Madame's assistant. If you'll come with me?"

"Dame," Rathe acknowledged, and followed her down the long corridor. The ceiling was low, but painted white and gold to match the false panels; oval windows like portholes offered the only light, and brief views of a narrow garden to one side and a graveled yard on the other. He caught a glimpse of a gate wide enough for wagons, and then the corridor turned sharply to the right, and Telawen tapped briskly on the closed door.

"Adjunct Point Rathe, madame," she announced, and flung the door wide.

The smell of tea filled the room, sweeter than any teashop, and Rathe lifted his head in spite of himself. He could make out smoke and the rich vegetal scent of one of the dragon-bush teas, but there were a dozen subtler flavors as well, green and herbal fragrances he couldn't recognize. The room was well-lit, with a skylight above the workbench and long windows on the courtyard side. The workbench itself was covered with small containers and blown-glass bowls; there was an enormous black stone mortar and pestle at one end, and a set of balances at the other. An iron stove was lit in one corner, and a kettle simmered loudly. Meisenta sat on a tall stool at the workbench, but turned gracefully to face them, dusting her hands with a clean cloth.

"Adjunct Point. I understand you had further news for me?"

"I'm afraid so."

Meisenta's mouth curved into a wry smile. "Not good news, then."

"Nor bad, madame. Point of Sighs has required that we enforce the letter of the bond, that's all."

"And what does that entail?"

"Someone from Point of Dreams will have to see Mattaes—in person—every day until the bond is lifted or the matter goes to the courts."

Meisenta grimaced. "Not very trusting, the folk at Point of Sighs. Tell me, Adjunct Point, should I have turned my brother over to them and spared myself this trouble?"

"Not if you believe he's innocent." Rathe heard his tone sharper than he had meant.

"Hah." Meisenta sounded genuinely amused. "A fair point, that. Mattaes has always been a peaceful sort—he'd always rather talk than fight, from when he was a child. And none of us in the trade have any time for murder."

"I understand it's your busiest time of year," Rathe said, tentatively, and Meisenta laughed again.

"My dear Adjunct Point, you don't know the half of it. And this year is worse than most." She gestured to the table behind her, though her pale eyes didn't follow. "Our ships are all driven ashore south of here, or never came at all. And for most houses, that's profoundly inconvenient, and costs them money, to be sure, but for us...." She turned abruptly back to the worktable, long hands moving easily among the litter of tools and containers. "Our Old Year blends are the best to be found in the city. We have an arrangement with the Malassy, they own two of the finest plantations in the Bight of Ghar. We buy their final thinning sight unseen, and at a price that ensures they've no reason to look for another buyer. It's all Dragon's Beard, there, on stony ground—there's nothing better even in a bad year, and this year was excellent. But we've only received a third of what we paid for. Another dozen chests sit on bes'Anthe's ship, damn the man, and the rest is—we hope!—somewhere along the coast and making its way north by caravan. But we won't know that until it arrives." She brushed her hands as if ridding her palms of old tea leaves. "And in the meantime, I must contrive something we can sell that doesn't disgrace us utterly."

"If everyone is in the same position," Rathe said, "surely you'll suffer no more than any other house?"

"Most likely," Meisenta agreed, "but I'm in no mind to cut my losses unless I have to. When I create a blend that pleases even in these conditions Staenka will be first among the tea houses."

Rathe couldn't help lifting his eyebrows at that. Staenka was certainly one of the important families, but Three Ships and Mazeline House and even Filipon and Daughters generally ranked above them. And Perrin and Pett was more profitable.

"Are you a tea drinker, Adjunct Point?" Meisenta gave a hard smile. "What's your choice?"

Rathe hesitated, hoping this was not the prelude to offering a fee. A man had offered him tea once, when he was much younger, and it had taken all his will to turn it down. "Unsmoked ordinary. Davyt Sisters makes a decent stone-and-iron ordinary at a reasonable price."

He had hoped to discourage her with the mention of the least important of the city's tea merchants, but instead she nodded thoughtfully.

"That's not a bad choice. Here, smell this." She held out a metal cylinder, and Rathe advanced to take it.

"Smell it," she said again, and Rathe lowered his head obediently.

It was tea, of course, but such a tea.... Rathe closed his eye in spite of himself, savoring the heavy scent. A smoked tea, not usually his favorite, but this smoke was lighter, smelling of burnt leaves rather than oily ash. Smoke and a hint of pepper, but most of all a deep, rich tea, better than anything he'd ever tasted. He took another deep breath, and handed it back with some reluctance. "It's lovely."

"That is last year's Old Year—Golden Dragon, I called it, for the pot-gold petals."

That would explain the touch of pepper. Rathe glanced back at the cylinder, and now that he was looking, picked out the flecks of bright yellow among the twisted leaves. "I imagine that would be hard to match."

"Hyris, brew us a tasting cup—the Golden Dragon and this year's batch."

"Yes, madame," Telawen answered, and turned to the stove.

Meisenta held out a second cylinder. "See what you think of this."

Rathe took it, realizing that the outer surface was scored with dozens of horizontal lines. A way for Meisenta to tell one size of container from another? But that was hardly the point. He sniffed: more smoke, sweeter than before, and a definite hint of wine; the smell of tea was not as strong or as deep as the Golden Dragon. He hesitated, looking for tactful words, and Meisenta laughed again.

"Even you can smell it—I mean no insult, Adjunct Point, but we both must admit your senses are nowhere near an expert's. It's a good tea, but not what we usually produce. It's possible no one can make better this year, but I'm reluctant to put this out without knowing that for certain.

If you were looking into raids on other tea blenders' workshops, Adjunct Point, you'd have leave to look at me."

"The teas, madame," Telawen said, and Rathe turned to see her holding out a tray with four small cups. "On madame's right is the new blend, and on the left is the Golden Dragon."

Meisenta reached across, not quite unerring; her fingertips brushed the edge of the tray, and she adjusted instantly, taking a cup of the new blend. "Please, help yourself."

Rathe took the cup, the plain glaze hot under his fingers, and sipped warily. It was still smokier than he liked, but it didn't try to claw its way down his throat the way the cheaper smoked blends did. Brewed, the smell of wine became a hint of berries, a sweetness that would sit well with a spoonful of honey. And with cakes, he thought, taking another drink. Philip would like this.

He had finished the cup in spite of himself. Telawen pushed the tray forward, and he set it back where it had been. A moment later, Meisenta set hers down as well. "Your thoughts?"

Rathe shrugged. "It's better than anything I usually drink. It's—sweeter? Lighter? I know someone who'd like it a lot."

Meisenta's expression twisted. "Yes, that's exactly the trouble. It's good, but…. We must strive to do better." She gestured to the tray again, and Rathe took the other cup. He tasted it, and sighed in spite of himself. This was definitely the best tea he'd ever tasted, made what he kept in his tea chest seem like dried dishwater. The overlay of leaf-smoke and pepper only emphasized the extraordinary flavor.

"You see?" Meisenta said, and Telawen shrugged, the cups rattling.

"You can't make a Golden Dragon every year, madame."

"No, but I can do better than this." Meisenta set her own emptied cup back on the tray, visibly shaking herself back to other matters. "Adjunct Point, we have other things on our minds than one tea captain's fees."

"And yet the man is dead," Rathe said.

"Mattaes should have paid what he asked. Instead, he came home to ask what he should do. I wouldn't have him hang for inexperience." Meisenta settled herself on her stool, while Telawen bundled the tray back into the corner. "I'll tell the household to expect someone from Dreams—and I'll tell them to admit her, whatever the hour, and be sure that Mattaes obliges. Will that suit you?"

"Thank you, madame."

He started toward the door, but Meisenta spoke first. "You're the one who doesn't take fees."

He felt himself stand taller. "That's right."

"When this is settled, whatever way it goes—if I were to offer you an ounce of the Golden Dragon at the dealer's price, would you count that a fee?"

"Possibly not," Rathe said, after a moment, "but I still doubt I could afford it, madame."

"Wait and see." Meisenta smiled and turned back to her table.

THE CLOUDS HAD closed in again by the time he left the Staenkas' house, and the wind had strengthened, coming hard from the west carrying a promise of cold rain at its core. Rathe tugged up the hood of his cloak and considered where he might find the cap'pontoise. Properly speaking, the pontoises' headquarters was at the Chain Tower, at the city's western edge; the pontoises were in charge of the great chains that could be raised to block the river against an invading fleet. Not that anyone had dared try to take the city that way in centuries, but the merchants resident were practical souls. It cost them little to keep the chain in order, and put everyone on notice, Leaguers, Chadroni raiders, and poor nobles alike, that the city was not to be trifled with. But that was a bitter walk, in this weather, and there was a decent chance Cambrai might be at the boat-house below the Queen's Bridge, where Sighs and Graves met. Besides, it would be easier to catch a low-flyer along the river if he had to go all the way to the Chain.

The open yard in front of the boathouse was busy, an apple-seller with her cart at one end and a boy with a tray of crisp sugared cakes at the other. A fire was lit in the iron basket in front of the boathouse's wide doors, and a blue pennant flew from the flagpole jutting from the eaves, warning of higher tides than usual. That was no surprise, given the rain and the generally bad weather, and Rathe paused, looking for familiar faces. He didn't recognize any of the pontoises sitting on the benches under the wide eaves, but one of the men at the apple-seller's cart looked up sharply.

"Rathe! What brings you to the river?"

"Saffroy," Rathe said, with some relief. Saffroy was Cambrai's tillerman, his personal second-in-command: if anyone would know where Cambrai was, it would be Saffroy. "I was looking for the cap'pontoise, actually."

"Were you, now?" Saffroy pocketed his apple. "That's fast for word to travel."

Rathe frowned. "I had a question for Euan, that's all."

Saffroy's shoulders relaxed. "Well. I expect he'll be glad to have a word with you."

"What's going on?"

Saffroy started toward the boathouse, beckoning for him to follow. "A man was seen to fall from the Hopes-Point Bridge an hour or so ago. Euan took the boats out, he should be back any minute now."

"A leaper?" Rathe asked. "But, no, you said 'fall.'"

"That was the word we had." Saffroy waved to a bench turned into a corner of the boathouse, sheltered from the wind, and Rathe settled himself, glad of the protection. For the first time, he realized that two of the three long rowing boats were missing from their slips. "It's an odd time—too much traffic for a suicide, someone would be bound to stop her. And it's hard to have an accident on that bridge. Graves, now, there's spots where the gutters drop straight to the water, and the gratings are none too well tended, but Hopes…that's another matter."

Rathe nodded in agreement. The Hopes-Point bridge was crowded with shops for most of its length. "You'd think the same would apply for an attack, unless you dropped someone out a back window?"

Saffroy spread his hands, the nails black with tar. "You know what I know."

A whistle sounded from the water, three shrill blasts and then three more. Saffroy shot to his feet as the other pontoises came running. "Stay here, Rathe," he said, and darted toward the center dock.

Rathe flattened himself against the rough wood of the wall, watching as half a dozen pontoises scrambled out on the center dock, some carrying heavy boathooks. The whistle sounded again, followed by indistinct shouting, and the blunt nose of one of the pontoises' rowing boats poked into the dock. The pontoises with the boathooks caught it, dragging it forward, and the heavy craft surged into the narrow space, thumping heavily against the leather fenders. All sixteen oars were raised upright like masts, and the oarsmen held them steady while their fellows secured the boat to the dock and someone shouted for a doctor. One of the pontoises detached herself from the group at the dock and darted away, and at the boat's stern another group lifted free a dripping bundle. A body, Rathe amended, naked and drowned, one arm trailing like river-weed, and the group rushed past to lay it on the ground by the fire.

It looked safe to move now, most of the pontoises already in the courtyard, only the last few busy securing the boat, and Rathe moved cautiously toward the doors. One of the pontoises knelt by the body, working the flaccid arms like pump handles, while another pounded on the chest and thighs: sovereign remedies for drowning, Rathe knew, but they didn't seem to be having much effect.

"Nico!" Euan Cambrai detached himself from the group around the body. "How'd you get here so fast?"

"He says he came on another matter," Saffroy said, sliding into place at Cambrai's side. He was carrying a towel, and the cap'pontoise took it gratefully. He was stark naked and as wet as the dead man, golden hair plastered to his head: presumably he'd gone into the river after the body, Rathe thought.

"It'll have to wait," Cambrai said. "Oriane's tits, where are my clothes—"

"Here you are, Cap," one of the younger men said, and passed over a bundle of linen.

Cambrai snatched at it, found the patched smallclothes and tugged them on, hastily looping the tapes at his waist. He was shivering, Rathe saw: no surprise, in this weather. He waited until Cambrai had pulled on shirt and breeches, and then said, "Your dead man?"

"Dead?" Cambrai stopped, blue eyes going wide. "No, he's not dead—not yet, anyway. But you can help me put a name to him, I think."

"Me?" Rathe followed Cambrai as the junior pontoises made way for them. The doctor had arrived—the local apothecary, by the badges on her coat—and was kneeling in the dirt to prop the man on his side while he choked and coughed up a thin stream of river water.

"Let him down," she said, and the pontoises at her side rolled him carefully back onto his back. Rathe winced at the sight. Someone's fists had blackened both his eyes, split his lip and broken his nose, the skin angry red and swollen even though the Sier had washed away most of the blood. There were more bruises along his ribs, and a deep gash gaped purple beneath the lowest rib on his right side. The doctor was busy packing it with clean rags, but the man didn't move.

"Beaten and stabbed," Rathe said aloud, "and likely robbed first."

Cambrai nodded. "Look again. Do you know him?"

"No." But as Rathe spoke, the features seemed to shift in his mind. "Astree's—it's Edild Dammar, isn't it."

"That's what I thought," Cambrai said, his voice grim. "Saffroy! Send to Point of Sighs, see if they're missing an adjunct—and don't mention Rathe, he's here on other business entirely. Aren't you?"

"In point of fact, I was," Rathe said.

"In the meantime," Cambrai said, "take him—should we move him, Galais?"

The apothecary looked up. "Let me get him wrapped up first, he's a mess. Then—yes, better to bring him into the warm, see if that won't help. You can lodge him in my surgery, I've a good fire there. But it's even odds if he'll live no matter what we do."

"That's the Sier for you," Saffroy said. "I'll see to it, Cap."

Cambrai nodded, another shiver racking through him. "Good. Come on, Rathe, let's within."

The cap'pontoise merited a tiny enclosed workroom at the corner of the boathouse, with oiled paper in the window in place of glass or horn, but at least the walls and door cut the wind. Cambrai pulled a coal from the stove to light the single lamp, and Rathe said, "Let me."

He built up the fire while Cambrai finished dressing, pulling on thick stockings and a knitted vest beneath a battered leather coat. A full kettle sat on the hob, and Rathe pulled it to the front. He could see the river's muddy bank through the cracks between the floorboards—falling tide— but the air above his knees was beginning to warm.

"There's tea on the shelf," Cambrai said. "The red box. I'd take it kindly if you'd start a pot."

Rathe did as he was told, measuring the leaves into the heavy pot. After the Golden Dragon he'd tasted that morning, this smelled plain and bitter, but he told himself he'd no better at home. After a taste he set down his cup. He did keep better.

"Right," Cambrai said. "So what brought you here on what turns out to be the most eventful day of the quarter?"

"I had a question about business on the docks, but now what I really want to know is what happened to Dammar."

"My advice is to look for a man with a grudge and bloodied knuckles."

Rathe sighed. "True. But I think this was more than a grudge." Though a man like Dammar must collect enemies as efficiently as he took fees. "At the moment Dammar's got a dead man on his books and has called the point on the son of a tea merchant." He ran through the events of the previous nights, and poured them each a cup of tea when he had finished.

"I don't suppose this Mattaes could have done it?"

Rathe shook his head, and settled himself on the guest's stool beside the stove. "He's young, lightly-made, not a fighter. I don't see him being able to beat Dammar that badly. Not unless his hands were tied, and I didn't see any sign of that, did you?"

"I did not."

"It's a bad business, a senior pointsman beaten and stabbed and dropped in the river. Even a man like Dammar...."

"Oh, I know his kind," Cambrai said. "Took fees, didn't stay bought.."

"Tell me what happened. I thought Saffroy said someone fell?"

"That was the cry that went out. A man seen to fall from the Hopes-Point Bridge, near the middle of the span. The tide was on its way out, so we launched from here—just luck I happened to be here and not at the Chain—and we rowed upriver after him. Took us some little time to find him, he might have been held under somewhere, but we picked him up maybe a quarter-mile upstream of here. And the rest—well, you saw. Someone had a score to settle with that man, I'd say."

"It's a long list."

"I'm not surprised."

Rathe groaned. "About how long did it take you to find him? Sighs will be asking about Mattaes."

Cambrai bit a nail. "A good hour. Maybe a bit more, from the time the cry went out."

That should rule out Mattaes. Rathe leaned back against the wall and sipped at his tea, trying not to compare it to the brews he'd tasted that morning. Cambrai stretched his stockinged toes toward the stove.

"So what was it you came to me about?"

"It seems very small all of a sudden. But we've heard whispers in Dreams, talk that there's a new gang on the docks, or an old gang wanting new fees? They want more than ever before and they want to be paid in coin, not goods."

Cambrai flushed and his lips twisted. "I don't suppose you've got someone who'll make a complaint?"

"Not I." Rathe shook his head.

"Neither have we," Cambrai said. "And, yes, I don't doubt we've heard the same stories. Doubled fees, coin only. And if the fees aren't paid, instead of cut ropes or cargo gone missing, women are turning up hurt—"

"I've not heard that part."

"They're too afraid to swear a complaint," Cambrai said, "but we've seen broken arms and a few sets of bruises that would rival Dammar's. We have a claim to the docks and I've told people that we'd press it, if they'd just make the complaint. But no one's been willing. I think there's a single hand behind it, one gang covering all the docks, but I can't prove it and I can't put a name to it.."

"If it's mostly in Sighs," Rathe said, "what are the odds that this attack on Dammar's part of it?"

Cambrai offered a grin that showed a chipped tooth. "He's our business now. I intend to pursue this, even if it takes us on dry land."

"I'd be very interested in anything you find out," Rathe said.

CHAPTER 4

To Eslingen's mild surprise, Coindarel himself was at the barracks, very fine in an ivory wool coat embroidered with a border of tiny golden flowers. His buttons were larger gold flowers, as was the pin that fastened the peach and lavender cockade that graced his hat. Estradere, who was dressed for riding, looked more than a bit put out, and Eslingen hesitated at the workroom door.

"No, Captain, do come in," Coindarel said, with a wave of a much-beringed hand. "The matter can wait—can't it, Patric?"

"Not forever," Estradere said grimly, but straightened, closing the ledger that he'd been consulting. "Well, Philip?"

"There's been a bit of a development," Eslingen said. "Chief Trijn at Point of Dreams wants our help."

He was pleased to see his words got their undivided attention. He went through the events of the previous day, and finished by drawing the Staenkas' letter of hand from his own cuff and laying it on top of the ledger. "Trijn has also asked that we keep the bond."

"Doesn't she trust her counterpart at Sighs?" Coindarel steepled his long fingers, pressed them thoughtfully against his lips. Estradere unrolled the bond, examining first the seals, and then the sharp lettering.

"I don't know that she does," Eslingen said. "Not entirely. And certainly there's cause to want a neutral party involved."

"And she's willing—Trijn's willing—to consider us that?" Coindarel grinned. "She's changed her tune."

"She's doing what the queen has ordered." Eslingen couldn't keep a sharp note from his voice.

"Written in haste." Estradere re-rolled the bond as though neither man had spoken. "But it'll do the job. We can keep it in the strongbox here safely enough, I believe."

"Chief Trijn would take that kindly," Eslingen said, after a moment, and Coindarel nodded.

"Yes, by all means, we must cooperate with the points—and before you say anything, Patric, I know it was agreed."

"The surintendant's written again?" Estradere asked.

Eslingen winced. The Surintendant of Points, Rainart Fourie, had not taken well to the notion of sharing power with another organization, least of all one specifically intended to police the non-resident nobility. Compounding that dislike, his stars lay in complete opposition to Coindarel's, so that the two men could barely be in the same room without quarreling.

Coindarel heaved a sigh. "No. No, he has not, not since the last—but we will let that pass. Yes, Philip, we will certainly hold this bond for Sighs and Dreams, and you have my permission to act on behalf of the Staenka family."

"They're merchants resident," Estradere said. "Our writ was the nobility and non-residents, the people the points can't touch. Not freeholders of the city."

"They want an advocate with the points, not an investigator," Coindarel retorted. "Isn't that right, Philip?"

"More or less," Eslingen said, cautiously.

"Then I see no problem in helping them," Coindarel said firmly.

"Of course you don't," Estradere muttered, quietly enough that the prince-marshal could pretend not to hear.

Coindarel waved his hand, dismissal this time. "Keep me informed, if you please."

"Of course, Colonel," Eslingen said, and backed away.

In the hall outside, he nearly tripped over Balfort de Vian, who blushed to the roots of his bright hair. "Excuse me," the boy said, and tried to slip away, but Eslingen caught his sleeve.

"Did you want something, Balfort?"

"I was just bringing a report to the colonel," de Vian answered, another wave of color sweeping over him. He pointed to the table beside the workroom door, where an untidy pile of papers lay beside a locked dispatch-case. "It's there."

Eslingen nodded, but didn't bother to look. "And you weren't listening?"

De Vian bit his lip. "I couldn't help but overhear. The Staenkas—Meisenta Staenka is my sister's leman's brother's wife. So I had some right."

"We all swore an oath to be impartial where we could and to withdraw where we couldn't. Where do you stand in this?"

De Vian glanced over his shoulder at the workroom's closed door, and Eslingen let himself be tugged further down the hall. "She's my sister," de Vian said. "How can I not be...well, *partial*? But I can't believe any of the Staenkas would stoop to murdering anybody. Mattaes least of all."

"What makes you say that?"

"He's...careful, I suppose you'd say. It's all about the trade with him." De Vian shrugged one shoulder, looking momentarily even younger than his years. "And anyway, Mattaes is too tidy to attack someone who's heading for the privies."

And that, Eslingen thought, was the difference between an eight-quarter noble's son and the son of a merchant resident. "Tell me again how you're related?"

"My sister Aliez—she's the Vidame d'Entrebeschaire now that Mother's dead—Aliez swore lemanry with Elecia Gebellin. She was supposed to marry the younger son, Oleguer, but our mothers couldn't agree on the contract, and then when Mother died Madame Gebellin said we were too chancy. I don't think they could afford the marriage-portion Aliez wanted—but that's not important. The older son, Aucher, he'd already been married to Meisenta Staenka, and he and Elecia took Aliez's side when she quarreled with Madame Gebellin. Elecia's gone to work for the Staenkas with Aucher."

"So the Gebellins are a tea family, too?"

De Vian nodded. "They don't have their own firm yet. They were factors for Perrin and Pett, but then Madame Gebellin made a killing on a side shipment, and persuaded old Madame Staenka to let Meisenta marry Aucher. He's trained to keep the books, you see, and of course Meisenta being blind, she needs help with that."

They had reached the courtyard, and Eslingen winced at the bracing wind. "Here," he said, and towed de Vian into the shelter of the arcade that faced the barracks building. Out of the corner of his eye, he saw Rijonneau watching from the stables, and as their eyes met, the other man touched his hat in ironic salute. Eslingen suppressed a sigh—of course Rijonneau would be the one to see him steering the prettiest of the would-be guardsmen into private conversation, not two days after defending the boy's right to the position—and pointed to one of the benches that stood against the wall instead of going inside out of the wind. De Vian seated himself obediently, folding his hands between his knees. It was tempting to sit beside him, shoulder to shoulder against the wind, but Eslingen leaned instead against the pillar opposite. "How do the Staenkas feel about this, now that their mother's gone?"

De Vian looked blank. "They seem happy enough. Aucher's useful, Aliez says—he knows what he's doing. There's no child yet, but it hasn't been but a year and some. And Meisenta and Elecia are good friends."

Eslingen tucked his hands behind him, bracing one foot against the pillar. It sounded to him as though Madame Gebellin was more than commonly ambitious, even for a merchant resident, if she'd succeeded in marrying one son to the eldest daughter of a major tea family, and had been angling for a vidame's heir. Not that d'Entrebeschaire was an important title, not if its previous holder had been one of the Mistresses of the Wardrobe—one of the queen's accountants, important within the household, but not a post that required nobility. And it was interesting that the daughter, Aliez, hadn't inherited her mother's post. No, if he were betting on the matter, he'd guess that the Staenkas were regretting that marriage—an excellent reason to postpone a pregnancy—and that d'Entrebeschaire thought she was well off to be free of a man who didn't bring a decent portion. Except that she was leman to the sister: perhaps it wasn't so simple after all.

"But you see, I can be useful," de Vian said. "There's a lot I can tell you."

"I don't doubt it. But if I take up your offer—there's a chance I'll find out all your family's secrets, even ones you'd rather I didn't know, and an even better chance that I'll have to use them in a way that will make your sisters angry. And they'll blame you, not me."

"There's only one sister," de Vian interjected. "Just Aliez. And then there's me and three brothers."

"That's not the point," Eslingen said. "If you're going to do this, you're choosing the Guard over your family."

"I'm here, aren't I?"

"Your sister nominated you."

De Vian made a face. "I asked her to. I have the stars for it, when I haven't for anything else useful, and I want—I want to serve the queen's justice."

For an instant, Eslingen wished Rathe were here to hear that declaration, and to tell him what to say to it. That sort of fervency was nothing he had heard in any of the companies where he'd served. "There's a reason the points don't ask their people to act against family and friends," he said, as gently as he could. He saw the disappointment in de Vian's eyes, and held up a hand. "I'm not saying no. I won't deny that you could tell me some useful things—you've already done so, and I'm grateful. But if you're to work any more closely on this, I need to know that I can trust you completely. And that means I need to know you've thought the matter through. Take today and tomorrow, if I remember right, the stars are good for contemplation, and give me your answer the day after. There's no shame in either choice, mind you, and I won't hold either one against you. But you need to be certain you can stand the consequences."

De Vian looked up at him, and for a moment, Eslingen thought he saw the shadow of the man beneath the still-childish face. "I will. Thank you, Captain."

"I'll talk to you on the third day," Eslingen said, and turned away.

He couldn't help thinking about the boy as he made his way back across the Hopes-Point Bridge and into Dreams, dodging the usual traffic without paying much attention. He remembered what it had been like at that age, to want to give oneself over totally to something, whether it was a cause or a craft or, as in his case, a lover. He hadn't thought of the man in years, remembered him with wry affection as much as anything: Sijmon Stalla had been another Leaguer, a big, bearded man who'd taught him the finer points of pike and sword, fended off his excesses of affection, and sent him on his way in the spring with the bribe of a promotion to the cavalry. He had been sure his heart was broken, and had even tried his hand at poetry to prove it, but a week with the horses had cured him of that. This, though…this had the potential to end badly, and he found himself hoping de Vian thought better of his offer. He misliked the way things were shaping between the families, regardless of whether Mattaes had killed the captain or no, and didn't want to see de Vian disowned—especially if that meant his sister would no longer sponsor him for the Guard. Though surely Coindarel could be persuaded to keep him on, if worst came to worst, and the more so if he'd lost that sponsorship in helping with the case…. And surely Rathe would have useful advice. It could hardly be an uncommon problem.

The steps in front of the Staenkas' house were scrubbed spotless in spite of the weather, and the knocker was newly polished. Eslingen used it gingerly, aware that he was leaving smudges on the brass, and the door opened with gratifying speed.

"Captain vaan Esling," Drowe said, with what might pass for actual enthusiasm. "Won't you come in?"

"Thank you." Eslingen followed him into the hall, and relinquished his hat and cloak to the waiting maidservant. "I'd like to speak to either Madame Staenka or to her sister, if that's possible."

"Madame has gone to the factor's, but Dame Redel will be glad to see you. If you'll wait here?"

He ushered Eslingen into a narrow library, pausing only long enough to open the upper shutters, and then disappeared again. Someone had already had a fire in the narrow stove, and it wasn't quite out yet, giving the room a ghostly warmth that dissipated as soon as the wind rattled against the tall window. It was clearly a working room, books stacked beside drifts of papers on the worktable, and the inkstand held four colors of ink as well as a selection of well-used pens. The shelves were crowded, too, books of every size and shape jammed in according to some unknown organizational system. He recognized a Great Herbal, given pride of place in its own stand, but the others bore only abbreviated labels, or authors' names stamped on the leather spines. Most of them carried a house tag, a bright-red seal in the shape of a poppy at the base of the spine, but its exact meaning he couldn't guess.

The door opened behind him, and he turned to make his bow. Seen by daylight, Redel was much prettier than her sister, the blade of a nose softened, her figure more generous—softer in general, Eslingen thought, though he doubted that applied to more than her looks. Even the second daughters of tea families understood their place in the business; they were no more likely to falter than the sons of the Ajanes, turned out with a sword and a horse to find their fortunes.

"Captain vaan Esling. I hope you've come to tell us you can take our part."

"The Prince-Marshal has agreed to hold your brother's bond, and I'm allowed to act for your family in the investigation. But I must warn you that I can't withhold evidence. If I find proof that your brother is guilty, I will hand it to the points."

"Mattaes has always been our peacemaker. Would you hold it against me if I say I've regretted that? In way of business only, you understand." She waved toward the nearest of the room's chairs. "Please, do sit down, Captain. I've taken the liberty of ordering tea here—less chance that we'll be interrupted, and I'd like the chance to talk plainly."

"So would I." Eslingen seated himself beside the stove, and Redel bent to stir up the fire before she took the chair opposite him. She was more neatly dressed than he would have expected for an ordinary working day: there was fine lace at her wrists and peeping above the neck of her bodice, a stiff lace cap perched high on well-dressed curls, and an expensive set of pearls, necklace and earrings both as fat and round as mistletoe. And as waxy-pale, too, which made them easily worth a petty-crown, perhaps even a full crown—very much not jewels for everyday, and he wondered exactly what she was trying to prove. A maidservant appeared with a table and tray, and Redel fussed with it, making sure the pot was warm and the tray of cakes properly arranged, then dismissed the girl and poured out tea for each of them. Eslingen took his cup with another half-bow, his eyebrows rising as he sipped at it. He had expected nothing less than good, but this was outside of anything he'd tasted.

Redel grinned, an unexpectedly gamine expression. "I'm glad you like it. It's this winter's house blend."

"I hope you charge what it's worth," Eslingen said. From the taste of it, it would be well outside anything he could afford.

"Of course." Redel shrugged one shoulder. "We have something of a reputation as purveyors of winter teas."

"Which must be difficult this year." Eslingen took another sip, as though they hadn't settled down to business.

"Just so." Redel offered the plate of cakes, and Eslingen took two of the crisp wafers. One was stamped with Seidos's rearing horse, the other with the Dolphin, and he wondered if that was an omen. "It has not been easy—though to be fair, none of the houses are going to find keeping any reputation easy, given how early the passage closed."

"Which is an argument Dreams is willing to use against your brother," Eslingen said, when she did not continue. "If everyone is desperate, every-one has a reason to kill to keep their cargo."

Redel smiled again. "Perhaps they should have called the point on me. Or Meisenta—though they'd have trouble arguing that against a blind woman, surely. Either of us would be more plausible. We were raised to the business."

"And Mattaes wasn't?"

"No more than any woman's son. He was intended to marry one of Amial Banneron's daughters—they deal in Chadroni goods, fine carvings and the like."

Eslingen cocked his head. "I don't see how that advantages your house. Did they match for liking, then?"

Redel snorted. "Mother had some idea of importing fancy containers for some of the blends, or some such thing. But Mattaes didn't really like the match, and the girl didn't much take to him, so when Mother died, Meisenta let the arrangement slide. Dame Banneron wanted a ridiculous portion for him, anyway. But the result was, Mattaes spent the last six or seven years assuming he was marrying into a house of merchants-venturer. He was never taught much of the trade."

"Yet he's handling some matters for you now?"

"We needed him. With Meisenta blind, there's only me to handle the warehouse and the docks—and Elecia, I suppose, but I'd rather the job went to closer kin. I'll give him his due, he's quick to learn. He did well for us last year."

"Then what went wrong with bes'Anthe?" Eslingen watched her narrowly, hoping to surprise some reaction from her, but instead she shrugged.

"We chose badly there. Perhaps I should admit I chose badly. His reputation was—let's say equivocal—but Elecia said he'd proved reliable for them. The man did not meet our expectations."

"Then you believe Mattaes when he says bes'Anthe asked for more money?" Eslingen reached for another of the little wafers.

"Oh, yes. I don't know how much you hear of what goes on around the docks, but there are new fees being demanded, and I'm sure bes'Anthe wouldn't have had the cash to pay them. And he would have felt it was our business to cover at least some of the cost, it being our cargo." Redel sighed. "I wish Mattaes had had the sense to just say yes when he was asked."

"Why didn't he?"

"You'd have to ask him that."

Eslingen lifted an eyebrow, and Redel sighed again. "He took offense, I think. He said he didn't think he should commit that much money without Meisenta's agreement, though it was only a few pillars over the original fees. He could have pledged that. I expect bes'Anthe treated him like a child, and that put his back up."

Eslingen nodded. "So then Mattaes came back here, and talked to you and your sister? What time was that?"

"We'd already dined, so we were in the parlor when he came in—half past eight, maybe? He and Meisenta and I argued about what he'd done, and he stalked off to bed. The points came half an hour after that."

"And did you see any blood on your brother's clothes? Or did he change before he joined you?"

"He'd changed," Redel said. "It was a miserable wet night."

So much for a simple proof, Eslingen thought. "What do you make of his claim that the shirt isn't his?"

"Well, he would say that," Redel said, with a grin, and sobered quickly. "No, that's the thing that worries me most, that shirt. I don't see how it could have gotten here, and yet—I just can't see Mattaes knifing a sea captain twice his age."

"He says it's not his shirt," Eslingen said.

"It may not be. The laundry's mixed things up before. But the blood on it…. I'm not so much afraid that he killed bes'Anthe, Captain, as I'm worried about what he might have done. Or that he might know something, and be too afraid to speak. Or think—I don't know what." Redel sighed. "Maybe he'll talk to you."

"I'll press him," Eslingen said, "and so for that matter will Dreams and Sighs."

"Adjunct Point Rathe spoke to him already today," Redel said, with a sidelong glance, and Eslingen nodded.

"I'll try him tomorrow, then. But I wonder…if Mattaes didn't do it, do you know of anyone else who would attack your man?"

"I've no idea." Redel shook her head hard for emphasis.

"But you admit bes'Anthe had an equivocal reputation."

"Oh, well, if you're thinking that way…." Redel shrugged. "He's a chancer, always out for one little thing more. At least, that's what Elecia said, and Andia Jannessen, she'd hired him last season. But we were giving him a chance to better himself, working for us, and we thought—Meisenta and I thought—that would be enough of a bonus. If I were looking, I'd look along the docks for someone else he's cheated. I don't think you'll find there's a shortage."

"AND THE SAD thing is, I think that's true," Eslingen said, leaning close to Rathe at one of Wicked's corner tables some hours later, "but I don't think it does us any good."

"I'm afraid you're right," Rathe said. "That's Sighs' business, and I can't think it's likely Trijn could persuade Astarac to let me ask any questions."

Rain rattled against the shutters above their head. Another nasty night, Eslingen thought, shivering. He hadn't managed to make it to Wicked's before the rain set in—and shouldn't have expected to, either, with the stars against him—and Wicked had taken his cloak to dry by the fire, leaving him in clothes that were merely damp. Rathe had somehow managed to evade the worst of the weather, but his hair was curling tighter than ever in the damp air.

"Not even with Dammar out of commission?" That had been a bit of a shocker: people didn't generally attack the points, though from everything Rathe had said about the man, Eslingen could well believe that Dammar might be the exception.

"Especially with him out of commission like this," Rathe said. "Astarac will be run off her feet without him, and she's not going to admit it, much less let any of us in." He sighed. "And if I were in her shoes, I wouldn't, either."

"So what can we do?" Eslingen poked at the remains of the pie they had shared between them, the shell nearly empty of the thick lamb-and-vegetable gravy that had filled it. He broke off a piece of crust that was soaked in sauce and popped it into his mouth, savoring the rich taste. Rathe refilled their glasses, careful to keep them even.

"Talk to the boy again, I suppose—your turn, I think. Talk to the pontoises, see if they know anything about bes'Anthe, any rumor he was in trouble."

"Yours," Eslingen said.

Rathe nodded. "You might ask Young Steen the same question, and his owner, for that matter."

"If they'll talk to me," Eslingen said. "I'll send a note, see if they'll meet me away from the docks. He was very touchy about this gang, Nico."

"That's a good thought."

"I've another question for you," Eslingen said, before he could think better of it. "It seems one of the boys who's trying to join the Guard has some connections to the Staenka family and has volunteered to help. He's sincere, I think, but—I'd welcome your advice on the best way to handle it."

"Depends on how pretty he is," Rathe said.

Eslingen froze, then made himself reach for his wine.

Rathe's eyebrows rose. "That pretty?"

"Very pretty." Eslingen kept tone and expression indifferent. "And all of seventeen. More to the point, he's—let's see, now, Meisenta Staenka's good friend's leman's brother, which is a way into the household."

"He's what?"

Eslingen ran through the genealogy again, grateful for the distraction, and Rathe shook his head.

"A way into the household, sure, or just maybe a way for them to get into our investigation."

"He swears his loyalty is to the Guard," Eslingen said.

"Well, he would."

"I believe him," Eslingen said. "He has the stars for it. He wants to see justice done."

"He's taken a liking to you," Rathe said.

"I assure you, he has not!" Eslingen felt himself blush, and was glad of the dim light to hide it.

"Do you think I haven't seen this before? Any apprentice who talks about seeing justice done is hoping to win her superior's favor. And don't tell me Coindarel forbids it."

Eslingen blushed even deeper at that. "And are you telling me you didn't join the points to see justice done?"

"What makes you think I didn't have a desperate passion, too?"

"For who?" Eslingen couldn't stop the question.

Rathe blinked at him. "You really don't see it, do you?"

"There's nothing to see."

"If you say so." Rathe tapped two fingers on the table. "Even assuming that's true—I wouldn't do it, Philip. There's too much chance he'd end up at odds with his family, and that's doing him no favors. If he was one of ours, we'd take him off the case."

"I told him that." Eslingen drained his glass. "He said he'd take the chance."

"If he were my apprentice, I wouldn't let him." Rathe leaned back, balancing his stool on two legs. "I wonder what the alchemists had to say about bes'Anthe's body? Fancy a trip to the deadhouse, Philip?"

"Not really. Probably not a bad idea, though. If they'll talk to you."

"I won't know until we ask," Rathe let the stool fall with a thud, and reached into his pocket to bring out a very dirty single-sheet almanac. He unfolded it on the tabletop, frowning at the tiny print. "If we go first thing tomorrow, we should catch Fanier."

Fanier was one of the two senior alchemists responsible for the city's untimely dead. Eslingen groaned. "What do you call 'first thing'?"

"If we're there about nine, they should be done with the night's work, and not yet started on the day's."

Eslingen heaved a sigh. "I imagine it'll be raining, too."

"Very likely." There was a note of laughter in Rathe's voice.

Eslingen gave a smile in return, though if truth were to be told, he was thoroughly sick of the current stars. It happened to everyone, of course, temporarily dominant stars coming into conflict with the stars that ruled one's birth, and it wasn't nearly as bad as the twice-a-year ghost-tides were for, say, necromancers, but it was certainly unpleasant enough. And it looked as though it would be a week or longer before the influence waned.

He made himself look around the taproom, trying to draw cheer from the fire and the warm lights and the good-tempered crowd that filled most of the room. The Acrobatikon, the last of the city's unroofed open theaters, had closed when the rains set in, another casualty of the unseasonable weather, and the Tyrseia had reduced the number of its shows in hopes of keeping down the costs of heating its enormous space, but the smaller closed houses and the handful of private houses were in full swing, doing their best to make their money before the enforced hiatus of the midwinter masque. Neither the play nor the cast had been announced yet, nor would be for some weeks, but already it seemed as though every actor in the city was competing for a place. Thank Seidos I'm not involved, Eslingen thought, not for the first time. He'd been part of the previous winter's near-disaster, when a discontented noble had attempted to use the masque to destroy the queen, and had no desire to take part in another. In fact, he planned never to set foot in a theater again unless he paid for a ticket.

"Philip?" Rathe gave him a searching look, and Eslingen forced another smile.

"Sorry. Thought I saw Siredy, that's all." Verre Siredy was a former colleague in the Masters of Defense, and also the lover of the actor Gavi Jhirassi, currently their upstairs neighbor. A very vigorous lover: they had heard the bedstead thumping more than once.

From Rathe's grin, the same thought had crossed his mind. "Surely not, I think Gavi's playing tonight."

"Must've been mistaken." Eslingen looked at the remains of their dinner, then tipped his head to listen for the sound of the rain against the shutters. "Sounds like it might be slacking some. Shall we?"

"What, no sweet?" Rathe recoiled in exaggerated horror.

"I can live without."

Rathe waved to the nearest waiter, handed him a couple of coins. "Ask Wicked to wrap up a couple of the fried pies, please. And bring Philip his cloak."

"Right away," the man promised, and Eslingen shook his head.

"You didn't have to do that."

"It does sound like it's a little better out." Rathe paused. "These stars are really getting to you."

Eslingen sighed, unable to come up with a clever answer. "Yes."

Rathe's hand closed gently on his shoulder. "Not much longer, I hope?"

"At least a week."

"Ah, Philip."

Rathe's grip tightened, and Eslingen leaned for a moment into the touch. "At least I've got a nice murder to distract me."

"We're certainly got that," Rathe said, and the waiter arrived with the cloak and a well-wrapped packet.

They rose and breakfasted in the gloomy half-light of another cloudy morning, and Eslingen took Sunflower down to the garden to let him run before handing him over to the weaver's daughter, her hair frizzed to a cloud despite her attempts to contain it in a turban. Even Sunflower seemed subdued, and let her take his lead with no more than a half-hearted attempt to tangle himself in her skirts. Eslingen eyed him warily, wondering if he was sickening for something, and the girl shook her head.

"He'll perk up once he's had a chance to lie by the fire. I've a marrowbone saved for him, too."

"Lucky him," Eslingen said, and the weaver appeared behind her daughter's shoulder.

"Didn't know you could be bought so cheaply, Captain! I'll bear that in mind." She closed the door before he could think of a clever answer. In its pen beside the house, the goat gave an almost human snicker.

"Ready?" Rathe asked, coming across the garden, and Eslingen hunched his shoulders under the not-quite-dry cloak.

"Is anyone ever ready to visit the deadhouse?"

"Point granted," Rathe said, after a moment. "At least it's not raining."

They stopped at the corner grocer, where the owner was just lowering the shutters, and Rathe bought apples for later and paid an extra demming to send one of the apprentices to carry a note to Point of Dreams.

"Not that Trijn would object to my being late," he said, "but it's better if she knows where to find me."

Eslingen nodded, and they made their way toward the Hopes-Point Bridge. Fog was still curling off the water—close to high tide, Eslingen noted, though he couldn't have said whether it was rising or falling—and it mingled with the smoke from the shops that lined the bridge to blur the edges of the buildings, and turn the pedestrians to ghosts. At least it wasn't raining, he repeated to himself, and a pamphlet pinned to the frame of a bookseller's door caught his eye. The woodcut on its cover showed the Hopes-Point Bridge, the familiar pile of buildings at each end and the brief gap in the middle, but beneath its central arch a hooded figure rose from the waves, a skeletal hand reaching toward the nearest pillar. Fish surrounded her, the same dogfish that had decorated the broadsheet; in bold letters, the title read *The Custom of the City, or, Old Tales Newly Expounded.* He slowed, beckoning to the apprentice sweeping leaves into the gutter.

"How much?"

"A spider, sir, and it's just out today."

That was more than twice the price of even the most questionable broadsheets, but Eslingen reached into his pocket anyway, came up with a single copper aster. He flipped it to the apprentice, who caught it neatly, and unpinned a fresh copy to hand it over with a flourish. "There you are, sir, and thank you."

Eslingen touched his hat in answer, aware that Rathe had slowed and was looking back over his shoulder.

"Philip?"

"Nothing important." Eslingen tucked the pamphlet into his sleeve, and stretched his legs to catch up with the other man.

They reached the deadhouse a little after the clocks struck nine. Rathe rapped sharply on the door, and after a moment one of the apprentices peered out at them.

"Pointsman?" he began doubtfully, and Rathe sighed.

"Adjunct Point Rathe, Point of Dreams. I'd like to speak to Fanier, if he's free."

The apprentice blinked, then composed himself. He was perhaps fifteen or sixteen, with an awkward length of limb, but he managed a reasonably graceful bow. "Please to come within, sir—sirs. If you'll wait here, I'll see what I can do."

He led them into the main hall, the stone floor spotless, and then past the fountain to a smaller room where a stove was lit and there were benches along the wall, then disappeared into the hallway. Rathe shook his head. "That one won't last."

"Oh?"

"Too polite."

Eslingen laughed. That was what had been odd about this visit: he'd never before been treated with anything like respect. But then, in this house, the alchemists' loyalty was to the dead, not the living. "I suppose they need someone who can treat with grieving kin."

"Maybe." Rathe's smile was wry. "I've just never met one."

The apprentice returned minutes later, accompanied by an older journeyman still wiping his hands on a stained towel. "Fanier says if it's about the tea captain, he can't tell you any more than he told Point of Sighs."

Eslingen saw Rathe's lips twitch—that was more what one expected from the deadhouse—and had to look away before he laughed.

"I don't expect any more than that," Rathe said, "but I still want to talk to him."

The journeyman tucked the towel through his belt, letting it fall with the stains to the inside. "All right, then, but I'm to say I warned you."

"Understood," Rathe said, and they followed the boys through the maze of corridors.

To Eslingen's relief, they finished up at one of the workrooms, not one of the wide examination rooms. The air was still chill, and weirdly scentless, but there were no visible signs of the bodies that filled the building. Fanier himself was standing beside a worktable, looking over the shoulder of a fair-haired journeyman who was busy copying something from a holder. He looked up as they came in, and removed his brass-framed spectacles, tucking them into the front of his loosely-knitted sailor's jersey. A second pair of spectacles sat atop his head, held by his unruly gray hair.

"Did they tell you I don't have anything new?"

"They did," Rathe said. "But the problem is, I haven't seen your old report."

Fanier nodded. "I wondered if that was it. I'm having a copy made."

"Thanks." Rathe gave a crooked smile. "Would you be willing to answer a few questions, before Sighs tells you not to?"

"Oh, is it likely to come to that? And what's this I hear about Edild Dammar throwing himself in the Sier?"

"I doubt he did it himself," Rathe said. "He was beaten and stabbed first, he's damned lucky the pontoises found him as quickly as they did."

"Not a lovely man," Fanier said, "but I don't wish that on anyone." He shook his head. "Should I be expecting you to take on this tea captain?"

Rathe grimaced. "Not officially. But Sighs has called the point on the tea merchant's son, and he's Dreams' responsibility, plus Philip here has been asked to keep an eye on things for the family."

"And we didn't like to disturb Sighs when they're bound to be in disarray over their man being attacked," Eslingen put in, with his most guileless stare, and surprised a laugh from Fanier.

"Well, they've not said anything to the contrary, so you're welcome to a copy of the report. Do you want to see the body, too?"

"Not really," Eslingen said, "but I suppose we'd better."

bes'Anthe's body lay in the deadhouse crypt, down a curved stair that brought them into a vaulted space lit with mage-lights. Eight temporary coffins stood on racks along the wall, and Fanier counted silently until they reached the fifth. "This is him," he said, and began unfastening the clamps that held the lid. Eslingen braced himself for smells and discoloration, but the body in the coffin seemed almost untouched, eyes closed, broad-boned face slack, hands upturned at his side. Even the knife-wound at the base of his ribcage had been washed clean, could have been a scar or a birthmark; it was just the waxy tone of the skin proved that the man wasn't sleeping.

"Not a trained blow," he said, shaking himself back to business, and Fanier nodded.

"No, but a lucky one. Caught one of the large blood vessels, the man died quick."

"Not something I'd like to rely on if I wanted to kill a man." Rathe reached into the coffin and lifted the man's right hand, studying the palm and then the fingernails. He repeated the examination on the other hand, and laid it down again, careful to put it back in its original position. "No sign that he fought."

"My guess is, he was taken by surprise," Fanier said. "And since he was taken from the front, he saw his killer. I imagine he didn't think to run away."

"Which could mean it was either a total stranger, or someone he knew well," Rathe said. "Sadly, from what we know of the circumstances, it could be either one."

"But less likely to be Mattaes," Eslingen said, "since they'd just had a shouting match. I can't see him letting the boy just walk up and stab him."

"Unless he didn't take him seriously as a threat," Rathe said. He shook his head. "Anything else we ought to know?"

Fanier shook his head. "He's a most *unremarkable* dead man. Do you know if he has kin? I'd be glad to have him taken away."

"You're full up," Eslingen said, looking at the coffins, and Fanier laughed.

"The river's running fierce this autumn."

"It's not those dogfish people are talking about, is it?" Eslingen said. He looked at Rathe. "I thought you said they were invented."

"Oh, has that reached the broadsheets?" Fanier asked.

Rathe lifted his eyebrows. "Please tell me you're not saying yes to that question."

Fanier chuckled. "There haven't been greater dogfish in the Sier in two hundred years. But by the look of these poor bastards, there are some exceedingly large ordinary dogfish out there. The pontoises pulled a body—as yet unnamed, though he's probably a sailor—pulled him out of the river four days ago, just above the Exemption Docks. Something had eaten about a third of the corpse. I suspect a pack of dogfish."

"I thought they were solitary hunters," Rathe said.

"Maybe they were spawning." Fanier shrugged. "We don't have so many tests that are specific for being eaten by fish."

"Sounds as though you might need to develop some," Rathe began, and the door at the top of the stairs slammed open.

"Adjunct Point! There's a runner for you from Point of Dreams!"

"That's never good," Eslingen said involuntarily.

"No," Rathe said, his voice grim, and started for the stairs.

The runner was waiting in the main lobby, still panting as though she'd run most of the way. She held out a folded slip of paper, and Rathe took it, unfolding it with a frown that deepened as he read. "Did you walk?"

The runner shook her head. "I took a low-flyer most of the way."

"Good."

"What is it?" Eslingen asked.

Rathe crumpled the paper and tucked it into his pocket. "Fourie wants me. And Trijn, I suppose, she says I'm to come to Dreams first." He paused. "I have to go."

Eslingen nodded, swallowing the obvious question. Whatever the Surintendant of Points wanted, it was unlikely to be good. "I'll talk to Mattaes. And Steen, if I can find him."

"If he pulls me off this," Rathe began, and stopped again, shaking his head.

"Don't borrow trouble," Eslingen said, and pushed him gently toward the door.

CHAPTER 5

RATHE MANAGED TO wave down another low-flyer by the University gates, leaned forward in his seat as though he could urge the two-wheeled carriage faster through the traffic that clogged the Queen's Bridge. By the time they reached Point of Dreams, the clocks had struck half past ten, and Trijn was pacing the main room, skirts swirling around her ankles.

"Where the hell have you been?"

"At the deadhouse," Rathe answered. "I had the flyer wait."

"Good." She looked him over, shaking her head. "By the Scales, don't you have a better coat?"

"Not here," Rathe said, though a part of him wished there were time to fetch his best from his lodgings. "How much of a hurry is he in, Chief?"

"Enough of one to say we should be there before noon." Trijn was at least respectable in a plain green skirt and bodice, the latter fastened to her chin with bright brass buttons. "What have you been up to, Rathe?"

Rathe spread his hands. "Nothing that I know of. I hoped you could tell me."

"Apparently we're both to be surprised," Trijn said, and led the way to the waiting flyer.

They arrived at the Tour de la Cite in good time, a few minutes before eleven by the clock in the tower opposite. Like many of the properties taken over by the Points, it had once been part of the city's defenses—one of the gatehouses, when the walls had enclosed a much smaller city—and the heavy stone walls and narrow windows gave it a brooding, brutal look. The low-flyer clattered to a stop in its shadow; Trijn paid it off, and they climbed the broad steps in silence. The inner corridors held a chill damp, despite the lamps and the red-coated clerks of the judiciary who scurried back and forth, and Rathe was glad when they reached the old South Tower, where the Surintendant of Points kept his office.

They were expected—late, in the carefully unspoken opinion of the austere woman who acted as the surintendant's secretary, who led them to a half-open door. "Chief Trijn and Adjunct Point Rathe, sir."

"Enter."

Rathe suppressed the desire to roll his eyes, and followed Trijn into the room. It was larger than most work spaces, with two long windows overlooking the square, and smelled strongly of beeswax and lamp oil. Lamps were burning in brackets on either side of the windows, throwing extra light on the neat piles of paper that covered the surintendant's table. Rainart Fourie himself sat squarely between the windows, his face in shadow; a plain falling collar and undecorated cuffs gleamed white against the unrelieved jet of his narrow coat. His hair was cropped close to his scalp as well, adding to the impression of austerity, but Rathe suspected the choice had more to do with vanity: longer hair would sit ill with that high forehead and the long and melancholy face.

"I'm glad to see you." Fourie's tone gave no such indication, but Trijn nodded anyway.

"We came as soon as we could. I had to send for Rathe, he was working."

"So you said." Fourie moved a slip of paper—a note from Trijn, Rathe guessed—from one side of the table to the other. "At the deadhouse, Adjunct Point?"

"Yes." Rathe had learned long ago that it was better not to volunteer anything; let the surintendant say what he wanted first, and answer accordingly.

"The matter of the tea captain, bes'Anthe."

"Yes," Rathe said again.

"Sighs has called a point on one of our residents," Trijn said. "We've been asked to act—and so has the City Guard."

A flush of color rose on Fourie's thin cheeks, but he said only, "So I've been informed." He waved to the chairs that stood ready, straight-backed hard wood. "Be seated."

Rathe risked a glance at Trijn at that, but she looked just as wary as she settled herself, spreading her skirts neatly over her knees.

"You will have heard the other news from Point of Sighs," Fourie said. "About their senior adjunct."

Rathe glanced at Trijn again, who started to shrug, and then thought better of it. "That Edild Dammar was beaten and stabbed and thrown in the Sier? A story like that travels, sir."

"And you were there, Rathe, when the pontoises brought him ashore." Fourie steepled his fingers.

"Purely by happenstance," Rathe said, and knew he sounded guilty. "I wanted to talk to the cap'pontoise about another matter."

Fourie reached for another sheet of paper. "The pontoises' report was somewhere terse. Tell me what you observed."

"I saw the boat come in, and the pontoises carry him ashore," Rathe answered. "Cambrai asked me to take a look at him—I assume he'd recognized him, but it took me a minute. If I had to say, I'd guess Dammar had been in a fight. One he lost." He went through the rest of what he'd seen, knowing that he wasn't adding much to the information Cambrai had already shared, and he was unsurprised when Fourie shook his head.

"Most unsatisfactory. Still, I trust we'll be able to correct that." He glanced at Trijn. "There is other news from Point of Sighs, I'm afraid. Chief Point Astarac—you knew she was increasing?"

Trijn's eyes widened. "She's a bit old for that, surely." She composed herself. "Sorry, sir. No, I didn't know."

"She and her eldest daughter are both with child, so I've just been told, and the daughter has been ill with it for a couple of months now. Astarac is further along, and this morning her remaining adjunct sends to me to say that Astarac had a fit in the night and has been taken to the Maternité." He reached for another slip of paper, this one torn on an odd angle. "Astarac says she'll be back to work as soon as possible, but I doubt the Demeans will release her any time soon."

Trijn straightened. "If you're planning to take my adjunct—"

Fourie lifted one finger. "Temporarily only. And you have a full complement, do you not?"

"Yes, but—" Trijn took a breath, visibly forcing down annoyance. "Sir, Rathe is my right hand, not to mention that he's in the middle of a dozen things that require a certain expertise. I can't spare him."

Fourie tapped his fingertips against one another. "And I dislike the notion that someone would feel free to attack one of my people. However questionable I may find Dammar's behavior, he remains one of us. I want someone I can trust to investigate the matter without fear or favor."

"You think someone at Sighs did it," Rathe said.

"That thought has crossed my mind. I'm aware of Dammar's reputation, and I've heard the talk of more extortion than usual on the docks.

The situation is volatile enough that I don't want to give this business to anyone who remains at Sighs—and the truth of the matter is, the junior adjunct has only been in the place a year. Not quite that, in fact. I would want to send someone else to take Dammar's place regardless."

Trijn swore under her breath.

"In that case," Rathe said, "there's no reason for me not to pursue the question of bes'Anthe's death."

"I'd prefer for you to concentrate on Dammar," Fourie said. "Let the rest of Sighs deal with bes'Anthe, or turn it over to the Guard, if you think that would be best."

I don't have a choice, do I? Rathe swallowed the words, and looked at Trijn. "I can hand over my books to Auzeri, we've been working hand-in-glove on most of it anyway."

"All right." Trijn glared at the surintendant. "But I don't have to like it, sir."

"That's not required." Fourie reached for a silver bell that stood on his desk. He shook it once, the piercing jangle enough to cut through conversation outside, and a moment later the secretary peered in the door.

"Show in Adjunct Point Sebern, please."

"At once," the secretary answered, closing the door again behind her. Rathe glanced again at Trijn, saw her visibly reconsider another protest. The door opened, this time wide enough to admit a stocky woman in a neat blue-gray suit. Winter-sea blue, the color was called, Rathe remembered, and it made the most of a sallow complexion. Her leather jerkin hung open over skirt and bodice, a badge of office rather than protection, but the truncheon at her belt was as large and potentially effective as his own. She might be his own age, or perhaps a few years younger, given that she was still the junior adjunct—or she might be a year or two older, and risen more slowly in a more crowded and prosperous station even than Dreams.

"Adjunct Point Sebern, this is Adjunct Point Rathe," Fourie said

Sebern gave a jerky nod. "I know his reputation."

"Then you won't find it a surprise that I'm assigning him to Point of Sighs—temporarily, of course," Fourie added, lifting a hand to forestall complaint. "Until either Chief Astarac or Adjunct Point Dammar can return to duty."

Sebern opened her mouth, closed it, took a breath and tried again. "With all respect, Surintendant, we can manage Sighs without outside help. Aside from the chief and Dammar, we're at full strength."

"I'd prefer to have another senior person in the station." Fourie's gaze narrowed. "And I'm sure you're not telling me that you don't want some-one from another station seeing your books."

Sebern paled, though from the set of her mouth it was hard to tell if the driving emotion was fear or fury. "If you insist, sir. I just don't want to take Adjunct Point Rathe away from his usual duties."

"I think we have enough people to manage," Trijn said. She looked at Rathe. "I'll want you to turn your books over to Auzeri before you make the move, though."

Rathe nodded. This wasn't the sort of job anyone liked, coming into a station as a resented stranger, and his reputation ran against Sighs' in ways that would only make it more difficult. On the other hand, it was at least a chance to examine Dammar more closely, and to find out what the station already knew about bes'Anthe's death. But how it would intersect with Eslingen and the Guard, or the pontoises.... There was no way to tell. Fourie smiled benevolently, as though he were completely unaware of the tension.

"Excellent. That's settled, then. Rathe, I'd like regular reports, please. And—that will be all, I think. Good day."

It was clear that no further objections would be permitted. They mum-bled their answers, and backed awkwardly from the workroom, then stood staring unhappily at each other in the antechamber until Trijn shook her head.

"Right. Well, we'll have to live with this. Rathe, I want you to go over your book with Auzeri."

"I'd like to go to Sighs first," Rathe said, with enough emphasis that Trijn blinked and nodded. He looked at Sebern. "We might as well get it done."

Sebern nodded, though she didn't look pleased. "If that's how you want it."

"Are you telling me there's a better way?" Rathe tried a wry smile, and to his surprise one corner of her mouth curved up in answer.

"Not that I can think of."

Rathe caught Trijn's sleeve as she turned away. "I'll be back before the night watch, Chief," he said, and wished it didn't feel as though he were telling her when to send rescue.

IT WAS NOT a terribly long walk back to Sighs, just over the Hopes-Point Bridge and then east along the waterfront. This was Bonfortune's Walk, wide and well swept, the cobbles ground down by the passage of four

centuries of wagons. On the north side, the river side, a jumble of two-
and three-story buildings were jammed between the broad passages that
led onto the wharfs, bare masts jutting above the roof-tiles. Pennants
hung at the head of some of the passages, bright strips of red and blue
and gold, some more faded than others, but each with a house-mark;
strands of smaller pennants hung above the doors of some of the lower
buildings, marking them as factors' halls, where the merchants resident
could come to bid on cargos as they arrived. The rest of them were chandlers and small shops and bonded warehouses, the last conspicuous for
their lack of windows and heavy ironbound doors. On the south side of
the street, the buildings were taller by two stories, narrow, once elegant
houses long ago converted into trading rooms and counting houses for
the families who had long ago moved into better neighborhoods. Perhaps half still had shops or showrooms on their ground floors, but their
shutters folded back to reveal leaded glass windows, and a well-dressed
knife watched most of the doors. You were there to buy mostly by invita-
tion, Rathe guessed.

Sebern saw where he was looking, and cleared her throat. "We do
things differently here in Point of Sighs."

And all of Astreiant knows it. Rathe kept the thought to himself, knowing he couldn't afford to antagonize her any further. "I've no intention—
it's not my place to change anything."

She stiffened, then consciously relaxed, rolling her shoulders. "No?
The sur seems to have something in mind."

"I'm sure he does, but he hasn't shared it with me. He's told me he wants
Dammar's attacker, and that's all I know."

"What about bes'Anthe? Edild told me you and Trijn were protecting
the murderer."

"I'd like to know who killed the man," Rathe said carefully, "and I don't
think Mattaes Staenka did."

"Everyone in the Bear and Bush heard them shouting at each other."
Sebern ticked the items off on her fingers. "But only a third of them think
they saw the boy leave. bes'Anthe went out to the garden and never came
back in; when someone finally wondered what had become of him, they
found him dead in the bushes and called us right away, so we know there
weren't any other quarrels that night. When we were finally allowed to
make the point, your own woman found a bloody shirt in his room."

"The quarrel and the shirt are your best arguments. Though the shirt's
not his, we proved that by the laundry-marks."

Sebern waved a hand in dismissal. "It happens. Someone's shirt or shift gets sorted into the wrong basket."

"Richer houses keep close track of that," Rathe said. "Because they can. And they've got extras to lose." He waited, and Sebern gave a grudging nod. "Mostly, though—first, the boy's no fighter. If he'd tried to take on bes'Anthe, he would have lost. Second, I can't see bes'Anthe letting him walk up and stab him, not after they'd just been shouting at each other."

Sebern made a face. "Maybe."

"What I want is to call the point on the murderer," Rathe said. "But I want proof."

"Edild was sure it was the boy," Sebern said.

"Show me the proof," Rathe said, "and I'll hand him over."

They had reached the end of Bonfortune's Walk, an open square with a central fountain. There were stables on the southern and eastern sides, and carters' yards further on, and apprentices were coming and going with buckets on heavy yokes. The smell of horses was stronger here than the scent of the river's mud. Sebern gave him a sidelong glance.

"You think you mean that."

"I do mean it," Rathe said wearily. There were any number of things he could have said—that he didn't take fees precisely because he wanted to be free to act against whoever the facts showed was guilty, that he and Trijn had come to an understanding long ago, that she respected his choice even when she didn't agree—but none of them would do any good. For most of Astreiant, a pointsman who didn't take fees, who couldn't be bought, also couldn't be trusted.

Her eyebrows rose, but she had the grace not to ask further questions. "We'll take the shortcut."

She led him toward a short alley that ran between two of the stable blocks that seemed to end in another brick wall. Sebern started down anyway, and Rathe followed, wrinkling his nose at the smell of urine.

"I don't imagine you use this much after dark."

Sebern grinned. "There's a lot of back alleys I wouldn't venture in without at least one sun up. But, yeah, this is one of them. It's convenient by daylight, though."

As they got closer, he could see that the alley took a sharp right turn, and then a left, to emerge at the corner of the square where Point of Sighs' station stood, squat and square to block access to the river. Supposedly a southern wall had been planned, with Sighs as its central gate, but like so many things southriver, the money had gone to other things, and the city had gone its own way around the square. Still, the massive entrance remained, big enough to drive a cart through. One of the half-doors was open, and even from across the square Rathe could see that the hall ran all the way through the building to a matching open door.

"Don't you find that a bit...chancy?" he asked, and surprised another grin from Sebern.

"It's had its tricky moments, but the doors and the bars are all iron-bound. Once they're closed, there's not much short of cannon that can open them. Now, if we were Point of Knives...."

"The gods forbid any of them get their hands on artillery," Rathe said. "Though—surely some of your sailors have cannon?"

"We try not to give them cause to use it on us," Sebern said, the moment of humor vanishing. "Come on."

The square was quiet, lined with respectable-looking shops and a pair of taverns that seemed to cater to the merchant classes. Rathe caught a glimpse of a girl reading to a double row of knitters, each with a half-finished stocking twitching on busy needles, and another narrow window showed a haphazard pile of thick Silklands tapestries and carpets: a good neighborhood, and prosperous, especially for the southern side of the river.

There were no steps to block the great doorway, though a slab of granite had been laid as a sill at some point, and the ceiling was a great arched vault like the inside of a barrel. Mage-lights clustered on the pillars and at the joints of the arches, and a pair of tables had been set facing each other, each one blocking a door that led deeper into the building. There was no fireplace, of course, and the air was chill; stoves had been set against the walls, low, hulking stone monstrosities, and there were benches and stools gathered haphazardly around them.

Both the duty points looked up sharply as Sebern entered, and the other points lounging by the stoves came to swift attention. Sebern eyed them without particular favor, and pointed to one of the younger men.

"Hirn. Go inside and fetch out anyone who's not doing something actually important. I only want to say this once."

"Yes, Adjunct Point," the young man answered, and disappeared through the left-hand door. One of the women made an abortive movement toward the other one, and Sebern nodded irritably.

"Yeah, right, go on, might as well check."

"What's over there?" Rathe asked.

"Stores, mostly. The armory. Usually there's nobody in there."

A knot of points emerged from the left-hand door, most of them young and disheveled: the junior points poor enough to settle for garret rooms at the top of the tower. The woman reappeared in the right-hand doorway, shaking her head, and Sebern clapped her hands.

"All right, listen up! You'll have heard that the chief's been put to bed at the Maternité until she delivers, and I know you've all heard about the Senior Adjunct. While they're both out of commission, the surintendant has sent us help from Point of Dreams. This is Nicolas Rathe, he'll be acting as Senior Adjunct until further notice."

There was a somewhat ambiguous murmur in answer, and the woman in the doorway said, "How's Edild?"

From her age, Rathe guessed she was one of the senior points, who might have considered herself in line for promotion to adjunct if Sebern had stepped up. Sebern wagged her hand. "Not as out of it as he was, they tell me, but not fit to talk to anyone. There's a physician sitting with him, we're to be called if anything changes."

The woman nodded, evidently satisfied, and Sebern said, "That's Bellin, she's the senior for the day watch."

Rathe suppressed a groan, knowing what was coming, and let himself be taken round the room. It was impossible to match names to faces as quickly as Sebern moved, and he guessed she was doing it on purpose. She was not going to make this easy for him. He smiled anyway, and kept voice and expression deliberately mild until they'd finished, and the group had started to move away.

"A word, if you please." The words were mild enough still, but he let his tone carry an edge. It stopped them in their tracks, and they turned back to look at him. "As Adjunct Point Sebern says, the surintendant has assigned me to Sighs until Chief Astarac and Adjunct Point Dammar are able to resume their duties. I'm here specifically to find out what happened to Dammar, not to involve myself more than is necessary in the station's business. I'm also already involved with the murder of the tea captain, bes'Anthe, and I'll say to you all what I've already said to Sebern. I want the murderer, nothing more, nothing less. I expect your cooperation in this."

There was an answering mutter, less antagonistic than he'd feared, and he looked at Sebern. "I'll need a workroom. It doesn't have to be Dammar's—I'd rather it wasn't—but I need the space."

"We can set you up." She glanced around the room before pointing to a tall woman with spectacles. "Ormere! Rathe is taking the smaller break room. Get a table in there, and a decent kettle." She looked back at Rathe. "In the meantime, I suppose you want to look at Edild's books."

"That would make a start," Rathe said.

DAMMAR'S BOOKS WERE, to Rathe's surprise, impeccably neat and seemingly carefully maintained. Sebern fetched the most recent volumes from the senior adjunct's workroom, going back half a year, and Rathe paged slowly through them. The daily notes were bland and unhelpful, a bald record of fines collected, the occasional point called, visits and conversations with the local merchants, with nothing to tell a reader why Dammar made his decisions. Rathe pushed on anyway, pausing only when Ormere reported his workroom ready. It was on the upper floor, like all the others, and still showed signs of its hasty repurposing from a common space. But it had a table and a stove, and Ormere had already set a kettle to boil.

"I've brought tea as well—it's our common stock, but I hope it will do until you can bring your own."

"That'll do fine," Rathe said, glancing around again. The space was shallow but wide, a room sliced from the end of the tower, with shelves at each end and a narrow window as well as the usual mix of mage-lights and candles. There was an oil lamp, too, set on the table with a battered set of pens and a chipped inkwell: more things to bring from Dreams, he thought, and put that aside. "Are you Dammar's second?"

Ormere shook her head. "Amanuensis—well, secretary, I suppose. The adjunct didn't really have a second."

"That's unusual." Rathe set the stack of Dammar's record books on the table, and settled himself in the single chair. The room was pleasantly warm: the senior points were going to have one more thing to resent about his presence.

"He used to work with Gerrijs Neulle, but he was transferred to Customs Point." Ormere shrugged. "He hasn't worked with anybody steadily since."

That was one way to leave your options open, Rathe thought. "Did he have you keep these books, then?"

"I made the fair copies." Ormere glanced at the stove. "The water's boiling. Shall I make a pot?"

That was more than he had expected, and Rathe gave her a wary glance. She looked faintly chagrined, however, as though she'd forgotten for a moment to whom she was speaking, and that was perversely reassuring. "Yes, please. Thank you. And if you have a minute, I'd like to ask a few questions."

"I'm at your disposal." She dragged a stool to the other side of the table, then poured out the tea as well. Rathe's head lifted as he caught the first whiff of the steam.

"That's...very nice."

Ormere shrugged again. "The tea dealers club in to supply the station. We do a lot of work for them this time of year."

Gifts like that were not uncommon in the trading districts, Rathe reminded himself. At Dreams it was always possible to get a ticket to any play no matter how popular. He took a sip, the liquid green and strong and spiced with the familiar pepper of pot-gold, and told himself he would enjoy it while he was here. Maybe it would ease tensions a little with the station.

"My first concern is with Dammar," he said aloud. "I'm not seeing anything in the books recently that would provoke an attack like that. Any idea why someone would try to kill him?"

"The adjunct didn't put down everything," Ormere said. "None of the seniors do. The chief's been ailing, even before this, and her daughter's been ill the last five months. We were trying to spare her."

And look how that's worked out. Rathe controlled himself and said, "So what's not in the books that might shed some light on this?"

Ormere spread her hands, nearly spilling her tea. "Not much, that's the thing. We may be on the south bank of the river, but we don't see much in the way of violence—"

That was such an unlikely statement that Rathe felt his eyebrows rise in spite of himself, and Ormere flushed.

"Well, except on the docks, of course. And most of them would rather deal with the pontoises anyway."

"Can't imagine," Rathe said, in spite of himself, and her color deepened. She had the sense not to say anything more, and he sighed. "So if there were some sort of extortion happening on the docks, you'd expect the sailors to go to the pontoises about it?"

"Well, no. They should come to us, of course, it's our district—and we do act on all the complaints we're given. It's just that the dockers and the sailors would rather deal with the pontoises than make a formal statement to us. The pontoises have a reputation for...informality."

Better to let that go for now, Rathe told himself, though he was appalled by the attitude. If that was how most of the station approached the sailors' problems, it was no wonder the extortion gang felt free to threaten even the ships' owners. "So who'd want to kill Dammar?"

"That's the rub," Ormere said, pushing her spectacles back up on her nose. "We've all been wondering. Mostly he's been dealing with theft—warehouse theft, some petty embezzlement. Nothing that would mean more than a fine or a woman losing her job, nothing to kill for. Except, of course, for bes'Anthe's murder. He was certain the Staenka boy did it, too."

"I'm keeping that in mind," Rathe said. "But the Staenka family has gone straight to the law on this. They brought in my chief, they've enlisted one of the Guard, and they've posted a sizable bond. Why do all that, and then try to kill Dammar?"

Ormere paused, considering. "That's a fair point," she said, after a moment, and Rathe felt himself relax. At least she was willing to think about alternatives. "And of course if you're right and the boy didn't kill bes'Anthe, then the woman who did it might have tried for Edild—though, no, he'd be her best protection, since he was set on calling the point on the boy. Unless...."

She stopped, the color rising again, and Rathe said, "Unless he'd taken a fee, and decided later that the matter wasn't fee'able after all." That was the least offensive way he could think to put it, and Ormere nodded gratefully.

"Though I wouldn't think—he took fees, Adjunct, but no more than most of us. Murder's a different matter."

Rathe nodded. This was not the time to press the question, though he was sure it would come later. "What else? You helped keep his books."

"One fraud case that was bigger than usual," Ormere said. "The merchant resident, a silk dealer, claimed her sister's man had deliberately bought poor-quality silk so that the sister could take over the business. Family quarrels can be nasty."

"True enough. So, what, the sister's man attacked him?"

"Or hired someone to do it. Edild took a pretty fee on that one—from the dealer."

Rathe reached for his tablets and made a note in the wax. "Worth checking. What else?"

"The pontoises."

Rathe looked up at that, and Ormere met his eyes determinedly.

"I told you, there's a long-standing argument about jurisdiction, and Edild took it somewhat personally. If he'd fought with one of their tillermen, and they went further than they meant."

"And then plucked him out of the river when they could have left him to drown?" Rathe asked.

"Why not, if they didn't know what their fellows had done? Or maybe it wasn't the pontoises themselves, but some of the dockers who'd rather deal with them than us."

That sounded considerably more plausible, and Rathe made another note. "I've heard a rumor that a group of dockers is asking more than the usual fee for unloading safely. Is there anything to it?"

Ormere shook her head, too quickly. "No one's complained to us."

Rathe thought that was probably the literal truth. He hoped Eslingen could get Young Steen to talk to him. "All right. If you can think of anyone else, any other case that might have provoked the attack—or if you know where he kept his daily notes?"

Ormere shook her head again. "I just copied what he gave me, I never saw anything else. I don't think he kept notes, just wrote it down straightway."

And this was why you kept your books up-to-date, and worried more about putting down information than about how neatly it was phrased. Except, of course, if Dammar was taking unreasonable fees, and not keeping his word, careful notes would only betray him. "I'll want to see the daybooks tomorrow," he said, "and I'll keep these for a while. Maybe something will stand out once I've been here longer."

"Right, Adjunct." Ormere pushed herself to her feet, accepting the dismissal. "But if I were you, sir, I'd look long and hard at the pontoises. They're nothing but trouble on the docks, and have been ever since they had to give way to us."

He spent the rest of the afternoon reading the last six months' entries in Dammar's books, making notes on cases that might provoke an attack. As Ormere had said, there were few of them: Dammar seemed to spend most of his time on complaints from the local merchants, complaints that, however petty on the face of it, had the chance of bringing solid fees. If he was fee'd for even half the cases that made it to his book, Rathe thought, he'd come close to tripling his official salary. It was probably worth taking a look at how well he and any family lived.

Except, of course, that he was supposed to be finding the person who'd knifed Dammar, not investigating whether he took fees and stayed bought. And neither Dammar's records nor the station's daybooks offered much to steer him in the right direction. He looked at his list—half a dozen names, none of them particularly likely—then picked up the last daybook and headed down the stairs.

As he'd hoped, the hall was quiet, most of the points out on the last patrol before the day-sun set, and the woman Bellin was sitting behind the one occupied table. Rathe slid the book over to her, and she took it with a not unfriendly nod.

"Done with it, then, Adjunct?"

"Yes, thanks. You're the senior on the day-watch?" It was a guess, but he'd been fairly sure of it, finding her in charge when the others were out.

She nodded, seeming equally unsurprised at the question. She was a stocky woman, strongly muscled, with a stiffly upright posture that spoke of the sort of heavily-boned stays that would turn a knife. "Any luck?"

Rathe shrugged. "I've some questions to ask. Is there anyone you'd point to?"

"It's docker business," Bellin said, "and that means the pontoises. I know you don't want to hear it, being friends with them and all, but they're still fighting over our rights. Easy enough for something to get out of hand."

"I've worked with the pontoises, yes," Rathe said, keeping his voice mild with an effort. "But I'm a pointsman, first and always. If any of them are responsible, I'll be down on them like a ton of bricks." And so would Cambrai, but he knew better than to make that argument. "What makes you say it's docker business?"

"There's always more trouble on the docks than anywhere else in Sighs." Bellin reached for the daybook, set it carefully back in its case with the others. "It's the nature of the beast, and also no surprise this year, with I'd say a quarter of the ships left trapped in the Silklands. Well, maybe not so many, a number have come straggling in or put to port south of here, but it's cost any number of families a goodly part of the winter trade, the tea merchants in particular. They were all waiting for that last shipment, the Old Year teas and the last thinnings, and half of it never got here, and the other half isn't the best of the crop." She shot Rathe a sudden glance. "All that's background, you understand."

Rathe nodded.

"So tempers are already running high, and money's short, and we're seeing more thieving along the warehouse rows. There's trouble in the taverns. When we make our patrols, we see more black eyes and torn coats and bloody knuckles—but not a one of them comes to us with a complaint. Ask, and they walked into a door or tripped down a ladder, got caught by a stray rope. Something's brewing, and if they won't come to us, it must be the pontoises' fault."

"You'd expect them to come to you if there were problems, then?" Rathe did his best to keep his tone merely curious.

"Why not? They're sensible folk, they know where their bread's baked. And most of us don't ask so much in fees, not from poor folk like them."

"Good of you," Rathe said, in spite of himself, but Bellin didn't seem to hear the irony.

"It's the pontoises, Adjunct, I'm sure of it."

"I'll keep that in mind," Rathe said. "In the meantime, I'm out for the day. Ormere knows my lodgings if I'm needed overnight, the directions are in the book, and otherwise I'll be back in the morning."

"Very well, Adjunct," Bellin answered, and Rathe turned away.

The clouds were building again, promising more rain, and he quickened his step as he headed toward Point of Dreams. The day-sun was below the housetops, throwing the streets into shadow; occasionally a cross street ran straight enough toward the west to show a glimpse of the molten sky as the sun hung between the clouds and the horizon. The air tasted of rain and river mud.

The streets emptied as he made his way across Sighs, shops and workshops already closed for the night, shutters locked tight across the ground floor windows. He was almost back to Point of Dreams, though, where the taverns and theaters would be just opening up for business, and something prickled at the back of his neck, urging him to hurry. The quickest way led down Redillon's Row, lined with little shops and the occasional copper merchant's house; they were all closed, shutters barred and doors shut, but the last of setting sun spilled into the passage, casting long shadows. Rathe was halfway down before he thought he heard footsteps on the cobbles behind him. He glanced over his shoulder, but the sun-dazzle filled his eyes; nothing moved, and he heard nothing more, but he quickened his pace again. The sun slipped below the horizon, the light fading rapidly from the cloud-streaked sky, and he risked another look. The street seemed empty, but he thought he caught a movement just at the mouth of one of the little alleys between the shops. It was not repeated, and he turned back, only to hear the scrape of stone on stone.

And still the street was empty. He laid a hand on the truncheon at his belt. The heavy metal cap, the queen's seal above a triple band, was a potent weapon, but if his follower carried a knife, and was willing to use it, as Dammar's attacker had been.... He'd faced knives before with just the truncheon, and hadn't particularly enjoyed it. The noise was not repeated, nor did anything move in the deepening shadows. It might, he thought, have come from someone's garden, and struck badly against his stretched nerves. Better to keep moving, get to the safe bustle of Dreams as soon as possible. He lengthened his stride, wishing Eslingen were there, and kept his hand on the butt of the truncheon.

The Row ended in one of the smaller squares, this one centered on a respectable tavern, its doors open to the night and the usual handful of patrons standing to chat on the threshold. Rathe allowed himself a sigh of relief. No one would be fool enough to attack him under the eyes of three of Dreams' most prosperous printers; they might not help, but they would certainly bear witness against any attacker, and even run for help if he needed it. And maybe it had been nothing after all: he'd seen nothing, and heard nothing that couldn't carry another explanation, but he couldn't quite rid himself of the feeling that he had been followed.

He reached the station's gate as the clock struck half past and swallowed a groan at the thought of the work he had still to do. There were his books to update and hand over, and whatever else Trijn needed from him—probably he should send a runner to warn Eslingen that he was going to be late.

"Adjunct Point!"

He turned to see a boy in the pontoises' long-tailed cap, panting as he dragged to a halt.

"Adjunct Point! The cap' wants to see you, soon as may be."

"Is it an emergency?" Rathe asked.

The runner hesitated. "No, sir, but he'd like to talk to you tonight. He's at the Cockerel. He says, sir, he'll buy you dinner this time."

The Cockerel was one of the smaller taverns, frequented by shopkeepers and craftsmen—a place, Rathe thought, where he might talk to Cambrai unobserved. "Tell the cap' I'll be there within the hour," he said, and pushed through the gate before the boy could protest.

To his relief, there was less to do than he had feared. It didn't take long to update his books and hand them over to Auzeri, who did her best to contain her glee at the temporary promotion. Trijn had left for the day, and left no messages: all to the good, Rathe thought, surveying his workroom. There were things he could bring with him, things he wanted—he had the place arranged exactly to his liking, from the locked chests for his books to the chair and the heavy teapot. But if he was going to bring one thing, he'd want to bring them all, and the position at Sighs was emphatically temporary. It would only make things worse if he looked as though he was settling in.

He signed out with the night-watch, and made his way back through the streets. It was raining again, not hard, and he hoped Eslingen had made it home before it started. But, no, there he was, just turning away from one of the apple-men. Rathe lifted a hand, and Eslingen waved in turn, stepping away from the shopfronts just as a wagon rumbled past. One wheel hit a puddle, sending a sheet of water cascading over boots and breeches. Eslingen swore, and Rathe hurried across the street to join him.

"Are you—?"

"Wet." Eslingen scowled as water dripped from the apple he still clutched in one hand. He glared at it, but dried it and tucked it into his pocket. "Even wetter than I was before."

"I didn't think I'd see you. I'm supposed to meet Cambrai at the Cockerel. You could join us?"

Eslingen shook his head. "I'm no use to anyone like this. I'm going to go home and sit by the stove until the stars change."

Rathe ventured to pat his shoulder, and Eslingen scowled again, but didn't move away. "I'll bring you something."

"It doesn't—" Eslingen began, then stopped. "That would be kind."

"Go get dry," Rathe said, and Eslingen turned away.

Rathe watched him go, the skirts of his coat dragging, back stiff with irritation, then made himself turn toward the Cockerel. To his surprise, Cambrai was sitting on one of the benches beneath the overhanging roof, pipe in hand and the runner still at his side. He rose at Rathe's approach, and waved his pipe in a general greeting.

"Was that Eslingen? I hope his coat's not spoiled."

"His stars are bad for water," Rathe said, and saw the mockery in Cambrai's face shift to sympathy.

"Ah. It's an ill time for that, to be sure."

"Yes," Rathe said, repressively.

Cambrai shrugged. "Well, the man's a clothes horse. But no harm in it." He tossed the runner a coin that glinted silver in the lamplight. "All right, Gilly, be off with you."

"What did you want?" Rathe asked, as the boy darted away.

"A word with you away from both our stations. Seems to me this will serve."

The main room was dark and crowded, especially by the enormous fireplace that filled most of the right-hand wall. Rathe caught Cambrai's sleeve and towed him to the left, where the crowd thinned, fetching up at last at an empty table against the wall. No one was currently in earshot, and if they kept their voices down, even the neighboring tables would be hard pressed to hear.

Cambrai sat down. "I thought we could get a room…."

"That would definitely cause talk," Rathe said with a smirk. "And Moricia overcharges for them."

Cambrai leaned back, balancing his stool on two legs, and one of the waiters came slouching over, wiping his hands on his apron. They each ordered a pint of spiced wine, and waited in silence until the water returned with the steaming mugs. Rathe took a sip, grateful for the heat, and rested his elbows on the table.

"I'd like to talk to Dammar." Cambrai let his stool fall with a thump.

"In Astree's name, why?" Rathe tipped his head to one side. "Besides, that's Sighs' business."

"But we pulled him out of the river. So I see that makes him mine."

"He was knifed on shore, on the bridge or before, and he's Adjunct at Sighs."

"Sighs won't do a damn thing to help him," Cambrai said. "The folk there don't love him any better than you do."

"That's not what they say."

Cambrai snorted. "They have to, don't they? He's taken too much coin. I'd wager he's involved with whatever gang is pressing for fees on the docks now."

"Would you, now." Rathe took another sip of his wine. "That's a serious charge."

"I'm a serious man."

"Share the proof, then. He's still one of ours, I can't call a point without something solid."

"If I had that…." Cambrai's shoulders slumped. "I've only whispers—a woman who says she doesn't need our help after all, now that Dammar's laid up, a couple of captains who say they were told the points were in the dockers' pockets. But the entire waterfront is breathing easier at the moment, and that's a fact."

"But not one you can call a point on," Rathe said.

"I want to talk to him. Ask what happened, see if he'll put a name or a face to whoever attacked him. No one's gotten his story yet, have they?"

Rathe shook his head. "Not that I know of."

"Well, there you have it." Cambrai spread his hands. "Let me talk to him, and I'll gladly share whatever he says."

Rathe rested his shoulders against the wall. "I can't just let you walk into his house and question him. Most of Sighs blames the pontoises for everything that's going wrong on the docks."

"Only to cover up what they're doing."

"I'm acting senior at Sighs now—"

Cambrai's eyebrows rose, but he waved for Rathe to continue.

"Make a formal request, at Sighs, on the books, and I'll come with you. That'll get you what you want…what we both want."

"You can't just let me ask a few simple questions?"

"Your questions aren't ever simple. Besides, there will be a doctor there, and whatever family he has. You'll do better if I'm with you."

Cambrai sighed. "All right. I'll make a proper request, seven seals and all. But I'm warning you, Nico, you need to watch your back. Someone at Sighs is up to their neck in this mess."

Rathe thought of the footsteps he might have heard, tracking him down the emptiest part of his route, and couldn't suppress a shiver. It wasn't at all impossible, was in fact frighteningly plausible if the pontoises weren't involved…. He shoved the tangle aside, knowing he didn't have enough facts to deal with it now.

"Send me the request," he said, and Cambrai pushed himself to his feet.

"This had better work."

CHAPTER 6

ESLINGEN WAS DRIER than he'd been in days and knew he ought to feel content, but instead he felt…hollow, as though the water had worn him away like old stone. The stars were against him, he told himself for what seemed like the hundredth time, and this would pass. He moved the stand that held his coat closer to the stove, hoping that it would dry well enough that he could brush the worst of the mud from the skirts. He had already cleaned his boots, and hung stockings and breeches to dry, stood now in nightshirt and dressing gown, holding back his sleeve as he fed the fire. He had been too out of sorts to stop for food, but there was still most of a loaf of bread and a crock of butter, and he cut slices for toast, spearing each one on the long fork to hold them to the flames. Sunflower came to sit at his feet, not quite begging, but clearly willing to dispose of anything remotely edible that should happen to fall, and Eslingen fed him bits of the crusts before he finally closed and latched the stove's door.

He reached for the pile of papers he had taken from his coat's cuffs. Most were broadsheets, purchased not quite at random in Temple Fair as he'd passed back and forth to the Guard's compound, but among them was a folded quarter-sheet addressed to him in an awkward scrawl. Young Steen had agreed to meet, though he'd specified a chophouse near the Exemption Docks and hadn't signed his name. For a moment, Eslingen wondered if it might be a trap, but put the thought firmly aside. The easiest way to be rid of him was simply to ignore his requests; an attack would bring down the attention of the Guard, and of Coindarel. And of Rathe: he wouldn't let it sit, either, and not just because it was bad for the law. No, Eslingen thought, he'd keep the appointment and see what Steen had to say, and stop by the Staenka house on the way back. He'd spoken to Mattaes that afternoon, and gotten nothing more than a repetition of the boy's previous story. Redel, though, had made an appearance at the end of the conversation, looking as though she wanted to say more, but her sister had called her away before Eslingen could find an excuse. And, he admitted, he was curious about how de Vian's noble sister fitted in with such a determinedly mercantile family.

He reached for the apple he had bought just before he'd run into Rathe, and unfolded the broadsheets with his free hand, not really seeing the smudged woodcuts. He was a little sorry he hadn't gone to meet the cap'pontoise with Rathe—if anyone could shed light on this extortion plot, it would surely be the river's keepers—but the thought of sitting there, damp and steaming and probably smelling of the street mud, while Cambrai smiled and joked and displayed strong corded muscles and golden hair…. And that was pure vanity, he thought, with a rueful laugh. But no one showed to advantage when their stars were in their detriment, and he and Rathe were still new enough that he preferred to look his best.

He reached for the first broadsheet, topped with a woodcut of something that seemed to be meant for a mermaid. Only the mermaids he had read about were supposed to be beautiful, or at least seductive; this one had drooping breasts and weed-like hair and her crooked hands were tipped with alarmingly large claws. She had fangs, too, in the top and bottom of her mouth: not at all the sort of creature one would follow in bemused fascination. The headline read *The Masculine Tribute, or, An Inquiry into Ancient Rites Relevant to Recent Sightings Along the Sier*. The verse was tortured at best, but claimed to tell the tale of the Riverdeme, the river spirit Rathe had said was associated with the dogfish, who had demanded a tribute of nubile young men before the sages of the University had trapped her, destroying her power. Still, the broadsheet concluded,

> *Young men who walk by autumn's tides*
> *Should careful be their face to hide*
> *Or the Riverdeme will drag them down*
> *To make her meal 'neath waters brown.*

It did not, Eslingen noted, specify how a fish-tailed being would confront those young men walking on the bank, or say why any sensible person would stay to chat with something that not only intended to

93

eat them, but was clearly well-equipped to do so. The next three dealt with the dogfish sightings—universally agreed to be unfortunate—but quickly devolved into an astrologers' quarrel over which stars governed the fishes' reappearance, and the implications of the quincunx between the sun and the winter-sun. The last of those was more technical than he had realized, and he eyed the calculations with disfavor before putting it aside.

The last was the one that had first caught his eye, plain type without an illustration, but the headline easy enough to read as one passed the printer's stall: *An Accounting of the Drowned.* It was a double sheet, back and front, the front proclaiming that sixteen men had died in the river since summer's end, and the back listed each of them, and the date and place of their death. And if that was anywhere close to the truth…. He held the sheet closer to the lamp, studying the seal that indicated the publication had been officially licensed. It was hard to tell, but he thought it was a forgery. He didn't recognize the printer's name or her house, but he guessed Rathe would.

And this was certainly something Rathe would want to see once he got in. He tidied the stack together and set the lamp on it to keep Sunflower from knocking them over, then blew out the flame. He checked the stove, Sunflower pattering at his heels, and took himself to bed.

He woke to clouded morning light and a hand on his shoulder, rolled over to see Rathe waving a cup of tea in his direction. Sunflower scrabbled noisily on the floor, apparently looking for crumbs, and Eslingen pushed himself upright. "Sorry. I thought I'd hear you come in."

"You were dead to the world, and I wasn't far behind." Rathe paused. "I saw the broadsheets."

Eslingen stretched, trying to guess the time, but the clouds defeated him. They had moved the bed into the second room after they'd knocked out the plaster-and-lathe that had blocked the original connecting doorway, but the household clock stayed in the main room.

"Half past seven," Rathe said, "and you're lucky I let you sleep that long. Cambrai wants to talk to Dammar today, and that's going to be tricky. But I wanted to talk to you first."

Eslingen sighed. "Give me a minute, and I'm all yours."

"We don't have time for that." Rathe sounded genuinely regretful. "But there's tea."

Eslingen made a hasty toilet, and came out into the main room still in his shirtsleeves, his hair curling loose on his shoulders. Rathe looked as though he was about to say something, but handed him the toasting fork instead. Eslingen flipped open the front of the stove, pleased to see that the fire was already built up, and busied himself turning the slices of bread in front of the flames. Rathe filled the teapot, and by the time the plate was stacked high with toast, the tea was ready. Eslingen took his share gratefully, and stretched out his toes to the stove's warmth.

"I thought you'd want to see that one," he said, and pointed an elbow at *An Accounting of the Drowned.*

Rathe swallowed a mouthful of toast. "If that's even half true—surely someone would have noticed sixteen deaths."

"They don't offer any cause, just the list, but everyone else is linking it to the dogfish and this Riverdeme."

"I saw that, too," Rathe said. "The Riverdeme, she's just stories, scary ones, but—old. She's been bound a long time."

"By the bridges, you said."

"That's what I was taught." Rathe gave a sudden grin. "And being as they're all intact, I'd say there's not much chance she's involved."

"From the broadsheets, I have to say I'm glad of that." Eslingen reached for the broadsheet, trying not to leave greasy fingerprints on the paper. "All right, we can assume some of these are just accidents—and is this even an unusual number of accidents for the docks? I wouldn't know."

Rathe took the sheet back, tucking it into his pocket. "It's definitely something I'm going to ask Cambrai, and Sebern—oh. Yeah. I have a new assignment."

"Oh?"

"I'd have told you before, but there wasn't time. Fourie's put me in as senior adjunct at Point of Sighs."

Eslingen swore under his breath. "That seems —chancy."

Rathe shrugged. "Astarac, that's the chief, is confined to her bed—she's with child and having a hard go of it—and with Dammar laid up, Fourie announced that Sebern, she's the junior adjunct, was too junior to hande the station on her own."

And he's also glad to have an excuse to put his own man into the middle of what's becoming a peculiar situation, Eslingen thought, but there seemed to be no point in saying it. "Is this likely to be permanent, do you think?"

"All gods forbid," Rathe said. "I've never liked Point of Sighs."

Eslingen nodded slowly. He suspected that Point of Sighs returned the sentiment, but once again it seemed unhelpful to comment. "So you'll ask them about these deaths, then?

"I will." Rathe nodded. "It seems like a lot, though."

"I wonder if there's anything in their stars," Eslingen said. "Anything they have in common—or, for that matter, if there's some conjunction at work."

"Also worth asking," Rathe said. "But, since collecting horoscopes is a particularly thankless task, let's make sure it's worth the effort. One thing you could do, though—pick up another couple of copies of that one. It'll help if it comes to anything."

"You think it will."

Rathe shrugged on his coat, and then the stiff leather jerkin, hung the truncheon at his waist. "I'm afraid it might."

He was out the door before Eslingen could think of an appropriate answer. Sighing, he turned his attention to the mud-spattered coat, and managed to brush away the worst of it before he had to leave himself. The weather had eased overnight, and streaks of blue showed between the scudding clouds, though the wind coming down the Sier was cold. He made his way to Temple Fair, bought two more copies of the *Accounting*, and scanned the stalls for anything else in that vein. He saw the same sheets he'd bought the day before, and obvious variations, but nothing new. Whatever was going on in Point of Sighs and on the river, it wasn't drawing the full attentions of the broadsheet astrologers. He wondered if that were significant in itself, and put the thought aside to ask Rathe later.

As he made his way to the Guard's barracks, he found himself hoping that de Vian might have changed his mind. Rathe was wrong about there being any passion there, but he was right that it was all too likely to end with the boy estranged from his sister, which did no one any good. And it was hard enough figuring out how to do this new job without having to teach the boy as well. And yet a runner might be useful, someone to carry notes and run errands—track down horoscopes and all the other tedious bits of business. If de Vian had sense enough to refuse this job, it might be worth taking him on later.

Rijonneau was by the riding ring, but professed himself entirely happy to step into the shelter of the stables. "I hear you're on detached service for a bit."

"I've been told off to help the points." Eslingen gave a quick summary, and the other captain nodded.

"The Major-Sergeant said it was something like that, though I wasn't quite sure I believed it. I didn't think that was really our job, figuring things out. I thought we just knocked people over the head."

Eslingen gave him a sharp look, and relaxed as he saw the gleam of humor in Rijonneau's eyes. "If you wanted something that simple, you should have stayed with the Dragons."

"I thought the pickings might be better in the city," Rijonneau said, "and then they tell me there's to be none of that."

Eslingen grinned in spite of himself. "The question is, Matalin, can you handle the company for a week or so?"

"We're not doing much now but keeping the horses in training. I've men to spare for that. And surely this case won't last until the Galeneon."

The company was supposed to be formally sworn in at midwinter, and put on a show to prove their worth. They would all need to work on that if it was to do Coindarel credit. "I'll be done before then," he said, "or I'll come back here anyway. Have you seen Balfort de Vian today? I could use a runner."

"Is that wise?" Rijonneau cocked his head to one side.

"Quite possibly not. He's determined to earn a place here."

"I know. And we could do worse." Rijonneau sighed. "Last I saw, he was cleaning tack."

The stables were dim and quiet, a third of the horses drowsing in their stalls, the air warm with their scent and the sweet smell of hay. Eslingen had grown up in a stable, and the stalls always made him think of his childhood home. Not that his father's stable had been anything near this grand, nor had they owned but one horse of their own, a sleepy cart horse to be rented to unlucky merchants. But, like his father's, this had stone outer walls and wooden stalls and loft, and he had to shake memory away as he reached the tack room.

De Vian was there, as promised, perched on a tall stool while he buffed the leather of a well-cleaned bridle. He looked up at Eslingen's step, and smiled widely.

"You didn't forget!"

"No. Though I'm still not sure it's a good idea." Eslingen eyed him unhappily. "I'm asking you to maybe go against your sister, to do something that has the chance of hurting your family. No one, least of all me, will think worse of you if you say no."

"This is something I can do," de Vian said. "I know how the family works, that's useful."

"But your sister may well see it as betrayal," Eslingen said. "You need to be sure you've thought this through."

"I have." De Vian set the bridle back on its peg and laid the brush on its shelf, and when he turned, there seemed to be a new maturity in his face, like the shadow of bones beneath the skin. "I've considered the consequences and—I'm no worse off if my sister disowns me, she does nothing for my keep now. And I know I'm the youngest here, and it's unlikely I'll have a better chance to show my worth. I'll do anything to earn my place, Captain, anything at all. But mostly—most of all, it's what you said. This is what I swore to, this is my duty. It's in my stars."

That was all true, Eslingen thought, and also exactly why Rathe had recommended refusing him. But Rathe had never had his way to make in a company, not like this. "All right. For the time being, you'll act as my runner. I've arranged it with Captain Rijonneau."

De Vian reached out as though to take his hand, then seemed to think better of it, bowing deeply instead. "You won't regret it, sir, I promise."

RATHE HAD EXPECTED mornings at Point of Sighs to be busier than at Point of Dreams—the theater crowd tended to sleep late, and save their quarrels for the afternoon—and had arrived early accordingly. However, though both great doors were open and the duty points were at their tables, the hall was largely empty. One of the station's runners was building up the fires in the stoves, and a woman in a plain bottle-green skirt-and-bodice was talking to a pointsman, but his hands were hooked in his belt and from their smiles, it looked more like flirtation than business. He skimmed through the overnight entries, and found only tavern brawls and petty thefts, plus an unlucky climbing thief caught halfway up a drainpipe. He lifted an eyebrow at that, and the duty point looked aside.

"Garin got lucky on that, just happened to swing his lantern a little higher. We've got the man in the cells unless someone bails him."

Or Garin took a fee, and then decided to call the point anyway, Rathe thought. But he was not here to clean house, and the story might just as well be true—in Dreams, he wouldn't have doubted it. "The thief's known to you?"

"We've had our eye on him. His mother's a fence, though she mostly works northriver."

"She'll post bail, then," Rathe said, and the duty point gave a regretful nod.

"Unless she's thoroughly annoyed. We might get lucky."

"Will the householder prosecute?"

"She's a busy woman." The duty point gave the words a sour twist.

Rathe grimaced in sympathy—if a crime was stopped without loss, most women preferred to let the matter go than spend the time and money to take a case to court, and that was as true in Dreams as it was in Sighs—and headed up the stairs.

His workroom was as he had left it, though someone had built up the fire here as well. The kettle was empty, though, and he leaned out the door long enough to call for a runner, and looked again at the table. He had left Dammar's books stacked to one side, their spines neatly aligned; now they sat slightly crooked, as though someone had put them back not quite perfectly. Or maybe the runner who had fed the stove bumped against them, but Rathe was glad he hadn't left any notes in the station overnight.

The runner appeared, brought water and fresh tea. Rathe settled himself at the table again, one ear cocked for the arrival of Cambrai's request, and reached for Dammar's books. If the cap'pontoise was right, and someone at Sighs was behind the attack on the Senior Adjunct, he would do well to watch his back.

The clock had struck ten before he heard footsteps on the stairs, and Ormere put her head in the open door.

"Adjunct, there's a message from the pontoises—from the cap'pontoise, actually."

"Send it up."

Ormere shuffled her feet as though she was an apprentice again. "The chief doesn't like the pontoises coming into the upstairs."

Rathe bit back his instinctive response. "All right. Then I'll go down."

"But—" Ormere stopped, and Rathe lifted his eyebrows.

"If it's beneath her dignity to come down, and she won't let them up, what does your chief do when she gets a message?"

"Usually the duty point reads it." Ormere was scarlet.

"And this message is addressed to—?"

"To you, Adjunct Point."

"Then you can send it up, or I'll come down." Rathe waited, but Ormere couldn't seem to find an answer. "I'll come down."

Cambrai's tillerman Saffroy was waiting by the duty point's table, the long tail of his knitted cap tossed around his shoulders like a chain of office, and what looked like a small satchel tucked under one arm. He looked up at Rathe's approach. "Adjunct Point."

"Tillerman. I hear you have a message?"

Saffroy produced the satchel. "A formal request from the cap'pontoise, Adjunct Point. He'd like a word with Edild Dammar."

There was a murmur of disapproval from the listening points, but Rathe ignored it, unbuckling the straps of the satchel to retrieve the folded sheet of parchment. He unfolded it carefully, the enormous wax seals clattering—seven of them, as promised, from the cap'pontoise himself and the Regents and Trijn at Point of Dreams, which held jurisdiction over the land around the Chain Tower that was the pontoises' headquarters, plus a university physician and the Maternité—and, at the very bottom, not just the seal of the Tour but the surintendant's own embossed monogram. He looked up sharply—Fourie must have loved giving that, no matter how necessary it might be—and caught the ghost of a smile on Saffroy's lips.

"Adjunct Point Dammar's badly hurt," Rathe said. "It'll depend on what his physician says."

Saffroy pointed to the Maternité's seal. "His physician has already accepted, and the Maternité certifies it. He's well enough to talk."

"I assume his physician will be in attendance?"

"She can be if she wishes." Saffroy shrugged. "But the cap' very much wants a word with him. He's not been well enough to speak since we fished him out of the Sier."

Rathe ran a finger over the seals, pitching his voice to be sure the others heard. "I can't go against the surintendant's orders, of course. But I want to be present."

It was Saffroy's turn to look doubtful for the listening points. "I expect the cap' can agree to that."

"It's that or nothing," Rathe said, and Saffroy managed a sort of bow.

"May we say noon, then, Adjunct Point?"

"Meet me here at quarter of," Rathe said firmly.

"Agreed," Saffroy said, and turned away.

Rathe kept his expression neutral as he turned to face the others. "Ormere. You'll come with me."

"Adjunct." That was Bellin, her hair in a loose tail as though she'd been called before she was quite ready. "You're not really going to let the cap'pontoise question one of ours?"

"I don't have a choice." Rathe tapped the surintendant's seal again. "The sur's agreed, and the physicians, there's nothing I can argue to say no. I'll be there, and I'll make sure Dammar isn't harmed." Physically, at least, he thought, and was afraid from the dissatisfied expressions that the others guessed the thought.

THE EXEMPTION DOCKS were technically outside the city limits, though houses and shops had filled in what had once been a perceptible gap until it was hard to tell what belonged where. Presumably Customs

Point knew which of the crowded streets formed the boundary, Eslingen thought, and some of the buildings bore painted badges, proclaiming them either generally Exempt or belonging to some other taxing entity, but the sprawl of crooked buildings and dogleg alleys was enough to tangle less experienced folk. The chophouse was near the actual docks; Eslingen fixed his eyes on the masts visible above the housetops, and threaded his way through the rutted streets, de Vian wide-eyed at his heels.

"What is all of this?" the boy asked, as they stopped to let a string of laden carts cross their path, the oxen leaning heavily into the yokes.

"If your ship goes upriver past the Customs House, you have to pay the Queen's fees," Eslingen answered. "If you have letters of exemption, or if your cargo is going somewhere outside the city—if you don't have to pay those fees for some reason—you dock here, not in the city."

"Or if you're under contract to one of the League cities?" De Vian nodded to the house nearer them, which bore Lahyemeis's hunting horn on a shield in the center of its main door.

"That's where it gets complicated," Eslingen answered. "Yes, sometimes, but sometimes not. Sometimes it's the fees you pay, and sometimes it's who signed the letter of marque—and mostly it's not our business." Smuggling, petty and great, was Astreiant's second-favorite pastime, after the broadsheets and just ahead of the theaters: it would take more than all the points and pontoises combined to do more than cut into the profits. Rathe argued that the laws needed to change first, and then enforcement, but that was Rathe for you. The last of the carts lumbered past, and he shook himself back to the matter at hand. "Let's go."

The docks themselves were crowded, ships of every size jammed against the wharfs, spars and lines seeming constantly on the verge of tangling hopelessly and bringing the whole structure down. There didn't seem to be a single empty mooring, just ship after ship, nearly every one with a swarm of dockers hauling cargo. The air smelled of mud and tar and new-cut timber; at the end of the longest wharf, a streak of scarlet cut the air, the narrow pennant unfurling from a mast-top, and sails blossomed from the middle spars. They swelled, catching the scant breeze, and the ship began to pull out into the river, whistles shrilling signals as she turned south toward the sea. She wouldn't be going far this time of year, Eslingen thought, probably no further than the towns at the river's mouth, where it was cheaper to refit and wait out the season.

He made himself look away from the river, scanning the buildings that faced the docks: brick and timber, mostly, not the solid stone of older Astreiant, but sturdy enough. Most of them seemed to be factors' houses or warehouses, or the occasional chandler; there was a tavern as well, with a bright bush to proclaim it sold Leaguer beer as well as Chenedolle's wine, and a fiddler was perched on a barrel outside the door, scraping a tune for his dog to dance to. The dog looked a bit like a basket terrier—maybe its grandam had been purebred. Eslingen tossed a demming in the man's hat as they passed.

The chophouse should be a little further on, down the next side street—and yes, there it was, a low building set back from the others along the street, a carved and painted wooden bull hanging above the doorway. The yard was empty except for a line of benches pulled under the broad eaves; in the summer, Eslingen guessed, there would be tables outside as well, but it was too late in the year for that. A woman leaned against the open door, fanning her face with her apron, and Eslingen caught the unmistakable scent of roasting meat.

"Captain, I—if we're going to eat here…I haven't any money. Not for this."

"If we eat, I'll pay. Assuming we're not too early," he added, to the woman at the door, who straightened with a smile.

"Ready just now, sir."

Eslingen nodded, and she ducked into the main room. He followed, pleased to see that it wasn't empty, and saw a hand raised in the back corner. Someone had set a screen to conceal a pair of rear tables—that seemed to be the fashion here, rather than private rooms—and he could just recognize Young Steen peeping around its edge.

"This way," he said, to de Vian, and moved to join the sailor.

To his surprise, Jesine Hardelet was waiting behind the screen, bodice loosely laced over a swelling belly, and a definite look of annoyance on her face. "Who's the boy?"

"My runner," Eslingen answered, before de Vian could speak. "Yours isn't the only business I have today."

"That wasn't in the bargain," Young Steen said, his face setting in an obstinate scowl.

Eslingen sighed, recognizing an impasse, and reached for his purse. "Balfort. Buy yourself something decent and go sit by the fire until we're done." He handed over a couple of seillings, trying not to think about his dwindling funds, and de Vian turned away, trying to hide his disappointment. Eslingen looked at the others. "Satisfied?"

Hardelet gave a slow nod. Increasing women were supposed to bloom with health, but she looked worn, her skin pasty, with dark circles under her eyes. "I'm already taking chances."

Eslingen chose a stool where he could see past the edge of the screen and seated himself. "But it was you who wanted to see me."

Before the woman could answer, a waiter scurried over. "Pardon, dame, masters, but the roast is ready. May I carve a chop or two for you all?"

Nothing would be more suspicious than not ordering. Eslingen saw the same knowledge on the others' faces, and schooled himself to patience. They placed their orders—loin chops, seared with butter, with mushrooms and fried parsnips and a jug of cider—and Eslingen glanced sideways to see de Vian placing his own order. There were a few more people in the main room now, another group just vanishing behind their screen and a few more sitting by ones and twos across the room, and he turned his attention back to the others. The sound of a fiddle came from the yard, as though the fiddler moved on to a new stand.

"We've had more trouble," Young Steen said bluntly. "The motherless bastards doubled my fees for unloading—above and beyond what they'd asked the first time, and had the brass balls to tell me it was for talking out of turn."

"And when I complained," Hardelet said, "my mother had a note that said she was likely to lose a grandchild that way. My mother owns the larger share in the *Soueraigne*, you understand."

Eslingen nodded. "Who did you complain to, dame? The dockers?"

"The owners' consortium," Hardelet answered. "You understand, we're not a guild—"

By which she meant they had none of the backing of the city's regents. Eslingen nodded again.

"But we do combine our voices in circumstances like this. Mother's a senior member, we've supported them for years." Hardelet's expression was bleak. "But it doesn't seem there's a damn thing they can do."

The waiter returned then, and they all leaned back while he placed the steaming plates and the jug and the pots of mustard. When he was out of earshot, Young Steen said, "Usually the owners manage to get some kind of agreement on the dockers' fees. And on the fees to Point of Sighs, and the dock rates, for that matter. If you're a consortium ship, you get a better deal. But not this year."

"Do you know what the consortium did with your complaint?" Eslingen asked.

"Not for certain," Hardelet said. "Usually, one of our women goes to talk to the head of the dockers, or her representative, so I assume that's what happened this time. And usually we make some kind of bargain. But this time...."

"This time they went to your mother and threatened you and the child," Eslingen said.

"Just so." Hardelet nodded.

"We're going downriver," Steen said. "We paid, the *Soueraigne*'s unloaded and at dock here, outside the city, and when we're done with you, we're going south to Ostolas and spend the winter there."

"And do you plan to have the child there, dame?"

Hardelet's mouth tightened. "We'll see."

Eslingen felt his eyebrows rise in spite of himself. If the child were born outside the city bounds, Hardelet couldn't claim residency for her—oh, she was of a good family, merchants resident of long standing, it would almost certainly be possible to have the child added to the city rolls, but it was a risk few women would run if they had other options. "Your idea, or your mother's?"

"Mine," Steen said. "But they all agreed."

Hardelet nodded again: more proof, Eslingen thought, that they're taking this threat in earnest. Not that I needed it. Something was nagging at the back of his mind, something Steen had said at the beginning, and he carved himself a bite of his chop, trying to pry loose the question. "Ah. Steen, you said the dockers doubled your fees for—talking out of turn, was it?"

"Yeah."

"And this was before Dame Hardelet spoke to the other owners?"

"That was what she was talking to them about."

"You spoke to me, and I spoke to Rathe, and that's as far as your name went," Eslingen said.

"So you say," Hardelet said, but without conviction.

"Unless you spoke to someone else," Eslingen went on, and she shook her head.

"I didn't want him to talk to you, Captain."

"I'm not a fool," Steen said. "I know what's at risk. But—"

Eslingen nodded. "How? Were you that closely watched? Is there someone on your ship—forgive me—who could be bribed to watch you?"

"It's a good question," Hardelet said, her anger fading again. "And I don't have an answer."

"It's why I want us to winter in Ostolas," Steen said, quietly. "I want us out of it. But there is one thing more I can tell you—"

He broke off as the fiddler stopped with a discordant shriek, and something struck the chophouse door. Eslingen thrust himself to his feet as three men shoved past the expostulating waiter, clubs as solid as a pointsman's truncheon ready in hand. There was a fourth man at the door, holding it open and watching the street, and the fiddler and his dog had fled. Hardelet and Steen were on their feet as well, Steen desperately shoving himself in front of her, and Eslingen drew his knife.

"Here, now, we don't want trouble—"

The leader swung at him and he ducked left, the club hissing past his shoulder. One of the others slammed the screen to the ground, and someone screamed from the kitchen, fear and fury mingled. Hardelet put her hands under the edge of the table and heaved, flinging it up into the face of the third man, food and drink and dishes shattering, then fell back against the wall, grimacing, as Steen swung a stool at the next man. Eslingen swore, and stepped inside the leader's swing, blocking his arm with his free hand and stabbing for the shoulder. The blade skidded on hard-cured leather, then caught and ripped cloth and flesh down the fat of his biceps. The leader swore, shortening his grip, and struck for the kidneys with the butt of the club. Eslingen felt the shift just in time, caught it instead on his arm and ribs—painful enough to bring his breath short, but not crippling. He turned into the swing, pulling the man away from Hardelet, and shoved him hard so that he fell backward over an upturned stool. Eslingen kicked him below the ribs—there wasn't time to choose a better blow—and turned to catch the closer of the remaining attackers by the collar of his coat. He hauled him back, but the man rounded on him, swinging his club, and it was Eslingen's turn to leap back out of the way.

Out of the corner of his eye, he could see that the chophouse's other patrons were on their feet, not yet ready to interfere, and then a heavy-set man lunged out of the kitchen flourishing an iron spit, the waiters behind him. The leader of the attackers saw them, and the man at the door put two fingers to his lips and whistled sharply. The leader swore, and shoved Steen sideways so that he caromed into Hardelet, nearly knocking her to the ground. The man Eslingen had kicked staggered to his feet and took off for the door, the others quickly overtaking him. Eslingen started after them, but pulled up, flinching, as the bruised ribs caught him. De Vian had disappeared, and he looked around sharply.

"Your boy went chasing them," one of the kitchen-men said. "Not that he's like to catch them."

I hope not, Eslingen thought, but he knew he needed to finish with Hardelet. He'd have to trust that de Vian had sense enough not to try to stop them on his own.

"Dame!" That was the woman he'd seen when they arrived, hurrying to help Steen ease Hardelet down onto a chair. "Are you all right? The child?"

"I'm well." Hardelet cradled her belly, rocking slowly back and forth. A bruise was blooming on her cheek as though someone had struck her. "We're well. We're well."

Steen knelt to wrap his arms around her, tears of relief starting from his eyes. "Jesi...."

"Do you want the points?" the chophouse woman asked. "Shouldn't be allowed, attacking honest women over nothing at all—"

"No points," Steen said, and the woman frowned, looking past him at Hardelet.

"Better have them in, dame, we'll all bear witness."

"We're leaving Astreiant today," Hardelet said slowly. "I'd rather not waste the time."

"I could speak to the points for you," Eslingen said, and stretched his back again. "If you're willing."

"We'll be gone before the tide turns," Steen said, grimly. "Do as you please, I don't care."

"Steen." Hardelet held out her hands, and reluctantly he steadied her to her feet. "Dame, I'm main sorry for this trouble, I'd no thought this would happen. I hope you'll let me make at least monetary amends." She reached under her skirts for her purse, and the chophouse woman's eyes widened as she brought out half a silver pillar.

"That's very proper of you, dame," the chophouse woman said, and the coin disappeared beneath her skirts. "Will you have my man walk you to your ship? And our Emael, too. I don't doubt your men are strong enough, but there's safety in numbers."

Hardelet shifted her shoulders as though she was still feeling out her body, then nodded. "I'd take that kindly, especially since I think Captain vaan Esling has errands of his own to see to."

"Duly dismissed," Eslingen said, lightly, and sketched a bow that sent a jolt of pain across his lower back.

"We've given you all there is to give," Steen said, his voice grim, but Hardelet caught his sleeve.

"A name," she said, leaning close enough that it was unlikely anyone else could hear. "The man running the dockers. Jurien Trys."

It meant nothing to Eslingen, but Rathe was bound to know it. He nodded, committing it to memory, and let Steen draw her away. The men from the chophouse joined them, flanking them protectively, and they left together. Eslingen straightened carefully, feeling more bruises on his arms and shoulders, and slid his knife back into its sheath.

"Your boy ran off after them," the chophouse woman said. It was not quite an accusation, and Eslingen bit back a sigh.

"I'm with the City Guard, dame. I'll have a word with the points once I find my runner."

She looked doubtful at that, but then her gaze shifted. "And there he is coming back."

"Good." Eslingen turned just in time to see de Vian duck through the door, and moved to meet him.

"I'm sorry, Captain." De Vian was painfully out of breath. "They got away…they went down into the docks and it was crowded and I couldn't see which way they went."

"It's all right," Eslingen said. "It was a good try."

"Are you all right? Is the lady?"

"Yes, we're both fine." Eslingen pressed a cautious hand to his side, and decided he was only exaggerating a little bit. "Come on. We've still got things to do."

THE CAP'PONTOISE ARRIVED promptly as the clock struck the last quarter, escorted by Saffroy and a pair of burly young pontoises who had the grace to wait outside the station's hall. Rathe collected Ormere and a runner, ignoring Bellin's scowl, and together they walked west along Bonfortune's Walk and then turned deeper into Point of Sighs. Dammar lived in lodgings, according to Ormere, but had been taken to his sister's house where he could be better nursed. The sister was a pewter-smith, and her house was also her workshop, the shutters down to form a counter and the room behind it loud with the sound of hammers as an apprentice shaped the bowl of a spoon and an older woman fed lumps of coal into the small furnace. She straightened at their approach, wiping her hands on her apron, her eyes going from Rathe to Cambrai and the pontoises and back again.

"You're the new adjunct they've put in place of Edild?" She didn't offer her hand, and Rathe didn't try to force the issue.

"Nicolas Rathe. I'm taking his place temporarily, until Dammar's well enough to resume his duties."

"That may be some time." Her voice was dry, and had more than a hint of a country childhood. "He's none so well just now."

"His physician certified him well enough to speak with us."

"But not for long." She sighed, the defiance leaving her. "And where are my manners? I'm Edild's sister Sawel, this is my house and shop."

"Mistress," Rathe said, nodding. "I expect you know Ormere, she was your brother's assistant, and this is the cap'pontoise, Euan Cambrai, and his tillerman."

"That's too many to disturb him," Sawel said.

"The physician said he could speak," Rathe said patiently. "Cambrai and I will go in, the others can stay down here."

Sawel grimaced, still winding her hands in her apron. "Luce! Is Dr. Bael still there?"

There was a moment of silence, and then another woman, journeyman-aged but in an ordinary housekeeper's skirt-and-bodice, came clattering down the narrow stair to peer under the beam at them. "Yes, mistress, she's here."

"Tell her the pointsmen are here to talk to Edild."

"Yes, mistress." Luce disappeared up the stairs again, her clogs loud on the wood. The apprentice had stopped his work to stare, but Sawel glared at him, and he hastily bent over his workbench, hammer sounding with renewed vigor. The clogs came closer, and this time Luce clattered all the way down the stairs.

"If you please, mistress, the doctor says they can come up. But she says she'll send them away if they tire him too badly."

"You heard her," Sawel said, to Rathe, and Rathe nodded.

"We'll try not to trouble him," he said, and started up the stairs, Cambrai at his heels.

Sawel had done her best for her brother. He lay in the chamber above the kitchen, smaller than the main bedchamber, but quieter, and warmed by the stove below as well as by the fireplace with its narrow grate. The bed had been moved to be further from the window, and a rectangle of cloth as heavy as a saddle blanket lay on the stool beneath the shutters, open now to let in the best of the daylight. A tall woman in a Phoeban physician's saffron gown looked down her nose at them as they hesitated in the doorway. Beyond her, Dammar lay unmoving on a sloping raft of pillows, the bed curtains pulled back and the sheet and blankets pulled up to his armpits. His hands were lax on the covers, and nearly as pale as the linen surrounding him, but the bruises on his face and chest were still deep purple.

"Doctor," Rathe said, warily. The Phoebans had a reputation for both skill and a tendency to guard their rights like fighting rats; he had no desire to get on her wrong side just yet. "We were told it might be possible to speak with Adjunct Point Dammar today."

"The Surintendant of Points himself has been asking that daily since the man was stabbed," Bael said. "I'd like to know what the hurry is."

"The sooner we can ask a few questions, the sooner we can catch the one who did this," Rathe answered. He thought he saw Dammar's fingers twitch at that, but focused on the physician. "We try to take care of our own."

"A bit late for that." Bael turned back to the bed, laying one long hand on Dammar's forehead, then seized one wrist to test his pulse. "He's not fevered at the moment, and wasn't last night, and his pulse is as calm as could be expected. But I'll stay, and if you make him worse, I'll throw you out."

"Fair enough." Cambrai flashed the physician a smile but she only scowled.

Rathe said, "We'll do our best not to agitate him. All we want is a few answers to get us moving forward." He stepped up to the bed as he spoke, and Dammar's eyes flickered open.

"Rathe." His voice was a whisper, but clear enough. "I heard they gave you my place."

"Only until you're well again." There were stools against the wall; Rathe brought one over, and motioned for Cambrai to do the same. "I expect you know Cambrai."

"The cap'pontoise?" Something like a smile flickered across Dammar's face. "Pulling out all the stops, Rathe?"

"I pulled you out of the river," Cambrai said. "That makes you mine."

Dammar's mouth tightened, annoyance or pain or both. "I was attacked on dry land."

"The sur's given it joint jurisdiction," Rathe said.

"The sur's involved?" Dammar sounded alarmed, and Rathe frowned.

"Of course, he's not going to see his people attacked without taking a hand."

"No...."

"So we're here to ask what happened," Rathe said hastily, not daring to glance at the physician behind them, "and to ask if you can put a name to whoever did this."

"No." Dammar's voice was stronger again, and he managed to move his head side to side on the pillows. "I mean, I can tell you—it was a man, two of them, maybe a third? I'm not sure...."

His voice trailed off again, and Rathe heard the whisper of stiff satin as Bael stirred uneasily. "Start at the beginning," he said. "You were on the bridge—on points business?"

Dammar frowned. "I think—yes. There was a complaint, one of the bridge merchants said someone had been in her storage space—chambers in the pillars of the bridge? They rent for nearly a half-crown the quarter, but the shops are small to start with, and it pays a woman to keep her extra stock there, if she can afford it—"

"I know the bridge," Rathe said.

"Well, then. Yes." Dammar's eyes fluttered shut.

Cambrai leaned forward. "So you were going to—check the locks? Or had she given you a key?"

"I...." Dammar's head swung from side to side again. "I must have had a key. My memory's none too clear."

"And you went down into the pillar?" Cambrai asked.

That was more of an assumption than Rathe would have been willing to make, but at least it seemed to spark some response from the other pointsman.

"Yes. It's an iron stair and an open center."

"With a hoist for the goods," Rathe said. "I know."

"They were there ahead of me," Dammar said. "Two for sure, maybe three? We fought...and one of them stabbed me. The next thing I knew, I'm in my sister's bed with everyone telling me I'd been in the Sier."

It wasn't remarkable for a man to forget everything around such an injury, Rathe thought, but there were pieces that didn't quite add up. "Who was the shop holder? The one you were working for."

"What? Why?" Dammar blinked.

"The men were waiting for you, you said. I'm curious how they knew you'd be there."

"It wasn't her," Dammar said. "She's an honest woman."

Rathe saw Cambrai roll his eyes, and suppressed the desire to do the same. "I'm sure she is. But she might have said something that gave them their chance, or even someone in her shop spoke out of turn. What's her name?"

"Havys." Dammar's voice was a thread again. "That's her family name, Dame Havys, I don't know her forename. At the Two Rabbits."

"Adjunct Point," Bael said, and Rathe glanced over his shoulder, mustering his most harmless expression.

"Just a few more questions, please. We haven't much more to ask."

Bael subsided, and Cambrai leaned forward again. "Do you have any idea who they might have been? Or who sent them?"

"I never got a decent look at them," Dammar said.

"Who would have wanted to do this?" Rathe asked.

Dammar made a noise that started to be laughter and then caught painfully in his chest. "There are plenty of people who don't like me, Adjunct Point. Could have been any of them."

"Names?" Rathe said.

"Too many...." Dammar's voice was fading, and Bael straightened. "Ask Ormere. Or Sebern."

"Adjunct Point," Bael said. "Time for you to stop."

"One final question?" Rathe looked over his shoulder, waiting for her reluctant nod before he spoke again. "When you went down the stair, was it dark, or was there a lantern?"

Dammar blinked. "Dark? I—I don't remember."

"That's enough," Bael said firmly. "You need to leave now, and let the man rest."

Dammar's eyes fluttered closed, but for an instant Rathe thought he saw relief in the other man's expression. There was no arguing with Bael, though, and he pushed himself to his feet. There would be time to ask more questions—and better questions, too, once he'd had a chance to follow up the little Dammar had told him.

"Thank you, doctor," Rathe said, and gestured for Cambrai to precede him from the chamber.

In the hall, Cambrai stopped, glancing over his shoulder, and lowered his voice to a near whisper. "None of that made much sense. Why attack a man in the storage cells? They'd have had to haul him up in the cargo lift to get him out, and that's not exactly inconspicuous."

Rathe shook his head. "I shouldn't have assumed he was attacked on the bridge, let him tell me."

"They'd have had to carry him there otherwise, and that doesn't seen so likely," Cambrai said. "And why didn't he want to give up the shop holder's name?"

Rathe nodded. "Or any names of people who'd like to do him in. On his reputation, I'd have expected him to list half a dozen straight off, just because he owes them a bad turn."

"I'm none so sure he's that sick, either," Cambrai said darkly. "But that dragon of a doctor wasn't going to let us stay without a fight."

"No. But we've got time, Euan." Rathe started for the stairs. "The bridge is my territory, let me have a word with Dame Havys. Will you ask along the docks for anyone who might have hated him enough to take the risks?"

"It'll be someone he cheated out of a fee," Cambrai said. "You wait and see."

Rathe nodded. That made the most sense of the story: if Dammar had gone to meet someone who'd paid a fee and not liked the results, that would explain both the secrecy of the meeting and the attack, and was a good deal simpler than Dammar's explanation. If he could prove that—or, for that matter, confirm Dammar's work for Dame Havys, as unlikely as that seemed at the moment—then they'd have a place to start finding new questions. Or to press harder on the old ones. "I'll keep you informed if you'll do the same for me."

"It's a bargain, Adjunct Point," Cambrai said, with a grin, and they came decorously down the stairs to join the others still waiting in the pewter-smith's workroom.

CHAPTER 7

ESLINGEN AND HIS new ensign made their way back west along the Sier, crossing the river at the Customs House—and if anyone had been following them, or paying undue attention, Eslingen thought, he would either have been seen struggling to keep up, or have lost them in the surging crowds. He stopped at Customs Point long enough to make a brief and colorless report of an attack on a ship's captain in the Exemption Docks, and then struck out for Point of Dreams, de Vian still trailing at his heels. At least the walk was keeping him from stiffening up, though he'd pay for it later.

"I'm sorry I couldn't keep up with them," de Vian said, for the third time. "There were just too many people."

"You did your best," Eslingen said. "Besides, what would you have done if you'd caught them?" He'd meant it for a joke, but the color rose sharply in de Vian's cheeks. "You did well to try."

"So what did they want?" de Vian asked.

"To frighten Dame Hardelet," Eslingen answered. "Maybe to make her lose the child, they'd threatened that before."

De Vian's eyes went wide. "That's horrible. Why?"

Eslingen hesitated, but if he was going to use the boy, he needed to be able to share what was going on. Besides, Young Steen and Hardelet would be on the river by now, and well out of reach. "This is not to be repeated."

"Never, Captain."

"They complained about dock fees, she and her man. And apparently the dockers took offense. It's been a hard autumn for everyone."

"Not that hard," de Vian muttered. He shook his head. "To attack a breeding woman—that's low."

"But effective," Eslingen said, before he could stop himself. That was the trouble with years of mercenary service: you got used to tactics that no one should find easy. He frowned, annoyed with himself, and heard de Vian sigh.

"Will they be all right?"

"I doubt the dockers can chase them once they sail."

"They'll make them pay for it later, if we don't find out who did it," de Vian said, and the assessment was accurate enough that Eslingen shot him a startled glance. De Vian shrugged uncomfortably. "I told you, my sister's leman is in the tea trade."

"So you said."

"I don't know what she sees in her," de Vian muttered, then blushed. "But that's often the way of it. Please don't say I said so."

Eslingen shook his head. "No, of course not. Is that Redel?"

"No, Elecia Gebellin. Her brother Aucher is married to Meisenta."

"I haven't met her."

"She's...sharp."

"There are plenty of women who say more than they mean," Eslingen said, and saw the boy shrug again.

"I suppose so."

He'd missed something there, Eslingen thought, but it was too late to pursue it. He could feel de Vian's withdrawal, and made himself relax, turning the subject to the first of the hot-nut sellers. The word stayed with him as they wound their way past Jacinte's Well and took the short-cut by the Granary, scattering gargoyles that fluttered up to scold them from the low rooftops. Clever? Prickly? Edgy? A quality that de Vian didn't like, at any rate; well, he was likely to find out soon enough.

The Staenka house was busy when they arrived, a private carriage drawn up at the door and a cart wedged into the narrow alley between the house and its nearest neighbor. Still, Drowe greeted them with plausible good cheer, and escorted them into the library, promising to send Mattaes to them right away.

"Any idea what's going on?" Eslingen asked

De Vian shook his head. "No, sir. I didn't see any marks on the carriage, either."

"No more did I," Eslingen began, and turned as the door opened. The woman was no one he'd seen before, but there was something in the shape of her cheeks and chin that made him glance quickly at de Vian, to see recognition in his eyes. "Maseigne?"

"Captain vaan Esling." She came forward with both hands outstretched, and he took them perforce, bowing politely. Seen up close, she was unmistakably de Vian's sister, the same elegant bones and ivory skin, blue eyes made brighter in her case by neat lines of kohl. She was powdered, too, but the pearls that were woven through her light brown hair were glass, and her gown had been remade at least once. "Aliez d'Entrebeschaire."

"Charmed," Eslingen murmured, and saw her eyes slide sideways, brows contracting as she saw de Vian.

"Balfort?"

"I've taken him for my ensign in this business." Eslingen wouldn't say "runner," not to a noble of any quarterings.

"I hope you find him useful," d'Entrebeschaire said, and forced a smile. "Meisenta—Madame Staenka—asked me to make her apologies. They're just finishing a tasting, but she should be with you shortly."

"I've no wish to interrupt," Eslingen said, though he groaned inwardly at the thought of coming back. He was definitely starting to stiffen after the fight; when he was done here, he wanted nothing more than an hour at the baths and a pint of beer to take the edge off.

"No, no, not at all," d'Entrebeschaire said. "Meisenta would like to speak with you—especially if there's any news?"

"Nothing's changed, I'm afraid. Just more questions."

"We're of course at your disposal." Her tone was more doubtful than the words. The door opened again behind her, revealing a shorter, darker woman in tidy mercantile black: presumably the sister-in-law, Eslingen thought.

"The factors just left, Meisenta says she'll be ready in a few minutes."

"Elecia Gebellin," d'Entrebeschaire said, and Eslingen bowed again. "Her brother is Meisenta's—Madame's husband."

"Is there any news?" Gebellin asked, and checked herself. "No, of course not, or you'd have said so already. Forgive me, Captain, we're all very concerned for Mattaes."

But not so concerned that you'd offer food and drink, Eslingen thought. "We've made some progress," he said. "And as a result, I have more questions—in particular, about hiring bes'Anthe and your relations with the docks in general, so if that doesn't required Madame's attention, perhaps we wouldn't have to interrupt her."

The two women exchanged glances, and d'Entrebeschaire said, "That's you and Redel, isn't it?"

"And Mattaes, this year," Gebellin answered. "But I know Meisenta will want to hear."

Eslingen bowed again, feeling the muscles of his back and sides tighten toward cramp. "As you wish," he said, and resigned himself to awkward small talk.

To his relief, however, it was less than a quarter of a hour before Drowe opened the door again and escorted them all into the large parlor. It was a handsome place, the shutters thrown back to let in the afternoon light, and both the fireplace and the smaller stoves were lit. The air smelled gently of beeswax and spices. Meisenta Staenka sat in a high-backed chair by the fire, a tall man, dark and elegantly made, standing beside her as though waiting to do her bidding. The husband, Eslingen guessed, and was unsurprised when he was introduced as Aucher Gebellin. Redel and Mattaes were present, too, and Meisenta waved a hand toward the remaining empty chairs.

"Captain vaan Esling. Please be seated."

"Shall I take Balfort, then?" d'Entrebeschaire said, to Elecia, and the other woman nodded. "You'll excuse us, madame, I'm sure."

De Vian gave Eslingen a sharp look of protest, but Eslingen shook his head. "Go on," he said, and d'Entrebeschaire drew him from the room. "My assistant in this business, Balfort de Vian. I believe he's Maseigne's brother."

Meisenta inclined her head in thanks. "I hadn't realized you had a companion, Captain."

"Have you found anything?" Mattaes asked abruptly, and Redel scowled.

"Mattaes!"

"Why pretend? We've got the points in and out every day, not saying one useful word, and he's supposed to be on our side. Surely there's no harm in just asking!"

"He has a point," Meisenta said, with a slow and unexpected smile. "But I think the captain would have told us if there was anything new."

Eslingen lowered himself into the nearest chair, hoping he'd be able to get back up again without flinching. "I'm afraid Madame is right. But I do have more questions about your dealings with the docks. One thing we have heard everywhere is that the dockers are demanding higher fees from everyone, and they've threatened violence if they weren't paid."

"So you're thinking the dockers killed bes'Anthe when he wouldn't pay?" Redel asked eagerly. "I could believe that, he'd be fool enough to hold out, thinking we'd have to pay in the end—"

"Redel," Meisenta said.

"The points are looking into that," Eslingen said. "Was there anyone on the docks who'd kill bes'Anthe to harm you, either personally or the business?"

There was a little silence at that, Redel cocking her head to one side like a bird, Meisenta lifting one painted eyebrow. Mattaes said, "Not personally, surely...."

"We're not universally loved," Meisenta said, with another of her wry smiles, "but I can't see any of our rivals running the risk of murder. Not in a year when everyone is short of supplies. It would be simpler to pool their holdings and undercut our prices—which means the same argument holds for business. I don't think it's likely, Captain."

"I don't agree," Redel said. "The Petts would happily see a man dead if it would ruin us, and the more so if it was bes'Anthe. You remember, Elecia, they hired him last year and wouldn't give him a good name when we enquired."

"I can't see the Petts planning a murder just to make us look bad," Meisenta said.

"No, but suppose one of their men met bes'Anthe after Mattaes left him," Redel said. "They might have quarreled, too, and then when their man killed him, they'd be just as happy to let the blame fall on Mattaes."

"It's still not likely," Meisenta said.

Nor was it, Eslingen thought, but this was the sort of thread he was looking for. "The Petts?"

"Perrin and Pett," Meisenta said. "Angaretta Pett is the holder, her son Tibot is the blender. We sell to many of the same markets. But they're honest folk, in their way."

"Honest?" Redel's voice rose.. "After they scooped that cargo out from under us last year?"

"That's business," Meisenta said, and there was an edge of steel in her voice. "We've done the same to them, and no one's ever died of it."

And that, Eslingen thought, was the sum of their answers: there were plenty of rivals, but none who had ever shown themselves willing to commit murder. "And you?" he said, to Elecia. "Has your family had trouble with the dockers, too?"

Out of the corner of his eye, he saw Aucher wince, but Elecia's expression didn't change. "We currently trade in partial cargoes. Meisenta has been kind enough to carry our goods with hers."

Aucher cleared his throat. "I did talk to one or two of the folk we'd dealt with in other years, in case they could do better for us."

"I asked him to," Mattaes said, and Redel subsided.

"But no luck." Aucher shrugged one shoulder. "Someone's organized the docks this year, that's for sure."

And that was no surprise, the attack on Hardelet and Young Steen was further proof if it was needed, but it didn't get them any closer to bes'Anthe's murderer. "Going back to your competitors," he said. "Did any of them have any connection to bes'Anthe?" He was grasping at straws, and he knew it.

"Only the Petts," Redel said. "They'd hired him last year, and something didn't go right. They wouldn't say what, but they wouldn't give him a reference, either."

"And that's my fault," Elecia said. "I suggested the man, and I'm sorry for it."

"He'd made the passage in record time three years running," Aucher said.

Redel nodded. "The Petts were the only people who had anything serious to say against him. I'd still hire him, if he weren't dead."

"We all agreed to it," Meisenta said. "There's no use blaming yourself, Elecia."

"But I do." Elecia gave her a surprisingly warm glance, and Meisenta smiled wryly, as though she'd somehow felt it.

"And I say you mustn't." She held out her hand and Elecia took it long enough to bow over her delicate fingers, then stepped away.

"Would you say bes'Anthe was a generally difficult man?" Eslingen asked.

The others exchanged blank looks.

"He was a hired captain," Mattaes said, after a moment, and Redel nodded.

"He was quarrelsome, by all accounts, and not scrupulous about his cargoes, but that's—to be honest—what we paid him for. To get the best tea he could, through our factors or any other means, and bring it to Astreiant as quickly as he could. All of the rest—I just can't help you, Captain."

"I understand." Eslingen pushed himself to his feet, his back twitching. "You'll forgive me, madame, if I take my leave."

Meisenta dipped her head in regal dismissal, and Elecia said, "I'll see you out, Captain, if I may."

"Of course." Eslingen offered her his arm, and let her lead him into the hall.

Once the door had closed behind them, he disengaged himself, looking past her for de Vian, but Elecia caught at his sleeve.

"A word, Captain, if I might?"

"Certainly." Eslingen suppressed another wince, and shifted his weight to his right side. The tightness eased a little, and he did his best to smile.

"I don't know if you follow the broadsheets?"

"Some."

"Then you'll have seen the rumors of the dogfish returning to the Sier?"

"Yes, and young men going missing, possibly eaten by an unpleasant sort of mermaid," Eslingen said.

"The Riverdeme's not that," Elecia said. "Whatever she is, she's not that."

She seemed disinclined to continue, and Eslingen did his best to hold back his impatience.

"I'm not sure what all that has to do with a man stabbed on dry land."

Elecia managed a preoccupied smile. "There's bad luck everywhere, and I think bes'Anthe's just a part of it. He and Mattaes have fallen foul of some strange conjunction.... There have been accidents, Captain, all up and down the river, more than there should be even at this time of year. Drownings, too, and the fish—I'd swear I saw one myself, just at dusk, crossing the Sier back to our factor's house. I'd taken a boat from Point of Hearts, thinking it would be faster on the outgoing tide."

"Your own boat?" Eslingen asked, curious in spite of himself.

She shook her head. "A hired one. I saw the badge clear as day. But the wind was up and the river was rough, and we had trouble passing under the Hopes-Point Bridge, came far too close to the middle piling for my comfort. And then, just when I thought we were safe and the water had stilled a bit, I saw it—just its back first, with a line of fins down the middle and the scales as big as a pillar coin. The dogfish dove under the boat before I could do more than point, and came up on the other side, lifting its head and splaying out its front fins like it wanted a good look at us. Looked like the ones they carve on the pontoises' standards, big head and tusks like a boar in its lower jaw and teeth like razors. But the worst of it—the worst of it was it had a woman's eyes."

Eslingen felt a chill run down his spine, in spite of knowing better, and couldn't quite manage smiling disbelief. "Yet you're still here."

"Because I'm a woman." Elecia's smile was wry. "And the boatmen was a graybeard. The Riverdeme takes only men, and the young and the beautiful for preference."

"Oh, Elecia, are you telling tales again?" That was d'Entrebeschaire, de Vian silent and wary-eyed at her side as they emerged from the library.

"It's no tale," Elecia protested.

"If you say so," d'Entrebeschaire said. "Captain, I'm very pleased that Balfort's making himself useful to you and to the company. I knew he was young for the post, but he very much wanted to apply."

"We're glad to have him." Eslingen saw the color rising under de Vian's skin. There was nothing he wanted more than the baths, but he managed a polite half-bow. "And now, if you'll excuse us?"

"Of course," Elecia murmured, and d'Entrebeschaire gave a gracious nod. Drowe let them out into the street, and Eslingen allowed himself to stretch, wincing.

"We've done enough for today," he said. "Be at the barracks, I'll fetch you if I need you."

"With all respect, Captain, you ought to see a physician."

Eslingen slanted a glance at him. "That obvious, is it?"

De Vian blushed again. "You're—not moving right. Are you hurt?"

"Not seriously." Eslingen saw the concern in de Vian's eyes, and sighed. "One of the dockers put a stick in my ribs. What I need is the baths."

"I should go with you."

"That's—" Eslingen swallowed what would have been an ungracious answer. "Thank you, but there's no need. I'll send if I need you."

For a moment, he thought the boy was going to object, but de Vian swallowed any complaint. "Yes, sir," he said, and turned back toward the bridge.

RATHE PARTED COMPANY with Cambrai and the rest of the pontoises outside the pewter-smith's, and stood silent for a moment, watching them retreat toward the river. Cambrai was no fool, though the pontoises' methods tended to be more direct than his own; if there was a name to be found among the sailors and dockers, he'd turn it up. And that left this Dame Havys, and her shop on the bridge.

"Did we get anything useful, sir?" Ormere asked.

Rathe nodded. "We've a woman to see on the Hopes-Point Bridge."

"Sir?"

Rathe made the explanation as they walked, skirting the docks for the quieter approach along the border between Sighs and Hopes. "So if you know anything about this Dame Havys, I'd be glad to hear it. There wasn't anything in his book, I'd have remembered the name."

Ormere shook her head. "I don't know her, sir, sorry. But the adjunct, he didn't always give me an entry until he'd resolved the point."

Unsurprising, Rathe thought. Not to mention unhelpful. "Well, that's where he says he was, so it's where we have to start."

"Are you going to leave the rest of it to the pontoises?" Ormere gave him a nervous look. "Finding out who had cause to hate him, I mean."

"I've already asked at the station and suggested people look into it. I'm still waiting for the answers."

Dame Havys's shop proved to be a wax-chandler's, a narrow space barely wider than the door and the open counter, with a ladder at the back that led to a loft and a tall ledger-desk where a grandmotherly woman sat at her books, one eye on her inkstand and the other on the lanky apprentice who tended the counter. Tapers and cake-candles were laid out in trays, arranged by size and color, along with a handful of small wax rabbits that mimicked the sign above the door, and the shelves at the back of the shop were filled with pillar-candles, the biggest as thick as a man's thigh. The air smelled heavily of beeswax and perfume, drowning out the scent of the river.

"Help you, dame?" the apprentice said, to Ormere, and then faltered as the jerkins and truncheons registered.

"We'd like to speak to Dame Havys, please," Rathe said, and the woman closed her ledger.

"I'm Havys." Her voice became wary. "What can I do for you, points-man?"

"Adjunct Point," Rathe answered pleasantly. "I don't know if you've heard about Adjunct Point Dammar, at Point of Sighs?"

She shook her head.

"He was attacked and thrown into the Sier, from the bridge here, and he says he was on business for you." Rathe watched closely as he spoke, but she shook her head again.

"I hadn't heard that. I'm sorry."

"I'd like a word," Rathe said again.

She eased herself off the tall stool. "If you want to talk in private, there's a tea house just past the foot of the bridge. I've no space here for anything but my goods."

"Lead the way."

The tea house was small and shabby, but spotlessly clean, and lay on a side street that led down to the water. At this hour, the main room was only half full, and it was easy to find a table where they wouldn't be overheard. Rathe ordered a pot of tea and cakes to go with it, and leaned his elbows on the worn table.

"Edild Dammar said he was looking into something for you when he was attacked. I'd like to find out a bit more about it."

"What did he tell you?" Havys was pleating the edge of her bodice between her fingers, then seemed to realize it and laced her hands firmly together.

"Just that he had a job from you." Rathe frowned when Ormere seemed about to say more, and she subsided. "As I said, I'd like to hear it from you."

"He's done any number of jobs for me," Havys said. "I know his sister, we're old friends. He's been kind enough to handle some minor troubles for me without fuss."

"When did you see him last?" Rathe frowned at Ormere again, and she subsided.

"Sweet Heira, I don't know," Havys said. "A week, two?"

"Not these last few days?" Rathe's attention sharpened, and he saw a flicker of worry cross her face.

"Did he say so?"

"What sorts of trouble did he handle?" Rathe swallowed a curse as the waiter arrived with the pot and the plate of cakes, and Havys fussed with it, insisting on serving all of them.

"Ordinary bits of business, really." Havys stared at the cups as she filled them one by one. "There was a man owed me money, he'd bought one of my great candles on installments, and then wouldn't finish. My apprentice—not this one, the one before—got in a fight and he got the bail reduced. Things like that."

"Do you rent storage in the bridge pier?" Rathe asked, and this time he was certain a look of fear came into her eyes.

"You saw my shop, it's too small to keep a decent supply, and my house is on the border of Dreams—" She stopped, mastering herself with an effort.

"Had you lost goods recently, from there or from the shop?"

Havys hesitated and reached for one of the cakes to cover her uncertainty.

"Dame." Rathe drew the plate back an inch or two, and saw her flinch.

"I had…I thought Edild might help me, he's been good before."

"He said you'd asked him to look at your storage, that you'd lost goods from there," Rathe said.

"Yes. Yes, I had, from there and the shop." Havys's voice was pitched suddenly high, and she cleared her throat unhappily. "You understand, even the small pieces are valuable—even the damaged bits, I can turn them back to the makers, get credit. It's good beeswax I sell, none of your tallow or adulterine goods. And none of your cheap perfumes. I asked him to look into it."

"Can you tell me what was missing?"

"I told Edild. Gave him a list."

"It seems to have gone missing, too," Rathe said dryly.

For a moment, her face was blank, but then she rallied. "Some short tapers, a medium pillar. A handful of the rabbits, they're always popular, but they're so small you have to watch them."

"Color?"

"All colors—plain, mostly." Havys drained her cup and pushed her stool back from the table. "And I can't stay talking any longer, it needs more than the boy to watch the shop these days."

"If I need to talk to you again...."

She shook her head. "I've told you everything I know, there's nothing more. Good day, Adjunct Point."

Rathe leaned back on his stool, watching her bustle out of the tea shop, then reached for the pot to refill his own and Ormere's cups.

"She was lying." Ormere ducked her head as though it embarrassed her to have spoken.

Rathe nodded. "And I wonder why."

There was nothing more to do, Rathe thought as they walked back to Point of Sighs, at least not without a lot more information in hand. Havys had lied and he'd missed his chance to ask her for the key to her storage cell. On balance, it was probably better to wait on that: he doubted Dammar had been attacked there, though why he'd chosen that for his lie Rathe couldn't see. Instead, better to set a team to search the bridge to see if they could find where Dammar had been taken—and talk to the pontoises' witness who'd seen the man fall, he added silently, that might give them a hint—and come back to Havys when he knew better what questions to ask.

He made the arrangements once they were back at the station, choosing women he knew as reasonably honest, or at least likely to stay bought, and settled down in his workroom to compose a note to Cambrai. They needed the witness's account, and better still, the woman's name so that they could ask their own questions; the trick was to find a phrasing that would let Cambrai give it to them. He brushed the tip of his quill across his lips, trying to come up with just the right words, and looked up when the door opened.

Bellin scowled in at him. "A word with you?"

"Come in." Rathe set his pen aside, gestured to the nearest stool. "What's on your mind?"

"What's this order to search the bridge? That's properly the pontoises' business."

"Since when are you so protective of their rights?" Rathe asked. "The bridges belong to all of us, that's always been the agreement."

"And it's a waste of time," Bellin said. "We should be looking for who did it, not where it happened."

Rathe felt his temper snap. "I'd be very glad to do that, if you'd care to list some names. Every time I've asked, you and the rest of this station have sworn up and down that the man had no enemies. Give me names, and I'm happy to see them questioned."

"I may not have names, but I know the sort who hated him. Let me take the night watch down the docks—"

"And do exactly what?"

Bellin hesitated. "I'll take half the watch, sweep the waterfront taverns, pull the known troublemakers. That'll get an answer."

"You will not." Rathe lifted a hand to tick off the reasons on his fingers, aware that he sounded like Fourie and not much caring. "First, that's the perfect way to be sure no one ever talks to you again—you'll drive them straight to the pontoises. Second, what in Tyrseis's name makes you think you'll get useful answers? Half of them will tell you what they think you want to hear just to get free of this. Third, it's as much casting nets at random as searching the bridge—more so, without anything more to go on. You have a name for cleverness here in Sighs, I'd like to see some of it."

"There are names." Bellin looked ready to pull her truncheon. "Names and people, summer-sailors and dockers and the scum of the river, they all have cause to hate him—"

"Name them and question them for cause, or let it be."

Bellin blinked, then dropped her gaze. "Sorry, Adjunct Point, I spoke out of turn."

You did that. Rathe swallowed the words. "Bellin, if there are folk you think should be questioned, do it. But I also want the bridge searched."

"Yes, Adjunct Point." Bellin took a deep breath and turned for the door, but paused with it half open. "We're all on edge. Dammar—he's one of us."

Rathe nodded, the anger draining out of him. That was how things worked in most points stations: you might dislike a colleague, disapprove of how she handled her fees and her points, but you'd fight to the death to defend her, just as she would fight for you. "I want his attacker, too," he said.

"Not as badly as we do." She closed the door behind her before he could do more than nod.

Rathe swore under his breath, all the clever phrases he had been considering utterly vanished, and reached for a second, smaller slip of paper. He scrawled a note asking Eslingen to meet him at Wicked's, then rang the bell for a station runner, and sent the girl off in search of him. Dammar's books sat stacked on the end of his table, and he reached for the most recent, paging through it in the vain hope of finding some name, some incident that he had missed all the previous times. There was still nothing, just the same prim, unremarkable plot of complaint and solution, none of them seeming to have either passion or enough money behind them to have caused the attack. Except, of course, that a careful man wouldn't have written down anything compromising, and from the books, Dammar was a careful man indeed. If it were one of Eslingen's plays, there would be a secret book somewhere, a meticulous record in magist's ink that showed only at a secret word, or some elaborate code that concealed the enemy's name in a lover's sonnet.

He found no sonnets in Dammar's books, and when he rubbed the pages cautiously between finger and thumb, he didn't feel any of the odd greasiness that usually accompanied a magist's ink. Holding a page over the stove's heat did no better, and Rathe set them aside again, feeling himself flush. This was that sort of case, though, the kind that had you grasping at the thinnest of straws. And the only thing that ever broke a case like that was hard work and a thread of luck.

There was a knock at the door, and it opened at once to admit the runner, carrying a folded slip of paper. Rathe took it, recognizing Eslingen's handwriting in the name scrawled across the fold, and tossed the girl a demming. "Did he say anything else?" he asked, scanning the note—a request to meet at the Sandureigne, the most elaborate and expensive of the city's bathhouses, rather than a Wicked's.

The runner shook her head. "No, sir, was he supposed to?"

"No." Rathe tossed her another demming. "Thank you." It must be Eslingen's taste for luxury that led him to make the suggestion, and not something gone wrong. Still, he caught himself counting the minutes until he could leave for the day.

THE SANDUREIGNE LAY just west of the junction with the Queen's Road, and the evening clouds were thickening again, the scent of rain on the air as the day-sun set. He was glad to see the string of mage-fire globes that framed the entrance, thickening the shadows in the carved tracery that covered the pillared doors. At this hour, the baths were crowded, and he stopped just inside as the wave of noise hit him. The air was warm and damp, smelling of sweat and herbs; he could hear shouting from the fives-court, and from the great pool, and suppressed a sigh at having to share the space with a hundred folk all bent on amusement. A wrought-iron screen divided the narrow lobby from the baths and changing rooms, an attendant sitting at a desk beside the gate. She had a knife with her, a big man with heavy muscles and close-cropped hair, and there would be more watchers in the baths themselves. Enough coin changed hands here to make it a tempting target.

"I was supposed to meet a friend here," he said to the attendant, without much hope. "I don't suppose he left word?"

The woman smiled, but the expression didn't reach her tired eyes. "What's your name?"

"Nico Rathe."

She shuffled through some slips of paper, and her smile widened. "Ah. Here we are. He's taken one of the private baths." She lifted a hand, and a girl in a short shift, her sleeves rolled up to expose work-reddened hands and forearms, moved to open the gate. "Scilla will take you—the Serpent, please, Scilla."

The girl bobbed a curtsy and pushed the gate open. "This way, please, sir."

Rathe followed her through a maze of corridors, his shoes loud on the tiled floor. Its pattern was as elaborate as a Chadroni carpet, the reds and blues and golds vivid in the mage-light, and he wondered what had possessed Eslingen to spend the money on one of the private chambers. The enormous wooden tubs and waiters to bring wine and savories—a full dinner, if you wanted to pay those prices—but you paid in good coin for every amenity. Though if Eslingen had something to celebrate…. Rathe couldn't hide a smile at the thought of spending an hour or two neck-deep in hot water with no one to see them but the waiter. There were pleasures worth paying for.

Scilla stopped at a scarlet door, two enormous green and gold snakes twining across its upper half. She knocked briskly, counted to four— Rathe noticed her lips move—and then pushed open the door. "Your guest, sir."

Rathe handed her a demming—yet another expense of the baths—and ducked past her into the steam-filled chamber. The bath was sunk into the tiled floor, patterned red and blue stars against cream, and there were benches and a set of shelves piled with clothes. Eslingen was already in the bath, his hair piled high to keep it out of the water, and there was another man with him, a familiar shock of bright-gold hair. Cambrai lifted a dripping hand in greeting.

"Nico! Glad you could make it. Join us, and pour us all some wine while you're at it."

Sure enough, there was a large pitcher on one of the benches, and an unused cup. Eslingen looked grim and Rathe closed his teeth on a curse. If Cambrai was trying to cause trouble between them, that was the last favor he'd get—and why hadn't Eslingen sent him about his business, anyway? Rathe took a deep breath, controlling himself, and began to unlace his jerkin. "Was this your idea?"

"It was my idea," Eslingen said, with just enough of an edge of annoyance that Rathe felt some of his own unhappiness release. "The cap'pontoise wanted to talk discreetly with you, and this seemed as good a chance as anything. Though I'd thought we might talk elsewhere, and then you and I could bathe."

"No point in wasting the water," Cambrai said, with a look that said he was being deliberately obtuse. "I didn't want to be seen with you twice in one day, Nico."

"I expect that would ruin both our reputations." Rathe stripped off the rest of his clothes, leaving them piled on the end of a bench, then fetched pitcher and cup and eased himself into the water.

Eslingen's mouth tightened. "I'm hoping he can finish this quickly."

Cambrai ignored him, and refilled his own cup. "The captain's got some useful news, as well."

Rathe looked at Eslingen, who shook his head. "I do, in actual fact. I told you I wanted to talk to—the captain I mentioned—and I got a name from him, the man they think's behind the new extortion gang. Jurien Trys."

Rathe found a seat on the bench that ran around the inside of the tub, letting his feet float away from the hotter wood at the bottom. "I don't know him."

"But I do," Cambrai said. "What's more, I wouldn't doubt he is in charge of all of this. We'll go looking for him tomorrow, and I've a nice long list of questions once we find him."

"Ask him about bes'Anthe," Rathe said. "If the boy didn't kill him, and I doubt he did, I'd lay money it has something to do with the new fees."

"Eslingen already mentioned that," Cambrai said. "And I will."

"So what else was it you wanted?" Rathe asked. "Seeing as you've made such an effort to join us here."

Cambrai showed teeth in a grin. "What, do you grudge me the only respite I've had all day?"

"Now that you mention it," Eslingen began, and Rathe grinned in spite of himself.

"I'm sure you have other places to be."

"Two things I wanted to talk to you about. First, like I said, I don't think Dammar's half as sick as he pretends."

Rathe considered, tipping his head to one side. Dammar's fits of weakness had come too conveniently on the heels of the harder questions to be entirely believable. "I'll agree with that, yes. But there's not much we can do about it while his sister has that doctor to watch him."

"I sent Saffroy to have a word with that doctor," Cambrai said. "She allowed as how she'd expected him to be making better progress."

"I'd have thought the knife must have touched a lung," Rathe said, dubiously.

Cambrai shook his head. "That's the thing, Bael said it didn't. He was lucky, it missed nearly everything of importance, so the worst of it was the bleeding. And the beating, of course, but he's only got a few cracked ribs, and the broken nose, and they're healing nicely. She's been building him up with various tonics, but he isn't responding as quickly as she'd expected."

"That's…interesting," Rathe said. "Can't say it's conclusive, but—interesting."

"Something's gone wrong, and he's in it up to his neck," Cambrai said. "At least that's my judgment."

"I can't argue," Rathe said. "And his story about how he was hurt doesn't hold up." Quickly he ran through his conversation with Dame Havys, Cambrai nodding thoughtfully as he spoke.

"You think she didn't call him?"

"Not for this," Rathe said. "She's had dealings with him, and she's a friend of his sister, she'd do him favors, but—I don't think he was on the bridge on her business this time. I've set a couple of my people to do a sweep, see if they can find where he was attacked—particularly if it wasn't in the storeroom—and then we'll see."

"Let me know if I can help," Cambrai said.

"I will, if you'll keep me up on what you find about Trys." Rathe paused, stretching again in the blissfully hot water. His foot struck a leg—Eslingen's, for a mercy—and they both shifted, sending the water sloshing. "What was the second thing?"

"Eslingen said you'd seen the broadsheets," Cambrai said. "About the deaths on the river."

Rathe nodded. "I have."

"It's true enough from our point of view," Cambrai said. "I'd like to know what Point of Sighs knows."

"I've not had a chance to ask much about it," Rathe said. "But I'll pass on what I hear."

"Apropos of that," Eslingen said slowly, "what's this tale about the greater dogfish?"

Rathe rolled his eyes, but to his surprise, Cambrai looked uncertain. "What have you heard?"

"I've seen the broadsheets," Eslingen answered, "and I heard a story from a woman who said she'd seen it herself. But I'm no river-man, that's why I'm asking you."

Cambrai was silent, and Rathe leaned forward. "You can't be serious."

"I've not seen one," Cambrai said. "Nor Saffroy. But—two of my reliables have, and I believe they saw something close enough to make it plausible. And the talk is all up and down the docks."

"But surely it's not possible," Rathe protested.

"It shouldn't be, not as I understand it." Cambrai wiped strands of his sun-gilded hair from his face. "The Riverdeme was bound when the bridges went up, the Queen's Bridge and then Hopes-Point. The dogfish dwindled, became what they are today. And yet...."

"Some other sort of fish?" Eslingen asked, without much hope, and Rathe was unsurprised when Cambrai shook his head again.

"There's no other like it. Nico, you have friends at the university. Would you ask one of them what they make of all this?"

"Why don't you ask them yourself?" Rathe asked.

"I don't have friends there," Cambrai answered. "And, I don't want to give the broadsheet printers anything more to talk about."

"You can't seriously think the Riverdeme is—what, unbound? In the river somehow?" Rathe pushed himself upright as though that would help him think.

"I don't think so. But there are plenty of folk who do."

Rathe nodded. "I don't know anyone offhand who studies the river. But I'll see what I can find out. And then you can make a formal request."

"Thanks." Cambrai hauled himself out of the water, padded dripping to the rack that held the towels, and began vigorously to dry himself. He was a well-muscled man, neat and graceful. Out of the corner of his eye, Rathe saw Eslingen watching, one eyebrow raised, but he couldn't quite read the other's expression. "Well, I'll leave you to it—" Cambrai's grin was wide. "And I thank you for the help, Nico. I'll do the same for you one day."

"I'll make sure of it," Rathe said, and let himself sink back into the water as Cambrai finished dressing and closed the door behind him.

Eslingen breathed a laugh. "This was not precisely what I had in mind. I wonder if this is covered by 'stars bad for water'?"

Rathe reached under the water to touch his shoulder. "He's gone now."

"And I've had about as much hot water as I can stand." Eslingen straightened and winced. "Especially with the wine on top of it."

Rathe frowned. "Are you all right?"

"I had a bit of a fight," Eslingen answered. "I saw Young Steen, and Dame Hardelet—it was they who told me about Trys. They'd also come to say that they were taking themselves downriver to Ostolas, and with good cause. A trio of bravos attacked us—and in a Customs Point chophouse, not on the street. Big men with clubs. They meant to take Dame Hardelet, and she's a good five months' gone with child."

Rathe whistled between his teeth.

"She's all right," Eslingen said

Rathe cocked his head. "But you're not, or not entirely. Let me see?"

For a moment, he thought Eslingen would refuse, but then the other man stood, wincing again, and turned, lifting his left arm to show an angry bruise at the base of his ribcage.

"He was trying for my kidneys. If he'd hit where he meant, I'd've been pissing blood for a week."

"Good thing he missed, then." Rathe did his best to keep his voice light, but a part of him wanted to find the man and beat him into a bloody pulp "What else?"

"Nothing as spectacular as that," Eslingen answered. "But I'll be sore in the morning."

"I imagine you're sore now," Rathe said.

Eslingen gave a reluctant nod. "I thought the water would help, and I thought we might steal an hour or two together. But the stars are entirely against me."

And it was coming on to rain again, Rathe thought. The bruise on Eslingen's back was twice as big as a man's hand, and wrapped around to the front of his body, and now that he looked more closely, there were other marks on the pale skin. "Have another glass of wine," he said aloud, "and then we'll take a low-flyer home."

"I'll be drunk if we do that," Eslingen said.

"Then you'll be drunk." Rathe filled both their cups, and held his out to touch rims with Eslingen's. "Drink up."

"A man might think you were trying to take advantage of me," Eslingen said, eyes wide in mock innocence.

"Let's see how you feel when we get in," Rathe answered, and Eslingen sighed.

They finished the pitcher, then dragged themselves out of the tub, Eslingen wincing visibly. Rathe watched him as they dried themselves and dressed, and decided that the Leaguer had probably been telling the truth, though that one blow under the ribs was bad enough. In the lobby, he handed a footman a spider to find a low-flyer for them, and then bundled Eslingen into the damp box before he could protest any further. It was raining again, a sullen drizzle that left the cobbles slick with mud, and made the driver wrap himself in a stiff oilcloth coat and a long-tailed hat to shed the rain.

He got them back to their lodgings in excellent time, however, and Eslingen climbed down, flinching again, while Rathe fished in his pocket for the fare and a tip. He handed over the coins, and turned to find that Eslingen already had the gate open, and the weaver's daughter was waiting to hand over Sunflower.

"You go up," Rathe said, and forestalled further protest by taking the dog's leash. He walked Sunflower through the dripping garden, hunching his shoulders as the rain strengthened, and finally tucked Sunflower under his arm to climb the stairs back to their rooms. For once, Sunflower made no protest, content to hang over arm and hip, and he pushed open the door to see Eslingen straighten from the stove, both fists pressed into the small of his back. The lamp on the table cast an arcing shadow.

"He's very quiet," Eslingen said. "What's wrong?"

Rathe set the dog down, seeing him dive for the basket where he had last hidden a bone, and came to lay gentle hands on Eslingen's shoulders. "I might ask you the same question."

Eslingen gave a wry smile. "You saw the bruises. I'm sore, that's all. I'll be fine in the morning."

"Arnica," Rathe said, and gave him a gentle push toward the bedroom. "I've a whole pot of Dame Falluel's best ointment—doesn't even smell like horse liniment. Get your clothes off, and I'll even put it on for you."

131

For a moment, Rathe thought the Leaguer was going to object, but then he sighed. "I'll take that, and thank you." He reached for his collar, tugging at the stock that held it closed. "This evening was more expensive than I'd meant. Let me at least throw in for the low-flyer."

Rathe reached for the stock as well, brushing his hands aside. He was absurdly touched: Eslingen didn't count the cost of his little luxuries, but it was generous of him to offer, on top of everything he'd already spent for the baths. "It's not a night for walking," he said aloud, and unfastened the knot, letting the wilting linen gape to reveal a few dark hairs. Eslingen blinked, breath coming short, and then flinched as some bruise caught him. Rathe grimaced in sympathy and cupped his cheek, stubble prickling under his palm. "Now, go on. I'll bring the arnica."

"This was not precisely what I had in mind," Eslingen said again, but did as he was told.

Rathe found the pottery jar on the shelf where he had left it, the stopper still solidly in place, and carried it and the lamp and a couple of towels into the bedroom. Eslingen lay face down on the mattress, his clothes for once left in an untidy heap. He was naked in the dark, his head pillowed on his folded arms. Rathe set the lamp on the chest by the bed, and sat carefully at Eslingen's side. He could see one eye open, but Eslingen made no other move. The bruise looked even darker in the flickering lamplight.

Rathe worked the stopper out of the jar and dipped out two fingers-full of ointment, breathing on it to warm the chill ointment. He laid it gently on the bruised area, but in spite of his care, he felt Eslingen flinch. "That bad?"

"Cold," Eslingen said, his voice muffled, and then he sighed. "Yeah, it hurts. But it'll be better for it in the morning."

"I'll be quick." Rathe did his best, wincing himself as he felt Eslingen tense under his touch, but at last the bruised area was done and he could spread more ointment across the small of Eslingen's back. Eslingen sighed again, but Rathe thought it was release rather than pain. He could see a few more bruises on Eslingen's upper arms and treated those as well, keeping his touch feather-light, and saw Eslingen drift into sleep under his hands. That was the wine as well as the bruises, and the arnica salve might have an extra herb or two to encourage rest: the best thing for him, Rathe thought, wiping his hands on the towel and closing the jar again. He was still incandescently angry at the men who'd done this—even knowing it was folly, knowing that Eslingen was probably a better fighter than he was himself, didn't relieve the urge to find the docker and beat him bloody. That would do him no good, and certainly wouldn't help Eslingen. He sighed, putting the jar of ointment aside, and stood up to undress himself. He blew out the lamp and settled in the bed beside Eslingen, who stirred and shifted without waking, and a moment later there was a clicking of claws and a thump as Sunflower found his place at the foot of the bed. Rathe tucked one foot under the dog's warmth, obscurely comforted, and composed himself for sleep.

CHAPTER 8

ESLINGEN WOKE TO milky daylight, and braced himself to roll over with only a silent grimace. The hot water and Rathe's ointment had helped, though, and he was able to sit up without undue complaint. The other side of the bed was empty; he could hear both Rathe and Sunflower moving around in the outer room, and a part of him was grateful to make his first cautious movements without a witness. The bruise still ached, but there was none of the sharp pain that meant broken bone or a torn muscle, and when he used the pot there was no sign of blood in his urine. A bad bruise, then, and certainly painful, but nothing that he hadn't dealt with before. He stretched again, cautiously, testing his limits, and the door swung open.

"You're moving better," Rathe said.

There was an edge to Rathe's expression, excitement barely leashed, and Eslingen's eyes narrowed. "What's happened?"

"A runner just brought a note from Sighs. They've found where Dammar was attacked." Rathe held out the jar of arnica. "Want to come along?"

"Oh, yes," Eslingen said, and reached for the jar. "Where?"

"Dame Havys's storage room in the pillar of the bridge." Rathe showed teeth in a feral grin. "Which I'm bound to say I don't think she knew when she spoke to us."

"Give me a quarter hour," Eslingen said, and reached for his shirt.

One of Rathe's runners was loitering at the foot of the bridge, and came bustling up at their approach, a heavyset boy in a fisherman's jersey under his almost outgrown coat. "Adjunct Point! Dame Sebern says come this way."

"Sebern's here?" Rathe asked.

The boy nodded. "Daiva—Daiva Hockel, she's the one who found it—she sent for the adjunct first, and she told me to run for you."

Eslingen slanted a quick glance at Rathe, but the pointsman's expression was unreadable.

"In the storage area, you said?"

"Yes, sir." The boy nodded again, harder. "This way."

The bridge was already crowded with the morning's traffic, and at first they had to fight their way up the sloping approach. On the bridge itself, the narrow shops rose to either side of the structure, and they fought their way up the left side, carts rumbling slowly past along the center of the span. It was just wide enough for two carts to pass without crowding passersby into the walls, but collisions were inevitable, and Eslingen winced as someone bumped against his bruises. It was also ideal territory for pickpockets, but he hoped being with a pointsman would spare him that indignity.

A third of the way across, the runner darted abruptly sideways, toward a gap between two of the narrow buildings. A rusted iron gate closed the mouth of what would have been an alley anywhere else in the city, and the man waiting behind it straightened at their approach.

"Adjunct Point."

"You said you'd found the place?" Rathe barely made it a question.

"Daiva did, yes, sir." The pointsman unlocked the gate, flattening himself against the wall to let them through. Beyond him, the passage ended in a lattice-work railing, the river showing through its gaps. "It's just through there, down the stairs—you'll see the lights. Pol, you stay with me."

The runner rolled his eyes, but did as he was told. Eslingen followed Rathe, keeping one eye on the river churning beyond the rail. Not that it wouldn't take some effort to go over that wall, it was nearly breast-high, but it was far from impossible. And just as possible to throw a body over it, he realized, and saw from Rathe's glance in that direction that he was thinking much the same thing.

"I haven't seen Cambrai's report yet," Rathe said. "But it could be."

Eslingen nodded, not liking the images that conjured for him. Fugitive sunlight glinted on the rushing water, the faint sparks only emphasizing the speed and depth of the river.

Ahead, almost at the end of the space, the wall of the right-hand house bulged outward, a door set into the curve of the laid stones. Rathe pulled it open, revealing a round opening, half filled with a wooden platform. A hoist and chain dangled into the open center, and a stairway led down to the left. There was light below, the steady glow of mage-light, and Rathe leaned cautiously over the platform's rail.

"Sebern?"

"Down here." The voice echoed up from below, distorted by the curved walls. "Wait, let me send Bartei up, it's crowded in here."

Rathe stepped back, and Eslingen pressed himself against the cold stone between the door and the edge of the platform. He was almost on top of the hoist, the drum with its coiled cable glistening with oil: obviously it was much in use, and looked to be in good repair, the brake braced firmly in place. He looked up, and saw a hook and leather sling dangling just below the ceiling.

Footsteps sounded on the stair, and a stocky man appeared, followed by a slight woman whose truncheon tapped against the stones as she climbed. The man said, "The adjunct says, go on down."

Rathe nodded, starting down the stairs, but Eslingen waited until the points had stepped out into the alley before he followed. Not that there was much he could do, if they wanted to attack, not in this cramped space and outnumbered three to one, and in any case, he told himself, it was unlikely to happen, so unlikely that he should be ashamed. He followed Rathe down the curving stair, steep and chill, with only a wooden rail to shield them from the central open well. He touched the knife at his belt for reassurance, knowing that it was at least partly the river that worried him, and kept his other hand firmly on the rail.

The stairs ended in a round room perhaps ten paces across, smaller than he'd expected, given the width of the bridge, but then, there was probably a matching chamber accessed from the shops on the other side. The stone floor was scuffed and dirty, and the entire circumference of the wall was broken at regular intervals by doors half a hand taller than a man. Each one was marked either with a stamped-brass emblem or a painted mark, and each had at least one heavy lock. There was a second row of smaller doors above them, and a third above that, and a sturdy-looking ladder ran on rails to grant access, but the mage-lights hung below the first rank, so their details were lost in shadow. A stocky woman in a pointswoman's jerkin was standing at the foot of the ladder—the other adjunct point, presumably, Eslingen thought, and in the same moment Rathe said, "Sebern. What have you got for me?"

"Not proof, but a good indication," the woman answered. "Who's this?"

"Captain vaan Esling of the City Guard. He's here on my say-so."

Eslingen thought Sebern would protest, but she said only, "It looks like there was a fight here, and I'll lay bail that's blood."

The dusty floor showed a confusion of marks, lines that might have been made by a sliding foot or a knee or hip of a falling woman; half a handprint showed clearly at the base of the wall, but there was nothing else that Eslingen could read. He looked up, unable quite to pick out the sling waiting at the top of the tower. If one was hauling goods from storage up to the shops, would one leave similar marks? It was impossible to tell.

Sebern lifted a smaller lantern, went to one knee to cast its light on the base of the wall between two doors. Rathe bent over her shoulder, careful not to cast a shadow, and Eslingen joined him. Sure enough, the extra light showed a dark stain on the stone, the dust thickened and damped, and on the wall about waist height was a line of darker dots.

"It certainly looks like blood," Rathe agreed. "Better get an alchemist down here to be sure."

"I've sent to the deadhouse already," Sebern said, and Rathe nodded.

"So, stabbed here—beaten and stabbed, I should say, that could have come from either. I take it this is where Dame Havys rents a space?"

"Yes." Sebern straightened, and the marks disappeared back into the shadows as the light left them. "So that holds."

"Why attack a man here, though?" Rathe put his hands on his hips, turning to survey the space. "It's crowded with the three of us, there's hardly room to swing a cudgel."

"Room enough for a knife," Sebern said.

"Yes, but he was beaten, too." Rathe squinted up into the dark. "And then you'd have to carry him up the stairs unconscious—"

"Use the hoist, surely," Eslingen said.

Rathe nodded. "Yeah, and we should check that for blood, too. But if you knew he was going to be down here, why not wait and take him when he came up? Knife him then, and tip him over the rail at the back of the alley. No need to risk someone else coming down here and trap you with your dead man."

"We're just lucky no one else is dead," Sebern said.

"Possible." Rathe frowned at the marks on the floor. "He came down here—with his attackers? Maybe they had to lure him down themselves, and that's why he was attacked here."

"But you said he said he was here on Dame Havys's business," Eslingen said.

"So he said," Rathe agreed.

"He wouldn't lie," Sebern said.

"Business she knew nothing of," Rathe said. "Maybe that's what they used to lure him?"

Eslingen looked up toward the hoist again, then let his gaze skim back along the stones. The two rows of compartments above the line of mage-lights were barely darker shadows, reminding him of the ash-grave hills along the Chadroni borders. The folk there burned their dead, dug the ashes into little chambers in the side of a hill and covered them with stones, until the entire hill was honeycombed with rock, and filled with the ashes of the dead....

One of the dark squares looked different from the others, darker, its shape faintly elongated. He frowned, looked away, looked back again to see the same anomaly. "Nico."

Rathe turned, eyebrows rising in question.

Eslingen pointed. "I think one of those bins is open."

"Where?"

"Third from the left," Eslingen answered. He saw Sebern scowl.

"Surely—" She stopped abruptly. "You've got good eyes, Captain."

"It might just be unused," Eslingen said, reluctant to hope too much.

Rathe shook his head. "Not down here, there's a waiting list for the spaces." He grinned. "It's your find, Philip, want to go up?"

"Oh, yes."

"Take my light," Sebern said, and Eslingen hooked the lantern onto his belt.

He slid the ladder along its rail, then pulled himself up past the row of mage-lights. Even outside their circle, it was easy to see that one door sagged open, no more than a finger's breadth, but enough to distort the shape from below. He caught at its edge and started to swing it open, then hesitated, seeing the sign chalked on the dark paint. "What was the woman's shop sign, the one he was working for?"

"Two rabbits," Rathe answered.

"Then this is hers." Eslingen lifted the lantern, angling it to cast the best light. The space revealed was smaller than he'd expected, perhaps an ell square, and mostly empty, except for a few paper-wrapped parcels thrust toward the back of the space. He reached in, stretching, and winced as the muscles across his back protested. But his fingers had touched paper, and he braced himself and reached again. This time, he touched string, and managed to hook a fingertip under the loop to draw it closer. It was small enough to fit in his pocket, and he let himself back down the ladder, holding it out like a prize at the bottom. "There's three or four more like it up there, but otherwise it's empty."

Rathe took it from him, assessing the knot with a glance—a shopkeeper's loop, nothing fancy—and tugged the dangling end to release the tie. He folded back the paper to reveal half a dozen beeswax rabbits, a tiny model litter cupped in his hands, and Sebern touched one as gently as if it had been alive.

"She sells these, doesn't she?"

"Yeah." Rathe folded the paper back around them. "I saw them in her shop." He looked at Eslingen. "And you say there's only a few more packages up there? No candles?"

"No," Eslingen said. "As I said, there are three or four more like this one—small goods, and, what's more, pushed all the way to the back. Either she's not using the space, or something's been taken."

"Havys could have just brought up a load and not yet refilled the space," Rathe said, "but I'll agree your idea seems more likely. She won't have kept it empty, not at the rent they charge for these spaces."

"But what's a wax-chandler got that's worth knifing one of us?" Sebern said. "It doesn't make sense."

"Nor does it," Rathe said. "But that's what we've got."

Eslingen inspected his sleeve, then turned his arm to display it. "I swept my arm back and forth a few times trying to get hold of that package. If there was anything else up there, it didn't leave traces."

"No," Rathe agreed. "I think I'd like another word with Dame Havys."

"Sebern!" The voice came from the top of the stair. "The boy's here from the deadhouse. Shall I send him down?"

"Go ahead," Rathe said. "Vaan Esling and I will talk to Havys."

Sebern nodded, and Rathe started up the stairs. Eslingen followed, grimacing as the climb pulled at his back. But then at last they were at the top, the platform crowded now with the pointswoman Daiva and a journeyman from the deadhouse.

"Before you go down," Rathe said, "I've a question for you here. Daiva, can you bring the sling down to us?"

"Sure, Adjunct," she answered. It took a minute for her to release the brake, but she brought the sling down to chest level and swung it toward them. Eslingen craned his neck, and saw with some satisfaction that there was a dark stain on the leather. Rathe gave a grunt of satisfaction.

"The stain. Can you tell me if it's blood?"

The journeyman blinked, then reached under his leather apron to produce a phial no longer than his little finger. "I thought the blood was down there."

"It might be up here, too," Rathe said.

The journeyman steadied the sling against his chest and carefully let a single drop fall on the very edge of the darkened area. It hissed and sparked, and when it vanished, the stain was unchanged. "That's blood, all right. But I can't tell you if it's animal or human without more tests. Though I don't imagine you get much butchery down here. Or meat kept."

"I wouldn't think so," Eslingen said, in spite of himself, and Rathe nodded in wry agreement.

"I want to know if it's human, and if the other stains are also blood. Can you tell if it belongs to a particular person, if we can provide a sample?"

"I can't," the journeyman said, "but Fanier might."

"I'll see what I can do," Rathe said. "Come on, Philip, let's see what Dame Havys has to say for herself."

It wasn't far to the wax-chandler's, with its sign of two young rabbits curled together in a leafy nest. There were candles marked with painted rabbits, and more of the little wax rabbits, and Eslingen wondered abruptly if they were meant to bring on conception. There was no time to ask, however, as Rathe pushed open the half-door, and Eslingen put on his most harmless smile. A young woman in a long blue coat turned away from the shelves at the back of the shop, hastily tucking the cloth with which she had been dusting into a pocket beneath her coat.

"Good day, sirs, how may I help you?"

"I'm looking for Dame Havys," Rathe said.

"Oh, I'm sorry," the woman said. "She's taken ill. I'm minding the shop for her today."

"Do you think she'll be back tomorrow?" Eslingen kept his smile steady, but he could see the woman turning wary.

"I couldn't say, sir. Perhaps I could help you?"

"Our business was with Dame Havys. And it's somewhat urgent…." Rathe let his voice trail off invitingly, but the woman didn't take the bait.

"I'd certainly carry a message, if you'd care to leave one. Or you could try back tomorrow."

"We'll do that," Rathe said. "Are you her journeyman?"

"Not I, I'm sent by the Guild. She has an apprentice, but he's on an errand."

No point in questioning her, then, Eslingen thought, and saw the same disappointment in Rathe's eyes. They thanked her, and left the shop, threading their way back toward the center of the bridge until they found a corner where they could stop out of the line of traffic.

"Not much useful there," Eslingen said, "but below—"

Rathe nodded. "I'd say that was where Dammar was attacked, and whoever attacked him must have wanted something from the chamber—I suspect Dammar had his own key to it, whether Dame Havys knew it or not, he could have been keeping anything there."

"So someone went down with him, waited for him to open the chamber," Eslingen said, "and then attacked?"

"That's how I read it. Unless the boy from the deadhouse turns up something different."

Eslingen straightened his coat. "And then hauled the body up in the sling and tossed him over the rail." He couldn't help shivering at the thought, Dammar bleeding and beaten unconscious, swaying up the height of the tower. It wouldn't take much after that, just a moment's break in the traffic, and the body could be slipped over without anyone noticing. The sounds of carts would drown any splash.

"They'd have had to tie him so he didn't slip free," Rathe said, "and that will have left marks. We can prove it that way, though I suppose it doesn't much matter."

"And it doesn't get us much closer to who," Eslingen said. "Though I think this should rule out any question that Mattaes Staenka was involved."

"That'll disappoint some of my people, but I agree with you. Not that I really thought it was! No, it has to be someone on the docks, and I can't help thinking it might be related to this gang. But I don't know any of the river folk, not to ask this kind of question."

"I only know Young Steen, and he's in Ostolas by now," Eslingen said. "Do we try anyway?"

"We might?" Rathe sounded less certain than his words. "Northriver or south, I wonder?"

Before Eslingen could think of an answer, there was a shout from the street, and a boy darted toward them, barely missing the wheels of a cart.

"Adjunct Point!"

Rathe grabbed him by the collar of his jacket and drew him out of the path of a disapproving woman in expensive black. "Be more careful!? What's amiss?"

"It's Adjunct Point Dammar, sir," the boy said, between gasps. "He's dead…. The doctor wants you."

"What?" Eslingen couldn't stop the word.

"Dead, sir," the boy repeated. "And please…sir, Dr. Bael says to come at once…she wants to talk to you before she has to answer the sister."

"We'll come," Rathe said grimly, and they turned toward Point of Sighs.

They reached the pewter-smith's house in good time, to find Bellin on the doorstep and the shop in chaos behind her.

"What in Tyrseis's name?" Rathe began, waving a hand at the apprentices huddled in one corner while a woman servant wept in the corner, her apron flung over her head. Eslingen could hear raised voices from the chambers above, and Bellin gave them harried look.

"Thank Astree, the brat found you. The doctor says there's something wrong, and the sister's reaching hysteric rage. Will you go up?"

"Must we?" Eslingen murmured, as something shattered on the floor above, and Rathe shot him a wry glance.

"I don't see that we have a choice. Walk warily, Philip, the doctor's a Phoeban, and the sister—Sawel's her name—I think she cared for her brother."

Eslingen nodded and followed him up the stairs. Shutters were open at the end of the hall, letting in a wedge of cloudy light that fell across an open doorway, and a woman's voice rose beyond it.

"—dare you question my judgement?"

"My brother is dead through your carelessness! I spit on what judgement you have!"

Rathe grimaced, and knocked loudly on the door's frame, then stepped through without waiting for an answer. "Now, then, what's all this?"

Eslingen stayed close at his shoulder, ready to jump should it be necessary to separate the women. The doctor was unmistakable, tall and lean in a deep ochre gown that showed ugly stains at the cuffs; the other, then, was Dammar's sister, older and graying, strands of her hair coming down out of a braided bun, her cheeks streaked with tears. Rathe was right, he thought, she did love her brother.

"You," she said furiously, pointing to Rathe. "You have no business here."

"I sent for him," the doctor interrupted, "and if you will protest so much, I'll begin to think there's a reason."

Sawel's mouth dropped open for an instant, and then she launched herself at the doctor. She got in one backhand blow that knocked the doctor back on her heels before Rathe caught her other arm and swung her away. Eslingen put himself between them and the doctor, who swore under her breath, but had the sense to keep quiet.

"Enough of that," Rathe said. "No, no more, dame. If it was a mistake to send for me, let me find it out."

His voice was soothing, the words less important than the tone. Sawel drew breath as though to speak, and collapsed into racking sobs. Rathe caught her before she fell, and she put her head against his shoulder like a child as she fought for control.

"Edild's dead," she managed at last. "I raised him, all the child I'll ever have. Mother died when he was four and I was fourteen, and I raised him, saw him settled—and now this. He was doing better, Adjunct Point, I swear it, and then she failed him. And now she has the gall to cry poison."

Eslingen heard the doctor stiffen, and stepped back, pressing his heel lightly on her toe. She gasped, but had the wit to stay silent.

"He was one of ours," Rathe said, "and we take care of our own. If anything was wrong here, whether it was negligence or worse, we want to deal with it."

"He was doing better," Sawel said again. "He was well enough to use the pot himself, laughed at me when I scolded him."

"I don't doubt you," Rathe said. "Go downstairs, have Luce make you a pot of tea. There's a pointswoman there, her name's Bellin, she worked close with Dammar. If there's anything you need, she'll get it for you."

Sawel drew a shuddering breath. "I'm sorry, Adjunct Point. I'll go down. But you'll speak with me before you leave?"

Rathe nodded.

He turned toward the door, turning her with him, and Eslingen offered his arm. She clung to him without apology, and he eased her to the edge of the stair. "Are you all right going down?" he asked, trying to match Rathe's tone, and saw the maid Luce waiting at the foot, her apron smudged and wrinkled from her own weeping.

"I'll be fine," Sawel said, but even so he lingered until she was halfway down before turning back to the bedchamber.

Edild Dammar was unmistakably dead, the linen sheet drawn down to reveal a sturdy body that had already begun to heal, the bruises faded from ripe purple to yellow and green about the edges. Rathe and the physician were looking at him, but Rathe turned at Eslingen's step.

"She's downstairs," Eslingen said, in answer to his look, "and gone to the kitchen, I hope." You were right, he wanted to say, she loved him—like her child, she said, no wonder she's distraught. There was no time for that, however, and he said instead, "What did the doctor find that's so upsetting? By all accounts, the man was like enough to die."

"He was a luckier man than he had any right to be," the doctor said, indignantly, and Rathe held up a hand.

"This is Dr. Bael," he said. "Doctor, this is Captain vaan Esling of the City Guard."

"Another troop to plague us," she said, but her heart wasn't in the complaint. "Adjunct Point, the man had no reason to die. I told you before, the knife missed everything of import in his chest, didn't even touch his lungs. He had fever for a day, and then—well, he said he felt weak, picked at his food, but I swear I thought he was doing it to stay snug in his sister's house. I gather he lived in lodgings, no one to look after him there."

"So he did," Rathe said.

"That was a thorough beating," Eslingen said, looking at the bruises that mottled chest and arms and thighs. Dammar's face was badly marked, too, both eyes still blackened, and for a guess his nose had been broken and eased back into a semblance of its original shape. "Might it have affected his wits?"

"If it had, I would have known it," Bael answered. "So would she, for that matter, and complained of it. No, he was lucky there, too. There's no reason for him to be dead."

"And yet," Eslingen murmured, in spite of himself, and earned a frown from Rathe.

"I take it that's why you called us?"

Bael nodded. "I wanted to send him to the alchemists to settle the question, but she'd have none of it."

"That's a serious thing to ask," Rathe said. "It comes hard on a woman who's just lost her brother."

Bael scowled at the body. "If someone's poisoned him, surely she'd want to know."

"Is that what you think happened?" Rathe drew the sheet back up, covering Dammar's face.

Bael stopped, the anger falling away, and for the first time Eslingen heard the Phoeban precision in her voice. "This is a most unlikely outcome for this man. I cannot see how the wounds he had could have killed him, not at this point. I see no other wounds, nor was he fevered, nor showed any sign of illness."

"He was weak enough when I spoke to him last," Rathe said.

"That surprised me," Bael answered. "I thought it was more likely he didn't want to talk to you."

"Also possible," Rathe said. "So. Not his wounds, not sickness—why poison, then?"

"He was taken ill overnight." Bael lifted a small wax tablet, no doubt checking her notes. "Some time about half past four, they think, for he called for the maid a little after, and she heard the clock strike five as she was tending him. He was struck with cold chills, then vomited. He was well enough to be taken to the close-stool first, but he said then his legs were heavy and within the hour they could no longer bear his weight. They sent for me at first sunrise, and by then he was in deadly pain and having trouble breathing. He lost the ability to speak not long after, and died a little after the clock struck nine."

There were two or three poisons that could produce that effect, Eslingen thought, hemlock first among them. "Did he say anything?"

"Complained of the pains," Bael said. "Cried for his sister. I asked if he'd eaten or drunk anything, but he never answered."

"There's a pitcher by the bed," Rathe said. "But no cup?"

Eslingen stooped, peering past their legs. "It's under the bed. He might have dropped it—"

"Or it was knocked over in the rush to tend him." Rathe picked up the pitcher and shook it lightly, then sniffed the contents. "Smells like tea."

Eslingen took it from him and sniffed cautiously. That was exactly what it smelled like, the ordinary sort of tea everyone drank all winter, and he handed it back with a shrug. "I'm not tasting it for you, but, yes, I'd say it's tea."

"Fanier will need to have a look at this," Rathe said. "All right, doctor, I'm asking you now officially. On your oath, how do you believe this man died?"

"I hold he was poisoned," Bael answered. "He had all the symptoms of a man who'd eaten hemlock, or dramberry, it might be either. And for a guess it was in the tea that was left him for overnight, though without testing what's left, I've no proof of that. But I'll give my oath and say before the judiciary that I believe the man was poisoned." She paused. "But don't think that'll get the sister to agree to sending him to the dead-house."

Maybe if you didn't put it quite that way, Eslingen thought, but had more sense then to say it aloud. He caught Rathe's eye, and surprised a wry smile.

"We can only try," Rathe said. "Philip, would you send Bellin up? Tell Dame Sawel I'll need to have a word. And ask Luce about the tea if you get a chance."

"Of course," Eslingen said.

He found Bellin at the foot of the stairs, dividing her attention between the door that led to the kitchens and what she could hear of what was going on upstairs. The apprentices had been sent somewhere, and the shop door was barred. "Well?" she demanded, as soon as he was close enough that she could speak without their being overheard.

"Rathe wants you upstairs," he said, not sure if he should say more, and she clutched his sleeve, then released him as though the wool was red hot.

"Was it poison?"

"The doctor thinks so," Eslingen said. "And Rathe wants to talk to the sister once you're in place."

"The doctor." Bellin looked as though she wanted to spit. "A fine lot of good she did him."

"She expected him to live," Eslingen said, unsure why he was defending Bael, and Bellin brushed past him without another word.

The back door opened onto a short hall that led to the kitchen, and he tapped softly on the wall as he approached. "Dame Sawel?"

The maid Luce was busy at the fire—the house had neither stove nor range, just the old-fashioned open fire hung with pots and a stand for a spit, though at the moment only a large kettle was pushed over the flames. Sawel sat hunched at the table they obviously normally used for the day's work, though a large bowl and a cheese grater and a bunch of carrots had been pushed higgledy-piggledy aside to make room for her. She had clearly been weeping again, a handkerchief knotted and sodden in her hands, but she looked up at his voice.

"Well?"

"Adjunct Point Rathe will be down in a moment," he answered. "In the meantime, dame, I'd like a word with Luce."

Sawel shrugged, resting her hand on her cheek, and Luce turned warily away from the fire. "What do you want, then? And who are you to ask?"

"I'm with the City Guard," Eslingen said patiently. "We're concerned in this also. I wondered, did you leave him with food as well as tea for the night?"

"No." Luce shook her head for emphasis. "He'd had a good dinner, I didn't think there was need. But the doctor said he should keep drinking, and he liked the flavor of the tea."

"Can I see the leaves?"

"I used the last of it." Luce turned to a cupboard and produced a small box that bore the remains of a label. "There might be some crumbs left."

Eslingen took it with a nod of thanks, and pried open the close-fitting lid to peer at what was left. Luce was right, it was little more than dust and a scattering of leaves and a few wrinkled buds, plus a tiny scrap of pink that probably belonged to some flower. He sniffed, but it smelled like any dozen expensive blends. The original label had been torn away, but a slip of paper had been pasted to the lid, a name scrawled across it. He turned it so that Luce could see the writing. "Half Moon Blend?"

Luce shrugged. "We got it from his lodgings, Dame Sawel wanted to keep him content."

Eslingen's attention sharpened. "Then I'm guessing no one else drank it?"

"Not at that price," Luce said.

Sawel lifted her head again. "It was Edild's tea, an indulgence, not something to be shared out—not at the prices those thieves in the tea houses charge! There wasn't much left." Her face crumpled. "I hoped to buy him more."

"I'll need to take this little bit with me."

"Why?" Sawel demanded. "There was nothing wrong with it."

"We need to be sure of that," Rathe said, from the doorway. "Dame, I'm sorry. I don't think he died a natural death."

Sawel's breath caught in her chest, and for an instant Eslingen thought she would wail again. But she controlled herself, just her hands closing tighter on the wet linen to betray her feelings. "That Dis-damned doctor—"

"She did her duty," Rathe said gently. "And then some, I should say. Your brother was lucky not to be worse hurt, but she did good work on his face."

Sawel nodded, her voice catching in a little hiccup before she could speak. "I'll grant her that, she did. And he was vain, Edild was, he'd have hated to have his nose set crooked…." She shook herself. "Well. Poison, she said to me. Do you believe that, too?"

"It seems most likely," Rathe said. "And in the tea he had overnight, that's the only thing that wasn't shared. I'd like to have an alchemist look at him, to be sure."

Sawel's eyes flickered closed, fresh tears running down her cheeks, but she managed to nod. "It was no one here, Adjunct Point. I can promise you that."

"We'll know more once the alchemists have seen him," Rathe said, and gestured for Eslingen to come away.

It was another hour or more before the cart arrived, though Rathe was pleased to see that Fanier had sent a closed carrier, the sort they used for the respectably dead. Sawel saw her brother's body into the back with jealous care, wrapped in thick blankets for futile cushioning, and withdrew again into her sorrow. Bellin watched her go, then gave Rathe a morose nod.

"That's good, to tell them to show respect. I'll go with him, if you'd like."

Rathe shook his head. "No, I want to be there myself. Philip?"

"I'll come, too," Eslingen said, and Bellin frowned.

"How's it the Guard's business? No offense meant, of course."

"Better not have been," Rathe said. He waited until her gaze dropped before continuing. "It might have to do with bes'Anthe's death. There are indications. No, you stay here and get a proper statement from Dr. Bael."

Bellin nodded and turned away.

"Are you sure you want to visit the deadhouse?" Rathe asked, and Eslingen gave him a crooked smile.

"Don't you know that's the very zenith of my day? I'm curious about that tea, too."

"Yeah." Rathe touched his purse reflexively, where he'd stowed a borrowed bottle filled with the tea that had been left in the pitcher. Eslingen had the box that the leaves had come from: surely that would be enough to tell them where the poison had come from, if not who had placed it there. Chills and vomiting, followed by weakness and pain and trouble breathing: he could think of two or three poisons that might cause that, but hemlock was most common among them all. That wouldn't be much help, hemlock grew like a weed along half a dozen streams just outside the city's bounds and could be purchased from any number of apothecaries, but it was at least a starting point. "Let's go."

They crossed the Hopes-Point Bridge again, the crowds diminished by the thickening clouds overhead. By the time they reached the deadhouse, the wind had risen, driving dust and leaves in swirls across the paving, and the air tasted of rain. The first drops were falling as he lifted the knocker, and beside him he heard Eslingen's martyred sigh.

"Tell me we can take a low-flyer home."

Not at that price, Rathe thought, but swallowed the words, remembering Eslingen's bruises. "Let's see."

The door swung open to reveal a girl apprentice, brass-rimmed spectacles perched on her nose to magnify bright brown eyes. "Oh. Fanier said I was to bring you back directly."

"You don't need a name?" Rathe asked, shaking off the raindrops as Eslingen crowded in behind him, and the apprentice gave him a disbelieving stare.

"Who else would you be?" she asked, closing the door, and started down the hall without waiting for an answer.

Eslingen snorted, but softly. "Good to know we've made an impression."

"Pity it's because we keep bringing them bodies," Rathe answered.

The workroom was, as always, spotless and scentless and cold, mage-lights glimmering in globes suspended above each of the tables. Only one was occupied at the moment, a strapping journeyman folding the last of Dame Sawel's blankets to set with the others waiting neatly stacked, and Fanier turned away from the body, wiping his hands on a strip of linen. He was growing a beard, as wild and white-streaked as his hair, or else, Rathe thought, he'd forgotten to shave since the last time Rathe had seen him.

"Want to tell me about this one?"

"I was hoping you'd do that," Rathe answered. "He died this morning, and the doctor who was tending him fears it was poison." He ran through the story, trying to give facts without interpretation, and at the end Fanier nodded.

"Poison, eh? Sounds plausible."

"And it makes a change from fish," the journeyman said, opening a narrow box that held her tools.

"Fish?" Eslingen said, with a look that suggested he already regretted the question.

"Two this week—five this month, pulled out of the river and all more or less eaten," the journeyman answered. "We hope by fish, because the alternatives aren't pleasant."

"That's still happening?" Rathe asked, remembering his last visit to the deadhouse.

Fanier shook his head. "The river's running high, and it's taking its time releasing the bodies. That's all."

The journeyman opened her mouth to disagree, and Fanier stared her down.

"Lay out the simulacra, please."

She hurried to obey, taking a set of small brass objects from the case and laying them carefully on the body. They were all about the size of a large walnut, and even at a distance, Rathe could identify a heart and lung and something that was probably a liver. There were more, laid in a neat pattern, and when she stepped back Fanier turned his hands palm upward, bracing himself as though he were about to lift a heavy load. The air above the body seemed to thicken, as though somehow fog had crept into the room, and in its depths, wet shapes glistened, heart, distended stomach, an eyeball, a coil of viscera. Rathe looked away, tasting bile, and was mildly relieved to see that Eslingen was looking firmly at his own shoes.

Fanier gasped, and Rathe risked a quick glance, to see the shapes dissolving into the mist. The mist itself was slower to disappear, but it was fading, thinning into wisps. "Well, your man was damned unlucky."

"Damned disliked," Eslingen murmured

Fanier shot him a look. "That, too. But what I meant was, he'd done very well to survive that beating. A hair's breadth in any direction—a hair deeper, certainly—and he wouldn't have lived to be poisoned. But that knife didn't touch anything important."

"That's what the doctor said, too," Rathe said.

"And that was a thorough beating," Fanier went on.

"There's a cracked rib here," the journeyman said, "but it's already almost healed. And of course his nose."

Fanier nodded. "With those bruises, I'd expected considerably worse."

"So there's no chance he died from that attack," Rathe said.

Fanier shook his head. "None. Which leaves sudden illness, or poison."

"Apoplexy?" the journeyman asked. "A cold stroke?"

"Faintly possible," Fanier said, "but the others fit the symptoms better. And poison fits them best of all. Which would you look for first, given the symptoms?"

The journeyman frowned. "Hemlock, I think."

"Agreed," Fanier said. "Do you know the test? Then go ahead."

The journeyman stepped closer to the table, wiping her hands on her skirts, then braced herself as Fanier had done, but with her palms turned down. She closed her eyes, concentrating, then swept her hands the length of the body, drawing a series of mirrored gestures with the heels of her hands. There was a tiny crackling sound, like someone walking on distant ice, and a momentary shiver of sparks, barely glimpsed before it was gone again. The journeyman completed her gesture, her eyes flying open.

Fanier nodded. "Hemlock, all right."

Rathe reached into his purse and brought out the stoppered bottle. "He had tea in the night, probably just before he was taken ill. This is what was left of it."

"Let's see what it tells us." Fanier took the bottle and opened it, sniffing curiously, then handed it to the journeyman. She sniffed in turn and handed it back.

"Smells like tea to me, boss."

"And to me," Fanier said. "But we'll see." He gestured over the bottle's mouth, and a brighter flicker of sparks was shaken from the air, to fall and float for a breath on the surface of the liquid. "Well, that's conclusive."

"Hemlock in the tea?" Rathe asked, reaching for his tablets.

Fanier nodded. "No question, and quite a bit of it. Your man wouldn't have needed to drink much for it to kill him."

"I'd guess he had most of a cup," Rathe said, thinking of the cup beneath the bed and the small damp patch beside the bed.

"That would be plenty." Fanier eyed the liquid warily. "Be sure we dispose of this safely, Serra. I suppose the next question is, was it added to the pitcher, or was it in the tea?"

"As it happens, I can help with that," Eslingen said, and produced the box with a flourish. "The maid said she made the tea from this—it was Dammar's own, fetched from his lodgings. I gather there wasn't much in the box to start with, and Dame Sawel made sure it was saved for him."

"Interesting," Rathe said.

Eslingen nodded. "Rather begs the question of whether he was meant to be poisoned now, or if this is some other person entirely?"

"I refuse to believe the man had that many enemies," Rathe said, but even as he spoke he knew it was possible.

Fanier gestured again, frowned, and made another gesture. "That's interesting. There are traces of hemlock in what's left—in the dust, primarily, as best I can tell—but it's not as strong as in the tea itself."

"So could it have been some mischance that he got a fatal dose in that pitcher?" Rathe couldn't keep the skepticism out of his voice, and saw Eslingen's eyebrows rise.

"Nobody puts hemlock in anything," the journeyman said. "Not even a little bit."

"Serra's right," Fanier said, "and anyway, what's there is enough to kill a man." He handed the box back to Eslingen.

Rathe sighed. "So. He died by hemlock, administered in the tea his sister's maid brewed for him to drink overnight. After someone had failed to kill him by beating him, knifing him, and throwing him in the Sier."

"When you put it that way…." Eslingen said.

"It seems unlikely that there'd be a second person who'd want to kill him, but I can't rule it out," Rathe said. "Nor can I see anyone in his sister's house trying to poison him."

Eslingen agreed. "She loved him, that's clear, and I don't see any reason for Luce or anyone else to harm him."

Which left them no better than where they'd started. Rathe swore under his breath. "We'll need to question Luce and the rest of the household, but I'm afraid you're right, I don't think they're involved. At least not knowingly...." He grimaced, thinking of lost time, and the misery of questioning a grieving house, then shook himself back to the present. "Fanier—"

"I know, you want my report as soon as possible." The alchemist sighed. "I'll do the best I can. Shall I send a copy to the surintendant as well? I know you're not entirely settled at Sighs."

"Thanks," Rathe said. "Come on, Philip, I'd better get back to Sighs."

THEY PARTED COMPANY at the foot of the Hopes-Point Bridge, Eslingen to see if any of Young Steen's friends knew anything about Jurien Trys, Rathe to return to Point of Sighs. Unsurprisingly, the main hall was full of points, the off-duty watch as well as the day-watch, Sebern sitting on the edge of the duty-point's table as she listened to their complaints. At Rathe's appearance, she slid to her feet and came to confront him, hands on hips.

"Well? What's the news?"

"Poison," Rathe said bluntly, and was meanly pleased to see the shock ripple through the company. "So says Fanier at the deadhouse, and I've no reason to doubt him."

Sebern had gone pale, her eyes wide. "Poisoned how?"

"There was hemlock in the tea he drank overnight," Rathe said. "It, the tea, came from his own lodgings—it was an expensive blend that she thought he'd like while he was getting better. And he was getting better, if he hadn't been poisoned, he would certainly have lived." He watched the gathered points as he spoke, but no one responded to that with anything but shock and horror. "And that's what we know now. Sebern, I want a word with you. Bellin, too, if she's back."

They followed him reluctantly to his workroom, Ormere at their heels to fill the kettle and stoke the fire. Rathe waved for the others to sit and leaned back to rest his shoulders against the wall. "Fanier's report is on its way, and a copy will be going to the surintendant as well. Bellin, did you hear anything of use from the family?"

Bellin shook her head. "Not a word. I'll go back tomorrow, and I'll want to look over his lodgings, but I don't think the sister or her people had anything to do with this."

"I agree," Rathe said. "And that brings us right back to where we were before. Someone wanted Edild Dammar dead. I'm asking you again, who are his enemies?"

There was a little silence, the two women exchanging glances, and then Sebern let out her breath in a frustrated sigh. "Everyone and no one, that's the problem. There are plenty of folk who hold a grudge against us, and might take it out on Dammar as the senior adjunct, but most of them wouldn't go to these lengths."

"There's also the evidence of where he was attacked," Rathe said. "Whoever beat him knew Dammar had access to Dame Havys's storage compartment—and I'd be interested if you turn up anything that suggests that Dammar himself might have been keeping something there. Someone to do with trade, someone to do with the docks, someone angry enough to try to knife him and then poison him when that doesn't work."

"It's not a pretty picture," Sebern said, "but it doesn't ring any particular bells."

"Let me go through the docks," Bellin said. "We'll get answers that way, I guarantee it."

Rathe hesitated—it might come to that, much as he hated the idea—and to his surprise, it was Sebern who shook her head. "No, Rathe's right, we need names. Let's do this gently, we can always press harder if we have to."

"Begin with the bridge," Rathe said. "Maybe someone there saw something."

Bellin nodded. "All right. I'll see to that, Adjunct Point."

"I'll see what I can do to come up with a better list," Sebern said, rising to her feet. "You might talk to Ormere, she knew him as well as anyone."

"I'll do that," Rathe said. "Thank you."

Left to himself, he leaned back in his chair, and took another drink of the tea, abruptly conscious of all the nuances of its flavor. Was it more bitter than it should be? Did his tongue and lips prickle oddly? He put the cup aside, glaring at the single drop that had splashed onto the table's worn surface. Poison did that, sowed distrust in ways that other instruments of murder did not; even if he was hated, and he thought on balance the station was getting used to him, it would be folly to poison another adjunct point so close on the heels of Dammar's death. Even so, it took him a few moments to bring himself to drink again.

He set the cup to one side and reached for Dammar's books, turned methodically to the earliest entries. Maybe another reading would give him a name, a case, some thread to pull that would loosen this tangle....

"Adjunct Point?"

He looked up to find one of the runners in the doorway, holding out a folded slip of paper.

"This came from the university, sir. Point of Dreams sent it on."

"Bring it here." Rathe took the paper, turning it over to find a wafer seal embossed with Istre b'Estorr's familiar monogram. A professional note from one of the university's more prominent necromancers—because it had to be business, or the note would have gone to his lodgings—was unlikely to be good news. His frown deepened as he read b'Estorr's note.

I'd like to talk to you about deaths by drowning. Off the books if possible.

No, that couldn't be good, but it couldn't be ignored, either. Rathe muttered a curse, and searched through the litter of slates and papers to find a suitable scrap. He scrawled an answer, promising to visit the university as soon as he could, and sealed it with one of Sighs' bright blue wafers. He found a demming, and handed it to the runner along with the note. "Take that to the university, please, and see that Magist b'Estorr gets it."

"Yes, sir," the runner said, and backed into another runner who appeared behind him. They disentangled themselves with only minor scuffling, and the newcomer shouldered her way in.

"A message from the cap'pontoise, sir."

"Thanks." Rathe took the paper and broke its seal, scowling as he read Cambrai's scrawl.

No sign yet of Trys. He seems to have gone to ground, no one's seen him in a day and a half. We'll keep looking. Meet tonight—six at the Cockerel?

Rathe swore again. No good news there, and he had worse to share: he scrawled an acknowledgement, sealed it with another of the station's wafers, and handed it back to the runner along with a couple of demmings. "Give that to the cap's man, and you find Captain vaan Esling, ask him to meet me at the Cockerel at six."

The runner ducked his head, and disappeared, and Rathe tipped his head back to stare at the ceiling. Maybe together the three of them could find some way forward.

CHAPTER 9

THE COCKEREL WAS as unprepossessing a place as it had been the first time Eslingen approached it, although at least this time it wasn't actually raining. He kept a sharp watch for puddles, and was relieved to reach the opposite side of the square without getting more than a moderate film of mud on his already dirty boots. Inside, the tavern was dark and warm and not particularly crowded, and he was unsurprised to find both Rathe and Cambrai ahead of him, tucked into a table in one of the back corners, far enough away from both the fire and the serving hatch to make them inconspicuous. Eslingen wove his way through the maze of tables, and Rathe lifted a hand in welcome.

"Philip. Any luck?"

"Nothing." Eslingen pulled out a stool, angling it slightly so that his back wasn't quite to the door. "Nobody wanted to talk to me, and the ones who finally did, they didn't have much to say."

"You were looking for Trys, too?" Cambrai asked.

"Nobody likes him," Eslingen said, "and they're all scared of him, those are the main things I learned. But what he's done, or where he is—nobody wants to touch that."

"His sister keeps a resort-house by the end of Bonfortune's Row, and Trys generally holds court in a side parlor there," Cambrai said. "But he's not been there for two nights, and his people are starting to get nervy about it. And with Dammar dead, that raises some awkward questions."

"You think Trys had something to do with poisoning Dammar?" Eslingen said, doubtfully

Cambrai shrugged.

Rathe drew shapes in a puddle of spilled wine. "There's no proof. But if Dammar was attacked because of the extortion gang, and if Trys is in fact behind it—well, he might have cause to rid himself of Dammar."

"That's a lot of ifs," Eslingen said, after a moment.

Rathe sighed. "That's what I've got."

"Dammar's a dead end, unless your people have something to say," Cambrai said, and grimaced at the inadvertent pun.

"I've got a station full of women who'd like nothing better than to sweep the docks clear of anyone who looks even slightly less than law-abiding," Rathe said. "For all his faults, Euan, Dammar was theirs—one of us."

"I won't claim him," Cambrai said, and waved a hand. "I know, you have to."

"I'd—" Rathe closed his mouth over whatever he had been going to say. *I'd rather not*, Eslingen guessed it would have been, and repressed the desire to reach out and touch his shoulder. "He was one of ours."

"And Trys is mine," Cambrai said. "He's a docker, and what he's doing is dock business."

"I can't stop my people from asking after him," Rathe said. "And if the poisoning leads his way…."

"I'll expect you to come to me with it." Cambrai shoved his stool away from the table. "We'll keep looking for Trys, and we will find him. But keep your people out of my way—and that goes for you, too, Captain."

Eslingen lifted his hands. "My business is with whoever killed bes'Anthe."

"And if that's Trys?" Cambrai glared down at him.

"Then it is my business." Eslingen matched him stare for stare.

Cambrai snorted and turned away.

Rathe swore under his breath. "The trouble is, he's right, we haven't got anything more to go on."

"No." Rathe's cup was empty, and Eslingen refilled it, then waved for the nearest server to bring a fresh cup and another pint of wine. "So what do we do now?"

Rathe glared.

Eslingen lifted a hand. "No, I meant, this must happen. What's the procedure?"

"What I said. Go back to Dame Sawel's house, question everyone there. Send my people along the docks regardless of what Euan says. Keep turning over rocks until something turns up." He made a wry face. "Enforce the laws. That'll upset business enough that someone will turn Trys in, if only to get us off her back. It's only a matter of time."

"What if I were to take some of that tea to the Staenkas' house?" Eslingen asked. "The sister said it was expensive, a special gift, they might recognize the blend—and before you say it, while they might want to murder Dammar, I can't see how they could have done it."

Rathe rubbed his chin. "That's not a bad thought, actually. And in the meantime—Istre had an unofficial question about drownings. Want to come along?"

"I could be persuaded," Eslingen answered.

THE NEXT MORNING dawned colder still, and cloudy, the mist crawling along the edges of the garden while Sunflower took his morning run. At Point of Sighs, the fog hovered over the river, forming a wall at the end of each dock, the ships lost in its depths, and Eslingen shivered in spite of the stove in Rathe's workroom. The space was larger than the room he had at Point of Sighs, and better furnished, but for once the kettle was off the hob, and the teapot, when Eslingen lifted it, proved to be dry and empty.

"I'm a bit off station tea at the moment," Rathe said, and Eslingen couldn't help but nod.

Rathe had sent a note to the university, asking b'Estorr to set a time, and the runner returned before the clock struck ten, flushed and fog-damp, carrying a reply that said the necromancer would be free until early afternoon.

"No time like the present," Eslingen said, though he was not looking forward to the walk in the rising damp, and they made their way out into the fog.

The bridge was heavily shrouded, and less crowded than usual; it was hard to see more than a house ahead, and they both clung close to the walls for fear that a cart would overtake them without warning. This was the sort of day that you might well expect murder on the bridge, and Eslingen loosened his knife in its scabbard.

Rathe gave him a sidelong glance. "Seen something?"

Eslingen shook his head. "I don't like the weather, that's all."

They were at the apex of the bridge, where there was a gap between the ranks of houses. It stretched perhaps fifteen ells, where the roadway opened out and there was nothing but a chest-high railing between the bridge and the river below. On better days, the space would be filled with peddlers, apple-sellers and broadsheet criers, maybe a fiddler playing for demmings, but today it was empty, the stones slick with damp, the water rushing beneath the span, invisible but insistent. Eslingen hesitated for an instant, listening, wondering if he'd heard the sound of hurrying feet on stone, but the river washed away all other sounds.

"Come on," Rathe said, and Eslingen saw him shiver and shift a step or two away from the railing.

The fog was no better on the Sier's northern bank, but more houses had lit mage-lights, and there were torches in iron brackets in the smaller squares. A damp bonfire burned in Temple Square, its smoke hanging low to wreath the entrance to the Pantheon, and the outdoor booksellers hadn't bothered to set up their tables. The Pantheon seemed more normal, though, merchants-venturer in rich wool visible between the ranks of the outer columns, and Eslingen told himself that was a good sign.

The university gates were mage-lit, and there was another smoky bonfire in the enclosed yard, students hovering in black-gowned knots to roast apples while gargoyles scrabbled in the leaves that had drifted against the bases of the buildings. Eslingen followed Rathe across the open space, and together they climbed the winding stair to the rooms b'Estorr held by right of his university position. The door opened at once to Rathe's knock, and b'Estorr waved them in, closing the door firmly behind them. Eslingen braced himself for the unnatural chill that always seemed to accompany the necromancer—b'Estorr's ghosts, invisible and intangible but omnipresent—but the fog-bound damp seemed to conceal their presence. Eslingen wasn't sure that wasn't more unnerving than the cold and feathery touches.

"I didn't expect you to be able to come this quickly," b'Estorr said, "but I assure you, we are grateful."

The 'we' encompassed a small graying man perched uneasily on one of the b'Estorr's carved chairs, his dark blue gown open over a suit of russet wool. The gown's corded silk had been fine once, Eslingen noted, but the hems showed years of water-stains and the slit sleeves were frayed: poverty, or just changing his coat to match the weather? The suit was in better repair, so it was hard to tell.

"This is Hannes Raunkeleyn, who holds the Disputations Chair in the Faculty of Elements," b'Estorr said. "Hannes, these are Adjunct Point Nicolas Rathe, of Point of Dreams, and Captain Philip vaan Esling of the City Guard."

"I'm attached to Point of Sighs at the moment," Rathe said. "In case that makes a difference."

b'Estorr looked at Raunkeleyn, who managed a shy smile. "No, that— if anything, it might make it better? No harm, at any rate."

"Normally I'd offer wine," b'Estorr said, "but today tea seems more appropriate."

"Sounds good," Rathe said, and perched on one of the other carved chairs.

Eslingen accepted a cup, white-glazed pottery painted with a design of ships and clouds, expensive stuff to match the furniture, and he found himself wondering if it belonged to the necromancer or to the university. At the moment, b'Estorr had left off his gown and was at ease in a scarlet house coat over plain breeches and a fine linen shirt; the coat was block-printed with black and gold flowers, and not, Eslingen thought, bargained for in the Mercandry's secondhand shops. It was rumored that the necromancer had made some small fortune in the years that he served the King of Chadron, and Eslingen guessed it might be so.

"So," Rathe said. "What was it you wanted to talk about?"

"Off the books," Raunkeleyn said. "I need that understood."

"Why?" Eslingen asked, with his most guileless stare.

Raunkeleyn looked into the depths of his cup. "My chair is called the Disputations Chair because not only must the holder defend her theses against all comers, but because the holder must represent the faculty in any internal debates. So it's extremely important that my name not be attached to any controversies for fear that someone might get the idea that the Faculty of Elements intended to begin some dispute. And I have no intention of doing so, particularly over this matter. If any of what I fear is true, it's far too important for abstract argument."

"Have you seen this pamphlet?" b'Estorr held up a copy of *The Accounting of the Drowned*.

Rathe nodded. "I have."

Raunkeleyn set his cup aside and knotted his fingers together as though to keep himself from gesturing. "Is it accurate?"

"I don't know," Rathe said. "There have been more deaths on the river than usual, but I don't know if that list is strictly accurate. I've put the question to the cap'pontoise, but he hasn't answered."

And wasn't likely to, not in his current mood, Eslingen thought.

"I'm more interested in these deaths." Raunkeleyn reached beneath his gown and brought out his own copy of the pamphlet, considerably more dog-eared than b'Estorr's. "These where she claims they were eaten by fishes."

"I have heard at the deadhouse that there have been bodies that seem to have been attacked by fish," Rathe said. "Partly eaten, in at least some cases. But that's all I know. The alchemists are rarely wrong about the causes of death, though."

"They're very accurate." Raunkeleyn rolled the pamphlet into a cylinder, then seemed to realize what he was doing and spread it out again. "I expect you've heard of the Riverdeme?"

"That's a broadsheet horror," Rathe said.

"Not originally." Raunkeleyn fingered an edge of the parchment.

"It's made a comeback," Eslingen murmured. He said, more loudly, "I wasn't born in Astreiant, so I don't know any more than I've read in the broadsheets. And what I've read—something like a mermaid that lures young men to their deaths?"

"That's what she's become," Raunkeleyn said. "Originally, the Riverdeme—she had other names, but they've been lost to time—she was a tutelary spirit, a deity whose home was in the Sier and who may have demanded sacrifices, and certainly received them, from the people who first settled on the banks here. She had a proper cult, and at least one temple, but that burned when Astreiant burned in the reign of Queen Amarial."

Eslingen lifted an eyebrow.

"That was seven hundred years ago." Rathe looked back at the scholar. "I understood she was bound by the bridges."

Raunkeleyn nodded. "That's the account we have. First the Queen's Bridge was built, and the Riverdeme could no longer travel south to the sea. She took so great a harvest of young men then that the Hopes-Point Bridge was built upstream of the Queen's Bridge. Hopes-Point was built to confine her, and the Queen's Bridge was rebuilt with new symbols to hold her on the southern end, and the cult itself was rooted out on the grounds that it had actively helped the Riverdeme claim her prey. With such a narrow hunting ground, and no help from worshippers ashore, she dwindled and disappeared. Even the greater dogfish that were her emissaries and alternate shapes vanished from the river. But now the greater dogfish have been seen again, and young men are being pulled drowned from the water."

There was a little silence when he had finished, the fog pressing against the glass. Eslingen cleared his throat. "Both those bridges are intact, and there's even two more bridges downstream of them. How can she be loose?"

"The bridge at Point of Graves was duly warded," Raunkeleyn said, with a pleased smile, "though the bridges at Customs Point were not. Apparently no one deemed it necessary. But if someone were to revive the cult, or if the warding symbols were damaged or removed—or, I suppose, if someone were to dig a channel that let the Sier flow unimpeded again.…. Yes, the Riverdeme could once again demand her tribute."

Eslingen gave Rathe a wary glance. Certainly there were more deaths, and the stories of half-eaten bodies were worrisome, but who in their right mind would revive a cult like that? To what end?

Rathe said, "It seems to me that we can only say there's proof of two things, more drownings than usual, and the return of these greater dog-fish to this part of the Sier. Does that fit your pattern?"

Raunkeleyn nodded. "And I hope that we are only at that stage of the problem. The greater dogfish are her harbingers, you see. If they are here, then either she is here, or she will not be absent much longer."

"Why not raise this in the university?" Eslingen asked. "It seems to me this is exactly the thing the university is supposed to deal with."

Raunkeleyn blushed.

b'Estorr said, "Hannes has tried to bring the matter forward. Neither his faculty nor the Provost have found the argument…convincing."

And we should? Eslingen glanced again at Rathe, and saw the same thought in the other man's eyes.

"What exactly is it you want us to do?" Rathe asked.

"I want to know if the wards on the bridges are still intact," Raunkeleyn said. "I can't exactly go climbing around the piers myself, but you have the authority. And also, you'd do well to be sure the cult isn't operating again—that would be a true disaster even if she was still trapped be-tween the bridges."

There was just enough truth in the broadsheets to make it worth look-ing. Eslingen saw Rathe sigh.

"All right. I'll have the Hopes-Point Bridge checked, and see what I can do about Queen's. And if there is a cult—what should I be looking for?"

"They'll need sacrifices for the Riverdeme," Raunkeleyn answered. "That will be the easiest way to find them. Attacking people along the river's edge."

"The points generally frown on such activity," Eslingen said, and Rathe bit his lip as though to hide a grin.

The university clock struck the hour, and Raunkeleyn bolted up out of his seat. "Sweet Sofia, I'm late! Istre, tell them anything else they need, and thank you, gentlemen—" He was buttoning up his gown as he spoke, and was gone before the clock had finished striking.

Eslingen felt his eyebrows rise

Rathe fixed the necromancer with a stare. "Istre. Are you serious?"

"He is," b'Estorr answered. "His manner's against him, Nico, but I've always found him reliable."

"Right." Rathe shook his head. "Well, it's not like we have much else to do at the moment. Tell him I'll have the bridges checked."

"Thank you," b'Estorr said. "If he says something's wrong in the river, I think you should take great care."

THEY PARTED COMPANY at the university's main gate, Eslingen claiming business with the Guard, and Rathe turned with a sigh toward the Queen's Bridge. He supposed he had known that the bridges bore signs and seals of magistical importance, but he'd assumed they had to do with the building, or with keeping the bridge intact. Now as he made his way over the high arch he found himself looking for the symbols carved into the paving, and woven along the breast-high stone railing. They all seemed intact, the carvings inlaid with what looked like weathered brass. At the center of the span, mage-lights hung to guide ships under the highest point of the arch, the bases of their stanchions etched with more signs. At least the fog had lifted enough to let him see. A few strands still coiled on the water, but most of it had retreated to hang overhead as low clouds.

The person who was most likely to know more was Cambrai: the pontoises, after all, had been founded to watch the river and its bridges, though after their last conversation, Rathe wasn't eager to talk to him. But Cambrai needed to know about the Riverdeme, and at the base of the bridge he turned south toward the pontoises' boathouse.

The yard was quieter this time, the high-tide flag still raised, its folds hanging damply in the foggy air. A young man in the pontoises' long-tailed cap was standing in the open door, and straightened at Rathe's approach.

"Pointsman!" He stopped, eyes widening. "Adjunct Point Rathe? Thank the Bull they found you."

"No one's found me," Rathe said, a cold chill running up his spine. "I was looking for the cap'pontoise."

"And he's looking for you. They've found Jurien Trys, dead between the tide lines."

Rathe swore. Trys dead, unable to talk—it was entirely too convenient, especially coming hard on the heels of the other deaths. A body between the tide lines belonged to no one—the river was properly the pontoises' jurisdiction, while the land belonged to the Points, and the tidal span was arguably both or neither. "Where?"

"Above the Queen's Bridge, at the end of the docks where the flat-boats tie up. We were taking a boat upriver ourselves, we can ferry you if you'd like."

Rathe hesitated. To arrive in the pontoises' boat was already something of a concession, but it was also the fastest way to get there. "Yes," he said, and managed to add, "Thanks."

The crew was already aboard the blunt-bowed boat, and Rathe accepted the steerswoman's hand to steady him into the stern. The pontoises remaining on the dock gave the boat a hard shove, thrusting it out into the current, and the steerswoman leaned hard on the tiller to bring the boat around so that the oars could bear. Rathe clung to the edges of his bench, water sloshing around his toes, as the oars moved for a moment in seeming chaos, women and heavy wood moving in apparently random directions, the boat rocking wildly as the current hit it. And then all sixteen oars struck the water at once, and the boat straightened, pointing upstream as the rowers put their backs into it. The steerswoman tucked the tiller under one arm and leaned down to shout in Rathe's ear.

"The tide's with us, that'll help."

The Queen's Bridge soared ahead, stark against the white sky, a sailing barge with its mast down and steering sweeps out looming in the center gap. The steerswoman eyed it, then put the tiller over, aiming the boat for the gap between the southern pier and the bank. There was plenty of room, Rathe knew, but the water rose and frothed against the stones, and he clutched the seat again as the boat slid through. The rowers' pace had never faltered.

West of the Queen's Bridge, the river widened, bending north. The water was more crowded here, a dozen small boats riding the tide, a single larger barge wallowing upriver under a broad striped sail, and Rathe was glad the fog had retreated. A runner crouched in the bow sounded what sounded like a battered hunting horn, a dissonant bleat, and the smallest boats gave way.

Their boat surged forward, flattening the low waves, and the runner sounded her horn again. The steerswoman lifted her free hand. "Hard aport!"

The right-side oars lifted, the left-side oars dug hard, and the steerswoman leaned on the tiller. The boat swung, tilting, water slipping briefly over the side as a larger wave flicked against it, and then they were facing the southern shore. A dock stretched to meet them, a single caravel tied up at the end where the water was still deep enough to hold it; to the left, a few of the smaller fishing boats were grounded on the pebbled strand, heeled sideways at awkward angles. There were people at the rails, though, and on the caravel, staring and pointing, and another great cluster of women on the strand itself, gathered around something humped on the stones. Another of the pontoises' boats was beached just beside the dock, oars laid by as the rowers milled around at its bow, not quite joining the gathering, but not quite standing apart.

The steerswoman gave quick orders, and the rowers made a few quick strokes, then shipped oars as the boat ran up onto the pebbles with a grinding sound. The runner and one of the first-rank rowers leaped out to steady it, and Rathe pushed himself cautiously to his feet. On the fishing boat, a little-captain, obviously the owner's dog, raced to the down-sloped rail and barked furiously at them until her owner caught her up and silenced her, smoothing the thick black fur.

He made his way carefully between the rowers and out onto the beach. The stones were slippery underfoot, and the beach was dotted with shallow, foul-smelling puddles. He stepped wide to avoid what he hoped was a fish's rib cage, and made his way to the group. Sebern was there, he was pleased to see, as well as Cambrai, and he nodded to both of them.

"I hear you were looking for me?"

Cambrai nodded, his mouth tight and angry, and Sebern pushed between a pair of pontoises to grab Rathe's arm.

"It's Jurien Trys, dead as a fish—they're claiming rights."

Rathe looked past her, at a body on the strand, heaped bonelessly where the water had left it. He could see a bare heel splotched with crimson—the fish had found him first—but the rest was little more than a sodden pile of rags. "What happened to him?"

"They won't let us look at him. I told them Trys was above the tide-line, and that makes him ours."

Rathe looked up the slope to see the line of debris that marked the extent of high tide, and saw her scowl.

"It was low tide when he was found—"

"He came from the river," Cambrai said. "That makes him mine."

Another territorial dispute. It took an effort for Rathe to keep his voice steady. "He's between the tide-lines, there's no arguing that, which means we both have a claim on him. The tide's coming in. I say we need to share."

"River deaths are ours—" Cambrai began.

"And land deaths belong to us. And the law says that the strand between the tides is neutral ground. I'm willing to bet this death ties in with our troubles at Sighs, and I don't intend to let that go. I'll work with you."

There was a moment when it hung in the balance, old friendship poised against older rights, and then Cambrai looked away, conceding. "We want him, too, but I'll grant it's for the same reason. All right. We'll share—but it sets no precedent."

"None at all," Rathe agreed. "Have you sent to the deadhouse?"

"We did," Sebern said. She jerked her head toward the bank, where a young woman in an alchemist's leather apron and a heavy wool coat scowled down at them. "She's waiting up there."

Rathe raised a hand to beckon, and Cambrai gave some sign to his people. One of them fetched a short ladder, and the alchemist swung herself down to the strand.

"You do know the tide's turned, right?" she asked, striding through the gathered points and pontoises as though they weren't there.

Cambrai shrugged. "You'll need to hurry, then."

"Won't be my fault if I have to move him too soon." She went to one knee in the mud, holding out a hand over the huddled body. A wide-brimmed hat was perched on her head, its feather drooping with damp, leaving her face in shadow. "I doubt he died here."

She flipped the body onto its back, unfolding the contorted limbs. They moved easily enough, Rathe saw: dead for some time, then. Coat and breeches were ripped and torn as though they'd been caught on something underwater, and the body beneath was savaged. "Drowned?" he asked.

"Maybe." The alchemist sat back on her heels. "But he was knifed, too. Not by a skilled hand. Looks like he fought back. I'll know more once we have him in the deadhouse."

"Knifed?" Cambrai asked, and the alchemist turned back the sodden layers of coat and shirt to reveal a purpled slash between two ribs. There was a set of ragged gashes further down, but those had clearly happened after death.

"Might be the cause of death," the alchemist said, cocking her head, "Or whoever stabbed him might have dropped him in the river afterward, and he might have drowned." She picked up the nearest hand, and Rathe grimaced, seeing half the fingers missing. The palm was skinned and raw and the alchemist examined it curiously.

Cambrai pointed to a ragged tear on the thigh. "That looks like a bite mark to me."

The alchemist nodded. "Fish have been at him, that's for sure. They're all after death, though."

Rathe looked at Cambrai. "If he washed up here—where would he have gone in the river?"

"This side of Hopes-Point, I'd think, or I'd expect him to be a bit more battered from passing through the gaps. What I'd like to know is how long he's been dead."

"I can't tell you here." The alchemist stood up, wiping her hands on the skirts of her coat. "I've a wagon waiting, if your people will help me get him up. We'll do a proper examination at the deadhouse, and send you word."

Cambrai gestured to Saffroy, who whistled for his people, and looked back at Rathe. "Do you want to go to the deadhouse, or shall I?"

"I think you should send someone senior, and I'll send Bellin if she's here." Rathe drew the cap'pontoise further down the beach, out of earshot. "There's something else I need to talk to you about."

"More important than this?" Cambrai didn't pull away.

"Potentially." Rathe lowered his voice even further. "Euan, you wanted me to have a word with the university. About the Riverdeme. Well, I've just come from there. And I was summoned, I didn't have to go looking."

"What?"

"You've seen that pamphlet, the *Accounting*?"

Cambrai nodded.

"It's caused some concern for at least a few scholars, and one of them is afraid that the wards on the bridges might have failed—that the Riverdeme might have wakened. You're better placed to prove or disprove that than I am."

Cambrai whistled softly. "That—she's not a lucky thing to speak of, not on the water, and especially not between the bridges. Yeah, I'll check the bridges—and sooner rather than later, Nico, I promise."

"I'd like to go with you," Rathe said. "Just let me get a word with Sebern first."

"You think it's that serious."

"I don't think we can afford to think otherwise," Rathe answered

Cambrai gave a jerky nod. "No time like the present, then, and maybe we'll spot where Trys went in the water while we're at it."

Cambrai collected his crew, and they climbed aboard, Rathe scrambling awkwardly in their wake. He settled himself in the stern, just in front of Saffroy at the tiller. Cambrai helped the rowers shove the boat back into the rising river, and then made his way past them to drop to the seat beside Rathe.

"What else did this scholar tell you?"

Rathe ran a hand through his hair, feeling the curls drawing tighter in the damp air. The fog had lifted enough that it was possible to see the full height of the bridge, and for an instant he glimpsed a dirty brass circle behind the murk. The winter-sun was up as well, a brighter pinpoint burning through the clouds. "He seems to think the Riverdeme's behind these deaths—"

"Folly," Cambrai said, not quite under his breath.

"Istre b'Estorr thinks he's worth listening to." Rathe ran through what Raunkeleyn had told them, and at the end, Cambrai shook his head.

"He's got no proof at all, bar the deaths, and they're—more than usual, certainly, but not an outrageous number."

"The alchemists are seeing bodies half-eaten by fish," Rathe said.

"Even sensible folk say they've seen the great dogfish. But, Nico, the Riverdeme's been bound for centuries. How can there be anything left of her?"

"Do I look like a philosopher?"

Cambrai reached back to tug at the knee of Saffroy's breeches. "Lay us against the middle pier if you can."

The boat surged forward with each stroke of the oars, riding the rising tide toward the bridge. From the water, it seemed even larger than usual, the spare pale stone only a little darker than the fog. The bases of the piers were stained dark by water and weeds; the upper edge of the mark was still more than an ell above the water. Iron rings hung above that, in staggered rows, and two of the rowers shipped their oars as the boat came closer. One seized a boathook, while the other crouched in the bow, eyes fixed on the pier. The boat heaved and jostled as it hit the swirl of water around the pier. The rowers grunted and lost cadence, oars flailing for an instant, and the boat tipped sideways, sending a great swirl of water over the gunwale. Cambrai swore, tipping himself and Rathe toward the other side and the boat righted itself, Saffroy cursing behind them.

"Easy, there!"

The boat swung sideways, caught in the current, and for a moment Rathe thought they were going to be pulled through the gap and have to come round somehow to try again. The rowers heaved, one last short stroke, and the woman with the boathook managed to catch one of the rings. Instantly, another pontoise sprang to help her, and the boat swung into the stones of the pier with a soggy thud.

"Fenders," Saffroy yelled.

The boat swung back—undamaged, Rathe saw, with amazed relief— and on that side the rowers dropped their oars and hastily flung what looked like sacking bolsters over the side, to cushion the boat against the pier. The rowers on the other side leaned hard to balance them.

"Hold her!" Saffroy leaned hard on the tiller, pinning the boat against the stone, and two more pontoises caught at the rings, bringing the boat at last to a kind of equilibrium. "Alongside, Cap."

"All right, Nico, let's see what we've got." Cambrai eased forward between the lines of rowers, crouching to keep the boat balanced, and Rathe followed less gracefully, not ashamed to cling to shoulders for balance. At the center of the boat, Cambrai rummaged in a compartment set between two of the rowers' benches, and came up with a mage-light lantern with a single convex lens in its tin sides. He lit it with a word, throwing a beam of light that looked thick enough to touch, and let it play across the pale stone. Rathe crouched beside him, watching the light glint off the tiny flecks of crystal caught in the rock, and then the beam settled on a square of inlaid metal about a foot across.

"That's it?"

"That's one of them." Cambrai steadied the light with an effort.

From below, the knot of tarnished-silver metal set into the stone looked untouched, the strands coiling in on each other into a twisted figure that seemed to have a hole in the very middle. The light fell across it, but the dark point at the center never brightened. All of the lines seemed unbroken, and the square itself was solidly fixed to the stone.

Cambrai let the light fall. "I don't see anything wrong there."

Rathe looked again at the rows of rings, the pontoises standing braced against the pull of the boat. There were more symbols, smaller squares and triangles, like a decorative band above the rings, and he pointed to them. "Is that part of it, too?"

"A lesser part." Cambrai swung the lantern's light along a darkened section, more worn than the square, lines and sharp angles tracing out a set of knots.

Rathe pointed quickly. "There."

Cambrai froze, the circle of light rising and falling with the river's waves, and they both stared up at the pier. One of the lines looked darker and duller than the others, as though the metal was more discolored. No, Rathe thought, it was missing altogether, there and in several other spots along the same section of the pattern, as though someone had pried away some of the strips of metal.

"I see it," Cambrai said. "And there's more."

Rathe clung to the rowers' benches as Cambrai's light picked out more gaps. None of the were very large, the largest only as long as his forefinger, but there was no denying that there were breaks. "Do you think that's what he meant?"

"The patterns are nearly intact. All these turns, they're meant to reinforce each other, to stand up to wind and water. The main seal is untouched. I don't think this would be enough."

Rathe squinted, trying to count the gaps. Cambrai was right, there were only six, maybe seven, in a band that was easily half again as long as the boat. "You wouldn't think it would be that delicate."

"I wonder what the others look like," Cambrai said, and dropped into a crouch beside the storage chest. "All right, let's check the next pier."

Rathe imitated the cap'pontoise, curling himself uncomfortably between two rowers as the boat fell away from the pier.

The piers at Hopes-Point stood in pairs, like enormous tree-trunks rising out of the river, to join in a stone arch. The keystone was marked with another seal, and Cambrai rose cautiously to his feet as the rowers backed oars, balancing the boat against the current. He played the lantern's light over its surface, but from the water it was impossible to see more than the general shape of the figure. Still, its colors were uniform, the pattern neat and symmetrical, and Rathe was fairly sure that a closer inspection would show no damage.

They pulled alongside the upstream pier, rowers again dropping oars to catch at the dangling rings, and drew the boat alongside. Cambrai found the larger seal again, its pattern the reverse of the one on the downstream pier, and once again the tarnished metal showed no gaps. There were a few more breaks in the band above the row of rings, but again, nothing that destroyed the intricate pattern.

"I just don't see it," Cambrai said, letting the light play a final time along the sharp angles. "It's what you'd expect, time and tide. If someone was trying to break the bonds, I'd think they'd have to cut straight through."

Rathe nodded. "I'll ask Raunkeleyn, but from the sound of it, he was looking for something a bit more dramatic."

Cambrai offered a wry smile. "Best check the other piers first." He waved to Saffroy, holding them pinned against the stone. "North piers, Saffroy!"

The tillerman waved back, and loosed his grip on the steering. The rowers released their rings as well, and the boat sagged away from the pier. A couple of men in a smaller boat passed them on the shore side, pulling hard against the tide, and one of them shouted something that was lost in the rush of water. Cambrai made an obscene gesture in their direction, and clutched at the nearest bench as the rowers straightened them. The current caught the boat, driving it on and through the gap beneath the bridge, to emerge in a brief flash of sunlight upriver of the bridge. Rathe looked up, counting the shops that clung to the rail overhead. Yes, there was the gap where Dammar had been thrown from the span. Not a killing drop, on this side of the pier; the man had been lucky, neither the fall nor the beating nor the knife's blow had been fatal, but someone had been determined to see him out. Poison was a surer thing than most.

Cambrai saw where he was looking. "A bad business, Nico. I do know that."

"I know." Rathe braced himself as the boat heeled against the current, Saffroy turning them back to examine another pier.

"I do have a word for you that you may find useful."

"Yeah?"

"One of my women talked to a friend of her sisters, who said she had dealings with Dammar not quite a year back. Said he'd taken payment in kind—Leaguer sprits—and she delivered the keg to him in one of the pier storage rooms."

"One that theoretically belongs to Dame Havys."

Cambrai nodded. "I'd say so."

"An easy way to lure him down there. And presumably whoever killed him wasn't going to leave anything worthwhile behind, so they cleaned it out." Rathe sighed. "Which would be more helpful if I knew what he'd kept there."

"Hard to track who's selling something when you don't know what to ask for," Cambrai said.

"And now I've lost my best lead."

"Trys?"

Rathe nodded.

"Not a nice man," Cambrai said, with restraint. "With him dead, I'm hoping this problem on the docks will fall apart. And maybe we'll turn up someone willing to talk, now that he's gone."

"One can only hope." Rathe grabbed the edge of his bench as the boat lurched and tilted sideways, Saffroy fighting the current to line them up with the northern piers. He'd spent enough time on the river as a boy that he'd thought he was comfortable in boats, but the pontoises' flat-bottomed, blunt-nosed craft were faster and nimbler than he had expected. Or else the pontoises took more chances than most: with Cambrai in charge, that was probably true.

Saffroy brought the boat alongside the northern piers, eased them slowly downriver as thy examined the inlaid seals. They looked no different from the their fellows on the southern pier, and Cambrai shook his head, letting the light play a final time across the upper seal.

"I don't see anything wrong, Nico. Which, let's face it, is good news."

Rathe laughed. "So it is, though it doesn't help explain anything."

"It's a bad autumn," Cambrai said, abruptly serious. "The weather's been against us, and there's more people looking for work, more folk willing to take stupid chances. That's what's behind most of these deaths, I'd stake money on it."

"You're probably right," Rathe said, but couldn't entirely believe it. He shook himself. "I'll talk to Raunkeleyn anyway, tell him what we've found. If he has anything more of interest, I'll pass it on."

"Thanks."

"In the meantime…." Rathe suppressed a groan, thinking of the long hours ahead of him. "I'll set my people to see if they find any connection between Trys and Dammar."

"He was the sort to take fees from the likes of Trys," Cambrai said, "but try getting that out of a Sighs pointsman."

That had too much truth not to sting, but enough to keep Rathe silent. If Dammar had had anything to do with Trys—and, like Cambrai, he found it hard to avoid the thought—it was going to be hard to persuade anyone at the station to admit knowing it. Better to start with Trys's associates, and hope one of them was feeling vindictive. "Better put me ashore. I'll let you know what I find."

CHAPTER 10

THE FOG HAD lifted a bit by the time Eslingen reached the Staenka house, both suns showing briefly through the clouds. The butler Drowe greeted him with what might have been genuine warmth. Redel was at the warehouse, he said, and Mattaes in his rooms, where he'd been since being confined to the house, but Meisenta would be happy to see him. To Eslingen's surprise, Elecia Gebellin was sitting at Meisenta's side, to the patent disapproval of the small woman stirring up the fire, but she rose to her feet as Eslingen was announced.

"I must be going, then. But I hope this is good news, Captain."

She swept out without waiting for Eslingen to answer, and out of the corner of his eye he saw the small woman scowl. Personal dislike, he wondered, or just worry Meisenta was spending too much time with another woman's leman? A maidservant, one might have said, except for the quality of her skirt and bodice, and he was careful to include her in his bow.

"Madame. Dame."

"Captain." Meisenta gestured toward the pair of chairs drawn up in front of the fire. "Dare I hope you've brought us news?"

"You've heard about Adjunct Point Dammar, then." Eslingen seated himself as the second woman straightened from the fire and came to stand beside Meisenta's chair.

"Rumor reached us," Meisenta said. "Is it true he's dead?"

"Yes." Eslingen took a breath. "He was attacked on the Hopes-Point Bridge, beaten and stabbed and thrown into the river. He survived that, but was poisoned in his sister's house. The points are looking for his killer."

"Who cannot have been Mattaes." Meisenta gave a wry smile. "You'll forgive me if I sound self-centered, but my brother's situation has to be my first concern."

"Perfectly understandable," Eslingen said. "And as far as I know, Point of Sighs is looking to Dammar's connections along the docks. This doesn't absolve Mattaes of bes'Anthe's death, I'm afraid, but this and some other troubles among the sailors makes his story seem more likely. I also came to ask a favor." Eslingen reached into his pocket to bring out the box that held the remnants of Dammar's tea. "I have a tea here that I'd like to identify, and I hoped you might help me."

"Hyris," Meisenta said. "My assistant, Captain. Hyris Telawen."

"Dame," Eslingen said, with another half-bow.

The small woman took the box from Eslingen's hand and gave it to her mistress. Meisenta worked the lid free, and bent over it cautiously. Her eyebrows rose, and she sniffed more deeply, then reached in to feel the broken leaves that were all that was left.

"I smell hemlock."

"Yes." Eslingen dipped his head.

"This was the tea that killed him?"

"The very same."

Meisenta lowered the box to her lap, frowning over it as though she could see the crumbs, then brought it to her nose again. "A good base—an expensive base, and I would guess an expensive blend. Hyris?"

Telawen took the box and sniffed at it, slanting a wary glance at Meisenta. "Hemlock, certainly."

"I don't know the blend," Meisenta said. "Do you?"

Telawen hesitated, and finally shook her head. "No, madame."

Meisenta took it from her and held it out. Eslingen retrieved it with murmured thanks. He tucked the box back into his coat pocket. He wasn't entirely sure he believed her, though, or at least if he believed Telawen. There was a wariness in the small woman's eyes that made him suspicious. When Drowe showed him out, he paused for a moment, then turned toward Point of Sighs.

Most of the tea warehouses lay a street or two back from the river, and clustered along a wider section of Ordinary Lane. There were half a dozen tea shops as well, warmly lit rooms that sold brewed tea and cakes to eat at the tables set into their bowed windows, and loose teas and blends at the counter in the back. There was an ironmonger's as well, with a great iron kettle on display in her window, and shops where you could buy fine pottery cups and even glassware: everything for the trade of tea, or at least the best of it, could be found along the lane.

There was no mistaking the Staenka warehouse, a ship between two lighthouses carved and painted above the main door, and Eslingen stepped up into another warmly lit room heavily scented with tea. There were no cakes for sale, or teas served by the pot; instead, there were two counters at the back of the shallow room, and stoves at either end where apprentices tended kettles and journeymen brewed tiny tasting pots for favored customers. The walls were covered with old-fashioned wood panels, mellow in the lamplight, and a frieze of ships and flowers and lighthouses circled the room just below the ceiling. The place spoke of money, and Eslingen caught his own posture changing in response.

A woman in a long russet gown badged with the Staenka ship came to meet him, her eyes sweeping over him to assess the cut of his coat and the value of his linen. "How may we help you—Captain, is it?"

Eslingen bowed slightly in answer. "It is. Philip vaan Esling, to see Redel Staenka. I'm sure she's busy, but I promise it won't take long."

The woman, a senior journeyman, swallowed her automatic protest, and produced a small bow of her own. "I'll see what I can do, Captain. In the meantime...."

She showed him to one of the tall tables—there were no chairs; clearly the customers here were not meant to linger—and he rested one elbow on its scratched surface while she disappeared through a door set in the wall between the two counters. The rest of the room was certainly busy, Eslingen thought. There were at least half a dozen buyers between the counters and the various tall tables, but it was striking that none of them looked particularly happy. Even as he thought that, the woman nearest him pushed a box—a sample of leaves—back toward the blue-coated journeyman, who spread her own hands in helpless apology. The first woman sighed, shaking her head, and slowly pulled the box back toward her. He had seen nothing else that made the tea merchants' troubles so clear.

The door opened again, and the senior journeyman beckoned. Eslingen followed her through the gap into a hall that smelled even more strongly of tea and mixed herbs. Ahead, he could see an opening that seemed to lead into the warehouse proper, but the woman turned aside, leading him instead up a short flight of stairs. On the left was the barred door of the counting room, a bored-looking knife cleaning his nails beside it while a gray-haired woman moved coins on a counting board. Her fingers moved so quickly that there was an almost constant whisper of silver against itself. The workroom was on the other side, and the senior journeyman tapped briskly on the door before pushing it open.

"Captain vaan Esling, dame."

"Thank you, Moll." Redel rose from behind her table and came to meet him, both hands outstretched in greeting. Eslingen took them, aware that she was not alone, that both Elecia Gebellin and d'Entrebeschaire were sitting to one side. Elecia must have taken a low-flyer, to get here so quickly, he thought, but made himself focus on Redel first. "Dame. Thank you for seeing me."

"I've been hoping for good news. Elecia told me that Dammar's been killed."

"And rather thoroughly, too, by all accounts," d'Entrebeschaire said, with a faint smile.

"Beaten and stabbed and thrown in the river," Eslingen said, "and when that didn't kill him, poisoned. You could say they made a thorough job of it, Maseigne."

"I'm sorry, I don't mean to be flippant," d'Entrebeschaire said. "Surely this is good news for Mattaes."

"It very likely is," Eslingen answered, "though it doesn't remove him from suspicion over bes'Anthe's death. If nothing else, though, I think it will make the points take a second look at bes'Anthe's other enemies."

"And by all accounts there were enough of them," Redel said, with a glance at Elecia.

"So they say," she said.

Eslingen cleared his throat. "But that wasn't the only thing I came for." He reached into his pocket and brought out the box. "I was hoping you might put a name to the maker."

"Meisenta's better at that than I am," Redel said, wiggling off the lid. "But I'll try." She sniffed it, cautiously at first and then more deeply, her brows drawing down into a puzzled frown. "Is that hemlock?"

Eslingen nodded.

"This is the tea that killed Dammar?"

"It was his particular fancy, I'm told."

"Poor bastard." Redel must have seen something change in Elecia's expression, some doubt or question, for her own brows drew down again. "I've no liking for the man, but hemlock's a bad death." She took another deep breath. "It smells more than a bit like our own Midsummer Blend. What do you think, Elecia?"

Elecia accepted the box and sniffed cautiously. "I don't know...."

"There's a definite note of berries," Redel said. "Meisenta's the one who thought of it, and we're the only house that mixes dried red berries and lad's-love. And the ordinary smells like ours."

"It's hard to tell one ordinary from another." Elecia offered the box to d'Entrabeschaire, who waved it away.

Elecia shrugged and handed the box back to Redel. "And I'd say dog-mint, rather than lad's-love. But that's just my guess."

Redel poked in the box, turning the few fragments over with her fingernail. "No, that's lad's-love, I'm almost sure, and that's red berry, or what's left of the husk, that's definitely ours. I wish there were more here, I could tell for sure if I could see the flowers." She closed the lid again, and handed it back. "But I think it is our own Midsummer Blend."

Eslingen thanked them as he tucked the box away again. "I'm guessing it's not difficult to buy."

Redel grinned. "If he bought it—more likely demanded it as a fee. It's in the shops, or you can buy it here, we'll sell to the public. But we don't make much of it, and we stop making it on the first day of the Fire Moon. A box like that, I've have expected him to have finished it long before this, not have enough left nearly three months on to make a pot of tea."

"He might have kept it for special occasions," Elecia said.

Eslingen nodded. "That's the most likely thing, of course. But if he didn't, and you stop making it—where would he have gotten it?"

"From us," Redel said. "Any one of the family…we can always blend up a batch as a favor. Or from someone who works for us—the people at the warehouse could follow the blender's book if someone wanted it badly enough."

"The people on the wharf?" d'Entrebeschaire asked.

Redel shook her head. "I wouldn't think so. They don't have access to the recipes, or to the teas, at least not easily."

"There's the tunnel," Elecia said. "They could get in that way."

"Tunnel?" Eslingen asked.

Redel offered, "The tunnel to the river—most of the big warehouses have them, to make it easier to move goods. The shore's built up a good ten feet above the water. But we keep the gates down and the chains in place when we're not actually using it, and Meisenta would fire anyone she caught using it without her permission. No, it has to be someone who actually works here, in the warehouse."

"Or who did a favor for someone," Elecia said. "That stretches things very thin."

"So it does," Eslingen said easily. "But every thread of a connection's important." Telawen had recognized the blend, he thought, and Meisenta—had not? Had lied? He suspected the latter. The lie made the thread more important, though he kept his expression polite and friendly. "Dame, I thank you for your time. And your help."

"I'll walk you out," Elecia said.

Redel nodded. "Do you have any idea when Mattaes will be allowed to walk free?"

"That's a matter for the points," Eslingen answered, "but I'll find out what I can."

"If you'll come with me?" Elecia said, turning toward the door, and Eslingen followed.

She led him past the counting-room—the woman was now writing busily in a ledger, a strongbox open beside her—and down the stairs again, but instead of turning toward the entrance, she paused at the open door that led to the warehouse itself. "Would you like a quick look? I imagine a Leaguer wouldn't have had a chance to see how a merchant resident manages her stock."

"That would be very interesting," Eslingen answered, with perfect truth, though a part of him wondered exactly what she wanted him to see, and she beckoned him to the doorway. Eslingen came to join her, looking past her into the shadowed depths that stretched almost two stories to a broad-beamed ceiling. A few mage-lights shone at irregular intervals, revealing a stand of cabinets, each of the locked sections marked with pale paper labels, single spots of light in the gloom. Beyond the cabinets, he could see wooden and iron-bound chests piled in irregular stacks. To one side, a young man in a blue coat took notes while another young man laid out rows of smaller boxes, a mage-light swinging gently above their heads, and all the way at the back of the hall, tucked into a corner not blocked by the piles of boxes, he saw another light above an iron-barred archway.

"Is that the tunnel you were talking about?"

Elecia nodded, the curling strands of hair that had worked from from her braids like lines of ink against her fair skin. "It runs straight out to the river. It's easier to bring the chests in here that way than haul them through the streets."

"I expect it would be more convenient," Eslingen said, with what he hoped was convincing disinterest. She seemed determined to draw his attention to the river access, and he wondered what she'd do if he failed to take the hint. "Can I assume, with everything that's been happening, that in another year there would be more chests stored here?"

"You can indeed," she answered, and he couldn't tell if she was happy with the change of subject or disappointed. "This is less than half what the Staenkas should have at this time of year. But at least we've had word that another shipload is on its way from Ghise."

That was one of the smaller ports south of Astreiant. "We?" Eslingen asked, and even in the poor light, he thought he saw her skin darken.

"Aucher is married to Meisenta, so of course I think of his business as mine also. And of course Meisenta has been a friend for many years."

"Of course," Eslingen echoed.

Elecia turned back toward the main door, and opened it to allow him to pass through into the shop. "I hope you'll have good news for us soon."

"So do I," he answered, and moved away.

It was late afternoon by the time he left the warehouse, the clock at Point of Sighs chiming the quarter hour. Almost five o'clock, he guessed, from the fading light, and turned toward the station. If nothing else, he needed to give Rathe his news, and with a bit of luck, they might be able to go straight to Wicked's and a decent meal. The duty point greeted him with recognition if without warmth, and sent a runner to warn Rathe; the girl returned few minutes later, wood-soled clogs loud on the stone floor.

"The adjunct says, you're to go on up, Captain."

Rathe's door was open, and he looked up from a slip of paper with a welcoming smile. The kettle was bubbling on the stove, and a pot of tea sat ready: things seemed back to normal, though Eslingen would have been willing to bet that the tea came from Rathe's own supplies.

"Have you heard our news?"

"I don't think so." Eslingen settled himself in the visitor's chair and at Rathe's nod poured himself a cup of tea.

"Trys is dead."

"Oh, that's lovely."

"Isn't it? Also stabbed, not expertly, and dumped in the river. He washed up on the mooring strand just above the Queen's Bridge. I'd say he'd been in the water at least a day, and more likely two."

Eslingen swore under his breath. "And no witnesses, no whisper of what happened?"

"Of course not." Rathe lifted the slip of paper. "And now I've got a note from the deadhouse saying that this isn't a formal report yet, but Fanier says the man was worked to exhaustion and then stabbed, and do I have any idea how that might have happened?"

Eslingen blinked. "That's different. And not precisely helpful, either."

"Not that I can see, at least not so far." Rathe drained his cup, and Eslingen refilled it. "Ah, that's better. I've got my people out searching, I've a hope they'll turn up something useful, and of course there will be a full report later, but...."

"I had a chance to ask about the tea. Meisenta said she didn't recognize it, nor did her assistant, but I asked Redel as well, and she said it was one of their own blends. They both picked up the hemlock, by the way."

"That's interesting," Rathe said. "I'd have said Meisenta was the better tea-blender of the two."

"I think she was lying. I thought the assistant recognized it, that's why I went on to the warehouse and talked to Redel. And I'm damned if I can see why."

"Something about the tea itself?" Rathe asked.

"It's their Midsummer Blend, Redel said, and they stop selling it at summer's end—at the start of the Fire Moon, she said. After that, you can only get it if you know the family, or less likely someone in the warehouse who was willing to blend it for you."

"But that assumes Dammar didn't hoard his supply," Rathe said. "Save it for special occasions."

"Exactly. And while by everything you've said he made more than the average pointsman, my impression is that he didn't live like a rich man."

"I'd say not. At least not from what I've seen here. If anything, I'd have said he was a parsimonious sort. Liked having money more than spending it. But in that case—"

"Why not just say it was your blend?" Eslingen finished. "Maybe they fee'd him for other jobs, but I can't help wondering if there wasn't some connection with the Staenkas."

"I take your point." Rathe pushed himself up from the table and went to the door. "Ormere!"

The pointswoman appeared almost before Rathe could take his seat again, a tall, mouse-haired woman with brass-rimmed spectacles sliding down her nose. She pushed them back into place. "Sir?"

"Do you know if Dammar was involved with any other business involving the Staenka family before bes'Anthe's death?" Rathe asked. "Did he take fees from them?"

Ormere frowned thoughtfully. "I don't know offhand, but if it was something small I wouldn't necessarily remember. I could go through his books if you'd like."

"Do that, please."

Another woman tapped at the office door. "Adjunct—oh, sorry, Ormere."

"I'm done," Ormere said, and backed away.

Rathe looked at the newcomer.

"News," she said. "Edelm Ammis says he's found where Trys was killed. Or he thinks he has."

"That was quick work," Rathe said. "Where?"

"An alley between two warehouses just off Bonfortune's Row. He sent a runner if you want to see it tonight."

"Oh, yes, I want," Rathe said, reaching for his jerkin. "Philip?"

"I'd very much like to come."

The runner led them through the shadowed streets, the day sun already sunk below the rooftops. They were at the eastern end of the Row, where the elegant shops and busy warehouses declined to older buildings, less well kept and less busy. Gargoyles scrabbled for trash in the gutters, and rose with a rattle of wings to perch scolding on the roof of a tumble-down shed. Eslingen picked his way carefully, grimacing at the smell of the puddles, and saw Rathe's hand on his truncheon.

"Ammis?"

"Down here!" A figure peeked around the edge of the shed, and vanished again, but Eslingen saw Rathe relax, and took his hand off his own knife.

Beyond the shed, the alley was unpaved, and sloped gently down toward what looked at first like a disintegrating stack of hay bales, but as they got closer was revealed to be a somewhat battered stone wall imperfectly padded with the hay. A two-wheeled cart was tilted against it: the reason for the hay? Eslingen wondered. He could smell the river again, mud and decay, and looked over the wall to see a narrow stretch of pebbles, the water licking at the stones perhaps ten feet below.

"Here!" Ammis called again, and Rathe pulled a mage-light from his belt, adjusted the screen to cast a fan of light across the alley's end. In its beam, Eslingen saw a young man crouching at the base of the wall, a door open beside him. Another point stood beside him, her skirts tucked up as though she'd been wading. Ammis waved, and Rathe came nearer, Eslingen keeping close on his heels. The ground was covered with what looked like relatively fresh straw, but it had been strewn seeming at random—no, had been swept away from the base of the wall, where the ground and stones were darkly stained. Some of the straw closer to the stain was also darkened and crumpled, and Eslingen sniffed cautiously, and thought he caught a faint metallic tang above the scent of mud and damp.

Rathe crouched, bringing the lantern closer, then let the light play carefully along the base of the wall.

"We don't know if it's blood, sir," Ammis said, "but it comes up red when you rub it."

"We've sent to the deadhouse," the woman said.

"I don't know your name," Rathe said, looking up at her with a smile.

"Couenter, sir. Liez Couenter. I usually work the night watch. I do think it's blood, sir."

"Philip?" Rathe said, and Eslingen bent closer. The stain ran along the wall's base and across the dirty stone sill that extended half an ell from the building, then disappeared into the packed mud. In the lamp's light, it was nearly black: if it was blood, a dying woman would have needed to lie there for at least a quarter hour—easily time enough to bleed to death, and plenty of time for a murderer to find a way to cover her tracks. He leaned back, seeing for the first time that the alley curved just enough to hide this wall from easy observation, then stooped to rub an edge of the stain. His fingertip came away faintly red, and he grimaced.

"It looks like blood to me, too."

"Trys usually holds court at Crow Hall," Couenter said, "but he was last seen at the Crown and Anchor."

"Crow Hall's not as fancy as it sounds," Ammis said. "It's a wreck of a place, at the foot of the wharf that Filipon rents."

"Not a nice place at all," Couenter agreed, "but they say he hasn't been there."

"Did you ask them yourself?" Rathe rose to his feet. The light swept over the woman's face as if by accident, but Eslingen was not deceived.

"We went in together." Couenter tucked a loose strand of hair under her cap, looking awkward. "And my mother makes compasses. They won't cross her, so they tolerate me."

Eslingen felt his eyebrows rise at that—there were so often odd overlaps between the points and the professional lawbreakers—but Rathe merely nodded. "You believe them?"

Couenter nodded. "They didn't know he was dead. It was us who brought the news."

Rathe nodded again. "And the Crown and Anchor?"

"It's a dockers' haunt, tavern and eatery and a few rooms on the second floor." That was Ammis, this time. "Hook-hand Bregit, she runs it, she said Trys came in and asked for a room for the night. She assumed he'd be meeting someone, offered to sell him a dinner as well, but he said he didn't need it. She said he wanted to be let alone, so she did just that. He was gone in the morning when she went up, but he'd left her fee on the chest."

"Did she see anyone go up?" Rathe asked.

Ammis shook his head. "It was a busy night, and she wasn't watching."

"And there's a back gate and back stairs," Couenter said. "The gate gives onto Perman's Alley. I expect that's why he hired the room there, and not at Crow Hall."

"So you think he met someone there," Rathe said. "And then—came here?"

"It's not far," Ammis said, pointing. "Just around the corner to the left. Two doors down is the alley, and it's not more than a minute's walk here."

"I think someone told him they had business here," Couenter said. "Maybe brought him to look at something in the warehouse, we found the door latched but not locked. And then they knifed him."

"And threw him in the water here?" Rathe asked.

Eslingen frowned at that himself, thinking of the strip of beach he'd seen below the wall, and Rathe rose gracefully to his feet. He paced off the distance to the wall, then leaned against it, peering down into the water. "They'd have had to do it at high tide, then."

"And in the dark." Eslingen joined him, stretching to see over the rail. The tide was close to high, and the water just touched the base of the wall, little waves lapping against the stone. "How deep would you say that is?"

"Not very," Rathe said. "And the tide's in."

"They might have had help," Ammis offered. "Someone in a boat, maybe?"

"You'd be taking a hell of a chance," Eslingen said. He leaned out, trying to see the backs of the buildings on either side of the alley. They both seemed to have windows overlooking the water, and there was certainly enough traffic on the river even at this hour to make dumping a body a risky proposition.

"But you wouldn't want to carry a body any distance either," Rathe said. "And what about this worked to exhaustion that Fanier sent?"

"Chased here?" Eslingen shook his head, rejecting the idea as soon as it had formed. "No, he left the Crown and Anchor quietly, by their account."

"Though he might have been pursued," Rathe said. "Run to ground."

Eslingen looked back at the open doorway. "What's down there?"

"Nothing much," Ammis answered.

Eslingen brushed past him to peer down the short flight of stairs. Rathe joined him, opening the mage-light's shutter, but the light showed a dirty stone floor and more wisps of straw. He glanced at Eslingen, who shrugged one shoulder. Rathe grinned, and they started down the stairs.

The ceiling was low enough that they both had to duck under the beams that held up the floor above, and from the look of those beams, draped with dusty cobwebs, the place was not in use. The floor was scuffed, though, blurred marks showing in the dirt, and the smell of the river was suddenly strong. Eslingen frowned, and Rathe said, "Ah. Look there."

He lifted the mage-light as he spoke, and light glinted from water. A straight channel about three ells wide ran the depth of the cellar, from the river wall to disappear into the shadows toward the street. There was a heavy door set in the river wall, and as Rathe raised the light, they both saw the arrangement of chains and pulleys that opened it. It was barred, a lock the size of a man's fist looped through staples on the bar and the frame, and Eslingen looked over his shoulder.

"Where does it go?"

Rathe turned the light, to find another door in the far wall. It was barred, too, though there was no lock in evidence, and Rathe said, "That's under the street. The cellar's bigger than the house." He flashed the light around again. "Well, maybe not as wide, but certainly deeper."

"Redel said there were tunnels that led to their warehouse," Eslingen said, "and it's two streets back from the river."

"I've heard of those cellar ways. But they don't reach into Point of Hopes. They're only part of Sighs."

"Convenient for moving cargo," Eslingen said, "but it doesn't look like anyone's used this one in a while. Convenient for moving a body, do you think?"

"Possible." Rathe turned, letting the light point back up the stairs to where the points waited. Without it, the cellar seemed very dark, and Eslingen was suddenly aware of the faint sound of water, of little waves whispering against stone, against the closed door. The river-smell seemed suddenly stronger, and in spite of himself he took a careful step away from the channel.

"Ammis!" Rathe swung the light again. "What about the channel here? Could they have taken the body out that way?"

Ammis stooped to peer down at them, Couenter hovering behind him.

"The door's locked and barred," she said. "And we didn't see any blood."

"You'd have almost the same problem taking the body out that way," Eslingen said. "You'd need to wait for the tide to come in—there must be a channel dug in the shore."

"Must be." Rathe flashed the light around the cellar again, a familiar dissatisfaction on his face. This didn't make any more sense to him, Eslingen thought, and he was determined to sort things out. "Come on."

Eslingen followed him back up to the street, and together they leaned over the rail. Sure enough, there was a gap in the beach beneath the house's wall, and the shadow of a door in the stone wall.

"You could do it at high tide," Eslingen said, and swung to look at the river again. As always, traffic was heavy, a barge just coming abreast of them in midstream, half a dozen smaller boats between them and it, and he shook his head. "Except someone would see you. Unless it was the middle of the night?"

"The dark would help, but the river's busy," Rathe said. "The sailors have to take the tides when they come. Though a body flat in the bottom of a boat.... Couenter!"

"Sir?" She came to join them, leaning cautiously against the rail.

"You're sure nobody took the body out that way?"

"I'm not sure. But the door—you saw it, barred and locked from this side, and it didn't look like anyone's been keeping the mechanisms in good repair. We can ask around and see if anyone saw anything."

"Or heard anything," Ammis said, joining them. "That watergate must scream like a gargoyle when it's opened."

"What about the other gate?" Rathe asked. "The inner one. Where does it go?"

Eslingen felt rather than saw Couenter stiffen, heard a quick intake of breath before she controlled herself. "There was a channel under Bonfortune's Row, it probably joins that. But it was blocked years ago—a lot of the cross channels were, the ones that run parallel to the river. Too many people were using them to rob each other's warehouses. Most of the ones that are left run south, away from the river."

"There was no lock on that door," Eslingen said, watching the woman, and saw her freeze again before she relaxed with an effort.

"But it was barred, sir, from the inside."

Eslingen glanced at Rathe, saw him shake his head slightly.

"All right. Ask around, see if any of the neighbors saw or heard anything—probably the time to consider is the last few high tides, but I leave that to you. See if you can find anyone who saw the body put in the river." He clapped Ammis lightly on the shoulder. "Good job, both of you."

"Though for all that," he said some hours later, "I'd like to know what frightened her."

"Frightened?" Eslingen tipped his head to one side. They were sitting together on their bed, a last cup of wine between them, and he leaned one shoulder against Rathe, grateful for his warmth. "I'd have said worried…." But no, "frightened" was the word, wasn't too strong at all, and Rathe met his eyes squarely.

"I think so."

"Yes." Eslingen nodded. "Yeah, I think you're right. And you're right, that raises the question of what."

"The Sier's a chancy place," Rathe said, and leaned his head against the wall. Eslingen, who had acquired most of the pillows, passed him the wine. "It always has been, and this year it's worse than most, with all this talk of the dogfish. But also her mother works on the docks. I didn't want to push her then, not knowing her family, but if her mother deals with summer-sailors and the like, she might know something useful."

"And be too afraid to share it," Eslingen said. "At least not while her fellows are listening. Someone at Sighs must know."

"I'm sure they do," Rathe said, "but I don't know who I can trust to ask." He offered the cup again; Eslingen took it and drank, then handed it back.

"There was one odd thing," Eslingen said. "I didn't have a chance to mention it before, and I don't know even if it matters, but—Elecia Gebellin and Meisenta Staenka are very close."

Rathe drained it, and stretched to set it on the chest beside the bed. "I thought you said Elecia was the vidame's leman."

"So she is."

"That's—interesting." Rathe paused, considering, his eyes as slitted as a gargoyle's against the lamplight. "Is it just an ordinary falling-out, I wonder? Lemen part ways, it's hardly unheard of."

"I'd guess d'Entrebeschaire hasn't noticed? She doesn't seem the sort who'd let it pass." Eslingen shook his head. "But I don't know what that has to do with anything, except that someone's going to regret it."

Rathe grunted agreement. "I had another idea," he said, after a moment.

"Oh?" Eslingen raised an eyebrow.

"Only I'd like to have you go along, since you heard Raunkeleyn, too."

Eslingen felt a chill creep down his spine. "What exactly are you suggesting?"

Rathe looked away. "Tell me if I'm wrong."

"Well, I would, if I knew what you were suggesting."

That earned a quick smile, little more than a flash of teeth. "Didn't Raunkeleyn say that the Riverdeme could be raised again if the flow of the river were unimpeded?"

"Yes, but you said the seals on the bridges were intact."

"Euan says they are, and he'd know. But the other thing Raunkeleyn said that could break it was if the main channel was bypassed somehow."

"The tunnels," Eslingen said, and felt the cold grip the nape of his neck again. "Where exactly do they go?"

"That's the question."

"Your point, Couenter, she said they were blocked, had been blocked for some time."

"But if they were open…. It would explain why she was nervous."

"We could go back, see what's behind that inside door." The thought of walking along the banks of an underground canal with its slippery stone banks was entirely unappealing, and Eslingen was relieved when Rathe shook his head.

"Only if we have to. And I don't want to ask Couenter, or anyone else at Sighs, not until I know more. No, I thought we could talk to Cambrai. He may well know more, the tunnels would technically have come under the pontoises' jurisdiction, and we might be able to see some of the outlets from the river itself."

"I'm not eager to go out on the water just now." Eslingen had no love for water at the best of times, or at least any water larger and wilder than the cold plunge at the bathhouse. And he had slipped once, wading in the Sier, felt the current tug with unexpected strength, hurrying him toward the center of the current. But Rathe had caught his arm, and nothing had happened.

"I don't blame you," Rathe said. "But I could use your eyes."

The pontoises' boats were sturdy, larger than the cockleshells that carried passengers from bank to bank, or along short stretches of river, and solidly made, designed to stand up to the worst the river could throw at them. Surely that would be safe enough. "I'll come," Eslingen said, before he could change his mind.

IT WAS ANOTHER foggy morning, and colder, too, so that Rathe took the time to build up the fire a little and make a pot of tea before braving the garden. When he returned, Sunflower at his heels, Eslingen was making toast, already dressed in a heavy vest and coat and his thickest stockings.

"Not exactly a day for the river," he said, and held out a piece of toast.

Rathe took it, grateful for the stove's heat against his thighs. "We should talk to Euan anyway, see what he knows about the tunnels."

The fog was lighter than the day before, the suns brassy behind the drifting clouds, and the station was busy, lines at each of the worktables and at least one of the night watch still arguing with a pair of sailors in a corner. Rathe swore under his breath, and braced himself to work through the book: nothing that the duty points hadn't handled perfectly well, but also no further news of Trys or Dammar. The man from the night watch—Luet, his name was—was giving him a begging look, and Rathe swore again, but went to join him.

"What's the trouble, then?"

The older of the sailors, a stout, graying woman in a respectable skirt and knitted jerkin, put her hands on her hips. "Our business was with Edild Dammar. They tell me he's dead? And Astarac's in child-bed."

Was it, now? Rathe swallowed the words, keeping his expression blank, and nodded. "Dammar's dead, yes. And Chief Astarac is confined to her bed. My name's Rathe, I'm adjunct in Dammar's place for now. Can I help you?"

The two exchanged glances, and then the woman lowered her voice confidingly. "I'm Josset Cade, and this is my bosun Pauterel. Am I to take it you're handling Dammar's cases, then?"

"I have his books," Rathe said, and waited. Cade matched his silence, and Rathe couldn't hold back a quick smile. "All right, Luet, I'll take this from here. You're off duty now?"

"That's right, adjunct point."

"Go on, then, and I'll leave a note for your book."

Luet nodded and moved away, and Cade took a sideways step, pulling them further away from the rest of the crowd. "Now that you mention books.... We'd made an arrangement with the adjunct, Pauterel and I, but it was off the books. So I'm wondering, would it be you we talked to, if we wanted to affirm the arrangement?"

"It depends on what you wanted," Rathe said.

"We wanted respite from those thieves of dockers," Pauterel said, and Cade frowned at him.

"And Dammar said he could provide that?" Rathe fought to keep his voice from sharpening.

"Well, not exactly," Cade said. "We hadn't encountered them when we spoke to him. But he promised to clear our unloading, and I hold that covers these people, as much as it covers the usual expenses."

"He told me he could," Pauterel said.

"He did not." Cade glared at him.

"What exactly did he say?" Rathe interjected. If Dammar had promised—it wasn't proof of a connection between him and Trys's gang, but it was a reason to start pressing harder.

"He said he knew and that he'd have a word with someone," Pauterel said. "And he meant it. I'd lay money on it."

"I take that as a two-for-a-demming broadsheet," Cade said. "Tell the adjunct what he was doing when you talked to him."

"He still said it," Pauterel said, stubbornly.

"What's she talking about?" Rathe asked.

"Ah, I ran into him as I was leaving the tavern. I practically tripped over the man. And, yeah, Captain, he was in a hurry, but he knew who I was and he knew what I asked him. And that's what he said." Pauterel crossed his arms, glaring at Cade.

Rathe glanced over his shoulder, looking for Ormere, and waved for her to come over. "I don't know if you'd heard that Jurien Trys is dead?"

Cade and Pauterel exchanged glances, the bosun's mouth drawing up as though he wanted to spit. Cade said, "I hadn't heard."

"We believe this may change matters with the dockers," Rathe said. "And if you wanted to make a proper complaint—"

"I don't know about that," Pauterel began, and Cade elbowed him to silence.

Rathe pretended he hadn't heard. "Ormere will be glad to handle it. Or if you'd prefer to make it informal, she'll make notes on the problem and see if there's anything we can do short of an actual complaint."

Cade hesitated, then shook her head. "No complaint, Adjunct, I'd rather keep this off the books. But I'll talk to her."

"That would still be useful," Rathe said, and pulled Ormere aside. "They seem to have had some arrangement with Dammar about fees and unloading. I want to know if there was any connection between Dammar and Trys, or the docker gang in general—and I mean any connection, he may have had some other arrangement for keeping his own fee-friends safe."

He saw Ormere's expression relax slightly at the excuse, though he thought she knew as well as he did that if there was any arrangement, it was most likely that Dammar had been working with the gang. "I'll do that," she said, and led the sailors away.

Rathe looked around again, hoping no one else would need him, and moved quickly to the duty desk. "I'm off down the river," he said. "Business with the pontoises. I'll be late this afternoon."

"Very good, Adjunct Point," the duty point answered, scratching a note in the daybook, and Rathe turned away, relieved to find Eslingen waiting by the river door. But not alone, he saw instantly. Standing beside him was a boy in the Guard's blue coat, warm chestnut hair bright against the coat and the clouded day. He turned his head then, and his face in profile was as beautiful as a statue's.

"Nico." Eslingen straightened at his approach. "This is Balfort de Vian, who's been assigned as my runner. You'll remember I mentioned him to you. He was sent with a message, and I thought we might find another pair of eyes useful."

Another very pretty pair of eyes. Rathe fixed Eslingen with a sharp look. "I thought you were going to keep the vidame's kinsman out of this."

"See if you can find a low-flyer," Eslingen said, to the boy, who nodded and backed away. Eslingen leaned against the door's frame, lowering his voice as he spoke. "I know you thought I should keep him clear, but he needs to earn his place in the Guard. He's got nowhere else to go, and his living to make."

"With those looks, that shouldn't be a problem."

"He wants a place in the Guard. And, as I told you, he wants to serve justice." Eslingen shrugged, miming unconcern, but his eyes narrowed. "He knows a bunch of tales of the Riverdeme—he's heard them from his sister, apparently. I thought that might be useful."

"It might." Rathe took a breath, willing himself to step back from an argument he hadn't meant to have. "But there's no room in the boat. Talk to him later."

"I'll do that," Eslingen said, and started after the boy.

CHAPTER 11

To Rathe's relief, both Saffroy and Cambrai were at the boathouse, and the four of them crowded into Cambrai's tiny workroom. Rathe explained what they had found at the spot where Trys had died, and saw Cambrai's eyebrows rise.

"I think I see where you're going with this. Those tunnels should have been blocked centuries ago, but if they've been opened—"

"They've never been opened in all the years I've worked the river," Saffroy said. "When I was an apprentice, I worked in some warehouses that had tunnels, but the cross channels were all shut off."

"Shut how?" Cambrai asked, and Rathe closed his mouth over the identical question.

"The ones I worked at had barred gates closing off the connections," Saffroy said. "Heavy ironbound wood, like sluice gates, only tall enough to reach the ceiling. And the bottom of the channel, of course. There was one that was blocked with stone, so you could see that there was a tunnel, but it was dry even at high tide."

"What would it take to qualify as 'open'?" Eslingen asked. "I mean, how much water would have to flow for the channel to count as unblocked?"

Cambrai shook his head "I don't know. Your university man might."

"Surely more than just a trickle," Rathe said. "If the river needs to flow without hindrance, then surely there has to be water in the channels at low tide, too?"

"Unless it's only unbound at the high tides," Cambrai said.

Rathe sighed. "You're right, that's a question for Raunkeleyn. I'll send a note. But in the meantime, I wondered if we might be able to see more from the river than trying to tramp through women's cellars."

"Maybe," Saffroy said. "You can certainly see the tunnel entrances, and not all of them are barred at the river end."

"I don't know," Cambrai said. "There's one or two that are only really useable at high tide, but if we see water draining, that would be an indication of water in the channel. I think."

"At least it would be a place to start looking," Rathe said. "Will you take us out, Euan?"

"I will. We'll take one of the smaller boats."

"Do you want me?" Saffroy asked, and Cambrai shook his head.

"I want you here to keep an eye on things. This shouldn't take more than an hour or two." He reached over his shoulder to snag a battered sheet of paper. It proved to be a tide chart, which he turned so that everyone could see. "In fact, we'll want to get a move on. The tide's already on the turn."

The smaller boat was flat-bottomed and blunt-bowed, like its larger sister, but it was only eight or nine feet long, and seemed far less stable. Rathe saw Eslingen hesitate at the edge of the dock, and leaned close enough to say quietly, "I thought we'd have a bigger boat. You don't have to go if you don't want."

Eslingen hesitated, then shook his head. "I'll be all right. Just don't expect me to row."

Cambrai looked up at that. "Oh, surely a big man like you could handle it?"

"I'm not much one for boats," Eslingen said, tight-lipped, but stepped carefully aboard.

"I can row," Rathe said, following, and there was an awkward moment while he and Eslingen changed seats. They ended up facing each other, with Cambrai at Rathe's back, and Saffroy released the last line and gave them a shove toward the river.

It took him a moment to match Cambrai's easy stroke, but then they hit a mutual rhythm, and Rathe leaned into the weight of the boat. It had been a while since he'd been on the river, longer still since he'd had to do any of the work, and he wished he'd brought gloves. He could feel the places where blisters would begin, and the pull of muscles he hadn't worked in years. Eslingen crouched on the bench in front of him, sitting in the exact center of the boat, his shoulders hunched and his hands closed tight on the edge of the bench. Rathe tried a smile, and got the flicker of one in return.

The tide was against them, though not as strongly yet as it would be; it took extra effort to heave the boat through the gap between the piers of the Queen's Bridge, but Cambrai steered them through, and pointed them toward the southern bank. The current eased a little there, and Rathe risked a glance over his shoulder.

"Where away?"

"Let's just take a trip up the bank," Cambrai said. "Spot the tunnel entrances, see which ones are still in use. Damn, the fog's getting worse again."

Rathe grimaced. More strands of fog were curling up from the shore, drifting across the water. The Hopes-Point Bridge was a ghostly shape in the distance, a darker shadow against the curtaining fog, the roofs of its buildings completely obscured.

"A little further inshore," Cambrai called, and Rathe copied the changed stroke. As if to emphasize it, a horn sounded from the middle of the river, low and urgent, and shouts and splashing followed it. Cambrai shipped his oars, listening, and Rathe peered through the fog, trying to see the source of the sounds. For an instant, he thought he caught sight of a ship's hull, a wall of wood rising from the water, and then the fog closed in again. A volley of curses came from upstream—a smaller boat had nearly been run down—and the horn blotted them out again.

"A bit close, that," Eslingen said, through clenched teeth.

"They're all right," Cambrai said, and bent his back to the oars again.

"I wouldn't like to take a ship downriver in this," Rathe said. "I'm surprised they're even trying. What's the hurry, this time of year?"

"They probably cast off before it got bad," Cambrai said, "and you know it's not cheap to tie up again once you're under way."

"I'd pay," Eslingen muttered, and Rathe gave him what he hoped was a reassuring smile.

"If it gets much worse...." Cambrai began, and Rathe risked another look over his shoulder.

"What?"

"We might want to tie up under Hopes-Point, wait it out. Or pull all the way up to the Chain, though I'd rather not try that unless we have to."

"It doesn't seem to be getting worse," Eslingen said, sounding doubtful, "but it's not getting better."

There was no answer to that. Cambrai steered them still closer to the shore, and a shift in the air showed pilings and the end of the dock suddenly through the fog, not quite a man's height above their heads.

"Portain's," Cambrai said. "That's the longest."

There was a ship tied up alongside, high stern outward; a dim light showed in what would be the captain's cabin. Masts and spars were bare and hung akimbo: no one had plans to go anywhere, Rathe thought, at least not soon. It was harder to see the shore, the stone wall and the buildings beyond, but there were brighter lights in the alehouse windows, and an enormous ball-shaped magelight hung from the upper windows of a warehouse, bathing the bricks in stark light even through the fog. The silk-dealer Rochendor, Rathe remembered, and the light was to keep off climbing-thieves. There was no sign of a tunnel here, though a section of stone toward the middle might have been lighter in color, a newer replacement.

The next dock was shorter, and there were several smaller ships tied up alongside, the round-hulled, single-masted craft that carried trade from the Sier's mouth and back again. Lights showed aboard all of them, and a dog barked wildly from the nearest as their boat slid by. A woman joined her at the rail, hugging the little-captain to her side to silence it, and Rathe caught the smell of her tobacco as they slipped by.

There were two doors in the next section of walled bank, both nearly completely exposed by the falling tide. One was closed by a heavy wooden door, and the other by a rusted iron grill festooned with a thick chain and a lock.

"That one I know is in use," Cambrai called. "The one with the gate. But the channel access was bricked up a long time ago."

Rathe made a noncommittal noise in answer, wishing they'd had time to talk to Raunkeleyn before starting on this expedition. Magists' work so often involved a symbol standing for the whole, a fingernail paring for a woman entire. It wasn't impossible that a missing brick would be enough to let water through and break the seal.

"That door's half rotten." Eslingen tipped his head toward the bank, and Rathe leaned forward, squinting. Eslingen was right, the door's lower edge was discolored and split, the wood as ragged as if it had been chewed, and there was a gap at least a hand-span wide between that and the sill revealed by the receding tide.

"Well, that's one," Rathe said, and Cambrai grunted agreement.

They hauled the boat around the next dock, this one occupied by a pair of barges and another of the single-masted ships. A fire blazed in an enormous brazier, and Rathe smelled melting tar and heard shouted orders, the words deadened by fog. The fog was getting thicker again, coils of it rising from the narrow strip of beach now exposed at the base of the wall, and Rathe saw Eslingen shift unhappily.

"Do we go on?"

"We're safe enough between the docks," Cambrai heaved at the oars. "There's not much traffic in this weather."

"Might be a reason for that," Eslingen said, and straightened cautiously. "Hello, there's water coming out of that one."

Rathe shipped his oars to see better. A curtain of fog had drifted between him and the shore, but he could still make out the opening, black against the gray stone. This tunnel had neither door nor grate, and sure enough a small but steady stream spilled over its sill and carved a shallow channel through the pebbles and silt.

Cambrai swore, and Rathe hastily worked his oars to hold them steady. The fog was cold on his skin, chilling in spite of the exertion.

"I'm not liking this fog," Eslingen said.

"What do you mean?" Cambrai asked.

"Aside from not wanting to be run down?" Eslingen craned his neck to look toward shore. "Something my ensign said, that fog like this comes from the Riverdeme."

"The Riverdeme is bound," Cambrai said. From the sound of it, he was clenching his teeth, though Rathe didn't turn to look. "Don't talk nonsense."

"It shouldn't be this thick," Rathe said. "Not on the river."

"Stop talking foolishness," Cambrai snapped, and as the words left his mouth a billow of fog rolled over them, cutting them off from the shore. They could no longer see the docks, either, or more than a few feet of water; even the raised stern was blurred, veiled in mist.

"Ship oars?" Rathe asked, feeling the boat waver against the current.

"No! Hold us steady," Cambrai answered. "Slow strokes, we don't want to drift back into the pier."

Rathe did as he was told, matching Cambrai's pull, and heard a splash out of time with their oars. Eslingen looked up sharply, his face pale in the dim light, pointing.

"Dogfish!"

Rathe craned to look, his oars idle, saw only a ripple in the water, moving against the tide.

"There's no such thing." Cambrai pulled hard on his oars. "Nico! Match me unless you want us over."

Rathe shook himself, lifting the oars again, and on the second try fell back into rhythm with the cap'pontoise. "Should we run ashore?"

"Make for open water," Cambrai said.

Eslingen looked up sharply. "What's that?"

The splashing was louder this time, closer, and Rathe missed his stroke, the oar kicking back painfully.

Something moved under the water, a wave lifting against the current, and vanished again. Rathe didn't dare look, concentrating on keeping the boat steady, but he saw Eslingen's head turn, scanning the surface.

"There. On my left, about two ells—"

Rathe looked to his right and saw the water rise again, a humped shape heading straight for the boat's side. For an instant, a fin broke the water like a sail, and then it was gone. A moment later, something struck the bottom of the boat, jolting them all sideways.

"It's coming again," Eslingen said. "On the other side—wait, there's two of them." He slewed sideways, scanning the water. "Three. There's another one out there."

"Oars up!" Cambrai called, and Rathe heaved the blades out of the water, turning them so that they lay parallel to the water.

The two came on, humped shapes boring toward the side of the boat. The leader's head broke the surface, and Rathe swore under his breath. It was a dogfish, but nearly an ell long, ten times the size of any he'd seen before. Great eyes gleamed in a high-arched skull, flat and silver, its teeth just visible in the water. And then it was under again, and the two together struck the boat amidships, their force tilting it sideways. The water churned as though they were trying to get purchase on the hull, to tip it, and Eslingen cried out.

Rathe felt the boat tip again, automatically leaned toward the high side to balance it, and saw the third dogfish half in the boat, hanging on to the side with wide-spread fins, the spiny frill around its thick neck erect and all its teeth showing. Water sloshed over the side, soaking their feet. Eslingen drew his knife and stabbed at it, first overhand and then, when it hissed and snapped, reversed his grip and brought the point up under the thing's out-thrust jaw. The dogfish hissed again and flipped away unharmed, splashing back into the water, and Rathe scrambled back into his place, searching for the other two.

"Above the bridge," Cambrai shouted, and Rathe risked a glance at him.

"What if we beached here? It's a hell of a lot closer."

The boat rocked again, and a second time, the dogfish slamming into the hull as though they could shatter the wood. Eslingen clung to his seat, knife ready in his other hand.

"This was always *her* territory," Cambrai said. "Above the bridge, or by the seals, that's safer."

Not that it felt all that safe, venturing out into the main current of the river in a fog so thick they could barely see the end of the boat, but if this was the Riverdeme's territory...he should trust Cambrai's instincts. He adjusted his grip on the oars, and suddenly something seemed to grab the right-hand blade. He swore, falling sideways, and Eslingen reached to steady him, keeping his own weight on the other side of the boat. Rathe flailed the oar up and down, and the weight released with a splash. He recovered his stroke, hands and back burning, felt Cambrai putting all his strength into the effort.

"They're coming again," Eslingen called.

Rathe cursed, trying to spot the moving water, and heard Eslingen swear as well.

"On my left."

As he spoke, the water erupted in froth and fish, two of the dogfish now clinging to the boat's side, working their strong tails to pull the boat down toward them. Cambrai flung himself to the high side, but he was too far away to make much difference. More water slopped into the boat, and Eslingen thrust awkwardly at the one closest to him, trying to force it overboard without tipping the boat further. Rathe leaned to his left, unable to do more than struggle to keep hold of his oar. Cambrai lifted one oar and flicked the other out of the oarlock to sweep it clumsily along the gunwale. The dogfish dropped away, and Cambrai just managed to keep hold of the oar.

"Pull, Rathe!"

Rathe straightened, dug both oars into the water. Eslingen jabbed his knife under the remaining dogfish's jaw, and the creature dropped away, leaving a smear of ichor.

"Pull!"

Rathe heaved on his oars, the boat a dead weight against the pressure of the outbound tide. His hands were burning, his back aflame, and he kept pulling, hauling the boat toward the middle of the channel. Behind him, he could hear Cambrai fighting with his own oars, but didn't dare look. Something struck the boat's stern, a resounding crack, and water rolled forward over the boat's bottom, soaking Rathe to mid calf. Eslingen had taken off his hat, was using it to scoop water out of the boat, but if there was a leak, that would never be enough—

There was a sharp snap and the boat lurched forward: Cambrai had finally gotten his oars back in place and joined the stroke. The boat lurched again, swaying—was that a final blow from a dogfish hitting the hull?— and then settled to a smoother progress. The fog thinned, too, shredding away to reveal the now-distant bank and the faint shape of the Queen's Bridge downstream.

"Can you keep the pace?" Cambrai called, and Rathe managed a nod. "Good. We'll pass the bridge and put ashore at the Chain."

THE FOG THINNED again north of the Hopes-Point Bridge, and the force of the tide seemed to ease, but Rathe was still exhausted by the time they pulled into the boathouse at the Chain Tower. He shipped oars at Cambrai's order, glad to let the pontoises pull them into the slip, and staggered clumsily ashore. Eslingen followed, his whole body drawn tight, ruined hat crumpled in his hand. Cambrai came last of all, shaking his head at the station chief who came to meet him.

"Everything's fine, Josc, we just took some water. Have someone light the fires in my workroom, and then bring a pot of tea."

From the look on the station chief's face, he didn't believe it, but he wasn't going to contradict Cambrai in front of a pointsman. Cambrai nodded briskly, and led them up two flights of stairs to an odd, wedge-shaped room with long narrow windows that overlooked the river. Not quite arrow-slits, Rathe thought, feeling faintly giddy, but close enough. A fire was already blazing in the broad hearth, and an apprentice was busy lighting the second of two braziers. On an ordinary day, that would be too much, but at the moment Rathe was grateful for the warmth.

"The tea's making, sir," the girl said, bobbing a curtsey, and hurried away.

Cambrai shut the door firmly behind them, and came to stand by the fire himself, holding out his hands, and then turning so that the heat struck legs and thighs.

"You'll have to tell them sometime," Rathe said. It wasn't what he'd meant to say; he'd planned something more diplomatic, but the cold and the reaction had him shaking, blocked more sensible comments. He was wet from the knees down, heavy cloth soaked almost through, rough and chill against his skin.

"Here," Eslingen said, and drew him closer to a brazier.

"I'll tell them once I know what it is I have to tell," Cambrai answered. "By the Bull! If that wasn't a dogfish—"

"I'd like to know what else it might be," Eslingen said.

"Those weren't the dogfish that used to steal my catch when I was a boy," Rathe said, trying to bring the conversation back to solid fact. "I'll admit they looked like the great dogfish in the broadsheets, but if that's accurate...."

"Accurate enough." Cambrai broke off as the door opened again.

Two apprentices each carried a tray, one with mugs already filled with steaming liquid, the other with a swaddled teapot and a squat square bottle that carried the remnants of a paper label. They set them on the worktable, shifting papers to make room, and Cambrai waved them impatiently away.

"And shut the door behind you!"

He waited until it had closed, then handed round the mugs. Rathe sniffed his, recognizing river-tea, brewed thick and sickly sweet, full of herbs to warm and buffer the body against shock. It tasted like honey with an unpleasant hint of something old and musty, like mushrooms, and he saw Eslingen recoil from his first sip.

"Drink up," he said, and Cambrai nodded.

"Yeah, get that down you, and then there's better waiting."

Eslingen swallowed obediently, but his expression was pained. "What is this?"

"It's good for shock and drowning. Near drowning, anyway, and we came close enough." Cambrai shook his head. "Does that mean we've got our answer, Nico?"

"That the Riverdeme is unbound?" Rathe made himself take another swallow. It would go down better before it cooled, and he could feel the shivers easing.

"I'd say the proof nearly ate us," Eslingen said. "And my hat's ruined."

"Drink," Rathe said again, not sure if that was shock or not, and looked at Cambrai. "We have to assume she's freed."

"Ordinary fish don't try to upset boats." Eslingen drained his cup with a grimace, and Rathe couldn't control a shiver. If the boat had capsized, there would have been three of them in the water, a good twenty ells from the shore; even three of the great dogfish could have made a meal of them. He saw the same knowledge in Cambrai's eyes, and swore under his breath, thinking of the bodies at the deadhouse.

"What does she want, now that she's unbound?"

Cambrai tossed back the last of his tea. "The gods only know"

"We should have brought de Vian," Eslingen said. "His sister's full of stories about the Riverdeme, some of them might be of use."

"You can get them from him later," Rathe said.

Eslingen frowned as though he hadn't heard, and poured himself a cup of the better tea. "There was something he said, about a temple and a punishment cell?"

"I know that story," Cambrai said. "You, Nico?"

Rathe shook his head. "Not that I know of."

"Centuries ago, when the Riverdeme ruled the river, she had women ashore to do her bidding, servitors, priests and congregants who'd sworn to serve her. They were powerful as queens, and if anyone disobeyed them, they'd be put in the drowning cell. That was a chamber below their temple, below the tide line, nothing in it but an old-fashioned pump. They would put an accused woman in there, and if she could pump hard enough to keep out the tide, the Riverdeme was presumed to have favored her, and she was freed. If not...." Cambrai shrugged.

"If not, she drowned," Rathe said. This was the sort of thing he'd joined the points to stand against—how fair could such a test be, for someone old or unfit, a woman weak from sickness or prison? How easy would it be to jam the pump, or leave a woman in the cell for more than one tide cycle? Without food, without drink, drenched in river water—the strongest might manage to hold back the water for a second time, but not a third.

"An ugly tale," Eslingen said.

Rathe finished the last of his tea, grimacing, and poured himself a new cup to wash the taste away. "Is this true, Euan? Was there such a place? Or is it another river-story?"

Cambrai shrugged. "I've always taken it for true—it was part of the channel system under the south bank, so they say."

"And, in theory, closed up," Eslingen said. "It seems to me there's a question we haven't asked yet, and that's precisely how the Riverdeme came to be unbound. Not by accident, I'm thinking."

To Rathe's surprise, Cambrai shook his head. "No one's paid much attention to the cross channels these last ten years or so. It's the tunnels that are in use, so they get the attention. It's just possible that enough of the barriers have eroded that the river can flow, and that's freed her. If your magist's right, Nico."

"I'll pass it on as soon as I have it," Rathe promised. "But Philip's right, there's a looming question. Did someone open the channels for her? And if so, who?"

"I can't think who'd benefit," Cambrai said. "Or how."

Eslingen put aside his second cup. "What about the dockers? That gang seems to be at the back of everything that's been going wrong lately."

Cambrai lifted an eyebrow. "He's got a point there. But I don't see how it benefits them."

"If it's one of their threats, maybe?" Rathe shook his head. "But then they'd have to have her under their control, and by all accounts, that's not really possible. But it's a place to start."

"You really expect me to go up and down the river questioning folk about the Riverdeme?" Cambrai asked. "They'll think I've run mad."

"Start with the ones who don't," Rathe said.

It was another hour before their clothes were fully dry and by then the nearest clock had struck three. There was just time to get to the university before the day's lectures ended—with a bit of luck, Raunkeleyn would be able to explain what they'd seen, perhaps even point them toward something they'd missed. He said as much to Eslingen, who nodded.

"Worth a try. But I should talk to Balfort. I'm curious what other stories he might know."

Rathe's mouth tightened, but he had to admit that Eslingen was right. They needed more information about the Riverdeme, and the old tales might have hints the university lacked. "All right."

"What do you say we meet at the baths, and Wicked's after?"

It was a peace offering, and Rathe managed a smile. "Not the Sandureigne twice in one week. There's a perfectly good bathhouse not two streets from us."

"Did I say the Sandureigne?" Eslingen asked. "They've proved they lack...discretion. Deukeyn's will do for me, and then Wicked's. I'll even pay."

"I'll hold you to that," Rathe said, and turned away.

The long walk to the university gates loosened the muscles in his back and thighs—it had been a long time since he'd rowed that far, or that hard, and he flexed his hands, the rubbed skin pulling. It could have been worse, he told himself, and shouldered through a crowd of students to ask the gatekeeper for directions to the Faculty of Elements. The woman directed him to one of the older buildings on the far side of the compound, square-built of gray stone, the elemental symbols carved over the main entrance blurred almost out of recognition by time and weather. A porter sat in the box at the base of the stairs, knitting in hand and her feet propped on a lit warming-box, and she lifted her head at Rathe's approach.

"Can I help you? This is the Faculty of Elements, you know."

Rathe put on his best smile. "Yes. I'm looking for Hannes Raunkeleyn, of this faculty—the Disputations Chair, I believe? I'd just like a brief word with him, we've spoken before."

"He's not here." The porter shook her head for emphasis, but her needles never slowed. "You might try his lodgings—the west wing of the Scholar's Hall—but I don't know if he'll be there, either. He's been very flighty of late."

Her tone invited gossip. "Has he?" Rathe asked, but before she could answer the door above her opened, and a tall woman in a deep blue gown, the chain of a senior faculty member spread across her shoulders. The porter looked back at her knitting, her back suddenly straight.

"Not here, sir."

"Thanks anyway," Rathe said, and turned away.

He had no better luck at the Scholar's Hall: Raunkeleyn had said not to expect him for dinner, and hadn't said when he might be back, though he had a lecture to give at the end of the week. He would certainly be back then—assuming nothing had gone wrong. It would probably be wise to leave a note with b'Estorr as well.

He made his way back across the university precinct to b'Estorr's lodgings, half hoping to beg a cup of tea for his trouble, but the necromancer's windows were dark. He left a note with the porter—*Need to speak with Raunkeleyn as soon as may be, on the matter he inquired about, which has acquired some urgency*—and turned back toward Point of Dreams.

IT WAS TWILIGHT by the time Eslingen arrived at the barracks, the clouds obscuring what was left of the light of the true sun. The breeze had strengthened a little, driving away the remnants of the fog, and he was grateful for its chill touch. The dogfish had been unsettling—terrifying, if he was honest with himself—and he didn't need the reminder to keep him looking warily into the shadows. It was foolish—pointless, too; the dogfish couldn't come on land, not in any telling of their story—but he imagined he could still smell the river, still feel its chill in the marrow of his bones. He was lucky his stars had not betrayed him: it would do no harm to light a stick or two of incense at Seidos's altar.

Evening stables was just ending, a last stableboy trundling a loaded wheelbarrow toward the midden, and he allowed himself the indulgence of ducking through the feed-room door. He lifted an apple from the barrel that stood waiting, and made his way down the line of stalls to where King of Thieves stood waiting. The big gelding lifted his head from his hay when Eslingen called to him and thrust his head over the stall door to make a grab for Eslingen's hat. Eslingen fended him off easily and offered the apple instead. King of Thieves lipped it delicately from his palm, then made a half-hearted lunge at his cuff buttons before settling down to finish the apple. Eslingen patted his neck, feeling the winter coat coming in, drinking in the familiar sounds and smells of the stables. He had been born here, his stars were in their exaltation here, and he felt the river's threat recede. King of Thieves snatched at his hat again, and he dodged, aware of the training sergeant's disapproval, then turned toward the barracks.

De Vian was alone in the room he shared with one of the other candidates, a branch of candles lit and a pot of tea on the worktable along with a stack of paper. He had an inkwell ready, and a disreputable pen, and perhaps a third of the sheet was covered with much-corrected writing. Eslingen tapped on the door, and de Vian started to his feet, annoyance changing to pleasure as he opened the door.

"Captain! Welcome. Would you like some tea?"

Eslingen shook his head. "I wanted a word with you—how far have you gotten with these tales?"

De Vian gave the worktable a guilty glance. "Not very. I'm no storyteller, I'm afraid." He looked back, his expression sharpening. "Did you find something, sir?"

Eslingen hesitated. He had no particular desire to relive those moments on the river, particularly not in front of the boy, but if he'd heard all those stories, maybe he'd have some useful insight. "We were attacked by what looked like great dogfish. They came at us in the fog, tried to overturn the boat, but we were able to get away."

"You're all right?" De Vian's eyes widened. "You were lucky, she always tries to take the fairest—"

"We fought them off," Eslingen said, and hoped he sounded sufficiently repressive. "We got west of the Hopes-Point Bridge, and they didn't follow. Couldn't follow, I assume."

"Yes. Hopes-Point is one end of the binding. The Queen's Bridge is the other."

"So I'd gathered."

"But you didn't see her?"

"The fish were quite enough," Eslingen said, and couldn't quite hide a shudder.

"You were lucky," de Vian said again. "She would have taken you, and there wouldn't have been anything anyone could do about it." He paused. "You're not hurt, are you? They didn't draw blood?"

"Not for want of trying."

"If they had, they could have claimed you. She could have claimed you. Elecia has a story, from Queen Amarial's time. There was a man she wanted, and she sent the dogfish to mark him, but his mother was a noble of the queen's household, and she sent him into the army instead, sent him north against the Chadroni. That kept him safe for a year and a day, but then his mother died, and his sister, and another sister, and then his aunt and her daughters, until at last he had to come home. Even then, he tried to keep away from the river, but one night, on a high spring tide, he went out, not meaning to go further than the Horse Tower. But he never came home again. They found his chewed bones at Midsummer, wedged in a sandbar below Customs Point. They only knew him by his rings."

Eslingen grimaced. Probably it was nothing, a good-son's tale embroidered beyond all resemblance to the truth. But in the wavering light, with the memory of the dogfish all too fresh, it was easy to believe. "They didn't touch me," he said, and wished he were more reassured.

"Then she can't touch you," de Vian said. "Not now. Not yet! But you must be careful."

"I fully intend to be," Eslingen said. "Which is why I want everything you know about the Riverdeme."

"I'm trying." De Vian licked his lips nervously. "Won't you come in? If you'd talk to me, I know that would help me remember."

"I have an appointment." In the distance, a clock struck six, and he grimaced. "And I'm late already."

"With Rathe."

Eslingen gave him a sharp look, not liking the note in the boy's voice. "Not your business, but—yes. With my leman."

He hoped that would be enough to silence him, but instead de Vian's mouth twisted. "He doesn't deserve you. He's no one, a southriver pointsman—"

"And I," Eslingen said, with sudden fury, "am a motherless man from Esling."

"I don't believe you! I'd be so much better for you, I'd take proper care of you, I'd never leave your side—"

"Enough!" Eslingen glared at him, and saw the boy's eyes fill with tears.

"But I love you." De Vian took two steps forward, pressed both hands against Eslingen's chest. Eslingen caught his wrists before he could move closer, and they stood frozen for an instant before Eslingen stepped back, holding the boy at arm's length.

"No, you don't," he said. "You don't even—" He stopped himself, knowing what he would have said at seventeen if someone had told him he didn't know what love was. "You don't know me—all you know is that I have a commission and fine clothes and a handsome face."

"And that you saved the stolen children two years past." De Vian tried to press closer. "You stopped the plot against the queen. Of course I love you. Only let me love you."

"That's broadsheet folly," Eslingen said. "Something out of the playhouse, fine speeches and nonsense. It's not love." He shook his head, unable to find the words, knowing that even if he did, there was nothing that he would have believed at seventeen. Love is strange and complicated, he wanted to say; it kindles quick as tinder and it takes years to ripen. This is lad's-love, quick to flower, quicker to fade: and no one in the throes of that passion ever believed it. He set de Vian firmly at arm's length. "And even if it was, I don't love you. Now. You're a decent ensign, you've earned your chance with the Guard, but if you keep this up, I'll send you packing. What I want from you is an account of the Riverdeme's stories. Can you do that?"

"Yes." De Vian swallowed hard, his face full of humiliated fury, and Eslingen pretended not to see.

"Good. Then we'll talk tomorrow." He turned away without waiting for an answer, wishing he'd handled that better—wishing Rathe had been wrong. But now all he could do was hope it blew over.

DEUKEYN'S BATHS WERE crowded: some of the theaters were still closed, Rathe guessed, recognizing any number of actors using the main pool, and he was grateful to see that Eslingen had claimed one of the two-woman tubs and was defending it against all comers. As Rathe approached, he lifted a dripping hand in greeting, and Verre Siredy rose from his haunches with a rueful smile.

"Enjoy yourselves," he said, and moved off toward the communal hot plunge.

The wooden tub was set into the stone floor, and Rathe could feel the heat beneath it as he unwound himself from his towel and climbed gingerly into the steaming water. It smelled of rosemary, good for his rubbed hands, and he slid down into the water, letting it rise over his shoulders. Deukeyn's didn't offer the privacy of the Sandureigne, or the pricey extras like wine and food, but they were far enough from the other tubs that a quiet conversation would not be overheard.

Eslingen leaned back at his end of the tub, resting his arms on the sides. His loosed hair trailed in the water. "Any luck?"

Rathe shook his head. "I left a note for him, and for Istre, too, but he's gone off, and nobody seems to know where. You?"

Eslingen looked away, mouth tightening. "Not so much, either."

"I'd have thought your pretty ensign would tie himself in knots to keep you happy."

"Not funny, Nico."

Rathe lifted his eyebrows. "I'm not to make jokes about the boy?"

It hung in the balance for an instant, and then Eslingen said, precisely, "I have been an idiot, and I'm not happy about it."

Rathe closed his mouth over his first answer. "Made advances, did he? I told you he would."

"Yes, I know you did," Eslingen said. "And, yes, he did. And I'm mortified I didn't see it coming, and he's mortified I said no, and the upshot is, I left him writing down river stories and trying not to weep, and I'm left wondering how to be rid of him gracefully, because the only cure is distance."

"You really didn't see this coming."

Eslingen's eyes fell. "I thought if I ignored it, he'd get the message."

"Oh, Philip." Rathe felt a knot ease behind his breastbone, a tightness he'd been trying to ignore. "You said it yourself, distance is the cure."

"And I'll be glad to give it to him," Eslingen said. "Maybe I'll send him to the university, let him charm the librarians out of their books."

"It may come to that," Rathe agreed. "But at least the matter's dealt with."

"For now."

"And that's good enough for me," Rathe said. "On more important matters, let me remind you, you said you'd pay for dinner, too."

Eslingen was as good as his word, paying an extra two demmings for the masseur, who worked vigorously at Rathe's back and shoulders until he felt like a well wrung rag, then adding another few demmings for a decent bottle of wine and one of Wicked's tables with its own underfoot warming box. Rathe felt as though he ought to protest, but he could feel his body finally relaxing, the abused muscles easing. He was emotionally eased as well, now that Eslingen had finally acknowledged and rejected de Vian's crush—it wasn't so much that he'd thought Eslingen would accept the boy's favors, he realized, draining a third cup of wine, but that Eslingen refused to see it. Which was Eslingen for you, and annoying, but at least there was no harm done. Rathe allowed himself a fleeting smile, and pressed his shoulder against Eslingen's as they walked home in the dark.

They hadn't spoken of the dogfish or the Riverdeme since they'd left the Chain Tower, but now as he lit the lamp the shadows seemed full of splashing and the glint of teeth. He shivered, then scowled at his own reaction, crossed deliberately to the chest in the most shadowed corner and began to shed his clothes. Eslingen hesitated by the stove.

"I might stay up a bit longer. Read some broadsheets."

"Read them in bed." Rathe didn't want to be alone even in lamplight, not with the memory of teeth and fins and fog waiting to ambush him. Eslingen stood irresolute, then shrugged and collected the lamp.

It was colder in the bedroom—someday they would buy a second stove—and they pressed close together under the heavy blankets until the sheets warmed. Rathe tried to settle, closing his eyes against the fickle lamplight, felt Eslingen shift to see more clearly, and heard the rustle of paper as he sorted through the stack. He was drifting off himself, lulled by Eslingen's warmth and the aftereffects of the baths and the wine, when Eslingen's whole body jerked sharply.

"You all right?" Rathe propped himself up on one elbow.

"Fine."

Lying so close, Rathe could feel the quickness of his breath, felt the gasp and stretch as he got himself under control, and ventured to lay a hand on the other's shoulder. "You should get some sleep."

Eslingen snorted, but reached for the lamp, quenching it and letting the broadsheets drift to the floor in a flurry of paper.

"You're picking them up in the morning," Rathe said, and was relieved to feel the other laugh softly.

They lay for a while in silence, the night closing in. In the distance, the clock at Point of Dreams struck the half-hour; the clock at the Bells struck half a minute later, a dull and muffled sound. Was it raining again? Rathe cocked his head, but couldn't tell if he was hearing rain or just a rising wind. Wind would be good, would drive away the fog.

"That was...unpleasant," he said at last, and beside him Eslingen stirred.

"How are your hands?"

"Sore. They'll heal."

Eslingen shifted, drawing Rathe's fingers gingerly into his own hands, stilled instantly when he felt Rathe flinch. "Shouldn't you bandage that?"

"Nah, let the air get at it." Rathe turned again, winding himself around Eslingen so that legs and arms and all were well entwined. They didn't often sleep like that, and he was surprised and relieved when Eslingen shifted to match him, pulling him close under the blankets. Rathe closed his eyes, but couldn't banish the memory of the dogfish hauling itself into the boat, teeth as long as a man's finger ready to rend and tear. They were more than capable of killing a woman, Fanier had the bodies to prove it, and he pressed tighter against Eslingen, feeling only smooth skin, not the scars that were visible in daylight. The dogfish would have left scars worse than anything either of them bore—if they'd survived the attack. "Those damned fish."

Eslingen's hold tightened again. "I don't like your river, Nico. More to the point, I don't think it likes me."

"It'll be better when the stars change," Rathe said, and hoped it was true.

THE MORNING DAWNED brighter and almost clear, streaks of blue showing through the clouds. The wind was up, blowing away the last traces of the previous days' fog, and plucking at Eslingen's second-best hat as he made his way toward the Guard's barracks an hour past second sunrise. Rathe was already at Point of Sighs, chivvying his people to find connections between Dammar and Trys, and waiting impatiently for Raunkeleyn or b'Estorr to answer his note, and Eslingen hoped one of those would bear fruit. After last night, he doubted anything useful would appear in de Vian's stories, but he supposed he had to inquire. He had to act as though nothing untoward had happened, that was the only way they would both get through this, but his steps lagged as he approached Manufactory Point.

The arcade in front of the barracks was empty except for a few pots of struggling flowers, the stones swept bare of dust. Most likely, de Vian would be in the stables or riding, but it was better to be sure. Eslingen made his way along the row, and stopped to knock on the door that carried the plaque painted with the boy's coat of arms. There was no answer, and he stooped to peer in the uncurtained window, but saw only the pair of neatly made beds and two small, empty tables. He straightened, heading for the stables, and paused in the side door to let his eyes adjust to the dim light.

The air carried the familiar smells of horse and sweat and hay, and two of the junior company were mucking out stalls at the end of the row. From the look of their barrow, nearly full of dirty straw and droppings, they were nearly done, and Eslingen lifted his voice.

"Hoy. Either of you seen de Vian this morning?"

The older of the pair straightened, flipping her long braid back over her shoulders, and the younger man took the chance to lean on his pitchfork.

"No, Captain, not since dinner last night."

Sendoya was in the main ring, supervising a group of riders, and Faraut leaned against the rails, watching. She pulled away at Eslingen's approach and came to meet him, a broad grin splitting her homely face.

"Captain! Good news, the Major-Sergeant talked the prices down enough that we were able to get all the horses we wanted. Including my mare."

"That is good news." Eslingen looked past her, but none of the people on horseback were de Vian. "Have you seen de Vian?"

"I thought he was supposed to be your ensign," Faraut said.

"I sent him back to barracks last night to write up a report for me," Eslingen answered. "He was supposed to have it for me this morning."

Faraut frowned. "That's not like him, he's usually too eager. Wait, Rothas might know." She lifted a hand and waved to the boy trundling the barrow toward the midden. "Taliour! Over here when you're done!"

"Yes, Sergeant." Taliour couldn't release the barrow's handles to wave back, but a few moment later he had reappeared, pulling his working coat hastily over his shoulder. "Ma'am, Captain?"

"You share de Vian's room, don't you?" Faraut asked, and the boy nodded. He was a few years older than de Vian, hardly a boy any more, really, but with the big hands and slightly wary movements of someone not quite done growing.

"Yes, Sergeant."

"I'm looking for him," Eslingen said. "He was supposed to have a report for me this morning."

Taliour hesitated. "He said something about that, yes."

Eslingen frowned, and Faraut drew herself up to her full height. "Out with it. Where's he gone?"

"He said he needed something," Taliour said. "He didn't say what."

"Start at the beginning," Eslingen suggested.

"He said he had to write something up for you," Taliour said. "He didn't say what, just that it was complicated—he was trying to remember things, and kept tearing up the papers, and finally he said he couldn't remember and he'd just have to ask. And then he put on his coat and said he'd be back before curfew, only this morning his bed hadn't been slept in."

"And you didn't see fit to report that?" Faraut demanded.

Taliour braced himself. "No, Sergeant."

"Did it occur to you that you should have done?"

"No, Sergeant."

"Faraut," Eslingen said. He didn't like the way this felt, though he couldn't have said precisely why. "Did he say where he was going? Or who he wanted to talk to?"

"No, sir." Taliour's eyes were fixed on the barracks roof. "It was something to do with your report, something he couldn't remember."

"What else did he say?" Faraut demanded.

Taliour glanced at Eslingen, then fixed his eyes on the roof again. "It wasn't anything. I didn't pay it any mind."

"What did he say?" Eslingen repeated.

Taliour wouldn't meet his eyes. "He said—he said you didn't realize what you'd asked, that you didn't understand, and if he didn't come back, it would be your doing."

"Oh, for Seidos's sake," Faraut began.

Eslingen lifted a hand. "What time did he leave?" If de Vian had been having trouble putting together the Riverdeme's stories, the logical place to go was to the person from whom he'd heard them—Elecia Gebellin. Or even to his sister, but given the amount of time Elecia seemed to spend with Meisenta, it was likely that de Vian had gone to the Staenkas' house.

"Before dinner," Taliour answered. "Curfew's not till second sunrise, I thought sure he'd be back by then—and I was abed right after myself, I expected he'd come in. And then this morning I thought he'd stayed over rather than come home in the dark."

And that might still be true, Eslingen thought. It was too soon to worry. "Do you know where his sister lives? The Vidame d'Entrebeschaire?"

Taliour shook his head. "No, sir."

"Point of Hearts?" Faraut said. "I remember Balfort saying once he was glad to have a bed here, it was a long walk to get here from the Western Reach."

"She spends a lot of time at Staenka House," Eslingen said, as much to reassure himself as to disagree. "I'll try there first, and then on the vidame's residence. If he comes back in the meantime, Faraut, keep him here."

"Yes, sir," she answered, and Eslingen turned away.

He made his best speed across the bridge at Point of Graves, skirting the gallows at its foot, the thin sun warm on his woolen coat. If de Vian had gone to the source of his stories—well, what difference did it make? By the boy's account, she would have enjoyed retelling her tales of terror; the only real risk was that she would embellish them. And yet, too many threads knotted around the Staenkas' household. Mattaes accused of murder, Dammar poisoned with one of their teas—not important, in and of itself, except that Meisenta had lied about it. And Elecia was spreading tales of the Riverdeme. To what end? That was the real question, and he had no answer. It would be wise to walk warily.

The Staenka house looked brighter in sunlight, the carving above the door more clearly marked by the fall of light and shadow. One of the servants was scrubbing the already spotless stones of the step, but sat back on his heels at Eslingen's approach.

"Captain! Can I help you, sir?"

"I'm looking for the Vidame d'Entrebeschaire. I don't suppose she's here?"

"Since Dame Meisenta married that Aucher, we never seem to get rid of her, or Dame Gebellin either." The man glanced over his shoulder, grimacing. "Which I should not have said, sir, and I'd take it kindly if you'd forget it."

"Forget what?" Eslingen asked, and the man pushed himself to his feet, reaching for the knocker.

"If you'll allow me, sir."

A moment later, the door opened, and Drowe bowed politely. "Captain vaan Esling. Won't you come in?"

Eslingen picked his way up the damp stairs, trying not to disturb the servant's work. "I'm here on an off chance—I'm looking for the vidame, if she's here?"

"She is, sir, with Dame Gebellin." Drowe waved him toward the library. "If you'll wait here, I'll fetch them."

"My business is with the vidame," Eslingen said, but didn't know if Drowe had heard or even cared. He tuned back to the bookshelves, wondering if there were any books here that had given Elecia her stories about the Riverdeme. The majority were herbals and recipe books, mixed with what might be travelers' tales and a few slim, well-worn volumes that bore only two or three letters on their spines. He started to reach for one, curious, and the door opened behind him. He turned, preparing his best smile, and saw as he had expected both d'Entrebeschaire and Elecia.

"Captain," d'Entrebeschaire said. "Drowe said you were looking for us?"

"For you, actually, Maseigne. I wanted a word with you about your brother."

"Balfort, you mean?" D'Entrebeschaire frowned lightly.

"Yes." Eslingen waited, not quite sure why he held his tongue, and Elecia rolled her eyes.

"What of him? We haven't seen him since you brought him here that other day."

D'Entrebeschaire laid a hand briefly on her arm, and she subsided. D'Entrebeschaire said, "If he was looking for me, he would have gone to my house in Hearts. I was heading there myself, if you'd care to accompany me?"

"That would be kind of you, Maseigne," Eslingen said.

"Is this really necessary?" Elecia asked. "I'm sure Captain vaan Esling can find his own way."

"I daresay, but I've business of my own to attend to. Don't fret, Elecia, I'll be back this evening."

"Please yourself," Elecia answered. "Another time, Captain."

"Dame." Eslingen bowed, but kept his eye on d'Entrebeschaire, and saw her sigh.

"Walk with me, Captain," she said.

To his surprise, she said nothing more until they had reached the street, and then it was only to suggest they take Gardeners Street. Eslingen acquiesced, matching her easy stride as they passed iron fences wound with vines. They were bare now, at the end of autumn, or held only a few tattered leaves and a withered berry, and d'Entrebeschaire snatched at a leaf as they passed.

"You took Balfort as your ensign, is that right?"

"I did."

"And consider yourself responsible for him?"

"Yes."

"Then why in Seidos' name did you let him involve himself in this matter?" D'Entrebeschaire stopped abruptly, swinging to face him. "You must have known it would only bring him trouble."

"I didn't know that you and Dame Gebellin were so close to the Staenkas," Eslingen answered. "And when I did, I offered him the chance to step away."

"Which you knew he wouldn't take." D'Entrebeschaire's voice was bitter. "He'll never go back on what he sees as his duty. Which is why I've stepped in."

Eslingen lifted his eyebrows at that, and she raised a hand to silence him.

"Yes, he came to me last night. I did not tell Elecia. Nor did I let him see her, as he wanted. I…have had some concerns about her involvement with the Staenkas, commercially and personally, and I didn't want him complicating matters any further. If, as I begin to fear, there is something amiss—I want him clear of it. He's too young and has no standing to protect him."

"He is part of the Guard," Eslingen said, mildly.

"That will only make this worse, if…if what I fear is true. I'll make you a bargain, Captain. Keep my brother out of this. Let me take him home, say he's ill, let him not be involved when your leman calls the point, and in exchange, I'll give you information you'll find useful."

"What sort of information?" Eslingen asked.

"Your word first, Captain."

Eslingen took a breath, not liking the bargain but not seeing any better option. He wondered if she knew of her brother's misplaced passion, if this was her way of dealing with that as well. "Very well, if you keep him home—if you can—I'll make sure his witness isn't required and that his name isn't mentioned. Is that enough?"

D'Entrebeschaire nodded, the stiffness leaving her shoulders. "I was— I have always been fond of Elecia, I've done everything I can for her. But this needs to end." She reached beneath her outer skirt, through an open seam hidden in the folds, and came out with a heavy iron key. "She talks too much about the Riverdeme, she dotes on every broadsheet tale and spreads new ones when she can. And she spends too much time with the Staenkas. Not just with Meisenta—don't think this is just jealousy. I know she visits the Staenka warehouse on her own, without Redel or even Aucher to keep her company. There is something very wrong there." She held out the key. "Elecia had this key to the side door cut. I don't think any of the Staenkas know she has it."

"She'll be missing it," Eslingen said, but took it, the weight heavy in his hand.

"She thinks she lost it on the river and had another one made. I don't know what she's doing, but—" D'Entrebeschaire stopped with a little gasp, then made herself go on. "Perhaps it's nothing. I pray it's nothing. But there are too many dead."

"Thank you," Eslingen said. There was more he wanted to say, to acknowledge what she was doing, the sacrifice she was making, for even if Elecia were innocent, things could never again be the same between the lemen.

"Make it quick, Captain. I can't bear the waiting." And then she had turned on her heel and stalked away up the busy street, leaving him standing with the warehouse key clutched in his hand.

CHAPTER 12

ESLINGEN MADE HIS way back toward Point of Sighs, keeping one eye out for anyone taking too close an interest in his progress. He saw no one, just the city's ordinary traffic, but he couldn't get rid of the feeling that he was being played for a fool. D'Entrebeschaire's story was all well and good—and a part of him wanted to believe it, to think that she was trying to protect her younger brother—but he couldn't let himself trust her. At the worst, it was a trap, an attempt to lure him into the river-connected tunnels where almost anything could be waiting. And that, he told himself, was why he needed to talk to Rathe: if there was a way to use this safely, Rathe would know.

To his relief, Rathe was in his workroom, frowning over a stack of papers and notes scrawled on scraps and thin bits of slate. He looked up at Eslingen's approach and waved toward the guest's chair, his expression lightening. "Have a seat. Have some tea. Care to give me a fresh eye on this mess?"

Eslingen seated himself, though he didn't pour himself any of the stewed tea that waited on the stove, and gave the papers a wary look. He thought at least one of the sheets came from the deadhouse, but it was hard to read the spidery writing upside down. "What's all this?"

"You might ask what it isn't." Rathe added a slate to what Eslingen realized was in fact a pile—in fact, what looked like chaos seemed to have some pattern to it—and then drew the deadhouse report out from under a set of similar pages. "This is Fanier's judgment on Trys. He confirms that Trys died of being stabbed, but also that he was in a state of complete exhaustion when it happened. Might not even have been conscious when he was stabbed, that's how bad it was. And now I'm really wondering about Euan's story."

Eslingen blinked, then remembered. "The drowning cell?"

Rathe nodded.

"It's a nasty thought." The idea chilled Eslingen to the marrow, and it was too easy to imagine: the narrow room, the pump, the water rising inexorably no matter how hard you labored.

"Did your runner—ensign, sorry—come up with any more tales about it?" Rathe asked.

"No. In fact, his sister's pulled him out of the business, taken him home."

"And what does the boy have to say to that?"

"I don't know, I didn't speak to him." Eslingen sighed. "Which would worry me more if I didn't suspect she was trying to cure him of an ill-advised passion."

"Always possible."

"And she gave me this." Eslingen pulled the key from his pocket and laid it on the nearest pile of papers. Rathe eyed it dubiously.

"And that unlocks?"

"The side door of the warehouse," Eslingen said. "Or so the vidame tells me. She says she took it from Elecia, who had a copy unknown to the Staenkas." He ran through what d'Entrebeschaire had told him, and when he had finished, Rathe dug a hand into his untidy hair.

"I don't like it. It's too easy. Even if d'Entrebeschaire is willing to betray her leman, there's no saying that Elecia didn't leave the key for her to find. Or that Elecia didn't put her up to it."

"Or that she's not trying to get back at Elecia," Eslingen said. "She and Meisenta are a bit close for my taste, if Elecia were my leman."

"I saw that too."

Eslingen nodded. "I don't know what to make of it, though."

"No more do I." Rathe turned the key over and over between his fingers as though that would give him some answer.

"You think it's a trap," Eslingen said, and didn't know whether he was offended or relieved to have it out in the open.

Rathe set the key down carefully, as though it were made of glass. "It's awfully convenient, Philip."

"And yet—it's what she'd do if she had to choose between her brother and a lesser-born leman."

"You believed her."

Eslingen paused, considering. "I believe she was worried for Balfort," he said at last. "That was genuine."

"But doesn't preclude laying a trap for us," Rathe said.

Eslingen inclined his head in agreement. "So what do we do? Ignore the offer? Come back in daylight?

"Daylight's no good," Rathe said. "Too many people around who won't be part of this, and if this does involve the Riverdeme and if she's been released, we'd be putting them in danger."

"Ignore it, then?"

"I think we have to chance it," Rathe said. "But not without backup."

"What if we took a troop of the Guard down with us?" Eslingen asked. "They're only expecting two of us, maybe we could overpower them—whoever they are."

"I thought of bringing people from Sighs," Rathe said, "but I don't know who to trust. And I can't send to Dreams instead without starting a feud between our stations that'd last a decade. If I was sure we were going to find something, I might risk it, but—not without more proof."

"The Guard," Eslingen suggested again, and Rathe shook his head. "No jurisdiction."

It was, regrettably, true, and Eslingen dipped his head. "The pontoises? I know you can't ask them to come with us, but could they patrol the shoreline, stand ready to help us if we signal for help? Though I'm damned if I know how we'd do that."

"I think the pontoises are our best bet," Rathe said. "And as for signals—have you ever used signal flares?"

Eslingen grimaced. "I have, and no, that's a terrible idea." The flares were fireworks warranted to give off pretty colors and shapes, intended to carry orders through the smoke and din of a battlefield, but in his experience they were mostly good for frightening horses.

"The ones they use at sea are different," Rathe said. "Self lighting, and the light carries a long way, lasts a long time—it has to, to be seen from shore, or on another ship."

"I'm still not sure how much good that does us underground," Eslingen said.

"Fire one down one of the tunnels that leads out to the river, and anyone in a boat should see the light at the tunnel's mouth. We can pick up half a dozen at any chandlers." Rathe gave a wry smile. "And it's better than nothing."

"Anything would be," Eslingen murmured. "Do you think Cambrai will do it?"

"I don't know why he wouldn't," Rathe answered. "He wants this ended as much as we do." He sorted through the scraps of paper on his desk, finally found one that seemed mostly unused. He tore off the corner that still had writing on it, dropping it tidily into the stove, scrawled something on the remaining section, and reached for a box of seals. "Ring the bell, would you?"

Eslingen obliged, and a moment later one of the station's runners opened the door.

"Adjunct?"

"Take this to the cap'pontoise," Rathe said, and held out the folded message. The girl took it with a curtsey that suggested she had received a coin with it, and disappeared again.

"What next?" Eslingen asked.

"You and I will do some shopping—I was serious about the flares—and take a blameless supper at a tavern called the Little Captain," Rathe said, and slid the key back toward Eslingen. "And then—we'll see."

THE LITTLE CAPTAIN proved to be respectable enough, though most of its patrons were dock clerks and warehouse workers, with the occasional ship's carpenter or sailmaker thrown in to remind one that this was Point of Sighs. They had found a table in the back corner, a safe distance, Eslingen hoped, from the fireplace, considering the packet of signal flares that nestled between his feet. The ordinary was, as Rathe had said, decent if uninspired, and the remains of a mutton pie lay between them, Rathe still picking idly at the gravy-soaked crust. They had split a pint of wine, also decent, were waiting now for confirmation from the pontoises before heading to the warehouse.

Even as he thought that, there was a movement in the shadows, and Saffroy—almost unrecognizable in a foppish coat and tight breeches—appeared at the table. He smiled down at Rathe and said something in a voice too low for Eslingen to hear, but Rathe nodded and laughed, and Saffroy turned away. Eslingen controlled the unworthy urge to throw a piece of crust after him, and said, "We're on?"

"We're on. Euan will have boats watching in case we get into trouble—and ready to pick us up, too, though at least the tide is with us."

"Right." Eslingen nudged the packet between his feet, heavy for its size and stuffed with magist-treated gunpowder. "I suppose we'd better get on with it."

They weren't far from the Staenka warehouse, but they took their time, looping around through the side streets so that they came up on it at an angle, along the street that would eventually lead past the side door. The main windows had all been shuttered for the night, the entrance closed, though a mage-light flickered in a cage above the arch. It would discourage thieves from trying to meddle with the locks, Eslingen thought, but he couldn't imagine that a thief would try anything so public. The street was growing quiet, only a single clerk hurrying south toward dinner or lodgings, her fast pace revealing flashes of pale stockinged ankle. The side street was darker, overshadowed by the neighboring building—another warehouse, windowless on this side, and built of solid dark stone. They crossed to the door without haste, and Eslingen drew out the key.

"Wait." Rathe drew a bit of crooked wire from his own pocket, tapped the lock with it, then drew a quick circle around the plate. When nothing happened, he said, "Go ahead, there's no magists' work on it."

Eslingen slid the key into the lock and twisted gently. The key's teeth bit the tumblers smoothly, the wards turning over with only a soft click. He caught the door before it could swing too far open, and peered inside. The hall beyond was dark, and he glanced at Rathe, who shrugged.

Eslingen eased the door back far enough to slip through. Rathe followed him, pulling the door softly closed behind them, and they stood together in the dark waiting for their eyes to adjust. It was quiet, and the air smelled pleasantly of tea and spices and paper: any watchman was in some other part of the building. "Light?"

"I think we can risk it." Rathe found his little lantern, eased back the shutter just enough to cast a dim fan across the floor. They were in a side hall, and one that seemed to be used for random storage; the passage was narrowed by boxes and baskets, and the stone floor was strewn with small shadows that might be any sort of small object.

"Someone being clever?" Eslingen stooped to examine the nearest of those shadows. It proved to be a piece of wood the size of his thumb: not enough to trip a woman, unless she was remarkably unlucky, but in the silence the crack of wood kicked against stone would be clearly audible.

"I wouldn't doubt it." Rathe let the light play along the hall, not moving himself, and gave a satisfied sigh when the light picked out another tall door. "That way."

The inner door proved to be unlocked. Eslingen eased it open, noting the well-oiled hinges, and found that it gave onto an inner corridor beneath the stairs. Tiny mage-lights glowed in sconces the size of a hen's egg, offering just enough light to see, and Rathe closed his lantern again. "Watchman's lights."

Which implies that there's a watchman, Eslingen thought. "I don't see anyone."

Rathe shrugged. "No time like the present."

Eslingen pushed the door open further and, when nothing moved in the shadows, slipped out into the hall, Rathe at his shoulder. They eased the door closed again, and Rathe looked around. "Where to?"

"The warehouse is this way," Eslingen answered. "And it's worth mentioning that Dame Gebellin made sure I knew that fact."

"Did she, indeed?"

Eslingen nodded, his own smile wry. "Which rather supports your point, yes."

"If we run into the watchman—let's hope there's only one—we found the side door unlocked and came in to warn him," Rathe said, and Eslingen nodded again.

They groped their way to the main corridor, the tiny mage-lights just enough to find their way, and paused again to listen for a watchman. The doors at each end of the corridor were closed, and Eslingen hoped they weren't locked. Surely not, surely it would take too long to lock and unlock each door, give too much time and warning to a would-be thief.

There was a soft sound, so dull and muffled that it was almost impossible to tell where it had come from. Eslingen cocked his head, but it wasn't repeated, and he looked at Rathe. "The warehouse?"

Rathe shook his head. "Upstairs."

There were only two rooms upstairs, the counting room and the workroom where he had spoken to Redel. "Into the warehouse. Better make it quick."

Rathe was moving even as he spoke, slipped noiselessly down the corridor to test the latch of the warehouse door. A satisfied smile spread across his face, and he pressed the heavy latch, leaning close to muffle any noise. The metal gave way with only the smallest of sounds, and he eased the door open.

Another noise came from upstairs, a scuffle and then the sound of feet on the stair. Eslingen flinched, tapping Rathe's shoulder. "He's coming."

"Looks clear," Rathe said, and pushed the door open further. Eslingen slid through after him, and they closed the door behind them, wincing in unison as the latch clicked into place.

The warehouse opened before them, a cavernous shadow lit by another string of watchman-lights that hung from the central beam, casting deeper shadows between the stacks of boxes. A brighter light glowed over the rows of cabinets, and another showed in the distant corner. Eslingen pointed to it.

"That's the tunnel entrance. There's a barred gate, though."

"Let's take a look." Rathe drew him toward a gap between two piles of boxes. Eslingen followed, wincing as some bit of leaf crunched beneath his shoe, and they wound their way into the maze of stored goods. There was a soft click, almost too soft to hear except that he'd been listening for it, and the light changed as the door opened again behind them. Rathe breathed a curse, and they flattened themselves together against a stack of crates, putting it between themselves and the watchman. Surely he'd only check the cabinets, Eslingen thought. It would take four or five men to steal any of the crates, and that called for an entirely different sort of patrol.

He saw light flash against the ceiling, drowning the mage-light and flicking quickly over the beams and along the stones of the wall, but there was no shout, no sound except the faint shuffle of footsteps on the stones. The light flashed again, more distant, swinging across the crates on the other side of the warehouse, and then disappeared again. Eslingen waited, head cocked to listen, and at last they heard the sound of the door closing again. Eslingen allowed himself a sigh of relief, and Rathe peered cautiously around the edge of the crates.

"It's all right, he's gone."

"That should give us some time, then," Eslingen said.

They worked their way through the stacks of crates to fetch up at last in the corner where the tunnel ended. It wasn't much, Eslingen thought, just a stone-lined basin barely large enough to hold one of the smallest river barges. The outgoing tide had left the basin almost empty, barely a foot of water covering the stones, and the same falling tide revealed that the iron grate ended a few feet above the bared surface.

"You'd think they'd take better care than that," Eslingen said, and saw Rathe nod.

"I suppose they think no one can get a boat up here, and there's nothing to steal that doesn't require a boat?" He took out his own lantern, let the beam play over the gate and its mechanism, then shuttered it again. "I think it used to come down farther."

"Or it's part of the trap," Eslingen said.

"There is that," Rathe said. "On the other hand...."

"I know." Eslingen sighed. "There's even a ladder."

It was only wooden rungs lashed to metal staples hammered between the stones, but it proved solid enough. The bottom of the basin sloped toward its center, exposing a strip a foot wide of stone and gravel, and when they crawled under the grate, the tunnel beyond showed the same thing. It would widen further as the tide continued to fall—it would be useful to see how far, Eslingen thought, see if they were open enough to free the Riverdeme. Of course, it would all be full again at high tide, but by then they should be well gone—and anyway, he told himself, the walls of the channel were barely shoulder high.

Rathe cast his light around again. "There's a footpath up there."

Sure enough, a narrow walk ran along both sides of the tunnel, not wide enough for two to go abreast, but wide enough for someone in harness to help move a boat along. Eslingen dug his own lantern out of his pocket, whispered the word to wake the fire at its heart. "On both sides, it looks like. But no ladder. We could probably climb the stones, though."

"Let's walk down here a bit," Rathe said.

"You've seen something?" Eslingen let his light follow Rathe's.

Rathe shook his head. "Just a feeling."

They followed the tunnel for some hundred ells, ears cocked for the sound of any other presence. The air was dank, and smelled of mud, but seemed clean enough—a torch would burn here, Eslingen decided, and tried to feel reassured. He could hear moving water, barely a rustle of sound, softer than their own quiet footsteps, but it was enough to make him think again about the Riverdeme. If the water flowed freely through the system, bypassing the bridges and their bindings, she might well be loosed again. At least the water here was too shallow to hide a bait fish, much less anything the size of the dogfish that had attacked the pontoises' boat.

The sound of the water was growing louder, and Rathe stopped abruptly, dropping his light so that it focussed only on the ground at his feet. "Junction."

Eslingen shuttered his own lantern, and paused to let his eyes adjust. Yes, that darker shadow ahead was indeed a break in the smooth stone wall, though there were none of the helpful watchman-lights, and he eased closer to Rathe. "Hear anything?"

"Just water."

They moved carefully down the tunnel's slope. Abruptly Rathe flung out his free arm to block the way. Eslingen froze, and then saw it. The cross channel cut through the tunnel at a greater depth, and it was full of water, water that seemed to be flowing past at a healthy clip. Someone had lashed a set of heavy beams across the western opening, enough to keep a boat from passing but not enough to slow the flow of water; on the eastern side, a wooden gate completed the tunnel wall, though the lower edge had rotted away sufficiently that the water swept through there as well.

"That's on a spring." Rathe focused his light. Metal stretched diagonally across the boards, running from near the top of the gate to another staple fixed in the wall. When enough water pressed against it, Eslingen realized, it would overcome the force of the spring and let the gate open, but once the water receded, the spring would pull it closed again.

"That can't be as old as the wood," he said, "or it would have rusted out."

Rathe nodded and turned the light left and then right, reaching out into the channel so that the light went as far as it could. Eslingen leaned more cautiously after him, but it showed nothing but water and the arched roof of the cross channel. It was brick, chipped and crumbling, with the same narrow walkway on each side of the channel.

"Which way?"

Rathe lowered the lantern. "We're very nearly in the middle of Point of Sighs, I don't know that it matters much."

"It does suggest someone's been going this way on the regular."

"Yeah."

"And look." Eslingen opened his own lantern again. "There's another ladder."

This one was just the iron staples driven between the stones, but it was strong enough to hold their weight. They clambered up onto the walkway to discover a gap just large enough to admit a grown man between the tunnel's wall and the post of the door. Rathe shone his light through, shrugged, and shuttered it again, flattening himself against the stone to wriggle his way through.

"All clear," he said, and Eslingen closed his own lantern. It was a tighter fit that he liked, the stone cold and unrelentingly solid against his back, but he managed to twist and drag himself through the gap, pulling the lantern after him. Rathe was prodding at the door.

"It swings both ways," he said. "Look. There's another spring on this side."

"And a hook here," Eslingen said, playing his own light across the walkway and the sides of the arch. "So. You were right, this section, at least, is in use."

"Lovely." Rathe eyed the water uneasily. "I'd give a great deal to know how deep that it."

"Too deep for me," Eslingen said, with more feeling than he'd meant, and he was glad that the darkness covered his blush. "Eastward?"

"Eastward," Rathe agreed.

The walkway widened as they went, until it was almost wide enough to let them walk side by side. The channel remained the same, water flowing softly in its depths, though by the marks on the stone walls, at high tide the water would nearly overflow its banks. The further they went, the more worn the brickwork seemed, mortar crumbling to leave great gaps between the stones. Eslingen heard something squeak in the depths of one of those holes, and guessed they'd become a haven for rats. Although…. He cast his light around curiously, found neither tracks nor droppings on the worn stones. Rathe looked back.

"What?"

"No sign of rats."

Rathe cocked his head, considering, and let his own light play over the walls and the walkway on the opposite bank. "That's…odd."

Every city had rats, and Astreiant was no exception, particularly along the waterfront. They were so common that they were one of the signs of the lunar zodiac, and fat, long-whiskered rats capered cheerfully on many a purse or decorated a house-sign. Even cradles, though there they were totemic, warning away the real beasts from a child born beneath their own sign…. "Rats belong to Bonfortune," Eslingen said aloud. "And he'd stand in opposition to the Riverdeme, wouldn't he?"

"The god of the merchants-venturer against the river's spirit?" Rathe considered. "You could argue that." He paused. "You think loosing her has driven off the rats?"

"I'm thinking it's possible," Eslingen answered. "At the very least, it's one more sign."

"Yeah." Rathe opened the shutter of his lantern a little further. "Look there."

The brighter beam picked out a heap of rubble half blocking the walkway. It spilled down into the channel as well, though the water ran swiftly through a gap in the rubble. "You said these channels were supposed to be closed off."

"They didn't do a very good job," Rathe said. "It doesn't actually prove anything, there are plenty of smugglers and thieves great and less who'd be very happy to make use of these tunnels. I'm surprised we haven't seen more signs of them."

"That also seems suggestive."

"Yeah."

They were close enough now to see that what had looked like a random heap of stones and dirt had once been a more solid wall, built to block the channel as much as the walkway. Now the channel was almost clear—at high tide, Eslingen guessed, you could get a boat through, though it would be scraping the highest stones—and there was a break in the stones blocking the walkway where a careful woman could work her way through. It had the look of a well-worn path, and Rathe let his light follow it around the heap of rubble.

"Looks clear enough."

Eslingen resolutely did not look at the channel to his left. The water there was only a few feet deep, though a fall on the stones would be serious. "Be careful."

Rathe hooked his lantern onto his belt and climbed carefully onto the stones, bracing himself with one hand on the rocks beside the wall. He teetered for a moment, then found his balance and stepped quickly forward, dropping out of sight as he jumped down onto the walkway.

"It's clear."

Eslingen hung his own lantern on his belt and stepped onto the first stone, then onto the second. Dirt sloped sideways ahead of him, dirt and loose pebbles ready to slide out from under him and drop him into the channel. He scowled at his fears, leaned forward to brace himself against the rocks, and took two quick steps. Pebbles slipped under his shoes, and he flung himself forward, scrambling ungracefully over the rockfall. Rathe caught his arms and steadied him onto the walkway.

"All right?"

Eslingen nodded, not quite trusting his voice, and busied himself with his lantern. The channel was much the same on this side of the barrier, the long channel running straight between the paired walkways, the brick walls interrupted by arches of darker stone. The air was different, though, smelled more of the riverside, of rotten fish and decaying mud, and he couldn't help wrinkling his nose.

"I smell it, too," Rathe said.

"Lovely," Eslingen muttered, but followed him along the walkway.

The smell grew stronger as they went: something was unmistakably dead nearby, and had been for some time. Eslingen drew out his handkerchief and pressed it to his mouth and nose, wishing it carried more scent, and ahead of him Rathe gagged, and turned it into an unconvincing cough. They were approaching a tunnel—no, Eslingen realized, not really a tunnel, there was no connection to the river, but a break in the channel wall, one just large enough to hold one of the two-woman lighters that carried small cargos to and from ships moored away from the docks, and as they got closer, Eslingen could see that the gap in the walkway had been spanned by a wooden grate.

The smell was so thick and rotten, that Rathe pinched his nose shut, cupping his palm over his open mouth, then went to one knee at the edge of the grating. "Astree's—"

He broke off, gagging again, and Eslingen pressed his handkerchief tighter to his mouth. Rathe's light swept the gap below, picked out a hump of clothes and torn flesh lying in the foot-deep water—a man's body, Eslingen thought, but you'd know it only by the clothes. He focused his own light, and found a second body, caught on a sloping ledge just short of the water. Another man, a sailor by his cap and the shredded jersey, though the head had fallen back at an angle that left the face mercifully in shadow. His torso had been ripped open from chin to crotch, what was left of guts and organs spilling out as though the fish had been at him—as though he had been fresh catch, Eslingen thought, swallowing bile, gutted on the fishmonger's slab.

"What now?"

"Nothing we can do for them," Rathe said, his voice muffled, "and there's no way to get down there to see who they were."

Thank Seidos for that, Eslingen thought, but the thought of searching those bodies, stinking and devastated, was beyond him.

Rathe let his light play over the grate, searching for breaks or weakness, then grabbed Eslingen's arm. Eslingen braced himself, leaning back as Rathe put his weight on the wood. It held, and Rathe nodded, clapping his hand over his mouth again. "We go on."

They crossed the grate without incident, following the channel as it curved gently to the south. They were following the line of the river as it bent toward Point of Graves, Eslingen guessed, and wondered how long they'd been walking. Certainly the tide was still running out, the water falling in the channel: plenty of time left, he told himself, but he wasn't sorry to cross another tunnel. It was closed by barred gates, but there was enough space between the edge of the grate and the channel walls for them to squeeze through. The tunnel was nearly dry, the channel cut deeper than its silted bottom, and it was easy enough to climb down and cross the tunnel dry-shod. There was even another ladder on the far side, and Rathe paused to examine it and the gate closely.

"I'd say this one was in regular use. I wonder where it goes." He turned his light down the tunnel, looking for house-marks on the walls, shook his head when he found none.

Eslingen shrugged. He'd lost all sense of how the underground passages matched the streets and buildings above, was grateful that the channel had been a single path so far. "Those men back there—sailors, I think?"

"I'd say so, yeah." Rathe hauled himself up the ladder to the channel's walkway.

"What do you think killed them?" Eslingen climbed up after him, pulled the lantern from his belt to examine the path ahead. It looked exactly the same as the areas they'd already passed through, and he suppressed a sigh.

"I couldn't tell." Rathe did the same, carefully not meeting his eyes. "What we saw—that could have been done after they were dead."

"But by what? Fish?"

"We're both thinking dogfish," Rathe said.

Eslingen glanced at the water in the channel. It looked deeper here, the current moving more smoothly over the stones. Still not deep enough for one of the big dogfish, he told himself firmly, and made himself look away.

The tunnel receded behind them, and the channel made a sharper turn, the water running more quietly in its bed. The light from Rathe's lantern found a set of chalked symbols on one of the arches, and a heavy iron ring set into the side of the channel.

"Smuggler's marks," Rathe said, frowning. "But not—that one should be 'safe anchor' but it's been scored through."

Sure enough, someone had crossed out the mark with two slashes of chalk, bright and new-looking in the lantern light. "Trys, do you think?"

"Or someone who didn't want to deal with him. Or who was afraid of the rumors."

"I'm starting to think they're more than broadsheet fare," Eslingen said, and his tone wasn't as light as he had intended. "This feels different, Nico."

Rathe nodded. "A little further. We've still an hour or so before the tide turns."

That was encouraging to hear. Eslingen opened his lantern a little further, but the light seemed puny against the darkness ahead, shadows that seemed somehow darker than before. The air was different, too, smelled not of mud and decay, or even of the bodies they had passed, but something heavy, vegetal, like the heaps of waterweed left to decay on the river's banks after the spring tides. There was salt, too, and an iron tang, like old blood.

Ahead, the channel widened suddenly, ended not at the edge of a tunnel but a sudden circular basin nearly fifteen ells across. Arches crisscrossed an enormous dome, and as Eslingen looked up, he thought he could see a paler circle at the height of the ceiling. A distant light? An opening to the outside? It was impossible to tell.

There was no crossing this. Not without a boat, or unless you wanted to swim, and there was nothing Eslingen wanted less than to drop down into that black water, stirred by only the faintest of ripples as the water from the channel flowed into the pool.

"A turning basin," Rathe said, determinedly practical. "Look, there's another tunnel."

Sure enough, a quarter of the way around the pool, on the inland side, another arch gave onto a dark opening. Eslingen started toward it, playing his light over the wall as he went.

"There were lights here once," he said. "Dozens of them." The niches were about an arm's-length apart, set into the brickwork; some still had twisted iron hooks that must have held lanterns—and must once, Eslingen realized, have looked more than a bit like a dogfish. Each of the niches had been outlined with tiles, but they had all been broken away, leaving only a few fragments of terra-cotta and here and there a speck of color. "Nico! Take a look at these niches. I don't think this was a turning basin, or not just that. Didn't Cambrai say something about a temple?"

Rathe turned his own light on the wall that curved back toward the channel. "He did, but—" He stopped. "Yeah, I see what you mean."

Eslingen turned, surveying the cavernous space. "There must have been a hundred lamps here. Maybe more." He couldn't imagine it, not with the dark pressing in on him, rising up from the water, sidling in from the open tunnel. Once the place would have been filled with light, each one a hundred times brighter than the lantern he carried, light to drive back the shadows, to make the water glow agate-brown as boats slipped through the narrow spaces. Now there was only the darkness, silence and the smell of wet iron.

Something fell into the water, a splash so soft that he could almost have convinced himself he imagined it, except that he saw Rathe stiffen.

"Was that you?"

"Not me," Eslingen answered, and swung his light over the pool.

Where the surface had been still, barely moving, ripples appeared, chevron shapes turning to point toward their side of the pool. The ripples swelled, became waves, and there were more waves behind them, taller still, rising impossibly from the basin.

"This way!" Rathe shouted, and Eslingen turned toward him as the first wave struck. It slopped over the edge of the walkway, soaking his shoes. He swore, and the second wave hit, catching at his ankles.

"Philip!"

Rathe was almost at the mouth of the channel, one hand clutching at the brickwork, the other waving his lantern.

"Come on, Philip, over here!"

The next wave knocked Eslingen sideways, landing hard against the bricks; he stumbled, went to his knees on the walkway, the lantern clattering away from him. He could see the next wave rising, brown and weighty, scrabbled frantically for something, anything, to cling to. His fingers scraped the stones, and the wave came down on him like a pile of stone. He felt his nails tear, and then the water tumbled him away.

RATHE CLUNG TO the piling at the edge of the walkway as the wave rolled over him, soaking him to the waist. He saw Eslingen fall, shouted his name, and the next wave rose. He saw Eslingen vanish into the water, and then the water hit him breast high, ripping him loose from his hold. He rolled out and down, felt the edge of the walkway strike him just above the knee, and the surge of water carried him further up the channel, away from the basin. It dropped him, coughing and choking, on his hands and knees in the debris at the edge of the channel, and he rolled clumsily to his feet, leaning against the channel wall. The water was over his knees now, deeper than it had been, and he fumbled for his lantern, still mercifully tethered to his belt, the light shining valiantly beneath the surface of the water. He recovered it and opened the shutter, relieved to find that he was still within sight of the basin.

"Philip! Philip, can you hear me?"

There was no answer, not even an echo, and he started back down the channel, swearing under his breath. Eslingen's stars were bad for water, he knew that, had known that all along; he should never have let him come with him, not here, not into this place....

"Philip?"

Still nothing, though it would be hard to hear anything softer than a shout over the sound of his own splashing. He pushed forward, an unnatural current slowing him, streaming up the channel against the tide. There was mud on his face, in his mouth, and he hawked and spat, trying to rid himself of the bitter film. The wave had carried him a good fifteen ells, and the current still pressed him back; he moved like a man in a nightmare, fighting for every step against a pressure that seemed to grow stronger with every heartbeat. He heard a distant splashing, out of synch with his own movements, and fought to hurry. Eslingen could swim, he knew that much, but with the stars against him—he cut off that thought, and struggled forward.

A wave loomed above him, surging up from the basin, a wave with teeth that glinted from the brown water in the lantern's light. An instant later, the teeth resolved to the shadow of a dogfish, and he yanked his truncheon from his belt as the water crashed down on him. He felt the dogfish brush past him, its teeth catching for a moment in the thick leather jerkin and then ripping through his sleeve as it lost its grip. He staggered, stumbling half to his knees, and dragged himself upright as a smaller wave rolled back toward him, the dogfish riding its crest. It had lifted itself half out of the water, front fins spread, the bottom of its toothy jaw just skimming the surface, and Rathe swung the truncheon with all his strength. He felt the blow connect, felt teeth splinter, and the fish vanished in a swirl of bloody water.

"Philip!"

Still no answer, and the water was gathering again, a rushing wave sweeping toward him. The water was up to his hips now even at the side of the channel; he braced himself, holding his breath, and the wave bowled him over, sent him tumbling, bouncing painfully off the stones. He felt something squirm past him, another dogfish struggling against the current, kicked out hard as something touched his ankle. And then the water was receding, the dogfish circling against its pull, seeking him through the dark water. He'd lost his hold on the lantern again, and it bobbed just below the surface at the end of its tether, leaving just enough light to see the ripples on the water's surface. He shifted his truncheon to his left hand and drew his knife, circling to put his back against the channel wall. The water was still rising, though the tide should be nearly dead low.

He kicked at a shadow, and a dogfish drove in from his other side, nearly oversetting him. He staggered back, bracing himself against the wall, swept the knife through the water where he thought a fish might be. The blade met nothing, but something sliced along his calf, drawing a swirl of blood and searing pain. He struck left-handed, felt the truncheon connect, struck again as though he was gaffing a fish at the end of a line. The dogfish rolled away, but there was more blood in the water.

The water was still rising, rolling up in a long slow wave that was cut by the fins of three more dogfish. Rathe kicked as something grabbed his other ankle, shearing through stocking and shoe leather and flesh, and dropped his knife as the wave rolled closer, jumping for the edge of the channel wall. The water lifted him, and he caught it, kicking at yet another of the fish, then scrabbling for a toehold in the rough stones. His right foot caught, the stronger, and then the weaker left, pain shooting through ankle and knee as it took his weight. He tossed the truncheon onto the walkway and used both hands to pull himself up, the lantern dragging behind him in the water. One of the dogfish struck at it, catching it like a fisherman's hook, and the new weight nearly jerked him backward into the stream. He clawed for purchase on the rough stone, wedging one foot hard into a gap in the stones, and then the tether parted, the magelight vanishing into the depths.

Rathe hauled himself up onto the walkway, feeling with battered hands for the tunnel wall. Without the light, there was no way to tell if the water was still rising, no way to know what else might be waiting in the dark. Something splashed in the water, almost at his feet: one of the fish, presumably, but he couldn't feel how close it really was. He crouched there for a moment longer, letting his breathing slow, then drew himself to his feet, keeping his back pressed against the stones. He was still bleeding, but he didn't think the cuts were bad; his hand stung when he gripped the truncheon, but the real problem was the lack of light. Without the lantern, there was nothing he could do.

He tasted bile then, fear and guilty fury tangling in his gut, but the cold sense that had made him a better than average pointsman held him still. He'd lost the lantern, he couldn't search without it. But outside, on the river itself, Cambrai was waiting with his people. Get back to them, and they could come after Eslingen. Half a dozen pontoises would be a help against the dogfish.

If he could get back to them. If he could find his way out. Something splashed again at his feet, and he snarled silently at it. He wasn't that far from the last tunnel, and by all the signs, it had been in use. If he could just get there, he had a chance. Of course, he was on the wrong side of the channel, but the water had been much shallower there, the bed of the tunnel dry in spots. He would take that chance when he got there.

He took a breath. He had flint and steel in his pocket, though it was even odds if the tinder would have stayed dry enough to catch even in its waxed box. Nothing to burn, though, except his soaked clothes, and they wouldn't make much of a torch even dry. The flares would light, they were meant to light at sea in storms, magist-spelled to keep off salt and wind and water, but they just spat out a single ball of light, with enough power behind it to soar hundreds of feet in the air and still keep burn-ing....

Maybe that would help, if he could lodge the ball in the stones of the ceiling. Maybe that would give enough light to let him feel his way along the footpath. At worst, it would give him a glimpse of the situation. He found the packet of flares and carefully extracted one, feeling along the tube to find the firing end. He pointed that down the channel, aiming for a low arc, and hooked a finger in the loop of string that dangled from the other end. He pulled it once, and again, harder, and felt the trigger give.

Light exploded from the tube, blue-white and blinding, soared down the length of the channel and slammed into one of the arches just beside the keystone. For a second, he thought it would bounce back, but it stuck, clung hissing to the stones. It wasn't as good as the lantern, but it was enough to see the path, enough to see that the water in the channel was sliding slowly back and forth, against all normal forces that ruled the river. A frilled fin cut the surface, and vanished again: the dogfish were still waiting.

Rathe kept his back to the wall, and edged along the walkway, trying not to cast a shadow or draw the dogfishes' attention. If they were the Riverdeme's eyes and ears, if he could just avoid their notice, get ahead of them, then maybe he could get away. He held his breath with each step, trying not to disturb even a single crumb of gravel. Two ells, ten, a dozen, and the water in the channel seemed lower, less affected by the weird movement. He moved faster now, his ankle throbbing. Ahead, the light seemed brighter: he was drawing closer to the arch where the flare had struck.

And then he had reached the arch, the harsh light showing the water in the channel almost normal, no more than a couple of feet deep. Looking back the way he'd come, he could see the wave rising and falling but never coming closer, as though it was held by an invisible barrier. Eslingen was somewhere behind that, taken by the Riverdeme, and surely, surely she wouldn't kill him outright. Surely if the tales were true he was handsome enough to be one of her chosen, and surely that would give them time to find him and break him free.... Maybe there would be time—Astree, Oriane, Seidos, let there be time—but there was certainly none to waste. Rathe ducked past the arch and hurried up the channel, heading for the tunnel he had seen earlier.

He found it at the edge of the flare's light, and set off another to guide him to the river's edge. He had lost all sense of time, was shocked to find himself walking dry-shod down the edge of the tunnel, with barely half a foot of water in the center of the passage. Still the ebb tide, still the Riverdeme's detriment, though the stars were more in her favor than he would have liked. The flare was nearly out by the time he reached the barred gate and hauled it open with a shriek of hinges.

After that noise, he would have expected some call, some response from a watchman on the streets above, but he staggered out onto the empty shingle without drawing any notice. It was raining, a thin, steady drizzle, and the beach stretched almost three ells to the water. The nearest dock was a quarter mile away, the ships black shadows unmarked by any lights; there were lights on the far bank, and on the Queen's Bridge, and Rathe reached for the last of his flares. He pulled the string to set it off, and watched the ball of light rise like an unnatural star over the river. If Cambrai hurried—if they could find Eslingen in time—he shook his head, drowning fear in anger. They had to find him, and they would.

CHAPTER 13

THE PONTOISES' BOAT scraped ashore, the oarsmen driving half its length onto the shingle. Rathe stared at it, shaking, unable for a moment to focus. The river's cold had driven deep into his bones, seemed worse in the open air even as his clothes dried on him. Someone was speaking to him, but the words refused to resolve into sense; mage-light surrounded them, heatless and bright, and he could have wept at its useless touch.

Something touched his lips, the neck of a bottle nudging at him, and he opened his mouth and nearly choked on brandy and strong herbs. He recognized it, though, the pontoises' rescue cordial, and managed to get most of it down, only a little spilling down his chin.

"Another," Cambrai said, and Rathe swallowed obediently, feeling new warmth seep through him. He was still shivering, but not as hard, and someone had wrapped a blanket around his shoulders.

"Philip…the Riverdeme took him."

Cambrai hissed softly. "You're sure?"

"I wouldn't say it otherwise."

"Perrine!" Cambrai waved to one of the pontoises. "Dry clothes, quick as you can. Come on, Nico, strip, and tell me while you're changing."

"We need to go after him."

"You'll do him no good if you can't stand for shivering." Cambrai was already plucking at the clasps of Rathe's jerkin, and reluctantly Rathe moved to help. He grudged every moment, but he knew that Cambrai was right, that there was nothing he could do until he was capable of clear thought again.

"Where would it take him?"

232

The pontoise, Perrine, brought shirt and breeches and a loose coat. None of them fit well, but Rathe dragged them on, folding fabric where it was too big and pulling his own belt tight to hold everything in place.

He saw Cambrai and Perrine exchange unhappy glances, and knew what they were thinking.

"Yes, if he's not dead. We have to assume it, have to assume he's alive, or we won't find him. And it took him, Euan. It could have killed both of us, but it drove me off and took him."

Perrine gave the ghost of a shrug. "The stories say she takes men."

"The stories say she kills them," Cambrai said.

"You have to look," Rathe said, through clenched teeth. "We have to look."

"And we will," Cambrai said.

Rathe grabbed his arm, tightening his grip until Cambrai winced and swore. "Really look, Euan. Like you mean to find him alive."

For an instant, he thought Cambrai would protest further, but then the cap'pontoise shook his head. "That means we move now." He lifted his arm, and Saffroy came loping over.

"The tide's on the turn, Cap."

Cambrai took a breath. "Take out every boat we have, send them up and down the southern bank—concentrate on the area between the bridges, but check below and above just in case. Every place a body—a woman might be washed out of the tunnels."

"If she took him," Rathe said again.

Cambrai gave him an unhappy look. "The drowning cell. Only I don't know where that is."

"No one does," Saffroy said, and Cambrai glared at him.

"Go on, get the boats in the water. Leave me Perrine and half the crew. And Benet, he knows the old tales better than most."

"Right, Cap." Saffroy touched his forehead and backed away.

"We have to find it," Rathe said.

"If we went back the way you came out," Cambrai said. "Go in force, plenty of light—"

Rathe dug his hands into his filthy hair, trying to think clearly. "It wouldn't be hard to backtrack, and maybe we can find something in the basin, it looked important."

Cambrai beckoned to his people. "Into the tunnel. Nico, you'll need to show us the way."

ESLINGEN CAME TO himself in darkness, oddly surprised to find himself undrowned, and not entirely certain that he was, though as his thoughts cleared he could feel bruises enough to convince him that he was still alive. He was on dry ground, pebbles and shells and all the familiar debris of the river's shore meeting his questing hands. There was a stone wall behind him, the same sort of rough-hewn blocks that lined the river's edge, and for a terrified instant he feared he'd been flung blind onto the shore. But no: he was beginning to distinguish faint changes of light and shadow, and when he looked up, a brighter circle showed overhead. Not daylight, or even the winter-sun behind clouds, but definitely light, maybe ten or twelve feet above him.

"Hello?" His voice sounded hollow, deadened by the stone. He cocked his head to listen, but there was no response. "Hello!"

Still no answer, not even the scrape of foot on stone, but he stood for a long moment anyway, until the possibility of an echo had died.

He ran his hands over the stones, searching for a handhold, but the stones were too tightly fitted to offer any purchase. He felt his way along the wall, looking for any break, any change in the pattern, but the wall curved gently to his right, bringing him around in a slow circle. After a while, he scuffed a mark in the ground and found a paler stone to place in it, then followed the wall again until he came back around the circle. It was smaller than he had thought, maybe ten feet across, which meant the darkness in the center of the cylinder was something more than shadow.

He had lost his lantern, but there were still two flares left in his coat's torn pocket. He pulled one out, unwinding the thin oilcloth that covered it. There was always the chance that the flare would fall back on him—there was nothing else to set on fire, as far as he could tell—or the less likely possibility that it would shoot through what might be a gap at the top of the cell and vanish into the dark, but all in all it seemed worth risking. He took a deep breath, pointed the flare toward the ceiling, and pulled the string.

Light blasted upward, golden as sunlight, rising with a hiss like a hundred lizards. Eslingen shaded his eyes, ready to dodge, and caught a brief glimpse of smooth stone rising all the way to a cross-barred grating. The light struck one of the bars, clung for a moment, then fell back, still hissing. Eslingen moved quickly out of its way, and it landed at the foot of the opposite wall, a spitting ball hot and bright as a furnace. In its light, the thing in the middle of the cell came suddenly clear: a pump, an old-fashioned sailor's pump, with a cylinder as thick as his thigh and a single long lever for a handle. There was water at its foot, glittering in the flare's light.

The drowning cell.

The breath caught in his throat. He had feared it from the instant the wave washed over him, feared it on waking, and even so the knowledge was like a knife blade to the heart. He was meant to die here, to struggle and fail and die, the very stars condemning him out of hand. He looked up at the grate again, twice a man's height above him, a paler circle against the dark. If Rathe had been there, they would have had a chance—Rathe could have climbed on his shoulders, he would have been just tall enough to reach the grate, and he could pick any lock ever made. But of course the drowning cell was meant for one person at a time, one slow and savored death.

"Hey!" He stopped, cleared his throat, and tried again. "Hello! Anyone out there? Hello?"

There was no answer, just the hissing of the flare against the damp shore. At the base of the pump, the water shimmered, reflecting its fire. Was the water spreading? They had to be approaching low tide; it had been falling the whole time he and Rathe searched the tunnels, and eventually it would turn. Would the pump even work? By all accounts, the drowning cell had been abandoned, unused and unmourned, for hundreds of years.

He reached for the lever before he could change his mind and pulled down hard. It moved easily, no suction behind it, but he could hear the parts sliding smoothly over each other. Possibly it was functional—something might be broken deep inside, but at least the outer parts worked. At least there was a chance. He was strong, unhurt, and if he was cold now, the exertion would surely warm him. He could pump for hours if he had to. And in those hours, Rathe would find him.

THE GROUP RETRACED Rathe's passage through the tunnel, torches and lanterns at the ready, traveling as quickly as they could along the narrow walkways. As they got closer to the basin, Rathe could see the signs of the waves that had rolled over him, debris washed into new piles, new water in the central channel. There was far less, however, than he had expected, only a little more than there had been when he and Eslingen first passed that way. Behind him, the pontoises whispered to each other, trying to match his pace without making unnecessary noise.

Ahead, the mage-lights showed the first shadow of the opening that gave onto the basin, and Rathe swung his borrowed light along the bottom of the channel. Surely the wave had reached this far—yes, that had to be the arch where he had lodged the flare's light—but the water had drained away, leaving nothing behind but the same sort of debris he had seen the first time. Out of the corner of his eye, he saw Cambrai give him a wary look.

"You sure we're going the right way?"

Rathe nodded. "The basin's just ahead."

"It's just—" Cambrai stopped, visibly choosing more tactful words. "I don't see any signs of flooding."

"This is the way," Rathe said, tight-lipped, and one of the pontoises behind them called out softly.

"Cap'! Take a look."

Rathe turned with Cambrai to see one of the pontoises leaning over the edge of the channel, holding her torch so that the smoke streamed up thick and black, but the light picked out a metal object at the base of the wall.

"That your lantern?" Cambrai asked.

"Yeah." Rathe swallowed his anger, and saw Cambrai nod.

"Right. Let's move it, you lot."

They reached the basin without attracting any attention, and Rathe paused on the edge of the walkway. The place looked different—the water was lower, which shouldn't be possible, and it seemed less dark, the niches in the walls clearly visible. There was no body floating in the basin or crumpled on the walkway, and in spite of himself he gave a sigh of relief.

"Turning basin," Perrine said, and Cambrai gave a considering nod.

"Take a look at these hooks," Rathe said, and lifted his lantern so that the light played over the nearest niche. The twisted hook showed clearly, but it seemed less suggestive of the dogfish than it had before.

Cambrai pursed his lips. "Benet? What do you make of this?"

That was the man who knew the old tales, Rathe remembered. The person who worked his way forward was small and wiry, with hands that looked too big for his skinny frame. He tucked the tail of his cap over his shoulder and met Cambrai's eyes squarely.

"Turning basin it may have been, but there's talk of a place like it. She had a temple down here, you came to it by water. This could be part of it."

The light seemed to fade, for an instant, as though a shadow had passed over the suns, and the air seemed heavier. Rathe braced himself against another attack, but the water remained quiet, the surface ruffled only by the most ordinary of ripples.

"All right." Cambrai looked back at Rathe. "Where now?"

"I was standing about here," Rathe said. "Philip was further along, heading for the tunnel there. My guess is he was taken there."

Cambrai nodded, though he let his light play for a moment longer across the water's surface. Rathe followed it unwillingly, afraid to see shadows beneath the surface, not dogfish, but a hand or an arm or a twist of sodden clothing, a swirl of dark hair. There was nothing but the brown water, and he made himself turn away.

The group paused at the tunnel entrance, focusing lights ahead of them into the dark. The beams picked out the familiar walkways and the still brown water—deeper here, deep enough to carry a small boat, though the passage itself was barely wider than the boats the watermen used to carry passengers up and down the Sier.

"Not meant for cargo," Perrine said, and Cambrai nodded.

"Benet?"

The old pontoise shrugged. "Like I said, she had a temple here. Or so they say."

Rathe let his own light play along the nearest wall. It was brick, and old, once sharp edges worn away, the mortar failing in spots, gray crumbs scattered across the stones. "This has to be it."

He saw Cambrai purse his lips, but finally the cap'pontoise nodded. "Everybody, stay sharp. Anything we ought to do, Benet? Or not do?"

Benet shrugged one shoulder. "Be respectful, Cap', that's all I can say."

Lovely. Rathe swallowed the word, and eased cautiously along the walkway. The others followed, silent except for soft footfalls and the occasional scrape of stone on stone as the bits of mortar grated underfoot. The tunnel ran straight—due south? Rathe wondered. That might make astrological sense. Eslingen would know, and the thought was like a knife to his guts. He fell back a little, forcing himself to search the surface of the water, but the light found only ripples, not even a floating leaf or stick to break the glassy surface.

Ahead of them, someone swore, and he looked up, to see the lights focused on the tunnel ahead. Tunnels ahead, he amended, his heart sinking. Ten ells ahead, the tunnel split, dividing not into two but into five separate branches, five arches opening into the dark. Rathe shoved his way to the front as though a clearer view might change what he saw, and Cambrai caught his sleeve.

"Nico. There's no way on."

Rathe flashed his light at the water. "How deep do you think that is?"

"Oriane only knows," Cambrai answered. "And you'd be a fool to swim it. Who knows what you'd wake if you tried?"

Rathe swore himself, knowing the cap'pontoise was right. "Just to get across…I wouldn't be in the water very long.…"

"Which one would you pick?" Cambrai's voice was almost gentle. "We should go back—try from above ground."

"Hold me," Rathe said, and leaned out over the edge, angling his lantern to send as much light as possible down each of the openings. Cambrai cursed, but leaned back to balance him. There was nothing but smooth brown water and the pale stone of the walkways—no, something poked above the surface of the middle tunnel, rocks or broken stone, and behind him someone grunted.

"Never get a boat down that one."

Rathe pretended he hadn't heard. "Look, we can at least keep on down the right hand tunnel, the walkways connect."

Cambrai pulled him upright. "Look." He pointed, and another pontoise obligingly swung her light in that direction. More stones poked above the surface, not a solid barrier, but a jagged line stretching into the dark. "I don't think that's the way."

"If we went back for a boat," Perrine said. "One of the collapsibles, maybe."

Cambrai nodded. "We'll do that." He looked at Rathe. "But it's going to take a hour or more to bring one, plus the time to carry it back here, and the tide's turned. I think we can do more from the surface."

"Such as?" Rathe shook his head, unable to think of anything but Eslingen trapped somewhere in the tunnels, Eslingen drowning, Eslingen dead.… He shook his head again, forcing himself to think calmly. Cambrai was right, it would take too long to search here. They needed a boat, and they needed more people, and most of all they needed more time. Someone at Point of Sighs might know—Couenter, for one, had seemed nervous on the subject—and Benet might know more people. "No, you're right."

"I'll send Saffroy down," Cambrai said. "With boats and enough people to search properly. And you and I will work from the surface. We'll find him, Nico."

ESLINGEN CROUCHED AGAINST the wall at what he thought was the highest point of ground. The flare had gone out some time ago, but it seemed as though more light was seeping in from the grating overhead, so that he could make out the shape of the pump and its handle, and the bars of the grate itself were very dark against a pale circle. He could see his own hands, pale shapes resting on his knees, and the trail of his cravat across his waistcoat. Of course, one didn't need to see to be able to work the pump, assuming the pump worked at all.

The still air was filled with the soft sound of water, a gentle murmur against the stone. The pool at the base of the pump was growing deeper, and its edge crept slowly up the slope. It had almost reached the stone he had placed a double handspan from his last marker: the tide was definitely coming in, and faster now than before.

He pushed himself to his feet, muscles twinging with every move—whatever had brought him had left him bruised and sore on top of the bruises he'd gotten in Customs Point—and reached for the pump handle. He pulled down, feeling no resistance, pushed up and pulled again without any better result. A part of him wanted to flail frantically, pump hard and fast until the pump was primed and finally began removing the water, but he made himself stop and turn away. He would need all his strength later, if he was to make it through high tide. Surely the pump would work once the water rose high enough.

The edge of the puddle had overlapped his marker stone now, and he moved it a careful handspan further up the shore. There was still room to sit, though the ground was cold and damp, and he made himself settle again. Patience was what he needed now, patience and calm. The water was rising, but eventually it would rise far enough that the pump could take hold, and then he was strong enough, disciplined enough, to last a long time. To last though the turn of the tide, he amended; he only needed to hold on until the water began to recede, and then he could rest. And by then, Rathe would have found him. Rathe knew Astreiant like the back of his hand, better than most women knew their lemen; he'd find this place, wherever it was. All Eslingen had to do was hold on.

The water was lapping at his marker again, and he suppressed a curse. The tide was definitely on the way in, running faster now with every step. He rose and tugged at the pump handle again. It felt heavier this time, and he let himself take two more strokes, but the pump did not quite engage. Next time, though, he thought, and settled himself to wait.

Something moved above him, a scuffling of boots on stone, and he shot to his feet, staring up at the grating. "Hello? Anyone there?"

There was no answer, but the circle brightened, and then Eslingen flinched away from the sudden glare of a mage-light lantern.

"Hello! Hey, down here!"

"Captain?"

Eslingen frowned, shading his eyes. "Balfort?"

The light wavered, was withdrawn to the edge of the grate. "It's me." De Vian sounded breathless, as though he'd run some distance. "Wait, I'll get you out."

"It's the drowning cell," Eslingen said, and heard his voice waver. He cleared his throat, and tried again. "The tide's turned, it's coming in—"

"I'm working on it, sir." Eslingen heard soft thumps, as though the boy were searching through a pile of debris. "There's no key, but—this might work."

Eslingen shaded his eyes, stepping around the curve of the room to keep de Vian's shadow in sight, and caught a glimpse of a sturdy-looking piece of wood as de Vian brandished it happily. Then it and de Vian disappeared, and Eslingen heard a grunt of effort as de Vian did something out of sight.

"Almost, sir!" De Vian shifted position, and there was a sudden snap of breaking metal. "Got it!"

"Good job, lad!"

De Vian heaved at the grate, dragging it sideways—it seemed to move on a single pivot-point—and leaned over the opening. "Are you all right?"

"Fine," Eslingen said. In the new light, he could see how far the water had risen, an inky pool filling the center of the cell, the pump rising from it. "Is there a ladder, a rope?"

"I'm looking."

There were more sounds of scuffling, and then a pleased exclamation.

"Anything?"

"Rope ladder, sir!" De Vian reappeared, busied himself with something at his feet, and then a rope ladder with wide wooden rungs unrolled itself and clattered down the side of the cell. Eslingen eyed it hungrily, and gave it a sharp tug. It felt solid, and he reached higher, letting his full weight dangle for a moment from the ropes.

"Excellent—"

There were sudden footsteps above, loud on the stone, and de Vian screamed. And then he was falling, a twisting shadow against the light. Eslingen hauled himself up the ladder, but metal shrieked against stone, and the ladder sagged sideways under him. He dropped free, cursing, and the ladder slithered down the cell wall, the wooden rungs battering against the stone. Eslingen swore again as a woman leaned over the opening. There was no mistaking the Vidame d'Entrebeschaire.

"Maseigne! What in Seidos' name do you think you're doing?"

"You should have stayed clear." She hauled the grate back across the opening.

"You'll leave your brother to drown?"

The grate slid home with a clang. "He made his choice."

"Aliez…." De Vian's voice was weak, but it carried far enough.

"Worthless, spineless bastard! Mother should have drowned you at birth." D'Entrebeschaire caught her breath. "Be damned to you."

"He'll die here—" Eslingen began, and she cut him off.

"One of you certainly will. Maybe not this tide, you're strong enough, and hale, and Balfort's no weakling either. Maybe not even the next one. But the tide will come. She'll take one of you."

"You don't have to do this!"

D'Entrebeschaire laughed. "I owe the Riverdeme a death."

She turned away, the light receding with her, and Eslingen shouted after her, "At least leave us a light!"

"Please…please, Aliez…." De Vian's voice was thick with tears. D'Entrebeschaire hesitated.

"You may regret what you see," she said, but hung the lantern from the grating's edge. The cold light spilled down, sparkling from the water still rising around the pump.

"Aliez!" de Vian cried again, but she turned away, her footsteps receding across the stone. In the new silence, the sound of the water increased, and de Vian caught his breath.

"Don't we need to pump?"

Eslingen shook his head. "Not yet—it's not deep enough to engage the pump properly, we should wait until it's worth the effort." And now there were two of them, he thought. With two of them, they'd surely survive the first tide, and maybe another, and maybe even the third, and long before then Rathe would find them. And then de Vian's awkward position, half sprawled, half sitting against the cell wall, fully registered. "Are you all right?"

De Vian tried to stand, but succeeded only in sitting up all the way with a cry of pain. "My leg—I landed wrong."

And just like that, the hope was gone. Eslingen took a careful breath, made sure his voice stayed relaxed and easy. "Let's take a look."

He splashed through the spreading puddle to kneel at de Vian's side, ran a hand down the boy's right leg. He felt the bone shift under his touch as he reached de Vian's calf, and de Vian drew breath sharply.

"There."

"Here?" Eslingen laid both hands on de Vian's calf, and felt him arch like a man lightning-struck. Both bones broken, if he was any judge.

"Yes." De Vian's breath hissed between his teeth, but he managed to shift so that he was sitting almost straight against the wall.

"All right," Eslingen said, and laid a hand on the boy's shoulder. "All right." That needed a splint; if he could brace it well enough, de Vian might even be able to take a spell at the pump, and there might be enough wood and rope in the remains of the ladder to do the job. He drew his knife and began sawing at the thick cable. At last he'd freed two of the wooden boards. They were too wide, clumsy, but they were better than nothing. The rope, on the other hand, was too thick to tie securely, and instead he unwound his cravat and knelt again at de Vian's side, sawing at the fabric to cut it into three long lengths.

"This is my fault," de Vian said. "I'm sorry. I thought…."

He let his voice trail off, and Eslingen gave him a quick glance. De Vian was deathly pale in the lantern's light, his lips bloody where he'd bitten them.

"Where are we?" Eslingen asked.

"Under our old house, the one we rent out…its deepest cellar." De Vian's breath caught as he shifted his weight.

"Where's the house?" Not that it mattered, Eslingen thought, not with them trapped down here, but it might give him some rough idea of how long it would take Rathe to find them.

"Off Bonfortune Row. Point of Sighs, not far west of the Queen's Bridge."

A chance, then, Eslingen thought. Rathe was learning Sighs, and what he didn't know, he could persuade his new station to tell. Assuming they weren't involved. He thrust that thought aside. "Your sister. Did she kill them—bes'Anthe, I mean, and Dammar?"

"I don't know. Probably." De Vian rolled his head from wide to side, wincing. "I knew our family served the Riverdeme, at least on grandfather's side, but that was centuries ago. I never thought she'd take it seriously."

I owe the Riverdeme a death, d'Entrebeschaire had said. Eslingen shivered, and made his tone as light as possible. "Too common for her?"

Something that was almost a smile flashed across de Vian's face. "We're not so noble, for all Aliez's graces. Our grandmother was a silver merchant, she bought Mother a place at court after the League wars."

And d'Entrebeschaire had lost that place on her mother's death, and had nothing with which to maintain herself and her younger brothers, but how freeing the Riverdeme helped that, Eslingen couldn't see. Unless she was working with Trys? "Do you know what she wants?"

"No." De Vian shook his head again. "Gods, my leg!"

"Almost ready," Eslingen said. He was no physician, knew little more than field aid, but surely that was all that was required. Except that the boards were too wide, and too short, and he had none of the tools, no sword or hand-axe to knock them into better shape.... He shoved that thought aside, and shrugged out of his coat and then his waistcoat. "Can you lift it?"

De Vian drew a pained breath, but managed. Eslingen hastily laid out the strips he'd cut from the cravat, then slid the folded waistcoat on top of them. De Vian gasped with relief and lowered his leg, and Eslingen wrapped the rest of the waistcoat fabric over it. He set the boards on each side of the calf and tied the fabric strips as tightly as he dared.

"Any better?"

De Vian's face was whiter than paper, but he managed a nod. "This is all my fault."

Eslingen sat back on his heels. "I don't see how."

"You don't understand." De Vian closed his eyes. "You'll hate me forever, and I only wanted—"

"What did you do?" Eslingen kept his voice even with an effort.

"I told her what you suspected. I was angry, it was stupid, but I went back to the house and I told her, and she said she'd make it right. As long as I stayed out of the way, she could fix things."

"Not so much." Eslingen stamped ruthlessly on his rising anger. This had all been a trap—Rathe had suspected as much, which made it worse—but there was nothing to be gained by shouting at the boy.

De Vian went on as though he hadn't spoken, his eyes open now and pleading. "She's—we've always rented out this house, even before Mother died, but when the last tenant left, Aliez didn't rent it out again right away. With all our bills due and the bailiffs at the door! I should have known she was hiding something. She made me promise to stay here, out of sight, but I followed her into the cellar and I found—" He waved one hand weakly at the walls around them. "This. I waited until I thought she was gone, and then I thought I could let you out."

Except that it hadn't worked. D'Entrebeschaire had known better than to trust her brother. Eslingen swallowed the words, and said, "Only she wasn't gone."

De Vian shook his head miserably. "I'm sorry, I only wanted—I was angry, but I couldn't let her leave you here. I've been a fool."

Yes, you have. The words were neither kind nor useful, and Eslingen swallowed them. "With two of us to pump, we have a chance. If you can stand."

"I'll try," de Vian said, but made no move to lift himself.

Eslingen wished for a moment that he had a flask of brandy, and swore at his own stupidity. Might as well wish they were safe at Wicked's, or drinking beer at the Old Brown Dog. "You may have to, but that's what the splint is for. It'll give you support if you need it."

De Vian blinked, and then grimaced as he understood. "If you can't keep up. If no one finds us."

The water was lapping at his outstretched foot, and Eslingen stooped to loosen the strings that tied Balfort's shoe. It ought to come off entirely, the boy's foot would swell, but he would need every bit of protection his clothes could provide.

He shrugged back into his coat, and reached for the pump's handle, drew it down against new resistance. The water was deep enough at last, and he heard something in the mechanism sigh heavily. He hoped that meant the water was being ejected, but there was no sign of it in the mage-light. He gave the handle five strokes, then ten, and felt the pressure ease. "Rathe will be looking for me. He'll find us."

"It's gone down," de Vian said.

Eslingen nodded, letting himself relax. The water was already creeping back, though, the dark pool now visibly swelling, and when it reached de Vian's foot, he gave the handle five more pulls. It was horribly clever, he thought: not enough time to truly rest between sessions, and at the same time, not enough time for the exertion to warm him. Though that would change as the tide came in—in an hour or three, he'd be wishing for this much rest. He worked the pump again, bracing himself for the night ahead.

THE WINTER-SUN WAS well up by the time they reached Point of Sighs, the station clock striking the first hour of the new day. The duty point shot to her feet as Rathe crashed through the half-open door, and the points gathered by the nearer stove swung with hands on truncheons, only to freeze as they recognized Rathe and the cap'pontoise behind him.

"Fetch Sebern," Rathe said, and a junior point leaped to obey.

She came down the stairs a moment later, wary frown deepening as she took in the scene below. "Rathe? What's going on?"

"The Riverdeme is loosed," he answered, and even in this extremity kept an eye on the room to see who was not surprised. "She has Eslingen."

Sebern swore, sounding genuinely shocked, and leaned hard on the duty point's table. "Where?"

"We don't know," Rathe said grimly. "Yet." No one in the main room had seemed anything but shocked, but more than half the night-watch was missing. "I want everyone down here, now."

Sebern nodded, and a pair of runners darted away, one up the opposite stair to the quarters, the other back to the workrooms to roust out anyone who hadn't heard the shouting. They responded quickly, stumbling down the stairs to join the others in the main room: slightly more than half the watch, Rathe estimated, and picked out the few familiar faces.

"All right. I've been patient about things here at Sighs, haven't pressed you about anyone who's taken fees or had dealings with Jurien Trys, and I haven't asked about the Riverdeme. My job here was to find out who killed your adjunct point, and up till now none of this has seemed relevant. But now...now the Riverdeme has taken Philip Eslingen. I want him back. And you'll help me, or I'll see each and every game and fee and fiddle of yours exposed."

There was a moment of shocked silence, so deep that he could suddenly hear the quiet ticking of the station's clock, and then at last Sebern cleared her throat.

"We're with you, Rathe."

Rathe nodded his thanks. "We think she took Eslingen to the drowning cell. Anyone have a guess where that might be?"

He was scanning the crowd for Couenter as he spoke, and wasn't surprised to see her shoulder out from among the others. "No one knows for sure, Adjunct Point. It was closed long ago—unless the pontoises know something?"

Cambrai shook his head. "We've got people going through the channels, but the tide's against us."

"There have to have been connections above ground." Rathe's hands were tightly clenched, and he made himself relax. "Some story, some old warning. A hint. Anything."

"The baths at Mother More's," someone said doubtfully. "They're supposed to have been some sort of temple once."

"That's just talk," someone else said, and the first speaker shrugged.

"But it is what they say."

"Mother More's baths," Rathe repeated. "Anyone else?"

Couenter wiped her hands on her skirts. "The cross channel under the warehouse where Trys was killed. They say things lurk in the dark there. Though to be honest, sir, that's as likely to be smugglers as the Riverdeme."

Rathe nodded. "We'll look."

"And the folk at Crow Hall, they might know."

"Crow Hall and the warehouse," Rathe said. "Any others?"

A runner raised her hand shyly. "The tower house on Destrier Street?"

Rathe waited, but the runner seemed too nervous to go one. Sebern swore. "She's right, that one was built on top of one of the Riverdeme's watchtowers. Might be worth a look, though I don't know if it even has a cellar."

That made four places, all equally possible, all equally unlikely. And the tide came fast. Rathe swallowed that thought, and said, "All right. Couenter. Take backup, and talk to the folk at Crow Hall. If they know anything, send straight back to Sighs. Fellson, you take a couple of people and look into Mother More's. I know you'll have to wake her, tell her it's points' business and an emergency and don't do anything that she can claim against us unless you have to. Is Ammis here?" Rathe scanned the group, and Ammis detached himself from the crowd.

"Here, Adjunct Point."

"Take a squad—and a couple of pontoises, Euan, if we can borrow them?"

"All yours," Cambrai answered, and Rathe hurried on.

"Thanks. Check out the channel under the warehouse. All of you be careful, I've already run into the Riverdeme tonight, and she sent the river against us. Her creatures are in the water, and the tide's against you. If you think you're onto something, don't push it, but come back and see if you can locate the same spots above ground."

He saw Ammis swallow hard, but the young man nodded. "Adjunct Point, what if we only find smugglers?"

"Squeeze them," Rathe answered. "In fact, if you know anyone who even whispered the name Riverdeme—I don't care if it's just to scare the man in bed beside them or to keep their sons home at night, I want them squeezed. Someone in Sighs must know where the drowning room is."

"Where do you want me?" Sebern asked.

Rathe paused. There was one more place to try, despite the hour: the Vidame d'Entrebeschaire had given Eslingen the warehouse key and sent them on their deadly search; whether she'd meant to do it, or, more likely, had been put up to it by one of the Staenkas or possibly a Gebellin, it was past time he talked to her. He didn't know where she lodged, that had been Eslingen's business, but the Staenkas would. "Stay here," he said. "If anyone turns up something useful, call out the day watch and go after them. We may not have much time."

"Should we inform the surintendant?"

Rathe grimaced. It was the only sensible thing to do, with the River-deme unbound and loose beneath the city, but he grudged every minute he'd have to spend scribbling an explanation. "Yeah. And the Guards, too. The more eyes the better. I'll write the notes."

Sebern nodded. "And then?"

Rathe collected Cambrai with a look. "Euan and I need to have a word with the Staenkas."

"Take Tiesheld," Sebern said, jerking her head at one of the biggest of the points, a good head taller than Rathe and built like a docker. "And Anhalt, too."

Anhalt was wiry and graying, her skirts short enough to show practical shoes and bright clocked stockings. The knife at her left hip was a good two inches over the legal limit, and Rathe nodded. "And a couple of runners."

"And at least one of mine," Cambrai said.

"If we need to, I'll call on Dreams," Rathe said, to Sebern, who grimaced but nodded in agreement. "And don't hesitate to call the day watch if you need them."

"No, Adjunct Point." She whirled away to organize her people, and Rathe drew a shaken breath. As long as it was in time—it had to be in time, there had to be time, if all the stories were true. The drowning cell gave its victims a chance, if they were strong enough, and Eslingen was stronger than most. Unless he had been hurt when taken by the dog-fish. Rathe thought of those terrible teeth...or worse, the Riverdeme had drowned Philip, rolled him over in the dark waters—

Cambrai laid a hand on his shoulder, and he jumped. "We'll find him."

"We'd better." Rathe seated himself at the duty point's table, not bothering to trim the pen, and began scrawling his notes to the surintendant and to Coindarel. Under better circumstances, he would have worried about his phrasing, about making things clear and concise, but tonight he couldn't spare the time. Get it all down, and then he could go. At last he was finished, and handed the papers to Sebern.

"See that the sur gets this. And the Prince-Marshal."

"They'll have questions," Sebern said, and whistled for a runner.

"Answer them as best you can," Rathe said, "and I'll answer them when I get back. Tell them it's all my doing."

Someone managed to flag down a low-flyer, and the driver let them all aboard with only a token protest, though Tiesheld and the smaller of the runners had to cling to the outside. The driver brought them carefully through the nearly empty streets and pulled up outside the Staenka house to give them a doubtful look.

"You're sure this is it?" he asked, and Rathe nodded, reaching for a payment he couldn't trouble to count.

"Yes. Wait for us, and I'll make it worth your while."

The driver glanced at the handful of seillings, thick eyebrows rising, and lifted his whip in acknowledgement. "I'll be here when you want me."

The street was dark, lights doused, the houses shuttered against the night—even the watchman's box at the far end of the street was closed, though Rathe thought he saw a flicker of light through the cracks in the wood. He ignored that—let the watchman shout, this was points business—and hurried up the steps to pound on the Staenkas' door. For a long moment, nothing happened, and he beat on the door again. Out of the corner of his eye, he could see lights wake in the house next door, and further down the street, and then Cambrai caught his hand before he could strike again.

"They're coming."

Rathe took a half step back, teetering on the edge of the step, and saw a light moving behind the shutters. He nodded sharply, and the door opened in front of him, the butler Drowe frowning out at him, anger turning to fear as he recognized Rathe.

"Adjunct Point? What's happened?"

"I need to speak to Madame Staenka and her sister," Rathe answered. "And is the vidame here?"

Drowe's frown deepened again. "She is not."

"The Gebellins?"

"Madame's husband is here." Drowe's back was stiff with offense, but Rathe was beyond caring. "And Dame Elecia."

"Get them, too." Rathe took a step forward, and Drowe fell back, letting them into the darkened hall. "And Mattaes. I want the lot of them."

"I'll inform Madame Staenka," Drowe began, and faltered at Rathe's glare. He was already backing away when he spoke again. "Wait here…."

"Nico," Cambrai said.

"I want answers," Rathe said. At the end of the hall, he could see a maidservant peeping out through the kitchen door, her hair fraying loose from the braid she slept in. "You. Light some lamps."

"And who are you to give orders in Madame's house?" Rathe recognized Meisenta's assistant Telawen, hurrying down the stairs in a hastily-donned skirt and bodice, her feet bare in her shoes and her hair stuffed hastily under an unmatching cap. "And at this hour of the night."

"Urgent business," Rathe answered, and there was a note in his tone that silenced her. She nodded to the maid, who ducked into the parlor, clutching her bedgown around her, and in the quiet house, Rathe heard the clatter of the fire irons as she stirred up the stove. "I need to see her now."

"I'll fetch her." Telawen hurried back up the stairs.

"Nico," Cambrai said again.

Rathe glanced over his shoulder, saw points and pontoises for once united in discomfort, eyeing the fine furniture uneasily. "I need all of them off balance," he said. He would not have had to explain to Eslingen, and suppressed the stabbing pain. "I need them hurried. I need them making mistakes, Euan."

Cambrai grimaced. "I'll follow your lead."

His tone was more doubtful than his words, but Rathe made himself nod back. "I'll hold you to that."

Lights appeared at the top of the stairs, a branch of candles held high, and Meisenta started down the stairs, one hand on the rail, the other on Telawen's arm. She was as plainly and elegantly dressed as ever, an expensive black wool gown that showed the fine white linen of her chemise at collar and cuffs. Her hair was brushed neatly back beneath her lace cap, and the shadows made her look momentarily younger than she was.

"What has happened, Adjunct Point?"

Rathe looked past her to see the rest of the family crowding down the stairs behind her, Aucher in his bedgown and Redel in a loose dress, her hair braided for sleep. Mattaes had at least managed to put on shirt and breeches and, yes, there was Elecia behind him, balancing on one foot as she put on her shoes.

"A question first, madame, and then I'll explain. Is the Vidame d'Entrebeschaire here?"

Meisenta's eyebrows rose. "Not to my knowledge. Elecia?"

"No." Elecia was still fumbling with her shoes.

"Where does she live?"

"In Point of Hearts," Elecia answered. "At the house of Oriane Flying, not far from the Chain."

"Go," Cambrai said to one of the pontoises, and Rathe nodded.

"We'll talk, madame." He waved his hand toward the parlor door, and then remembered. "In the parlor?"

"Make free of my house," Meisenta said, not without irony, and swept through the door ahead of him. Rathe waited until the others had gone ahead before he followed them.

Meisenta settled herself in her usual chair, but it was Telawen who stood beside her rather than her husband. Aucher hung by the fireplace, frowning sleepily, and Elecia said, "Madame—"

"Be silent." Meisenta didn't move, still as a statue in the enormous chair. "I am sure the adjunct point has good reason for bringing so much of the dock to our door."

"This past afternoon, the vidame gave Philip vaan Esling a key to your warehouse, madame, and told him there was something terribly amiss— that the old river spirit, the Riverdeme, had been loosed, and was responsible for several recent deaths." Someone gasped at that, but in the flickering candlelight, Rathe couldn't tell who had made the sound. "This fit with other evidence we had uncovered. We used that key, madame, to enter your warehouse—"

"Another of Sighs' lawful entries?" Redel snapped.

Rathe ignored her. "And search for signs of the Riverdeme. There we were attacked, and Captain vaan Esling is missing. Taken. I want him back. Now."

There was a murmur of voices, and Elecia's rose about the rest. "And you suspect the Riverdeme? She's a fairy tale. This is madness."

Redel gave her a sharp look. "You were happy enough to tell her tales."

Elecia shook her head. "They're stories, nothing more."

"She is history. A part of Astreiant. And the bounds that held the Riverdeme have been broken," Rathe said. "Did you think no one would realize? There are greater dogfish loose in the river, the pontoises have seen them, and the deadhouse holds bodies of men killed by them. The university has taken notice. The Riverdeme has my leman, and I will have him back."

"The vidame gave you the key," Aucher began, and Elecia broke in.

"Then she's the one you need to talk to."

"I should tell you, dame, that she spoke of your...obsession with the Riverdeme. She feared what you might do," Rathe said, and was pleased to see Elecia flinch.

"I don't understand," Mattaes began, but even as he spoke, his expression shifted, as though he were adding up a total that displeased him.

"It was your idea to hire bes'Anthe, you encouraged Meisenta to let me handle that business."

"Strange things have been happening in the tunnels," Redel said slowly. "I didn't believe the boatmen, but...." She looked at Elecia. "You heard their gossip."

"I did."

The painted clock on the mantel struck the quarter-hour, and Rathe flinched. The tide was on the rise, steady and inexorable, and if Eslingen was in the drowning cell and if it still functioned that was barely a chance of survival. And if he was not, if the Riverdeme had carried him somewhere else, if he was lying unconscious in some tunnel or cross channel, that was almost no chance at all. He could not, would not lose Eslingen this way. "I am out of patience," he said. "And I am out of time. Tell me where the Riverdeme has taken vaan Esling, or I'll see that Sighs calls a point on this house for every scheme, every misstep, every petty shortcut that has ever been mentioned within these walls. I'll find enough to see you locked in cells for the rest of your lives—and far less pleasant ones than Mattaes occupied—and the entire city will wonder at your fall." He heard Cambrai draw breath sharply. "Do you understand me?"

"You wouldn't...." Redel began.

Rathe bared teeth in something like a snarl. "Don't push me."

"I have heard enough." Meisenta, her hands clenched tight on the arms of her chair, spoke. "And more than you think, Elecia. I don't care whether it's you or your Dis-damned leman, if you've freed the Riverdeme, you've gone too far. Do not dare bring further shame to us. Tell Rathe what he wants to know."

"But I don't know!" Elecia spread her hands with a fair assumption of innocence. "Truly, Meisenta, I don't."

"I married your brother for the good of this house," Meisenta said. "Because you offered me promises, and, I will admit to my shame, because you were fetching and clever and flirted nicely, for all that you had a leman. Those tales you told me, when Aliez was absent, how you'd maybe made a mistake stepping so far outside your class, not a word of them was true, were they? You, he, brought nothing to the marriage, not even a pauper's dowry, just your clever tongues and your bright ideas. There's no contract to break, no husband's goods to return. I can repudiate him this minute—with but three words, Elecia, I can leave you penniless, homeless and helpless and friendless. Answer the man!"

"Meisenta...." Elecia went to her knees at Meisenta's side, both hands on Meisenta's knee. "I swear, we meant no harm. I made a mistake, a terrible one, and I shouldn't have shared it, but, oh, this house, I so wanted to be part of it, to be with you however I could—"

"You can bear witness, Adjunct Point," Meisenta said. "And I believe the cap'pontoise is here as well?"

Cambrai cleared his throat. "I am."

"Then understand I make this announcement formally," Meisenta said. "As it applies to my present husband Aucher Gebellin, and to all his kin. I renounce—"

"Wait!" Elecia clutched at her skirts. "Wait, please, Meisenta—"

"Tell him where his leman is."

"The drowning cell." Elecia gulped tears. "She'd have taken him to the drowning cell. We owe her a death."

A cold calm filled Rathe. This was what he had needed, the key that would save Eslingen's life. All they needed now was the place.

Cambrai asked, "Trys wasn't good enough for her?"

Elecia gasped again, looking wildly around as though seeking a way to deny him. "She didn't want him, he wasn't right. I don't know, it's Aliez's family that served her all those years ago. I just did what she told me."

"Take me there," Rathe said.

Elecia nodded frantically. "I will, I swear!" She looked at Meisenta. "Please be kind, please be kind."

"Madame Staenka, you and I have unfinished business, and I'll leave a pointsman here to secure things. But this won't wait," Rathe said.

"I'll stand the point," Meisenta said, and he believed her.

CHAPTER 14

ESLINGEN LEANED AGAINST the wall of the drowning cell, his breath coming in heaving gasps. The water was ankle-deep now, after the last session of pumping, but already he could feel it creeping higher, cold fingers tracing a path up his calves. His arms and shoulders burned from the unfamiliar exercise, and he was shivering violently as the sweat dried on his upper body.

"Balfort?"

"Sir?" De Vian's voice was shaking, but Eslingen pretended not to hear.

"Are you all right?"

"Yes, sir."

Eslingen could hear the boy's teeth chattering. He sat huddled against the wall, arms wrapped tight around himself. The water covered his outstretched foot, lapped around his hips, and Eslingen made himself straighten, stripping off his coat. The skirts were soaked, but the upper body was only sweat-damp, and maybe it would be better than nothing. "Here. Take this."

He waded around the curve of the room, steadying himself against the wall as things rolled and shifted under his feet, and Balfort took it warily.

"What about you?"

"I'm staying warm enough," Eslingen said, with an attempt at a smile, and tightened his aching muscles as another shiver wracked him. At least de Vian was too disciplined to call him a liar, though he saw the doubt in the boy's face. "At least I will be soon enough."

The water was rising, faster now, and he suppressed a groan. A thousand strokes, he told himself. Just that, and then we'll see. He turned back along the wall, and something slipped underfoot, sending him flying. He caught himself on hands and knees, swearing, soaked now from knee to neck, and flailed for a moment in the swirling water before he could get to his feet. The water was knee-deep now, he could hear it rushing in the channels, and he reached for the pump handle in desperate haste. He pulled hard, and nothing happened, the antique mechanism suddenly balky. He cursed again, thrusting up, and felt the lever engage. He braced himself, legs spread, and began to pump again, counting each stroke.

A hundred strokes, and the water was still rising. He counted three hundred before he was sure that that inflow had slowed, and then at last the water began to drop again. He counted five hundred, then seven hundred, a thousand, but the water stayed stubbornly at the middle of his calf. His arms and back were burning again, his palms raw, but he didn't dare stop. Always until now he'd been able to get ahead of the water, give himself a break, a chance to catch his breath and let his muscles unknot, but now the water was rising in spite of all his efforts, crawling toward his knees. Maybe he was imagining it, maybe it was just the waves caused by his movement, but the thoughts fell flat as the water crept higher still.

He was counting again, though he had lost his place and started over at least once, the lever stiff in his hands. Five hundred strokes, and the water was almost at his knees; five hundred more, and it was only a little higher, but arms and shoulders and back were on fire. His palms had blistered and split, the salt of his sweat and the river water burning on raw skin. Maybe he could cut a piece from his shirt, protect them that way—but that would mean stopping, and the tide was faster than ever now.

Surely they were approaching high tide. Surely the inflow would ease soon. He hauled on the handle again, and felt the mechanism shift and slip. He stumbled forward a step and caught himself, but when he pulled down, the handle moved too easily, as though something had come loose. He tried again, feeling the water surge against his skin, and still nothing happened.

"Balfort. Can you stand?"

"What's happened?"

Eslingen could hear splashing and then a cry of pain, but couldn't take his attention off the pump. He jiggled the lever sideways, felt something catch, and tried again. The pump caught, a solid half-stroke, and then slipped free again. "Damn it! There's a problem with the pump, I'm trying to fix it, but—"

He couldn't bring himself to finish the sentence, couldn't bear even to think it. Stars bad for water: did that mean even the pump would break under his hand? He worked the lever sideways again, felt it catch, and pulled down more slowly. This time, it held, and he could feel the water moving again with each stroke. He hauled up and down, not daring to move too fast, and thought the machinery would hold at least a little longer. Just until the peak of the tide, he thought. That can't be far off now. But he had lost all track of time, and the distant lantern-light gave him no help at all.

"The pump's broken?" De Vian's voice scaled up, and Eslingen shook his head, fighting to keep his strokes shorter than before. Too deep, too strong, and he risked damaging the antique mechanism even further.

"No, it's all right now—"

He heard splashing, and then a heavier splash and a cry of pain, and risked a look. De Vian sprawled full length in the rising water, his face contorted in pain as he tried to drag himself upright. "I can help—"

"I've got it," Eslingen said. "We must be almost at high tide, it's just a little longer."

More splashing, and another whimpered curse, and he saw de Vian roll over, dragging himself back toward the wall. Sitting, the water was nearly to his chin, and Eslingen swore under his breath.

"You need to stand, Balfort. The water's gaining. If you can stand, it'll be all right, I can slow it down long enough, but you have to stand up."

De Vian braced himself and heaved, tears mixing with sweat and river water, but slid back into the water with another heavy splash. "I-I can't. Dis Aidones, I'm so cold...."

Eslingen kept pumping, while his thoughts raced. The water was still coming in fast, but he could spare a minute or two to lift de Vian to his feet. It would be better if there were some way to keep him upright, something to tie him to, or something to tie him with, but he'd used his neck-cloth on the splint, and there was no time to tear his shirt into something usable.... And there was nothing to tie him to except the pump itself, no handy rings or iron staples set into the walls, but maybe that was better than nothing. He counted ten more strokes, feeling the water hesitate, and let go of the lever, splashed through water now nearly waist-deep to catch de Vian under the armpits and haul him upright. The movement set off new agony in his back and shoulders, and de Vian cried out in turn as his broken leg dragged hard against the ground.

"I'm sorry," Eslingen said. "But you have to stand. Just for a little."

De Vian mumbled something that Eslingen chose to take as agreement. Eslingen shifted his hold, trying to let the boy's injured leg float freely, and stepped on the remains of the rope ladder. His foot twisted under him, and he fell sideways, his head grazing the stones with sickening force. He curled in on himself, unable for an instant to do anything but cradle the pain, and a twist of rope looped around his elbow, holding him down. He fought it, by instinct at first and then as his lungs burned and he couldn't find the surface, with frantic purpose. His free hand found de Vian, and the boy's hand closed over his, tugging awkwardly. It was enough to orient him, and he managed to get his head above water. He dragged in a shuddering breath, freeing himself from the rope, and pulled himself upright, reaching for de Vian again.

The water was waist-high now, and climbing greedily, and the lantern-light seemed to have faded. Eslingen hauled de Vian to his feet, ignoring the stifled yelp, and dragged him through the deepest water until he could reach the pump itself. De Vian blinked dully, and Eslingen wrapped his arms around it.

"Link your fingers. That's right, just like that, well done. Lean on the pump, hold onto it, you'll be all right—"

He reached for the pump handle himself, the rags of his shirt floating around him like weeds, drew it down hard. It took an instant to catch, but then he felt the welcome resistance and leaned heard against it, heedless of the pain in his hands and back and head. Something was trickling down his cheek, and when he licked his lips he tasted iron and salt, the ugly taste of blood. Or river water, he told himself, the river was brackish, and all the gods knew filthy on top of it, he might not be bleeding, though his head throbbed with the beat of his heart.

De Vian clung to the pump opposite him, his thin face against the rusted metal, eyes half closed. His fingers loosened and Eslingen swore.

"Balfort! Wake up, boy, hold on."

The long lashes fluttered, and he straightened, his hands tightening again, though a grimace of agony passed over his face.

"Good," Eslingen said. "That's good."

De Vian managed the flicker of a smile in answer, and Eslingen groped for something more to say, something, anything, to keep the boy alive and focused. He didn't dare let go of the pump handle, not when the water was above his waist and kept there only by the constant effort. All he had was words, and he drew breath, knowing what a slim lifeline they could be.

"Balfort. Talk to me. You said your family served the Riverdeme?"

"Long time ago." De Vian's voice was a whisper, barely louder than the water. "My father's side, his grandfather."

And that had the sound of a noble house about it, Eslingen thought. Blame the father's family for all the ills. "Tell me about it. Were they mediums? Scholars?"

"Servitors." It was an old word, and at first Eslingen wasn't sure he'd heard it correctly, but de Vian spoke again. "That's what they called them, servitors. They served the temples, collected the fees—like the pontoises, they negotiated justice on the river. That's what Father said."

Eslingen's hands were on fire, the muscles in his back threatening to cramp as the cold crept higher. But the progress was slower, he thought, and dragged hard on the handle.

"But she also took young men," de Vian whispered. "That was what brought her down. Father said that, too—said she'd have taken me, and Mother laughed. I've been a fool."

"It's all right."

De Vian slipped downward, then dragged himself up again with a cry of pain. "I only wanted you to love me."

"Oh, Balfort." Eslingen's breath caught, though he couldn't waste his strength on tears. "You don't want me. I'm too old, I have a leman—you deserve someone who'll love you just as desperately, someone as bright and beautiful and brave as you. Someone to match you, to stand at your side—"

De Vian rolled his head back and forth in denial. "There's no one...."

"There will be." Eslingen put all the conviction he could muster into the words. "Someone is waiting, I know it—you just have to live for them."

"I'll live for you."

"Just live." Eslingen hauled hard on the pump, letting the anger spur him on. They had to keep talking, somehow, he had to keep the boy awake and holding on until the tide finally turned.

"Can you ever forgive me?" The words were barely a whisper.

Eslingen swallowed his first answer, knowing it would do no good. "It's all right," he said, and bent his strength to the pump.

THEY BUNDLED ELECIA into the low-flyer still weeping, though she controlled herself enough to give directions. Cambrai relayed them to the driver, and Rathe concentrated on keeping his seat as the coach rolled heavily over the cobbles.

"Where is this, exactly? And what is it?"

"Aliez—the de Vians own a house in Sighs," Elecia said. "It came to them from someone's husband, a few generations back, they kept it to rent out, and they've been living on the money ever since." Her face contorted, a bitter grimace revealed in the light of the lanterns outside the Sandureigne. "But it's old, older than the city proper, and the cellars are below the waterline."

Rathe swore under his breath. "Do they connect with the tunnels?"

"I don't know." She cringed from his glare. "I don't! Aliez didn't like anyone to know about the place, she thought it was beneath her."

"What about the tenants?" Cambrai asked. "What do they know?"

"There aren't any," Elecia answered. "She let the lease lapse, and didn't look for new ones. She let it stand empty."

Rathe fended her off as the low-flyer took a corner in haste. A picture was taking shape in his mind, nothing that he could prove, not yet, but there were too many coincidences and connections. "She let Jurien Trys and his gang use it. You both were up to your necks in that business."

"We never—"

"If you want any sort of clemency," Rathe said, "you'd better think hard about what you're going to say."

"Aliez had dealings with him," Elecia said. "I told her he was trouble, but she wouldn't listen. She thought she could do anything."

"And Dammar?" Rathe asked. "He was your agent, wasn't he? Your idea?"

"But I didn't have anything to do with his death," Elecia said. "That was Aliez."

The low-flyer was slowing, the driver looking from side to side to find the house markers. Elecia pointed. "There. The third one on the left."

It was an old building, narrow in a style that had been abandoned centuries ago, little more than a room and a stairway wide, wedged in between larger houses that had clearly been built on the remains of its gardens. All of them were shut tight against the dark, and the low-flyer's driver looked over his shoulder.

"Want me to wait again?"

Rathe nodded, and pointed to the runner. "Run to Sighs and let Sebern know we've found the house. Tell her to send a company."

"Yes, Adjunct Point," the boy said, and darted away.

Cambrai had already dropped down from the low-flyer, and was examining the main door. "Locked and barred. We won't get through that without axes."

Rathe looked at Elecia. "Another door?"

"Around the back." She pointed to a narrow gate at the head of the alley between the houses.

Rathe tested it, found it unlocked, and swung it open on well-oiled hinges. Cambrai caught his sleeve.

"We don't know who's in there, or how many."

Rathe looked up at the bulk of the house, the lower windows shuttered, the upper ones black and empty.

"If Trys and the vidame were in this together, half his men could be here," Cambrai said. "We're too few."

"The place is empty, Euan," Rathe said. "I feel it in my bones. And Philip is in there." He stopped, shaking his head. Cambrai was right, that was the problem: if there were guards—and he would be a fool to assume there were none at all, no matter how empty the house felt—he would be leading his people into danger. But Eslingen was in the drowning cell, and every minute counted. "I'll go first. If we run into anything we can't handle, we'll pull back and wait for Sebern."

"That'll give them a hostage," Cambrai said.

"If it means pulling him out of the drowning cell," Rathe began, and stopped himself. "I'll take that chance."

Cambrai nodded, and waved for the others to follow. "So will I."

They made their way quietly down the unpaved alley, the mud smelling only somewhat of rotting greens, fetched up in a narrow courtyard surrounded by new walls a good ten feet high. The windows on this side were shuttered all the way up, but the kitchen door beckoned, freshly painted wood and bright brass fittings. Cambrai grimaced.

"That'll be a beast to break."

"Let me try," Rathe said, and reached into his pocket for his set of picks. The lock itself carried no enchantment; he found the right pick on the third try, and eased the wards out of the way. As he pushed the door open, he could almost hear Eslingen's voice in his ear. *What unexpected talents you have, Adjunct Point!*

The door gave onto the rough pantry, with its shelves for the great crocks of flour and oil and other bulk goods; they were empty now except for one great tun too large to move, and the dusty floor showed a confusion of footprints.

"Someone's been in and out recently," Cambrai said.

Rathe nodded. "Let's hope it's the vidame."

The kitchen was equally barren, the great hearth swept clean of ash and the stone counters empty, and when Rathe checked the brick range, its fire pits were bare. There wasn't even a last sprig of herb hanging from the hook above the high window. Elecia had been telling the truth at least this far: no one was living here. At Cambrai's nod, Tiesheld and the pontoise melted through the door that led to the main part of the house, and reappeared a few minutes later shaking their heads.

"Empty," Tiesheld said. "Nobody's been here in a while."

But there were marks on the floor, Rathe thought, lifting his lantern. Scuffs of dirt and drying mud, and they led back to a corner where an unobtrusive door opened on the cellar stairs. He looked at Elecia. "Here?"

She nodded, swallowing hard. "There's another cellar below."

"Bring her," Rathe said, to Tiesheld, and saw her pull away.

"No. Please, I'd rather—" She seemed to realize she'd get no sympathy, and fell silent again.

Rathe nodded. "Let's go."

HE HAD RUN out of things to say, babbling about de Vian's future, about the Guard and the horses and the things they both had to live for. Eslingen dragged at the pump handle, bending his knees to put his weight on it and spare his back and shoulders. Every muscle felt as though it had been sculpted of molten lead, and if his fingers hadn't been locked with cold, he could not have gotten his raw hands to grip. De Vian was sagging, his eyes closed, the side of his face rubbed raw by the rough metal. Eslingen drove the pump handle down again. The water was above his waist, but steady there; it might, he thought, it might just be going down a little, and he shook his wet hair out of his face.

"We're almost there," he said, his voice so hoarse he barely recognized it. "Hang on, Balfort, the tide's about to turn."

De Vian didn't answer, his face sliding slowly down the pump's cylinder. His hands slowly opened, the interlaced fingers relaxing, and he sagged backwards into the water.

"Balfort!" Eslingen hauled at the pump handle. If he could get a stroke or two ahead, surely he could grab him, drag him back upright—shake enough wits back into him to hang on just a moment longer. "Balfort, damn it—"

The lantern's light dimmed suddenly, as though the shutter had been closed. Eslingen looked up quickly, but there was no movement beyond the grate. Instead, there was a presence, a shadow, rising up out of the water from the conduits that fed the cell, hard and cold and hungry.

"Balfort!" Eslingen redoubled his efforts at the pump, back and hands shrieking, and thought the shadow wavered. De Vian floated in the dirty water, arms outstretched, pale face and hands just above the surface. He was dying, Eslingen thought, maybe already dead, and he himself didn't dare stop pumping for fear that the shadow would return. That had been the Riverdeme, surely, ready to take her sacrifice, and if his efforts were keeping her out, that was all he could do.

And if he stopped pumping, he might never be able to start again. He was at the very edge of exhaustion, every movement energy he couldn't spare. The tide had not yet turned after all. "Balfort? Come on, answer me...."

Something moved in the water, a slithering ripple like the flick of a fish's tail. He couldn't see anything, though, just the movement, strongly against the still incoming tide. He swallowed a sound that might have become a sob, and bent his back to the pump again. He was getting weaker, he could feel it, was nearly at the point where all the will in the world couldn't force him to move. The shadow felt it, too; he could almost feel her smile, cold and satisfied. Not yet, he told himself. He could make one or two or a dozen more strokes—one more now, and another, and one more after that. He would keep going, because each stroke was one more chance for Rathe to find him.

"One more," he whispered, and leaned his weight against the lever.

The cellar was as empty as the kitchen above, and smelled of mold. The remains of a set of shelves was heaped against one wall, splintered, rotting wood, and there was a barrel taller than a man set in a cradle in the far corner, but there was no sign of a door. Rathe grabbed Elecia's arm.

"Where is it? The door?"

"I don't know—"

It took all his strength not to shake her, his muscles trembling with the effort, and he saw real fear in her eyes. "Tell me."

"Beside the barrel."

Rathe swept his lantern's beam across the dirt, over what might have been tracks or the marks where something had been dragged, and Anhalt, who was closest, hurried over, sheathing her knife as she went. Rathe could not remember seeing her draw it, but the sight of the blade cleared his head a little. They were almost there, this was not the time to make foolish mistakes.

"It's locked," Anhalt called, and Rathe shoved Elecia toward Cambrai, reaching for his picks again.

This was a better lock, which boded well, and he flinched as a magist's ward stung his fingers. He recognized the symbols cut into the metal case, and grimaced. There were subtler ways to break these wards, but they took time. Brute force was unpleasant, but effective, and he pressed his left hand flat against the lock, muttering the counter-ward. It snapped, a tongue of flame licking the center of his palm, and he jerked his hand away, swearing. But the ward was broken, and there was only a red mark in the center of his palm. He sorted through the ring of picks to find the right size, then gently felt for the wards. Too heavy: he changed the pick for a stronger one, and felt again. Yes, there it was, just there. He closed his eyes, concentrating on the press of metal against metal, pushed down to lift the wards. The lock resisted; he pushed harder, and the pick slipped out of position. He swallowed a curse—no time for that, no time for anything but his best, most perfect concentration—and felt for the wards again. And then he had it, the lock turning open with a heavy snap, and door sagged outward.

He caught it and pulled it open, teetering for a moment at the top of a spiral stair before he caught his balance. A wave of damp rose out of the dark, carrying with it the smell of the river, and he started down before anyone else could object. He heard Cambrai curse behind him, but Anhalt was at his back, and he held out his lantern, letting its light spill down the curve of the stair. There was no sound from below, no movement in the shadows, and he kept going, lantern in one hand, the heavy truncheon in the other.

As he passed the third turn, light blossomed ahead of him, faint but unmistakable, and he stopped, pulling the lantern back to narrow the shutter.

"Trouble?" Anhalt hissed at his shoulder, and he shook his head.

"Don't know. There's a light."

"Let me go first?"

Rathe shook his head again. "I've got it," he said, and moved before she could say anything more.

The stair opened onto a small and homely room, much like the buttery in the oldest houses, a round room with a shelf running at shoulder height around the circle from one edge of the door frame to the other. The light came from the center of the room—from a hole in the center of the floor, shining up from between the bars of a grate, and there was a broken lock and a heavy metal bar discarded on the stone floor.

"Philip?" Rathe dropped to his knees beside the grate, holding out the lantern. A second lantern hung from the grate itself, and in the doubled light he could see down into what looked almost like a well, water glittering as it caught the light. There was a pump in the center, and things floating in the water, and a pale and blood-smeared face looked up at him.

"Nico?"

"Oh, gods, Philip." Rathe grabbed the metal bar, levered the grate sideways with a great screech of metal on stone.

"No, wait," Eslingen called. "She's here."

"She'll have to take me first." Rathe swung on his haunches, looking for some way to get Eslingen out. There must have been a ladder, even just a rope, but there was no sign of one—no, there were eyebolts set into the stone just below the well's lip, and hooks in them, but the rope that had been attached had been none too neatly severed.

"By the Bull, you've found him," Cambrai said, and shoved Elecia toward the wall. Anhalt caught her by the arm before she could flee back up the stairs, pinned her against the stone.

"Rope," Rathe said, and Cambrai nodded, reaching under his jerkin to reveal a coil tied around his waist.

"Here. You don't spend your life at the docks without learning to carry line."

"Let me down."

"Better he climbs up," Cambrai said, busily wrapping the rope. It was just long enough, Rathe thought, and he looked down again to see Eslingen still dragging painfully on the pump handle. "The tide's still coming in."

"Philip! Can you climb?"

Eslingen tipped his head back, and Rathe winced at the streak of blood running down his cheek. "I'll try…. I'm not alone. De Vian's with me."

"I have to go down," Rathe said, to Cambrai. "If he's been pumping since he was taken—"

Cambrai nodded, looping one end of the rope through the nearest eyebolt, then stood to take a turn around his waist. "Go."

Rathe wound the rope around his own waist and lowered himself cautiously over the edge. He heard Cambrai grunt as the rope took his weight, and began walking down the stone wall. Eslingen was still pumping, but the noise of the water was louder, and Rathe let himself slide the last few feet, dropping into waist-deep water cold enough to take his breath away. What he had taken for Eslingen's coat resolved to a floating body—de Vian, all right—and he took a step toward him before shaking himself back to the important things.

"I'll pump. You see to him."

Eslingen nodded, grimacing as he uncurled his fingers from the pump's handle. Rathe caught a glimpse of raw and bloodied flesh, but then Eslingen stumbled away, splashing awkwardly across the cell, and Rathe made himself focus on the pump. He could feel the water rising, creeping up his ribs, and he braced himself to haul on the lever. It took all his strength to get it moving, and almost as much effort on the upstroke: if Eslingen had been doing this for hours, no wonder he looked half dead. He caught the rhythm, breathing hard, felt the water slow around his feet.

"Euan! Euan, how long before the tide turns?"

Cambrai leaned over the edge. "Not more than half an hour. Less. We'll get you out—"

The lantern's light flickered, as though something had moved between it and the depths of the cell. Rathe saw Eslingen look up sharply, then slap de Vian's face lightly.

"Balfort. Come on, son—" He choked, shaking his head, but tried again.

"Let him go," Rathe said, as gently as he could. Eslingen glared at him, bloodied face stark with grief.

"He was my ensign."

"He's dead." The light flickered again and faded, as though a cloud had moved over the sun. Rathe looked up, seeing the air thickening with mist, and felt something slip past his hip. "Philip!"

"She's here." Eslingen released the body and staggered toward him. He slipped, caught himself, then fell forward with an enormous splash, vanishing beneath the surface.

"Philip!" Rathe lunged for him, the pump forgotten, sweeping his arms through the opaque water. The light was fading further, fog thickening. Something brushed his ankle, then his hip, a cold and bony caress. Not the dogfish, he told himself, still groping through the water, it couldn't possibly be, and if it's her, I'll pretend it isn't. His out-flung hand touched something, cloth or hair, but it washed away from him, his fingers closing on water.

His foot struck something solid, something that gave soggily, and he held his breath and reached beneath the surface to find sodden cloth. He heaved at it, realized he had Eslingen's breeches, and worked his way up to find linen and skin. He hauled again, and Eslingen's head broke the surface, lolling loose on his shoulders, his hair spreading like a drowned man's.

"No," Rathe said, hardly aware he spoke aloud, and wound both fists in the front of his shirt, pulling him further out of the water. He freed one hand to grab Eslingen's hair, and Eslingen's eyelids flickered. He coughed, heaved himself to his feet, and Rathe loosed his hair, though he kept

tight hold of the shirt. The water was rising again, was almost to his armpits. "Philip, you have to stand, I have to pump now—"

Eslingen nodded, clutching painfully at Rathe's jerkin, and Rathe
reached for the pump again, hauling hard on the handle. It moved reluctantly, but it moved, and Rathe raised it again, fighting against the weight
of water and Eslingen's clumsy grip. It was darker than it had been, no
longer foggy but the dark of evening in spite of the lanterns overhead,
and he saw Eslingen's eyes widen.

"She's here," he said again, but Rathe couldn't spare the strength to look
over his shoulder.

He could feel her, though, a weighty presence, a chill breath down his
spine, a cold and considering hunger that could never be satisfied. Eslingen looked past him, sudden determination in his face, and Rathe said,
"No! Stay with me, that's our only hope. She can't take us, not while we're
pumping—"

Eslingen's breath caught, and he reached up, managed to hook one
raw hand over the lever and pull down. He closed his teeth tight over
pain, breath coming in short gasps, but he was, arguably doing the work.
Something splashed behind them, a hiss and flick of air like an angry
snake, and suddenly the Riverdeme was on the other side of the pump,
rising naked from the water, skin as white and speckled as a fish's belly
gleaming in what was left of the light. Her breasts were as flat and angled
as a fish's plates, and a dogfish's tusks rose from her lower jaw. She bared
her teeth at them, clawed hands outstretched, the webs between the fingers showing translucent as oiled paper.

Mine.

Rathe felt Eslingen flinch, but they kept pumping, matching each
other's movements. The Riverdeme hissed again, and sank back into the
water, dissolving into mist only to shoot out again barely an arm's length
from the pump. Her eyes were flat and perfectly round, reflecting the
light so that they shone like sequins, like mirrors in the dark. Her teeth
and claws were perfectly white, sharp as razors, ready to rend and tear
the moment they faltered.

Mine.

"You can't have him," Rathe said. "You can't have us, that was the bargain, that's the rule of the cell, you can't take us while we keep the water
out. And we are doing that, and we will keep pumping until the cell is
empty and you are gone."

Promised....

265

It was barely a word, might have been only a hiss of anger, but Rathe seized the sense of it, jerked his head toward the top of the cell. "If you want the one who promised, she's up there."

The Riverdeme reared her head at that, and dissolved again into fog. Something, not even a shape, shot upward from the water's surface. It passed between them and the lantern like a cloud, and then the light was back and above them Elecia screamed in shrill terror. Cambrai shouted something, and Elecia screamed again, the sound trailing off into a wet bubbling moan.

"I—she killed her," Eslingen said, blankly.

"Yeah," Rathe said. "Keep pumping."

There was a flat crack of light overhead, a thunderclap without sound, blinding and stunning and overwhelming. Rathe clung to Eslingen as something rained past them like ash and swirled away in the water, looked up with streaming eyes to see someone leaning over the edge of the cell. He blinked hard against the green clouds that covered his vision, but it remained Rainart Fourie. The surintendant gave his thin smile.

"Well, Rathe, you seem to have cut things a bit close this time."

"Not my intention, sir," Rathe answered, and a rope ladder unrolled down the side of the cell.

"Can Captain vaan Esling manage on his own, or do we need a sling?"

"Better get a sling," Rathe answered. "There's a body down here, too."

"Ah. Most unfortunate." Fourie turned away, presumably to give orders, and Rathe looked at Eslingen.

"You're all right?"

"Every muscle in my body feels like you put a hot poker to it, and my hands are flayed. But I'll live."

That was more honesty than Rathe had expected, and he put his arms around Eslingen as though that could help. The water was still chest high, but it wasn't rising, he realized, and there was no sound of it rushing in. "The tide's turned."

"Not before time," Eslingen said.

Another rope and sling appeared, and Eslingen was hauled wincing out of the cell. Rathe stayed long enough to help retrieve de Vian's body, then climbed out himself, and sat for a moment on the damp stones, shaken to the bone. Someone draped a blanket over his shoulders, and he huddled into it, grateful for its warmth. The lower cellar was crowded now: he recognized people from Sighs, and from Dreams, and to his shock there were three women in magists' robes and university badges. Raunkeleyn was with them, gesturing wildly, his own robe fastened askew as though he'd dressed in haste. There was a patch of something that was almost certainly blood by the door, and a fan of it across the wall as though someone had been killed flying, and he looked for Elecia's body.

"The alchemists have already taken her," Fourie said, and Rathe dragged himself to his feet. "It seems we came just in time."

"Thank you," Rathe said. He looked for Eslingen, and saw him leaning against the wall, another blanket wrapped around his shoulders. His eyes were closed, but he seemed to feel the look, for he straightened, eyes opening, and started toward them.

"The next time you discover that an ancient power has been loosed, Rathe, I expect you to inform me immediately," Fourie said.

"I told you as soon as I was sure of it."

Eslingen caught his elbow as he staggered.

"I profoundly hope there won't be a next time, sir." Eslingen gave Fourie his best smile, and to Rathe's surprise Fourie managed a thin smile in return.

"I never make assumptions, Captain."

"What happened to d'Entrebeschaire?" Rathe asked.

"She seems to have fled," Fourie answered. "I have a report of a woman matching her description passing the Queen's Gate an hour past midnight, claiming a deathly ill relative in the country. The Guard has been sent after her, though I expect it's too late."

Eslingen opened his mouth as though to protest, then closed it again. Rathe said, "The Staenkas. I don't honestly know how deeply they were involved."

Fourie held up his hand. "That can be decided later. For now, Adjunct Point, take yourself and your leman home—I'll send a physician see to you both."

"Yes, sir," Rathe said.

Somehow he dragged himself and Eslingen up the stairs and out into the street, and stood for a moment breathing the night air. The wintersun was past the zenith, only a hand's breadth above the western rooftops, and there was a hint of gray in the eastern sky. It was cold, and the air smelled of drying leaves and tar and faintly of the spices traded two streets over; he pulled the blanket tighter around his shoulders, wondering where he could find a low-flyer at this time of night, and if they could walk as far as Dreams if he couldn't.

"Nico." Eslingen touched his shoulder, and he looked up to hear the jingle of harness as the low-flyer's driver urged his horse into motion.

Rathe looked up at the driver, who touched his forehead in response. "You've been waiting all this time?"

"The Surintendant of Points said he'd have my license if I didn't," the driver answered. "And I'm done in, gentlemen, so if you wouldn't mind—"

Eslingen laughed, and Rathe couldn't help a smile. "Take us home."

EPILOGUE

ESLINGEN SPRAWLED ON the bed in the fading light of a winter evening, Sunflower at his side and a stack of broadsheets ready to hand. Most of the pain and stiffness had left his muscles, though his palms were still scabbed and healing, and he had found a pair of soft kid half-gloves to cover them until the doctor said he could remove the bandages. He had been back to the barracks in the morning, but Coindarel had watched him work, and sent him home for another day. It was just as well, Eslingen admitted silently. The Guard had failed to catch up with d'Entrebeschaire, losing her just south of Jandoc, and everyone was still on edge about that. He had kept de Vian's secret, the least he could do for the pack of younger brothers left motherless, sisterless, and unprotected; as far as the Guard knew, she had killed one of their own. No one liked to see her get away with that, and it was no consolation at all that Raunkeleyn claimed she could never go near running water without risking the wrath of the Riverdeme's kindred. That would only be satisfying if he was there to see it, and he doubted that was likely.

At least the stars had shifted. The worst of the rains had passed, and the last time he'd been caught in a downpour he'd been no more than reasonably wet: his planets had left their detriment. In the distance, a clock struck five, another chiming in a heartbeat later, and as they finished striking, he heard the main door open. He lifted his head, as did Sunflower, and Rathe stopped in the door, laughing.

"The pair of you."

"He's a good dog," Eslingen said, conscious that they had relaxed in the same moment as well, and fondled his ears. "Did they set a date for the Staenkas to go before the judiciary?"

269

Rathe shook his head, and came to sit on the bed beside him, kicking off his shoes. "Meisenta made an offer to settle the offense, which Fourie recommended the regents accept. It's a stinging fine, they'll be paying it for years, but if the sur says it's fair...."

"What's she doing with Aucher?"

"Said she'd keep him if he made a clean breast of it," Rathe answered. "And as a result he's been talking like a broadsheet chanter. He says it was all his sister's idea, hers and d'Entrebeschaire's, and they did everything either themselves or through agents—agents conveniently not known to him."

Eslingen dragged himself to a more upright position, adjusting the pillow behind him. "So he says they killed Trys."

Rathe nodded. "They'd freed the Riverdeme by then, and she was hungry, so they thought they'd kill two gargoyles with a single bolt—they were worried that her taking random sailors would give her away too soon. They dropped him down the drowning cell, but he was strong enough to hold back the tide, and the Riverdeme couldn't touch him. Elecia thought that meant she'd refused him, so she had him dragged out and knifed at the warehouse."

"And Dammar?"

"Trys did that on his own, or so Aucher says." Rathe shrugged. "Dammar was using the point on Mattaes to demand a bigger fee. Trys had his men beat him, and then d'Entrebeschaire decided that—with us sniffing around—she'd better silence him permanently. Aucher says he gave them the tea to bribe him with—and Meisenta doesn't exactly apologize for lying about recognizing the blend, but says she was afraid of getting Mattaes into deeper trouble if she admitted she recognized it. Myself, I think she was just as worried about Elecia, but she's not about to admit that now. In any case, Aucher says he has no idea where they got the hemlock."

Eslingen snorted at that.

"Oh, I agree, it probably came from the Staenka workrooms, they have it there. D'Entrebeschaire seems to have been the one who talked her way into his rooms after he was beaten; she's certainly the one who suggested to his sister that they bring him the treat from home."

"And the tea captain, bes'Anthe—the one who started all this?"

Rathe smiled without humor. "Aucher says that was Elecia, or maybe d'Entrebeschaire and one of her men."

"But why?"

"Because they thought bes'Anthe was going to tell Mattaes about the extortion ring— which he did—and that bes'Anthe knew that there was a connection between Trys and the Gebellins. Aucher says they thought bes'Anthe was going to ask Mattaes to use his influence to get Trys to take a lower fee. In any case, Mattaes is cleared, though what he plans to do with himself is anyone's guess."

Keep serving the family, Eslingen thought. Mattaes wasn't the sort to give up that security. Not like de Vian.... He shook the thought away. "Do you believe that? I can't see Elecia knifing him—and d'Entrebeschaire would have made a better job of it."

"I believe that's what they were afraid of." Rathe sighed. "But the rest—I think Aucher stabbed him, but he swears not, and I can't prove it. I think the bloody shirt was his, there was a mix-up over the household laundry a month or so before, four shirts sent to them that belonged to another house, and only three made it back to the laundry. I think he had some idea then that he and Elecia were wading into deep water, and after he'd killed the man, he left it in Mattaes's room. But, as I said, I have no proof." He stopped, his face bleak. "I told Meisenta, though. What she does with it is her business."

Eslingen lifted an eyebrow. "She's coming out of this well enough."

"She loved Elecia," Rathe said. "And I don't believe she knew what was going on. Or at least not about anything that would be more than the usual way of business."

"Astreianter merchants play for keeps," Eslingen said, not quite lightly enough.

"And there's damn all I can do about it." Rathe shook himself. "You were back to the barracks this morning?"

Eslingen nodded, accepting the change of subject. "It still hurts my hands to ride, so the Prince-Marshal told me to stay away until they're healed. Rijonneau and his company followed d'Entrebeschaire all the way to Jandoc, but she turned off the road there, and they weren't able to pick up her trail." He glanced sideways at Rathe as he spoke. This had been the Guard's first real assignment, and it was singularly without result: he could hardly blame Rathe for pointing that out, but Rathe was staring at the far wall.

"Raunkeleyn says the Riverdeme will punish her—well, the Riverdeme and her kindred spirits."

"Not very satisfying, though," Eslingen said.

"It's what we've got." Rathe rested his head against the wall, his shoulder pressing against Eslingen's.

Eslingen sighed. "There's a piece I haven't told you— haven't told the Guard, either, and don't intend to. After I turned him down, Balfort went to his sister and told her what we knew."

"I wondered," Rathe said, after a moment.

"Of course you did."

"Not at the time, but afterward...." Rathe shrugged. "I did wonder, the way it all fit together."

"It was stupid," Eslingen said, "stupid and petty and I think he knew it as soon as he'd done it. And he did try to help me."

"Without notable success."

"He was a boy," Eslingen said. "I shouldn't have taken him on. He'd be alive today if I'd listened to you."

"Maybe." Rathe kissed Eslingen's neck. "Or maybe he'd have done something just as foolish. But he made his own choices, and he stood by them at the end. You taught him that."

"Will you stay at Sighs?"

"Not after Astarac is brought to bed," Rathe answered. "Which, please all the gods, should be soon. I'm too junior to take Dammar's place on a permanent basis. No, I'll be back at Dreams, and happy to be there." He shook his head. "I don't like the way they do business."

There was something in his voice, a note not of discontent, but of unhappiness, that made Eslingen look curiously at him. "What did you do?"

"Threatened everyone at Sighs—I don't mind that so much, they shouldn't take fees, and they ought to stay bought when they do, but it's still not right. And then I told Meisenta that if anything had happened to you, I'd hound them to my grave." Rathe tipped his head back again, staring at the faded canopy with its embroidery of stars and suns.

"Oh, I heard all about that."

Rathe sighed. "I was bluffing, Philip. I couldn't—not even for you."

"I'd be dead then and I wouldn't care," Eslingen answered. He reached for Rathe's hand, closed it in his own. "Seriously, Nico, I'd expect nothing less of you."

There was a long silence, and then, very softly, he heard Rathe laugh. "Ah, Philip. I suppose we deserve each other."

"I'm content," Eslingen answered, and leaned companionably against him.

Acknowledgments

ONCE AGAIN, THANKS are due to editor extraordinaire Steve Berman—yes, you were right again—and to copy editor/designer Alex Jeffers, whose work on this book was helpful, thorough, and perfectly tuned to the book I wanted to write—and whose design makes it even more lovely. I'd also like to thank the patrons of my Astreiant Patreon, who not only offer material support, but remind me why it's so much fun to write in this world.

MELISSA SCOTT is from Little Rock, Arkansas, and studied history at Harvard College and Brandeis University, where she earned her PhD in the Comparative History program with a dissertation titled "Victory of the Ancients: Tactics, Technology, and the Use of Classical Precedent." She is the author of more than thirty science fiction and fantasy novels, most with queer themes and characters, and has won four Lambda Literary Awards, most recently for *Death By Silver*, written with Amy Griswold, as well as multiple Spectrum Awards and the John W. Campbell Award for Best New Writer. She can be found on Twitter @blueterraplane.

CPSIA information can be obtained
at www.ICGtesting.com
Printed in the USA
BVHW04s1522140518
516179BV00006B/702/P